HMAS SYDNEY

1941

Masterly Misled

Greg Bathgate

HMAS *Sydney* in October 1941 – a few weeks before her fateful voyage

Joseph Burnett (1899–1941)
Commanding Officer

Raider HSK *Kormoran*

Theodor Detmers (1902–1976)
Commanding Officer

Publisher: Inspiring Publishers,
P.O. Box 159, Calwell, ACT Australia 2905
Email: publishaspg@gmail.com
http://www.inspiringpublishers.com

A catalogue record for this book is available from the National Library of Australia

National Library of Australia The Prepublication Data Service

Author: Greg Bathgate
Title: Masterly Misled
Genre: Non-fiction
ISBN: 978-1-922792 -25-9

In 2008, a Commission of Inquiry had been authorised by the Federal Government to assess the circumstances of the clash between the Australian cruiser HMAS *Sydney* and the German auxiliary cruiser HSK *Kormoran* off the West Australian coast on 19th November 1941. It, however, went through the motions of finding in what amounted to a status quo position, one which broadly agreed with the Navy some 80 years ago, even though it had a lot more information at its disposal, including the location of the sunken ships, the wreck site images and archival files.

In a quest to explain various issues, the inquiry had erred in its assessments by falsely countenancing the statements of those few German officers who had failed to give an accurate account of the engagement. In this respect, the confined parameters of the scene of the action had proven their scenario could never have happened. Other questionable factors include the Royal Navy having knowingly sent the *Sydney* to its doom, the false position and day of rescue of German survivors by a British tanker, RAN Naval Intelligence involvement and the message received in Fremantle by the South Western Area Combined Headquarters on the day of the battle – plus other issues in which the inquiry had made the mistakes of the past.

It was an inquiry that had been necessitated because of intense opposition to the official story and it was meant to resolve any baseless issues, but for the most part it was an opportunity lost.

CONTENTS

Note: Unless otherwise specified, all references shown in the chapters hereunder have been taken from the Commission of Inquiry Report – index to Exhibit 252 (shown as Document ID). Others refer to messages and files from Australian and British Archives.

ABBREVIATIONS

AA	Anti-aircraft
ACH	Area Combined Headquarters
ACNB	Australian Commonwealth Naval Board
ADM	Admiral
ASIO	Australian Security Intelligence Organisation
B-Dienst	German signals intelligence
CAFO	Confidential Admiralty Fleet Order
CAMSI	Confidential Admiralty Merchant Shipping Instruction
CAPT	Captain
CDRE	Commodore
C-in-C	Commander-in-Chief (e.g., ADM Layton, C-in-C, China Station)
CMDR	Commander
CNS	Chief of Naval Staff (Chief of Navy)
CO	Commanding Officer
COIC	Combined Operational Intelligence Centre
COIS	Chief of Intelligence Staff
CPO	Chief Petty Officer
CWR	Central War Room
CZM	Commander-in-Chief The Netherlands East Indies Naval Forces
DCA	Department of Civil Aviation
DCNS	Deputy Chief of Naval Staff
DF	Direction Finding
DNI	Director Naval Intelligence
DNO	District Naval Officer (also Director Naval Operations)
DNOWA	District Naval Officer Western Australia
DSTO	Defence Science and Technology Organisation
EST	Eastern Standard Time
ETA	Estimated Time of Arrival
ETD	Estimated Time of Departure
FEDO	Far East Direction-finding Organisation

FLGOFF	Flying Officer
FLT	Flight Lieutenant
FOCAS	Flag Officer Commanding Australian Squadron
FRUMEL	Fleet Radio Unit Melbourne
FSF	Finding Sydney Foundation
G	Golf Time (GMT plus seven hours)
GMT	Greenwich Mean Time (zulu time)
GPCAPT	Group Captain
H	Hotel Time, WST Time (GMT plus eight hours)
HFDF	High-Frequency Direction Finding
Hm	Hectometre
HMAS	His Majesty's Australian Ship
HMAT	His Majesty's Australian Transport
HMS	His Majesty's Ship
HMT	His Majesty's Transport
HSK	Handelsstörkreuzer (German raider)
IJN	Imperial Japanese Navy
K	Knots/Kilo time, Eastern Standard Time (EST) – GMT plus 10 hours
kcs	kilocycles
LCDR	Lieutenant Commander
LEUT	Lieutenant
Mcs	Megacycles
MF	Medium Frequency
MMS	Mercantile Movements Section
MV	Motor Vessel
NAA	National Archives of Australia
NATSAR	National Search and Rescue
NB	Naval Board
NEI	Netherlands East Indies
NID	Naval Intelligence Directorate
nm(s)	nautical mile(s)
NOC	Naval Officer Commanding (e.g., Sydney Harbour)
NOIC	Naval Officer-in-Charge
PO	Petty Officer
POW	Prisoner of War
PRO	Public Records Office (Kew, UK)

PWSS	Port War Signal Station
RAAF	Royal Australian Air Force
RACAS	Rear Admiral Commanding Australian Squadron
RADM	Rear Admiral
RAF	Royal Air Force
RAN	Royal Australian Navy
RANR	Royal Australian Navy Reserve
RANVR	Royal Australian Navy Volunteer Reserve
RFA	Royal Fleet Auxiliary
RN	Royal Navy
RNVR	Royal Navy Volunteer Reserve
RT	Radio Telephony (voice)
SAR	Search and Rescue
SBLT	Sub Lieutenant
SFTS	Service Flying Training School
SIGINT	Signals Intelligence
SIM	Shipping Intelligence Message
Skl	German naval war staff
SS	Steamship
SWACH	South Western Area Combined Headquarters
TOA	Time of Arrival
TOR	Time of Reply
USS	United States Ship
VADM	Vice Admiral
VAI	Vessels in Area Indicated
VS	Visual Signalling (by light)
VHF	Very High Frequency
WAHQ	Western Area Headquarters (RAAF Perth)
WGCDR	Wing Commander
WIR	Weekly Intelligence Report
WRANS	Women's Royal Australian Naval Service
WST	Western Standard Time
WT	Wireless Telegraphy
z	zulu time (Greenwich Mean Time)

HMAS *Sydney* departing Port Melbourne in 1938

INTRODUCTION

Many of the findings made by the Commission of Inquiry on the action between HMAS *Sydney* and the German raider HSK *Kormoran* have been eroded by more recent revelations from ordinary crewmen. Even though the inquiry took no notice, statements that had been kept secret for some 50 years have been entirely disregarded by the Navy.

A background summary of the debate and an analysis of major inquiry findings, including evidence that has been overlooked or ill-conceived, will leave present and future generations in no doubt as to the circumstances and conduct of the battle.

In 1957, George Hermon Gill wrote the official history (*Royal Australian Navy 1939–1942*), in which he gave details of the *Sydney/Kormoran* action. LCDR Gill, journalist, naval officer and war historian, was commissioned to write this history because of his previous role as publicity censorship liaison officer in naval intelligence, his knowledge of naval historical records and for his good relationship with the press. He gave a seemingly plausible account of the *Sydney* disaster and his explanations were viewed favourably at the time.

Gill is said to have based his account of the action on information contained in various reports on the interrogations. He obviously had implacable belief in particular German versions of the battle in stating that 'the story of her last action was pieced together through exhaustive interrogation of *Kormoran*'s survivors. No room was left for doubt as to its accuracy'. He relied primarily on evidence given by the *Kormoran*'s senior officers, especially that of her commander, Theodor Detmers. Gill's description of the battle entailing his version of the German story was meant to be the final episode. It stood the test of time until questioned in the early 1980s.

As a result of his publication, *Who Sank the Sydney?*, Michael Montgomery (son of the *Sydney*'s navigator) aroused the public on the accuracy of the official history. His research led to the possibility of a cover-up by Gill, and in the absence of *Sydney* survivors he could not accept that Detmers's account could be totally believed if it could not be corroborated. It seemed to him that the German account did not add up and that they may have acted illegally to defeat a much superior warship.

Montgomery's book ignited public interest and it became the forerunner of many other publications, some of which rigidly defended the official history and the naval establishment. Those authors who were opposed to his book went to great lengths to discredit his research and they staunchly defended the story portrayed by Gill, whereas others foresaw the merit in some of his claims. Dozens of books and papers were written giving both sides of the argument and public forums were held in an attempt to get consensus on the truth of the matter. In 1997, a Senate Parliamentary Inquiry was constituted to publicly discuss the issue.

The purpose of the inquiry by the Joint Standing Committee on Foreign Affairs, Defence and Trade (JSCFADT) was to investigate and report on the circumstances of the sinking of HMAS *Sydney*. Its terms of reference also included the extent of the availability of archival material, the prospects of conducting a search for the cruiser, the identity of the suspected *Sydney* crewman on Christmas Island and the location of his grave site. [He was recently identified (using DNA) as Able Seaman Thomas Welby Clark, who had enlisted in Queensland.]

Witnesses called to give evidence and those who lodged submissions appeared evenly divided as to the truth of the German story and the circumstances of the sinking. However, in a departure from the official history by Gill, the Committee concluded (among others) that 'a strong case can be made that the *Kormoran*'s underwater torpedo capacity played a major role in the defeat of the *Sydney*'. It was the first time that an assessment of the claims and counter-claims had been publicly adjudicated. But this finding was not to deter those who believed in the version of events portrayed by Gill in finding that the *Sydney* had been struck by a torpedo from the above-water tubes of the raider *Kormoran,* while both vessels were sailing along at close quarters at about 14 knots.

Further public discussions were held, and still the protagonists could not agree. Attention then switched to the most likely location of the *Sydney* wreck site. Two locations were proffered as search areas – a northern sector west of Steep Point and a southern sector near the Abrolhos Islands on the western coast of Australia. After much debate, the Finding Sydney Foundation finally got approval to search the northern area in the vicinity of 26°S, 111°E where most German survivors suggested the battle had taken place. In 2007, British explorer David Mearns of Sydney Search Pty Ltd was appointed to lead the Finding Sydney Search Foundation expedition. As a result, the *Sydney* and *Kormoran* wreck sites were found in March 2008.

The locations of the wreck sites and the images obtained appeared to show that the German story was correct in many respects, and within a matter of weeks the Chief of the Defence Force appointed a Commission of Inquiry to inquire into and report upon circumstances associated with the loss of HMAS *Sydney* and on the consequent loss of life and related events. The president of the inquiry, Terence Cole, AO, RFD, was given wide powers on any matter of relevance that he saw fit to pursue. With such far-reaching terms of reference, this inquiry and subsequent report was meant to have been the final word on the saga. Cole's final report was delivered in August 2009.

In his report on the battle, Commissioner Cole concluded that 'there is no basis for doubting the essential elements of the account the German survivors gave of the engagement and the sinking of *Sydney*'. Although this finding fell short of countenancing G Hermon Gill's complete faith in the German story that no room was left for doubt as to its accuracy, Justice Cole still found there was no basis for doubting – this, despite the fact that the Germans could not all agree on crucial aspects of the battle and that some of the crewmen had changed their testimonies over the years.

The extensive report by President Cole, who held the rank of commodore in the Naval Reserve, was roundly accepted by the Navy and by the government which had initiated the inquiry. It was generally welcomed by historians, but it did not placate those researchers who continued to examine and question the basis on which some of the findings were made. To them, of the many different stories, there was reason for doubting the particular German story supported by Cole.

Some could not accept that such an inquiry, conducted by the Navy and with evidence given by civilians, could have achieved an impartial outcome. Besides, during this inquiry and well before all of the evidence had been presented, it was widely reported that Justice Cole had foreshadowed the likely outcome by stating that he would not be surprised if he found that the Germans had told the truth – the truth as envisaged by him. It was considered inconceivable that the announcement of a naval inquiry that was essentially inquiring into itself and its past actions could have led to a different outcome from that expressed by navy historian G Hermon Gill.

Most concerning was that the two major inquiries held in 1997 and 2008 had reached completely different conclusions in regard to the opening phase of the battle. Obviously, this could only have occurred due to placing more emphasis on the evidence of particular *Kormoran* survivors. As a result, one of these two inquiry findings had been incorrectly assessed.

In the first instance, the Senate JSCFADT Inquiry concluded that the underwater torpedo (which could not be launched if the vessel's speed exceeded three knots) played a major role in the *Sydney*'s defeat. This finding attached more significance to the evidence of those ordinary crewmen who implied that the vessels were stationary or moving very slowly when the action began. On the other hand, the Commission of Inquiry discounted the word of the bulk of the *Kormoran*'s crewmen in preference to the word of the Royal Australian Navy in 1941–2.

These dissimilar findings are perplexing because both inquiries had in their possession a similar array of evidence on which to adjudicate. However, it was not helpful to the inquiries that many of those at their battle stations and on the deck of the *Kormoran* during the opening phase of the battle could not estimate the speed of their ship or even indicate whether the vessel may have been stationary. And for those below deck, surely the sound and vibration of its diesel engines would have indicated that their vessel was either stationary, moving very slowly, or making considerable headway. Clearly, the raider was either stationary or nearly so, or moving steadily ahead.

Regardless of the viewpoints expressed by his crew at the time, the problem for Detmers was that he could not promote in the minds of the interrogating officers the idea that a stationary *Kormoran* may have fired its underwater torpedo. To do so would have led to the suspicion that the torpedo had been launched before he had made his declaration and as a consequence, he may have acted illegally under the rules of international warfare. But ironically at Perth on 1st December 1941, it was Detmers who initially let slip when being interrogated that after his vessel had been identified 'the cruiser signalled stop' via searchlight and then asked for the secret call from a distance. But thereafter he changed his mind and gave the impression to his interrogators and in the reports on the action that both vessels had continued to move ahead at the steady pace of about 14–15 knots.

Nevertheless, and despite the fact that Detmers had originally stated that the cruiser had signalled him to stop, the Commission of Inquiry based its deliberations solely on both vessels moving at the aforesaid speed, as well as saying that the stop order did not mean the vessel had stopped, although if he hadn't have at least slowed, Admiralty had instructed the arresting ship to open fire. Whether true or not, the inquiry scenario seemed persuasive enough because of the purported speed of the ships that he had stated, as well as being corroborated by other German reports on the action. Besides, Detmers had indicated that after an unsuspecting *Sydney* had steadily overhauled her quarry and as both vessels were moving at a steady speed on a parallel track some 900 metres apart, *Kormoran* opened fire with her guns, and shortly afterwards the cruiser had been struck by one of the raider's battery of two (deck) torpedoes.

With or without Detmers's knowledge and well before he had compiled his action reports, some crewmen had already expressed their views. For example, survivors rescued by the State Ship *Koolinda* told that the raider had been ordered to stop and an engineer officer said that when they could not reply to the secret letters, they were then ordered to stop. A member of the raider's gun crew said '*Sydney* told us to stop, which we did, or almost so…*Sydney* also more or less stopped'...and when interviewed 65 years later he again stated that both ships were almost stationary, adding that a small boat was being swung out. And evidence from the diary of a crewman that *Kormoran* had been ordered to stop at a distance signifies that she had remained at a very slow speed until the battle started.

The above quotations not only support Detmers's original statement that the cruiser had been signalled to stop at whatever distance, they also demonstrate that the *Sydney*'s Captain Burnett had stopped the *Kormoran* after having established its disguised name, *Straat Malakka*, and immediately afterwards had asked for her secret letters. That Detmers did not reply with the secret letters illustrates that Burnett had assessed the vessel as suspicious and as a consequence, stopped the vessel at a distance in accordance with the identification and challenge procedures issued by the Admiralty.

However, more recent comments by a wireless operator (who had been called a traitor by his fellow crewmen) confirmed the shot from the underwater tube: 'Yes, one shot and the first shot was from underwater...', and he again revealed that 'the starboard underwater torpedo was fired first – while at slow speed. This long-held secret was shared with many survivors... it was discussed and talked over in the prison camp. The torpedo personnel explained it and it was passed around in conversation. We had (more than) enough time to talk about it'. He further described that 'the guns opened fire when the torpedo hit'. And a torpedo mechanic wrote that 'the torpedo was already zipping through the water as the gun flaps opened'.

From these comments it seems as though Detmers may have delivered his concealed underwater torpedo unobtrusively and illegally before his declaration. Thus, the Commission of Inquiry might have erred in overlooking the significance of Detmers's 'stop order' statement as well as confirmatory evidence from his crew. This includes the interrogations notes of survivors rescued by the troopship *Aquitania*, revealing that the action 'started' from an estimated distance of '10 kilometers' – a similar distance that complied with the Admiralty's challenge procedures for stopping and identifying suspicious vessels from a minimum of 14,000 yards.

Evidence of the stop order and the subsequent first shot from the underwater tube can be further verified. For example, though most reports had indicated that three torpedoes were fired in the opening phase of the battle, one survivor was more specific in explaining that the two above-water torpedoes were in fact belatedly launched but both missed their target. It goes without saying that considering these torpedoes were about to be fired and because they were exposed to gunfire from the cruiser, it demanded that they be fired off in case they exploded due to the return fire from the *Sydney*. And in his diary account, an officer from the *Kormoran* had described them as 'two dud torpedoes' – both tubes being jammed on their ratchet mountings.

Although naval interrogators in 1941 were aware that the *Kormoran* was armed with underwater torpedoes, only scant reference of its specific use had been forthcoming from the Germans. They were forbidden to discuss the raider's secret weapons, especially during interrogations in case their comments were to have been construed as incriminating the Germans in an illegal act. Of the more recent evidence made available by the two inquiries, only the JSCFADT Inquiry took their comments seriously.

Now that the wreck sites of the *Sydney* and *Kormoran* have been located, crucial evidence that has been in the public arena since the 1940s accurately establishes the navigable parameters of the raider, which is proven mathematically absolute. In this respect, the position given by Detmers on the location of the battle site, the relevant positions shown in all three action reports and the nominated course sailed by the raider, confirms that Detmers had been ordered to dramatically slow from his speed of 14 knots.

In this sequel to my previous book, *Oversight* (which also had made known the confined parameters of the action site), *Masterly Misled* uncovers the intrigue and clandestine operations of the Australian and British Navies during the period of late 1941, which had resulted in the *Sydney* being sent to her grave.

❑ ❑ ❑

PROLOGUE

The Navy's battle account between the cruiser and the raider in November 1941 as it now stands has been concreted in the minds of the public over the past 80 years. However, what is largely unknown is that the story of the action as it is now told is not based on all the evidence available, rather it has been mainly assessed from statements made by a select group of *Kormoran* survivors – this, in the complete absence of survivors from the *Sydney*. The Navy claims that the story told by these few Germans seemed to ring true.

Findings made by the recent Commission of Inquiry in 2009 unequivocally support the Navy proposition from an historical perspective, but as archival records purporting to corroborate the inquiry findings were based on the evidence of a few, in many instances statements often flagrantly disregarded by the inquiry disprove these findings. An opportunity to reconsider the whole ambit of evidence has therefore been necessary.

The 2008 Commission of Inquiry had the following terms of reference:

To inquire into and report upon the circumstances associated with the loss of HMAS *Sydney* II in November 1941 and consequent loss of life and related events subsequent thereto. President Justice Terrence Cole had also been authorised to issue the procedural directions he considered appropriate, inform himself on any matter relevant to the inquiry as he thinks fit, determine whether any part of the inquiry should be conducted in private and direct that all oral evidence be given on oath or affirmation.

Commissioner Cole had thus been given wide powers to investigate the circumstances of the *Sydney*'s loss. He had the resources of the Navy for the purpose of conducting investigations and he had a plethora of archival evidence from which to draw upon, as well as photographic evidence of the wrecks of the warships. But throughout the proceedings his call was on others to provide evidence, which he compared with information already sanctioned by the Navy. And in many instances, those who gave evidence in good faith were looked upon as adversaries, simply because their evidence did not conform to the Navy's version of events, as attested in the transcripts.

Overall, it was an inquiry that had delivered the desired result the government had wanted and on which they had sought to end any further discussion. The German story as told by those few Germans had proven to be accurate, according to Justice Cole – this, well before all the evidence had been heard. Many observers had good reason to suspect his findings would be a fait accompli and this proved to be the case when he delivered his status quo findings, which just happened to be very similar to those made back in early 1942.

The inquiry found that the battle was fought as a result of a chance encounter and that the *Sydney*'s Captain Burnett was responsible for the loss of the cruiser because he had not followed his orders. It found that the cruiser was struck by one of the above-water torpedoes because the *Kormoran* was moving too fast to launch the underwater torpedo. It also found that the RAN had no knowledge of the battle until the afternoon of 24 November, five days after the battle.

President Cole gave compelling reasons why Captain Burnett would have been suspicious of the *Kormoran,* which had been disguised as the Dutch merchant ship *Straat Malakka*, but in his final deliberations he appeared to ignore them all. He found there was no basis for doubting the essential elements of the account the German officers gave of the engagement and the sinking of the *Sydney*, inferring that survivors gave similar accounts, whereas in fact many witnesses had portrayed the action very differently.

The inquiry also asserted that the *Sydney* was not at action stations but at cruising stations, and that Burnett obviously thought the disguised *Kormoran* was friendly and was taken by surprise after the cruiser had asked her to give the secret call sign. In simple terms, Burnett had been deceived by the vessel's appearance, did not take the necessary precautions when approaching and had flagrantly ignored the routine instructions for identifying a suspicious vessel. This is indeed a daft scenario for a captain of an Australian cruiser to display.

There is, however, compelling evidence that Burnett had been aware that he was facing an enemy vessel that he had been sent to intercept. A witness statement and an examination of the sailing schedules of a particular troopship, plus the fast return to the site of the action (for which permission from the Royal Navy had to be given), confirms that Burnett suspected that he was dealing with an enemy ship. Unpalatable as it may be to state it, this information had been made available to JSCFADT, but had been entirely disregarded by the Commission of Inquiry.

Even more outlandish was the finding that the observable damage to the *Sydney* is consistent with the German assertion that the *Kormoran* fired two torpedoes from her above-water starboard mounts, one of which hit the cruiser, even though underwater images of the damage to the bow do not indicate the origin of the torpedo, or indeed how many had been fired.

In some cases, the Commission of Inquiry made its deliberations on archival evidence alone, and in this respect, it can be argued that the findings can be justified. But much more was required.

It failed to investigate key documents and recent claims by German survivors hitherto entirely disregarded by the Navy.

The inquiry also failed to adequately address the message from Geraldton supposedly sent on the night of 19 November 1941, as well as failing to identify the emigrant from Germany in the 1950s purporting to be from the raider *Kormoran* who had stated that the *Sydney* had been finally torpedoed and sunk by a Japanese submarine. Detailed research has emerged rendering many other of Justice Cole's findings invalid.

Conspiracy theories are what they are – theories only. But when theory is supplanted by navigational fact, conspiracy becomes transparent and those initially responsible deserve condemnation. However, this is not to say that the present-day Navy should be censured as the originators or the perpetrators of the cover-up. Nevertheless, it should be borne in mind that these shortcomings are a product of wartime, during which unintended consequences often resulted in attempts to conceal the facts.

And history is not history based on the evidence of only a small sample of the hundreds of witnesses. Nor is it written and based on 'empirical' evidence that may appear to tell the full story. It is written only after an overall evaluation has been conducted and an independent analysis has been undertaken to confirm the evidence. The process of fact-finding is the only way to distinguish the truthfulness or otherwise.

On both counts, the inquiry failed to do the required investigative work before the commencement of proceedings, which resulted in a false portrayal of the action and to ultimately mislead the public and relatives of the *Sydney*'s deceased. The content of this book delineates the facts from the fiction from information that has been previously widely circulated. But due to the fact that the findings made in this book are in many instances contrary to the Commission of Inquiry findings, it is therefore imperative that the reader be acquainted with Justice Cole's ruling, which can be found at the many libraries in Australia, and on the website, 'HMAS Sydney II Commission of Inquiry'.

❑ ❑ ❑

Navigation at Sea: In 1941, well before the Global Positioning System had been introduced, navigators could determine the ship's position manually by sextant at midday local time to verify speed, the ship's whereabouts and take corrective action, if required. In ascertaining other purposes of navigation, such as for manual planning of course(s) to be sailed and for intermediate distance(s), they used another relatively simple method that was available only in those days:

LENGTH OF A DEGREE OF LONGITUDE			
Latitude	Nautical Miles	Latitude	Nautical Miles
4	59.9	22	55.7
5	59.8	23	55.3
6	59.7	24	54.9
7	59.6	25	54.5
8	59.5	26	54.0
9	59.3	27	53.6
10	59.2	28	53.1
11	59.0	29	52.6
12	58.8	30	52.1
13	58.5	31	51.5
14	58.3	32	51.0
15	58.0	33	50.4
16	57.8	34	49.9
17	57.5	35	49.3
18	57.1	36	48.7
19	56.8	37	48.0
20	56.5	38	47.4
21	56.1	39	46.7

Distance between all latitudes = 60nms
A nautical mile = 1852 metres
[Defined as one minute of latitude]
60 seconds = one minute
One nautical mile = 0.869 standard miles
Example:
From latitude 15°S, longitude 106°E to
latitude 29°18'S, longitude 112°36'E.
Bearing = 157°, tan 23° (trigonometry)
Distance = 932.21nm (Pythagoras)

(58.0)
23°
858nm
932nm
½ = (55.225)
6.6 × 55.225 = 364.485
(52.45)

Part latitudes are proportional to the relevant longitudinal values shown

The navigation used in the 1940s is applied throughout this book.

COVER-UP

In 2009, the Commission of Inquiry found that HSK *Kormoran* was not directed to intercept HMAS *Sydney,* a finding based on the assessment that the raider did not know the location or movements of the cruiser before the interception took place. No serious consideration was given to the alternate proposition or even that others may have known about the general locale of the battle site. Instead, the inquiry found that the *Sydney* had accidentally stumbled across the raider *Kormoran* on 19 November 1941, when returning to Fremantle from a routine escort duty. It was described by the inquiry as 'a chance encounter'.

The inquiry, however, had also failed to adequately identify the location of the UK troopship MV *Largs Bay* at the time of the encounter, even though Secret Intelligence Messages (SIMs) had established her general whereabouts. The inquiry was also told by the Naval Faculty that the Norwegian tanker *Bramora* was closest to the position of the encounter, but her sailing schedule proves otherwise. It will also emerge that the position of the troopship on 19 November has specific relevance to the *Sydney*'s encounter with *Kormoran*, and for the Norwegian tanker *Bramora*, SIM messages by the Navy establish that the position of the vessel has been wrongfully assessed.

Larger fast vessels, such as the 45,000-ton troopship HMT *Aquitania,* normally sailed direct from Singapore to Australia via Sunda Strait and Cape Leeuwin, but other ships (excluding large naval vessels) were routed via specific way points either east or west away from the main Indian Ocean shipping lane to avoid the possible presence of enemy vessels. For example, in November 1941, the tanker *Bramora* and the troopship *Largs*

Bay had been routed east and *Trocas* west. But that survivors from the *Kormoran* had been discovered by *Aquitania* may have been due to the fact that the vessel had sailed directly along the shipping route from Sunda Strait to Cape Leeuwin. Thus, in some respects, it can be claimed that *Aquitania* had discovered German survivors by chance.

During escort of the troopship *Zealandia* from Fremantle northwards to the Sunda Strait, HMAS *Sydney*'s Captain Joseph Burnett came under the command of the Royal Navy's Commander-in-Chief of China Station (ADM Geoffrey Layton) at latitude 13°S on 15 November at 1500z (GMT). He was then required to follow any orders from C-in-C China until the cruiser's planned return southward to the said latitude at 2330z on 17 November, thereby reverting to Australia Station RAN command.

Note: z time = GMT (Greenwich Mean Time)
G time = GMT + 7 hours
H time = GMT + 8 hours (WST)
K time = GMT + 10 hours (EST)

After delivering *Zealandia* to HMS *Durban* at 0400z on 17 November to position 7°56'S, 104°40'E (41nm short of the originally planned objective at latitude 7°15'S) for ongoing escort to Singapore, the *Sydney* allegedly set course and speed for her return journey direct to Fremantle for an arrival of 'PM on 20 November'. It is in this context that the chance encounter with the *Kormoran* is said to have taken place at 0900z on 19 November 1941.

If the above assessment was true, on sighting the raider the cruiser had travelled 1,149nm for a period of 53 hours direct from position 7°56S, 104°40'E reached at 0400z on 17 November (as advised by C-in-C China) to position 25°54'S, 111°20'E, the point of encounter with the *Kormoran* at 0900z on 19 November. This equates to an average minimum speed of 21.68 knots against the Westralian Current of about 0.5 knots, and in order to achieve this speed the *Sydney* would require an overall speed of at least 22.2K. Provided that approval had been given for this speed, the *Sydney* would have arrived in Fremantle a further 438 miles away (via 31° 25'S, 115°E) at approximately 2 pm on 20 November. Burnett would thus have fulfilled his estimated time of arrival (ETA) which he had signalled on 11 November after departing Fremantle.

A speed of 22 knots certainly required operational approval for the use of an additional boiler because such a speed is excessive and uneconomical compared with previous return trips from routine escort duties of about *18–19 knots on two boilers. The expenditure of additional fuel could hardly be justified for a routine mission. Clearly, this is not what Burnett had in mind nor would have contemplated.

***Note:** At 19 knots, the *Sydney* would have returned direct to Fremantle from the intended rendezvous position 7°15'S, 104°40'E at around midnight on 20 November (distance = 1623nm). It was only due to the slower than expected progress made by the troopship *Zealandia* that Burnett had arranged for the rendezvous with HMS *Durban* at latitude 7°56'S in lieu of 7°15'S. From the actual rendezvous position to Fremantle Harbour (distance = 1575nm), HMAS *Sydney* (also at max 19K) had been due back in Fremantle at approximately 2 am on 21 November. [The return journey is based on 18.5K against the current in each case]

Given that the *Sydney* had travelled 1149nm at a constant 22 knots for which Burnett required operational approval, he could only have been given permission to do so in China Station waters while under the command of C-in-C China in Singapore. More to the point, an order for such a speed or for that matter a more rapid rate (as later explained), raises the prospect that China Station had identified enemy presence off the West Australian coast by the Singapore-controlled Far East Direction-finding Organisation (FEDO) stations in Australia based at Harman, Melville and Jandakot and that for no other reason approval had been given for the cruiser to investigate. The finding by the Commission of Inquiry that HMAS *Sydney* had encountered the *Kormoran* by chance is therefore highly questionable.

The Naval Board had been previously informed that the troop-transport MV *Largs Bay* had been due to depart Singapore at 0500z for Sydney on 15 November via Thursday Island (message from COIS, 1514/14). She was to transport service personnel, mail and military equipment from Singapore back to Australia. At 14,000 gross tons, the UK-based *Largs Bay* (maximum speed 16 knots) had been requisitioned in August 1941 as a troopship. On this occasion, some 200 passengers were embarked, including civilians. Also stowed on board were hundreds of tons of aircraft and stores for the Army and Navy.

On 16 November, *Largs Bay* was re-directed to Sydney via Cape Leeuwin at an allocated speed of 14 knots. Secret Intelligence Messages (SIMs) confirming that *Largs Bay* did not sail as originally planned via Thursday Island (Cape York route) shows the vessel positioned well to the east of the Sunda/Cape Leeuwin shipping lane on 18–19 November. Cancellation of her Cape York route had been probably influenced by a report of a suspected raider sighted in the Western Pacific near Bougainville on 15 November. The wide route taken by the troopship indicates she had been advised to avoid sailing the normal Cape Leeuwin shipping lane in case of possible enemy presence.

According to her movement card, *Largs Bay* departed Singapore and arrived in Sydney Harbour at 2043z on 28 November, a journey of about 4,429nm at an average speed of 13.51 knots.

SIM latitudinal and longitudinal positions for 18–19 November generally accord with her estimated speed. For example, at 2000z/19 the vessel had travelled 1517nm from Singapore in 111 hours at an average speed of 13.67 knots. When the *Sydney* first saw *Kormoran*, *Largs Bay* was located near 18°S, 110°35'E, 476nm to the north. Only the tug *Uco* was closer to the position of encounter, inshore, approx. 140nm away.

Most significant, however, is that when *Largs Bay* had passed through the Sunda Strait to position 6°50'S, 105°E at approx. 0050z on 17 November, HMAS *Sydney* was located nearby, just over 50nm away from the rendezvous position with *Zealandia* and HMS *Durban*. An eyewitness account corroborates the fact that they were well-positioned to meet later that day.

A submission lodged with the 1998 Parliamentary Inquiry (Vol. 1, p95) conducted by the Joint Standing Committee on Foreign Affairs, Defence and Trade, described HMAS *Sydney* as having 'escorted' the *Largs Bay* between the hours of 4 pm and 6 pm local time on 19 November. But of course, this could not have occurred on that day because the troopship was then situated over 450nm north of the *Sydney* at the time the cruiser was about to engage the *Kormoran* in battle. The person who witnessed the escort, Lindsay Drake, is probably correct with the times he nominated, but the SIM positions confirm that the interception could only have occurred on 17 November and not on 19 November. Refer letter hereunder.

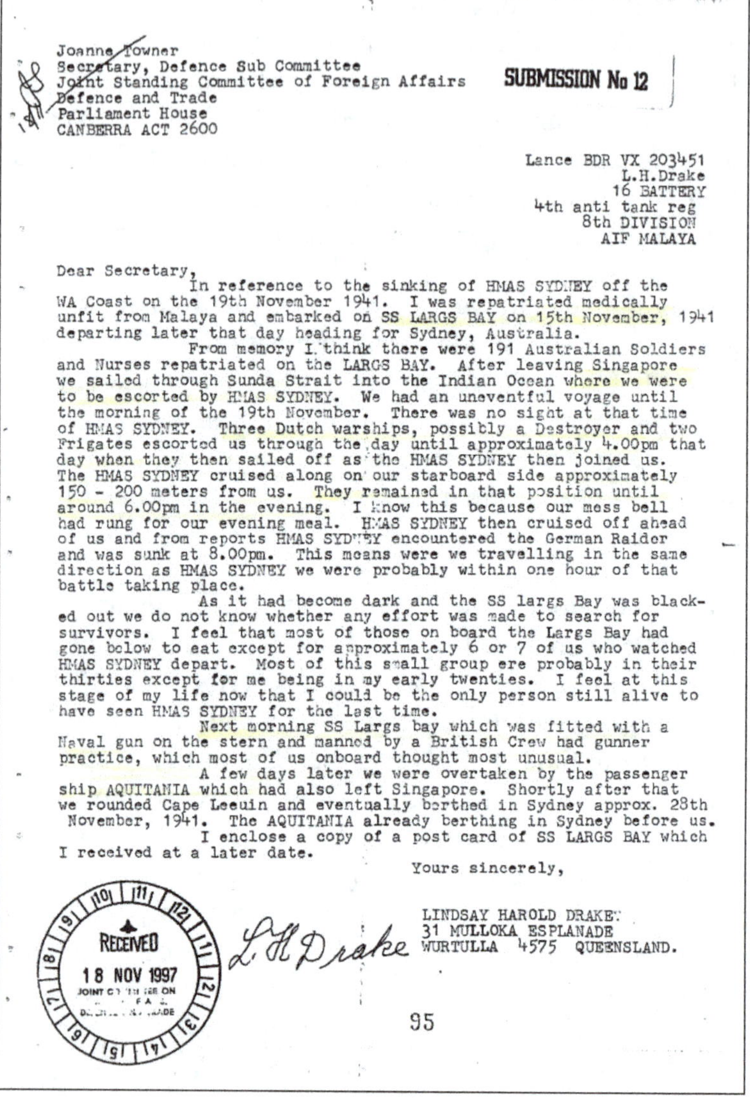

Joanne Towner
Secretary, Defence Sub Committee
Joint Standing Committee of Foreign Affairs
Defence and Trade
Parliament House
CANBERRA ACT 2600

SUBMISSION No 12

Lance BDR VX 203451
L.H.Drake
16 BATTERY
4th anti tank reg
8th DIVISION
AIF MALAYA

Dear Secretary,

In reference to the sinking of HMAS SYDNEY off the WA Coast on the 19th November 1941. I was repatriated medically unfit from Malaya and embarked on SS LARGS BAY on 15th November, 1941 departing later that day heading for Sydney, Australia.

From memory I think there were 191 Australian Soldiers and Nurses repatriated on the LARGS BAY. After leaving Singapore we sailed through Sunda Strait into the Indian Ocean where we were to be escorted by HMAS SYDNEY. We had an uneventful voyage until the morning of the 19th November. There was no sight at that time of HMAS SYDNEY. Three Dutch warships, possibly a Destroyer and two Frigates escorted us through the day until approximately 4.00pm that day when they then sailed off as the HMAS SYDNEY then joined us. The HMAS SYDNEY cruised along on our starboard side approximately 150 - 200 meters from us. They remained in that position until around 6.00pm in the evening. I know this because our mess bell had rung for our evening meal. HMAS SYDNEY then cruised off ahead of us and from reports HMAS SYDNEY encountered the German Raider and was sunk at 8.00pm. This means were we travelling in the same direction as HMAS SYDNEY we were probably within one hour of that battle taking place.

As it had become dark and the SS largs Bay was blacked out we do not know whether any effort was made to search for survivors. I feel that most of those on board the Largs Bay had gone below to eat except for approximately 6 or 7 of us who watched HMAS SYDNEY depart. Most of this small group ere probably in their thirties except for me being in my early twenties. I feel at this stage of my life now that I could be the only person still alive to have seen HMAS SYDNEY for the last time.

Next morning SS Largs bay which was fitted with a Naval gun on the stern and manned by a British Crew had gunner practice, which most of us onboard thought most unusual.

A few days later we were overtaken by the passenger ship AQUITANIA which had also left Singapore. Shortly after that we rounded Cape Leeuin and eventually berthed in Sydney approx. 28th November, 1941. The AQUITANIA already berthing in Sydney before us.

I enclose a copy of a post card of SS LARGS BAY which I received at a later date.

Yours sincerely,

L. H. Drake

LINDSAY HAROLD DRAKE
31 MULLOKA ESPLANADE
WURTULLA 4575 QUEENSLAND.

RECEIVED
18 NOV 1997
JOINT COMMITTEE ON F.A.D.T.

95

Submission establishing that HMAS *Sydney* met with *Largs Bay*

Drake's observation of HMAS *Sydney* meeting with *Largs Bay* has its inevitable conclusion:

When the troopship *Largs Bay* had entered the Indian Ocean from the Sunda Strait at 0050z on 17 November, the *Sydney* had relinquished escort of the troopship *Zealandia*. But by 0830z/17 (4 pm Singapore time), instead of returning directly to Fremantle, the cruiser had sailed easterly near position 8°18'S, 106°E, some 82nm east of the rendezvous position with HMS *Durban*. The cruiser had then intercepted the troopship at a leisurely 18 knots. Two hours later, HMAS *Sydney* departed from her near position 8°41'S, 106°16'E (*Largs Bay* had been en route to her allocated Way Point 14°S, 110°E). Upon encountering the *Kormoran* in position 25°54'S, 111°20'E, the cruiser had travelled at a far more rapid rate than ever for the return journey to Fremantle – 1,072nm at an average 23.3 knots against the current of about 0.5K [Total speed, approx. 24K].

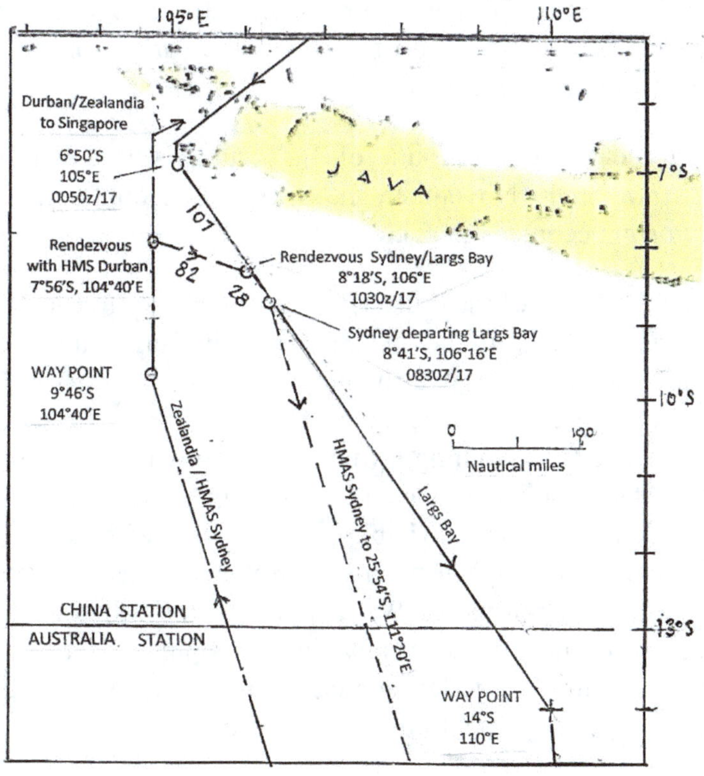

Interception of MV *Largs Bay* by HMAS *Sydney*

Acknowledgement by the inquiry that the *Largs Bay* could not have met with the *Sydney* on 19 November (as witnessed) is proven correct. This had been due to the Parliamentary Inquiry in 1998 and the Commission of Inquiry in not properly examining the claim by the witness, which would have revealed that the vessels had in fact met earlier – on 17 November, at the times claimed by Lindsay Drake.

MV *Largs Bay* and MV *Bramora* (both had sailed east of the shipping lane) were the first vessels to pass the vicinity of the *Sydney/Kormoran* action site. SIM messages reveal (by backtracking) that of these two ships, the troopship is suspected of reconnoitring the area of where the action took place, but the oiler had been due to pass approx 60nm due east of the battle site on 21 November – *Largs Bay* in the early morning and *Bramora* in the afternoon (WST).

Given the witness account of the cruiser's presence with *Largs Bay* on 17 November, the *Sydney*'s encounter with the *Kormoran* becomes much clearer:

On the departure of the cruiser, the responsibility for the safety of *Largs Bay* lay with the *Sydney*'s Captain Burnett and he had at hand the aid of his Walrus aircraft (range 520nm) to keep the troopship under surveillance further north in case it was attacked and for searching for possible enemy presence further south. At sunrise on 19 November, the gap between the vessels had widened too far for visible aerial contact with *Largs Bay*, but at about 9 am the *Kormoran*, approx. 250 miles to the south, came within range of the Walrus. However, in the event that Burnett used his Walrus at any time, stopping to retrieve the aircraft would have added immeasurably to the average speed required by the *Sydney* to intercept the raider.

In the case that the Walrus sighted the *Kormoran* (based on both vessels course and speed), it was a simple matter to calculate the point and time of interception, although Burnett's initial assessment of the errant vessel would have been an easy task because the VAI showed that no merchant ship was expected to be in the area. And his suspicions would have been aroused by the fact that if the vessel had remained unreported on Australia Station for a considerable time, his own experience in dealing with mercantile shipping during which very few arrived on Australia Station unannounced, would have led him to believe that it must be foremost presumed to be an enemy vessel.

Above all else is the secrecy of the interception with *Largs Bay,* for it is truly incomprehensible that the master (and officers) of the ship did not at any stage divulge to the RAN that HMAS *Sydney* had met with her. Their first opportunity was on berthing in Sydney Harbour on 29 November – this, at the time the Navy was still trying to establish the facts and fate of the cruiser. That complete silence on the matter has been maintained ever since points inevitably to the fact that the captain of the *Largs Bay*, who at that time (on 17 November) had been under the direction of China Station, had been ordered by C-in-C not to disclose the rendezvous with the cruiser.

Drake's view of the departure of three escorting Dutch warships and close escort by the *Sydney* ought to have been taken more seriously by the inquiry. After all, the disposition of warships on 17 November showed that only three warships had been assigned to the Sunda Strait area and the Port of Batavia (Tanjong Prick), two of which can be identified as the cruiser *Tromp* and the destroyer *Van Nes* (message from NB to DNOWA, 1618H/18). That these vessels regularly escorted allied ships arriving in the Sunda Strait and out of NEI waters indicates that Drake's claim is soundly based. [Other Dutch warships were based at Sourabaya and Balikpapan.]

Considering *Largs Bay* is found to have been in such close proximity to the *Sydney* does not mean that the cruiser intended to escort the vessel south all the way to Fremantle. In the past, the troopship had often sailed independently and she was armed with a stern gun that offered some protection. And for Burnett, who had signalled 'PM/20' as his expected ETA in Fremantle, keeping pace with the much slower troopship would have delayed his return considerably.

However, Drake should not have been confused about the identity of the RAN cruiser he had observed for two hours that was stationed approximately '150–200 metres' away because from this short distance it is highly unlikely that her distinctive features and white ensign could have been mistaken for any other type of warship of any other nationality. Obviously, HMAS *Sydney* had good reason to go out of her way to be there.

At a speed of some 24 knots to Fremantle (providing the raider had not been encountered), the cruiser would have returned much earlier than the planned 'PM' time of arrival. Thus, Drake's observation of the presence of the cruiser, plus her high-speed return over a distance of 1,074nms to intercept the *Kormoran*, again renders the notion of a chance encounter highly questionable.

Note: The encounter with *Kormoran* at 0900z on 19 November almost head-on had taken place on the western extremity of the shipping lane to Cape Leeuwin, approx. 25nm west of her previous return track from Sunda Strait on 5 October.

According to the archival files and due to the different frequencies used by the Royal Navy in China Station waters, HMAS *Sydney* did not receive any messages from Australia Station command while under C-in-C China control between 1500z/15 and 2330z/17. Burnett had been ordered to revert to China Station WT frequency during these hours while in waters above latitude 13°S, and for contact with HMS *Durban* during the rendezvous, the cruiser had been instructed to 'watch' on a frequency of 3835kcs (message to *Sydney*, 0311z/12).

These orders meant that on departing *Largs Bay* at 6 pm local (Singapore) time on 17 November, HMAS *Sydney* was required to revert to Australia Station command about 13 hours later at latitude 13°S (the dividing line between Australia and China Stations), and in order to reach this south latitude a minimum speed of 20.7 knots (against the current) was required over a distance of 269nm. But during this 13-hour period, the cruiser had been urgently despatched southwards and because contact by WT with China Station had been due to cease at 2330z/17, a measure of the maximum speed required for the *Sydney* to reach the encounter position from latitude 13°S can thus be obtained. For example, in the case of HMAS *Sydney* having been despatched when communication with WT China Station had been due to cease, the cruiser had travelled 803nm from latitude 13°S to the encounter position (25°54'S, 111°20'E) in 33.5 hours at an average speed of over 24 knots against the current (total speed required, approx. 24.5K) to intercept with the *Kormoran* at 0900z/19. Again, by way of comparison and with regard to travelling 1072nm direct from the cruiser's position at 1030z/17, a speed of 23.3 knots against the current was required.

British areas of station responsibility (blue)

Considering the cruiser had taken over escort of *Largs Bay* from the Dutch warships for approximately two hours, Burnett was unlikely to have received orders from C-in-C China during this period. But if so, he would have departed from the troopship earlier. He was much more likely to have received orders between the hours of 1030z and 2330z on 17 November – this, before the cruiser was due to revert to Australia Station command at latitude 13°S. And it was during this period that average speeds of between 23 and 24 knots were required to be achieved all the way to the encounter position.

It was completely out of character for the *Sydney* to have maintained such a high speed over such a long distance while on a routine return from escort duty, though Burnett would have achieved a much faster rate had the cruiser not sailed on a direct course to the encounter position or if he had stopped to retrieve his Walrus aircraft. On only one previous occasion had a high-speed run of 25 knots over 2,100nm from Colombo to Aden been undertaken, but that was an exception because it was a special operational order for the cruiser to join the Royal Navy fleet in the Mediterranean.

There is no evidence in Naval Archives that C-in-C China had informed naval authorities in Australia that the *Sydney* had been despatched to find a suspected enemy vessel or that the cruiser had signalled this same intention while under RAN command. A joint operation was not considered necessary because it was merely predicated on a suspicion that an enemy vessel had been detected. Besides, such an operation to identify and possibly arrest the errant vessel could have proven unwieldy. Incoming messages would be received by the cruiser, but as transmissions would not be advisable in an environment of strict radio silence until the suspect vessel had been intercepted, Burnett would have to rely on his own judgement, rather than from orders issued to him by the RN and/or the RAN.

After the *Sydney* had been classified overdue for 36 hours, a request by the Naval Board for the time and position in which the cruiser had departed company with the *Durban* (message 2333H/23), solicited a slow response from China Station. A reminder requesting 'any information...' (message from NB, 1009H/24), eventually drew a brief response in signalling the position of the rendezvous with HMS *Durban*, but they gave no further information whatsoever on *Sydney*'s presence in China Station waters (message to NB, 1251H/24). It was this reply that led the RAN to believe that the cruiser had sailed directly to Fremantle from the rendezvous point.

However, this last almost ambivalent reply received 12 hours after the Naval Board had sought any further information does not ring true. After all, C-in-C China did not disclose that the

Sydney had, while under RN command, intercepted *Largs Bay,* or had even made the Naval Board aware of her presence near the cruiser. And although the RAN had been made aware of the troopship's general sailing schedule and projected track to Sydney via Cape Leeuwin for inclusion in the VAI, Burnett had not received this information while in China Station waters. It is just not possible that he would have known her exact whereabouts for the purpose of interception if *Largs Bay* was to have observed the customary radio silence. Information on her location could therefore only have come to Burnett from C-in-C China, or via HMS *Durban*.

Furthermore, that *Durban* was by necessity cognizant of current Allied shipping movements in the Sunda Strait area, she must have been aware of *Largs Bay*'s approximate position at all times. And that the sailing schedule also confirms the presence of the troopship in the Sunda Strait early on 17 November, *Durban*'s knowledge of her movements is unquestioned. It would have been remiss of her not to have communicated the troopship's approximate position sometime before the rendezvous. Besides, a liner of her size and which transported troops and carried important military cargo was regarded as a prime target for an enemy vessel. But more importantly, communication between the *Sydney* and *Durban* had proven to be essential otherwise the amended rendezvous position with *Zealandia* could not have been arranged.

As there was normally no need for the cruiser to return at such a high speed, clearly, Burnett had received information on the possible whereabouts of a suspected enemy vessel and hence the urgency for the *Sydney* to investigate. But he simply had no good reason to justify the excessive speed and the expenditure of additional fuel over such a long distance. Unquestionably, Burnett could only have been ordered to do so from sources within China Station, which also had exclusive control on enemy direction-finding via its FEDO stations.

There is further compelling evidence that C-in-C China had been cognisant of the *Sydney*'s involvement in a battle:

SIM messages confirm that *Largs Bay* had planned to arrive near the scene of the battle in the Indian Ocean on the morning of 21 November at approximately 4 am local time. But even though the vessel had been assisted by the current from Cape Leeuwin to Cape Otway Signal Station she had attained an average speed of only 13.51 knots (0.49K below her allocated speed) for the journey from Singapore to Sydney. In fact, she was some 10 hours behind her schedule when she reported to Wilsons Promontory and 14 hours late arriving in Sydney. Such a large reduction in speed is in marked contrast to *Aquitania*, which had sailed almost the same route and had experienced similar sea conditions.

PORT	MESSAGE NOS.	ARRIVE 1941	DEPART	REMARKS	PORT
Singapore			0500 Nov 15	via C Leeuwin	Prom. E. 0758/27.
Sydney	41/13	2043 Nov 28	1150 Dec 12	Route 1351/16/11 →H.K. Route 42.	
Auckland	107/8	0222 Dec 17			

Movement Card Schedule for *Largs Bay*

Most obvious is that the above schedule shows that *Largs Bay* had not been assisted by the easterly current while traversing Australia's southern coast and because the much larger *Aquitania* had been assisted to the tune of 0.4K, there is absolutely no doubt that *Largs Bay* likewise would have exceeded her prescribed speed of 14 knots on this leg of the journey. In fact, all vessels en route from Cape Leeuwin to Cape Otway are assisted by this perennial current.

For instance, her movement card (below) shows this same ship had earlier departed Fremantle in November 1940 for Adelaide at 0825z, arriving four days later at 1326z in 101 hours, at an average speed of 15.1 knots for the 1,523nm journey. The troopship had thus exceeded her allocated speed of 14.5

knots by 0.6k. In order to account for the lack of speed on this last occasion in sailing at less than her allocated speed from Cape Leeuwin to Cape Otway, *Largs Bay* must have sailed a greater distance on the Indian Ocean leg within the available timeframe. This is very suspicious, which means the vessel had been diverted from its scheduled course, ostensibly to search the site of the action (see Edgar Emerich's observations below).

Movement Card Schedule for *Largs Bay* – Fremantle to Adelaide, Nov 1940

SIM messages at 2000z/19 confirm the position of the troopship and that she had reached the proximity of the action (25°54'S, 111°20'E) at 2000z on 20 November (0400H/21 Nov, WST). But backtracking from Cape Otway (where *Largs Bay* had been 10 hours behind schedule) and with currents in mind, reveals that this ship had also gained speed across the Great Australian Bight from Cape Leeuwin as shown on the above movement card, to the tune of about 14.4 knots and so it should have arrived in position 35°S, 115°E at 2200z on 22 November. Before that, she had been impeded by the Westralian Current and could raise no more than 13.5 knots against the current, 578nm from the scene of the action. This had meant that the *Largs Bay* had left the scene at approx. 0300z on 21 November (1100H/21 WST) and had searched the area for survivors for at least seven hours.

The only possible explanation, save for an engine breakdown (which is not recorded on her movement card) that can account for the slow speed of *Largs Bay* is that China Station had notified the troopship's Captain Roberts of the approximate position of where the battle had taken place and as his vessel approached the battle site, he had been re-directed to search the proximity of the site in the ensuing daylight hours.

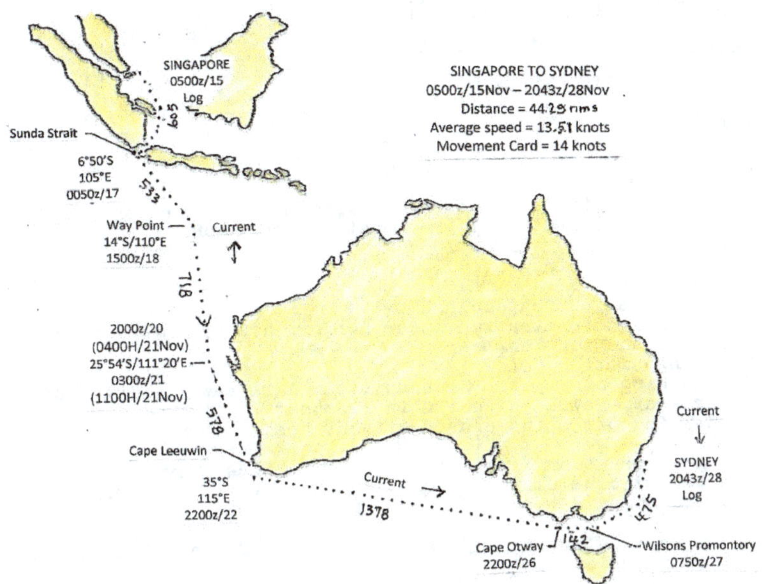

Track of *Largs Bay* from Singapore to Sydney

Edgar Emerich describes (under interrogation) what he saw from his boat while drifting – a merchantman with one funnel (*Largs Bay*), the only vessel in the area on the morning of 21 November.

Interrogation Notes 4.12.41.

EMERICH Edgar Erich Helmut.

Born 31.1.1916. Frankfurt / Main

Single.

N.N 733/37 S N. C. O.

In lifeboat with von Goesseln - wooden boat, seen by plane; taken on board small grey boat, armed 2 guns (Y D)
Volunteer in Navy since 1937.
Had been in Spain,
Italy,
Was on Warship "Deutschland".
Worked in Administration under Purser. 4th Division. More to do on land than on sea.
Fighting station below.
Saw nothing of fight. Came up after dark saw burning Cruiser far away. Developed boils in lifeboat.
A week in boat ships passed without seeing them.

1. A merchantman with 1 funnel - 7/8 miles away. No signals except blue cloth - 1 or two days after departure from "Kormoran."

2. 2 days later saw a passenger ship, 4 funnels 5 miles away, no signals.

3. Early morning saw a ship in the distance, looked like a tanker - funnel aft.

4. Monday a plane flew over them.

Aquitania had reached Cape Otway at 2125z/26 from Sunda Strait in excess of the allocated speed of 21 knots, assisted largely by the westerly current from Cape Leeuwin. At the very least, for the vessel to have been even minimally assisted by the current to the same extent as *Aquitania*, *Largs Bay* would have averaged 14.4 knots from Cape Leeuwin and have arrived there earlier. But SIM messages show that the vessel had been due to arrive at latitude 26°S at approx. 2100z/20 which, in turn, establishes that she had sailed the remaining distance to Cape Leeuwin (578nm) at the improbable average speed of 11.8 knots in 48.5 hours.

In the case that *Largs Bay* had sailed from latitude 26°S to Cape Leeuwin at a more appropriate speed of say 14 knots in 41 hours, it means that the vessel had been unaccountably delayed on this leg of the journey for at least seven hours. The corollary means that this ship had been instructed by C-in-C China to reconnoitre on the morning of 21 November (as Emerich's evidence confirms) and to then have continued her voyage to Cape Leeuwin that afternoon. This explains the below-average speed to Cape Otway, which resulted in the vessel being 10 hours behind schedule when passing the signal station at Wilsons Promontory on 27 November.

Finally, that *Largs Bay* had arrived 14 hours late (against the strong current) in Sydney Harbour, further explains the role of C-in-C China in secretly diverting the vessel to locate survivors of a battle. Note that the *Aquitania* had arrived in Sydney within an hour or two of schedule.

This signal 19 (above) marked Wilsons Promontory is most unusually prominent on her movement card. It is conspicuously noted separately. It had either been sent to or delivered by the vessel while passing by the signal station. The content of the message is unknown, but it can be taken to relate to her untimely schedule.

....

MV *Bramora*, a Norwegian tanker with a maximum speed of 10 knots (as shown on movement card) had departed Singapore at 0800z on 13 November bound for Adelaide via Cape Leeuwin. Her planned sailing schedule (the coordinates through which she would pass), including Way Point 13°S, 109°E (message from NB, 1934z/15), is clearly delineated on the diagram below. The tanker was due in Adelaide on 30 November and had been routed easterly away from the Cape Leeuwin shipping lane to avoid possible enemy presence.

In 2009, the RANs Naval Faculty claimed that at the time HMAS *Sydney* encountered *Kormoran*, *Bramora* was situated 427nm distant to the north. However, this is not consistent with the speed derived from the movement card, nor her location derived from SIM messages. In fact, her average sailing speed from Singapore (Dep. 0800z/13 Nov) to Adelaide (Arr. 1630z/30 Nov) via Cape Willoughby was approx. 8.86 knots over a distance of about 3,690nm. See below.

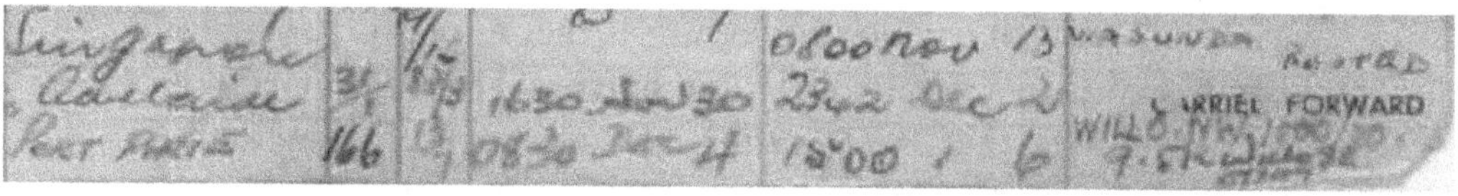

Movement Card for *Bramora* – departure and arrival from Singapore to Adelaide

The above schedule establishes that the fully laden *Bramora* had been allocated a speed of no more than 9 knots. But what is most perplexing is that each of the SIM messages provided by the Naval Faculty showing the position of *Bramora* (to the nearest degree) is demonstrably inaccurate for the period 18–20 November. For example, the SIM position 18°S 10°E at 2000z/18 represents an average speed of 10.2 knots from Singapore. But the laden vessel could not have travelled at such a rate (approx. 1,352nm in 132 hours) because she would have arrived in Adelaide a day earlier than scheduled. Also, SIM messages, in particular the position 22°S, 111°E assigned at 2000z/19, signifies an absolute minimum speed of 10 knots from SIM position 19°S, 111°E. This cannot be correct because it was only on occasions when the vessel had discharged its fuel that speeds of up to 10 knots have been recorded on her movement card.

The only explanation possible to account for her average speed of 8.86 knots on passage to Adelaide is that the tanker had passed the vicinity of SIM position 18°S 10°E at 2000z/19 – 24 hours later than expected. *Bramora* is then found to have achieved a more equitable speed of 8.5 knots from Singapore. The vessel had therefore sailed 1,326nm in 156 hours, not in 132 hours as shown in the SIM messages.

It follows that the claim made by the RAN that *Bramora* was 427nms away at the time the *Sydney* encountered *Kormoran* is incorrect. These SIM coordinates and time (2000z/19) are demonstrably wrong. Instead, it is established that the vessel had reached the vicinity of 17°S, 110°E, approximately 550nm distant from the *Sydney/Kormoran* encounter at 0900z on 19 November. Except for the *Uco*, the *Largs Bay* was closer to the action, some 460nm away.

There is, of course, another quicker way of checking the positions of these ships. For example, *Bramora* had departed Singapore at 0800z/13 and had travelled at her approximate allocated speed of 9 knots to Adelaide. At 0900z/19, she had sailed for six days and one hour (145 hours) for a distance of approx. 1,305nm, which locates her about 95nm north of *Largs Bay*, whose almost equivalent journey took 100 hours at a speed of 14 knots (1,400nm).

Note: On her journey southwards against the Westralian Current from Way Point 13°S, 109°E, the speed of *Bramora* (and for all other vessels) is affected by the head-on current, generally estimated to be 0.5 knots, that is, in this case from 9 knots to 8.5 knots (204nm/day). Conversely, when assisted by the strong easterly flowing current from Cape Leeuwin to Adelaide, the speed of the vessel should have increased to the tune of up to 1 knot in accordance with oceanic predictions. On this leg of approx. 1,230nm, the tanker achieved an average speed of 9.7 knots, 0.7k above her allocated speed and well within expectations.

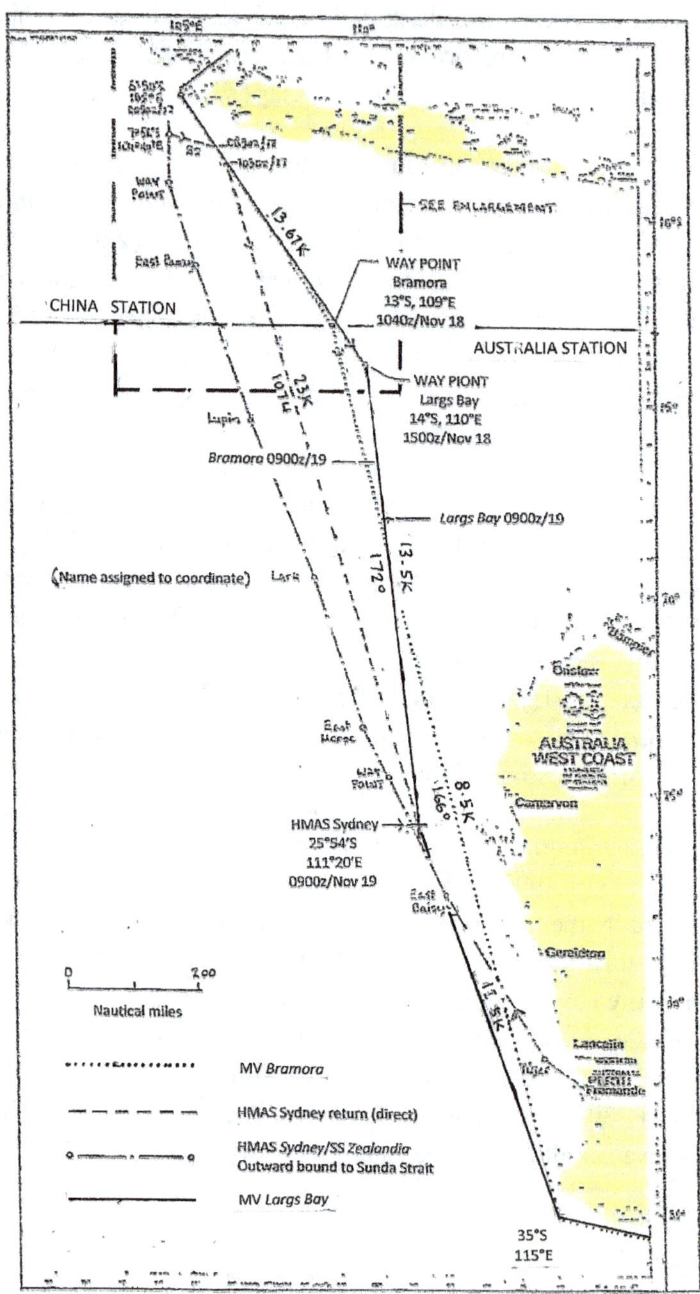

Routes taken by HMAS *Sydney/Zealandia*, *Largs Bay* and *Bramora*

Throughout *Kormoran*'s voyage, only a few high-frequency transmissions were made back to Germany, but one in particular would have been heard by C-in-C China's Far East Direction-finding Organisation (FEDO): 'Supply ship detached rendezvous 17th day following month Schiff 41' – this, on 24 October after *Kulmerland* had re-supplied the raider (from 17th to 24th). However, it is not positively known if other messages had been subsequently transmitted because precise details of her movements and of signals in her last operational area do not exist. Only those signals retained in the German archives have been made available for scrutiny.

In the case that transmissions were made (believed to be twice per month), such signals should have been detected by the secret FEDO HFDF station at Jandakot near Perth and possibly by direction-finding at Pearce RAAF station. If so, and even if intercepted by only one station, the direction (bearing) of the signal and the time interval between signals meant that only one signal would have indicated that the suspicious vessel had been moving up or down the coast at a certain speed. In fact, because HM ships travelled under radio silence, any HF signal detected in the Indian Ocean could safely be presumed to have emanated from an enemy vessel.

Also, it is known that *Kormoran* sometimes received HF signals in raider code, her HF receivers being in operation at all times, including regular nightly news broadcasts from Germany. It is, therefore, likely that some of these incoming signals had been detected at Jandakot. But although such world-wide HF signals could not be readily used to ascertain accurate distance and direction, in those days the receiving antennae could emit a significant amount of radiating energy (often referred to as antennae leakage). Thus, depending on the atmospheric conditions at the time, and providing the vessel was sufficiently close to the coast, it was always possible that these emissions could be directionally tracked by obtaining just a single bearing from errant radiant-emitting antennae on board the raider.

The proposition that *Kormoran* travelled up and down the coast in search of Allied shipping is clearly perceived to be a tactic to ensure maximum coverage of the merging sea lanes from Suez and Capetown to Fremantle and Cape Leeuwin, but in the process *Kormoran* was at risk of being detected by the direction-finding methods described above and/or by sightings made by Allied shipping. And even though naval intelligence does not mention specific knowledge of raider activity at the time off the west coast of Australia, the Combined Operational Intelligence Centre (COIC) had surmised that the Indian Ocean raider responsible for sinking a number of merchant ships could now be positioned in the vicinity of Fremantle.

Moreover, the RAN was not always privy to the latest information gathered by the British-controlled Far East Direction-finding Organisation. Signals from suspected enemy shipping in the Indian Ocean (e.g., from Jandakot), collated and controlled by the FEDO in Singapore, were sent to the RAN on a need-to-know basis.

As shown above, HFDF tracking was effective for detecting enemy emissions from transmitters and to a lesser extent receivers and that each HFDF station was controlled by British naval intelligence in Singapore, only China Station in Singapore had been cognizant of the general whereabouts of a suspected enemy vessel that might be off the West Australian coast.

Explicit knowledge of the area where the battle had occurred is borne out by *Largs Bay*'s untimely schedule and diversion to the vicinity of the battle site on 21 November. Again, that *Aquitania* may have inadvertently discovered survivors by chance on the morning of 23 November while on her normal course, but it is much more probable that the vessel had been alerted by C-in-C China to the possibility of finding survivors well before she had approached the vicinity of the battle site.

Contrary to the Commission of Inquiry findings, the following has been established:

- Whether from the proposed or final rendezvous positions, Captain Burnett had a commitment to return to Fremantle from the rendezvous position before midnight on 20 November. He could have achieved this at the economical speed of 19 knots as he had done in the past, but he could not have hoped to meet his ETA at this speed after being diverted to meet with *Largs Bay*.

- An eyewitness account verifies that HMAS *Sydney* intercepted *Largs Bay* at approximately 4 pm Singapore time on 17 November, not on 19 November as recalled. Except for the tug *Uco*, it was the vessel closest to the encounter position of 25°54', 111°20', approx. 476nm away. Three British ships had been seen by Edgar Emerich from his lifeboat on two different days, obviously searching for survivors.

- HMAS *Sydney* encountered *Kormoran* after departing from *Largs Bay*, but the high speed attained and the consequent early arrival in Fremantle is synonymous with Burnett being informed of the general location of a suspected enemy vessel while under C-in-C China command. There is no evidence that approval for such a high speed came from sources within Australia Station.

- SIM positions established on 18–20 November for *Bramora* have not been correctly identified, and in order to account for her actual sailing schedule the timetable is found to be 24 hours in arrears. The tanker was in fact about 595nm north of the *Sydney/Kormoran* encounter position at 0900z/19, not 427nm posited by the RANs Naval Faculty.

- SIM positions and timetables for *Largs Bay* accord with her sailing schedule to latitude 20°S, but not for the remaining journey to Sydney Harbour. That her movement card shows an inexplicable drop in average speed to the extent that she was 10 hours behind schedule at Cape Otway is compelling evidence that the troopship had been delayed for no reason other than C-in-C China had re-directed the vessel to search the approximate vicinity of the battle site.

- The fact that the *Sydney* met *Kormoran* almost head-on is evidence of Burnett's knowledge of the raider's final movements. The logical explanation is that the cruiser's aircraft had unobtrusively sighted the raider earlier on 19 November.

- FEDO tracking had led C-in-C China to believe that an enemy vessel was operating off the West Australian coast, but the fact that no vessel was expected in the area, Burnett was sure to have regarded the vessel as suspicious at all times. And previously as deputy chief of Naval Staff, he was kept fully informed on the operation of the RANs Mercantile Movement Section. The high degree of accuracy in plotting VAI positions was renowned.

The proposition that HMAS *Sydney* encountered HSK *Kormoran* by chance while returning directly to Fremantle from the rendezvous position with HMS *Durban* has been shown not to have occurred.

❑ ❑ ❑

Vessels in Area

HMAS *Sydney*

MV *Largs Bay*

SS *Zealandia*

HMS *Durban*

Tug *Uco*

MV *Bramora*

MV *Trocas*

HNLMS *Tromp*

HNLMS *van Nes*

HSK *Kormoran*

HMT *Aquitania*

QUESTIONABLE CONDUCT

C-in-C China's role in the HMAS *Sydney* affair is indelibly linked to the strange behaviour of the British tanker MV *Trocas* en route from Palembang's port of Pladjoe to Fremantle, which had reportedly rescued German survivors from a raft on 24 November – almost five days after the *Sydney/Kormoran* encounter. However, close examination of her voyage and claimed rescue position uncovers deceptiveness, apparently unforeseen by the Commission of Inquiry.

At 2333H (WST) on 23 November 1941, the Naval Board signalled C-in-C China Station requesting the time and position that the *Sydney* handed over *Zealandia* to HMS *Durban.* Then after further conversations with DNOWA late on 23 November it recommended a search for the *Sydney* early on 24 November on the basis that the cruiser had engine trouble and did not wish to break radio silence. This search NW of Rottnest proved negative, as did further efforts to contact the cruiser.

Then at 1009H on 24 November, the Naval Board again sought the information from China Station that had been requested 10 hours previously and informing that the cruiser was 36 hours overdue at Fremantle. Another search NW of Geraldton to locate the cruiser was arranged at 1212H. Thirteen hours after the Naval Board's first request, China Station revealed that the *Sydney* had parted company with *Zealandia* at 1200H on 17 November in position 7°56'S, 104°40'E. No further information was provided, the Naval Board presuming that the cruiser was to return directly to Fremantle.

However, shortly afterwards at 1616H on 24 November, C-in-C China advised the Naval Board that the British tanker *Trocas* had picked up 25 German naval men at 1500H in position

24°06'S, 111°40'E, asking that guards be sent to control the prisoners on board. From early statements by the Germans, it appeared that the *Sydney* had somehow been involved. The Naval Board then requested *Trocas* to report details of the engagement and at 2340H the DNOWA advised that the message had been passed on. All available ships were quickly redirected to the area seaward of Geraldton and Carnarvon to locate the cruiser. An escalation of the air search for the cruiser began in earnest at daylight on 25 November.

As the *Trocas* raft had been reportedly found in a position isolated from the *Aquitania* raft found early in the morning the previous day, it was expected that both rafts would have displayed similar drift characteristics. After all, these inflatable rafts were of the same rubber material, they had been launched from the stricken *Kormoran* at approximately the same time, they contained 25 and 26 men, respectively, they were both at the mercy of the wind and current and they had no means of propulsion (paddles only), yet the *Trocas* raft had drifted in a completely different direction. In fact, compared with the *Aquitania* raft and flotsam found by the search vessels, which had all drifted on an average bearing of 355° from the *Kormoran* wreck site position, this raft had drifted on an average bearing of 014° to about 55nm north-east of the raft found by the troopship.

Typical WW2 German inflatable rubber raft

[Larger capacity rafts were braced to prevent inward collapse]

As it is not possible to establish a separate credible drift path for the *Trocas* raft position in isolation of the *Aquitania* raft and other drifting objects found based on wind and current, a superficial assessment would suggest that the *Trocas* raft should have drifted generally along the path of the other raft. So when compared to the recovery position of the raft, the longitudinal coordinate (111°40'E) in particular, appears suspiciously awry.

Nevertheless, the Naval Board (yet to be told of the earlier rescue by the *Aquitania*) believed that the position given by C-in-C China was, in fact, accurate, so it became the focal point for the search. Early on 25 November, all merchant ships in the vicinity, including naval auxiliaries from Fremantle, were ordered to pass through position 24°06'S, 111°40'E and to keep a lookout for survivors. But a sea and air search on approach and in the reverse direction found nothing and *Trocas* could not be located on her course to Fremantle from the given rescue position. Intriguingly, 10 hours after C-in-C China had reported the rescue, *Trocas* contacted Geraldton radio VIN advising again of the same rescue position, adding that the survivors on the raft, who were now aboard the tanker, came from *Comoron* (sic), but the tanker did not give her position at the time.

Concern for the whereabouts of the elusive *Trocas* was also due to the possibility that the German prisoners could have captured the crew and the ship, and if so it had to be reasoned that because the tanker did not report her position the Germans could conceivably have taken control. At 1000H on 25 November, SWACH signalled RAAF Pearce and CWR to urgently carry out searches for the *Trocas*. SWACH had believed her 1200H position to be either 26°50'S, 112°50'E or 27°05'S, 112°10'E, speed 9 knots, these positions based on the belief that the tanker had passed through position 24°06'S, 111°40'E at 1500H on 24 November, as reported. The positions had been based on the presumption that *Trocas* had been approaching Fremantle either offshore on a normal direct course of 160° or further inshore on course 171°. Six aircraft had been allocated to locate *Trocas* and survivors, but still she could not be located throughout the day.

Finally, at 1845H, 18 hours after last contact, SWACH reported to CWR that *Trocas* had radioed her morning position (which had been nominated as the noon position in the SWACH logbook). This position is shown plotted at 26°47'S, 112°13'E on the MMS Plotting Sheet (**NAA MP 1049/5**). From here the tanker intended to meet with *Wyrallah* in position 29°18'S, 112°36'E (approx. 230nm NW of Fremantle) at 0630H on 26 November to take the requested men on board to guard the prisoners. The message also mentioned that the air search for *Trocas* had been cut short when she had reported her position, which had been verified by the means of direction-finding.

The whereabouts of *Trocas* had, indeed, remained a mystery for SWACH and the Naval Board ever since China Station had reported the rescue of the tanker's survivors 26 hours previously. Efforts to make contact had failed and air and sea searches had proved negative. It was not the normal behaviour of a British or Allied merchant ship, particularly as the search to find the missing cruiser was in progress. Plainly, the *Trocas* rescue position was impossible to substantiate by simple logic.

Trocas had initially departed from the Sumatran port of Palembang on 16 November en route to Fremantle. She did not sail a direct route from Sunda Strait, having been routed away from the main shipping lane by message 140 on 17 November (refer to movement card). During her journey southwards, *Trocas* is said to have rescued German survivors in the position stated by C-in-C China. It has also been claimed that this rescue was the first indication that the *Sydney* had been involved in an action. But it was unknown at the time that *Aquitania* had rescued a similar number of survivors from an identical raft at 0630H on 23 November, and that flotsam from the *Sydney* and *Kormoran* was to be subsequently recovered in an adjacent area about 55nm west of the given position.

Given that the wreck sites of the *Kormoran* and *Sydney* have now been identified, the survivors rescued in their life raft by *Aquitania* in position 24°35'S, 110°57'E had drifted northerly after casting off from their burning ship. Other partly submerged items from both ships had been subsequently found nearby. But what is most odd is that the *Trocas* raft is said to have been picked up after inexplicably drifting NNE away from the flotsam area.

Concerted efforts by aircraft to locate *Trocas* on her way from the so-called rescue position to Fremantle had proved fruitless, but that she eventually radioed her 25 November noon position at approx. 1800H that same day, strangely, is not recorded in the SWACH logbook. Also, the so-called evasiveness displayed by the *Trocas* does not suggest there was any urgency that guards be provided to control the prisoners and that efforts to locate the tanker by air and sea proved negative suggests she did not traverse through 24°06'S, 111°40'E on her way to Fremantle. Instead, she is suspected to have sailed seaward of the main search area, to an area that had yet to be adequately searched by aircraft.

The drift of the *Trocas* raft to the rescue position stated by C-in-C China simply cannot be justified. After all, those on board the raft had experienced the same sea conditions as those on the *Aquitania* raft, but that flotsam was recovered along an adjacent drift line is compelling evidence that the claimed rescue position is incorrect. And if, in fact, the *Trocas* raft had drifted in the direction of the *Aquitania* raft and to a location where other objects were found, the actual position can be more justly identified as 24°06'S, 110°40'E, 55nm due west of the claimed position (one degree of longitude).

Sea and air searches had been directed to the area where *Trocas* could not be located. But more to the point, C-in-C China had reason to falsify the rescue position because of their role in directing the *Sydney* at high speed to intercept a suspicious vessel that had proved to be disastrous. It was an operation that went wrong, effectively inducing the fictitious claimed position. And given that the RAN were not officially privy to the failed operation, it was deemed necessary that Royal Navy involvement be kept secret, though in any case there was only a slim chance that survivors from the *Sydney* would be rescued after five days at sea.

Trocas did not report her position for 21 hours, because that may have suggested she had not passed through 24°06'S, 111°40'E. But that she had subsequently reminded the Naval Board via Geraldton radio that she had indeed traversed the claimed rescue position (message to NB, 0100H/25), cannot be confirmed because her position at the time had been unknown. Nevertheless, the Naval Board had placed total reliance on the integrity of the given position as confirmation that the vessel had indeed passed through it, even though the tanker's subsequent movements had not been reported.

Not only is it suspected that China Station had falsified the rescue position, the tanker had been advised to again quote the false position. But curiously, no signals to or from the tanker had been detected by DF until she had radioed her noon position on 25 November. It therefore appears that this secrecy between the master of the *Trocas* (Captain Bryant) and C-in-C China had been paramount.

In order to dispel any knowledge of complicity between the master of the tanker and C-in-C China, it must have been considered appropriate at the time to advise the ACNB that the rescued survivors had been picked up in an area one degree of longitude (55nm) east of the actual rescue position, in an area where *Sydney* survivors were most unlikely to be found. After all, that as the message had spelt out the rescue coordinates, it was considered advisable to make only one minor change to the given position. Nevertheless, such a small alteration had far-reaching consequences for SWACH and for the Naval Board.

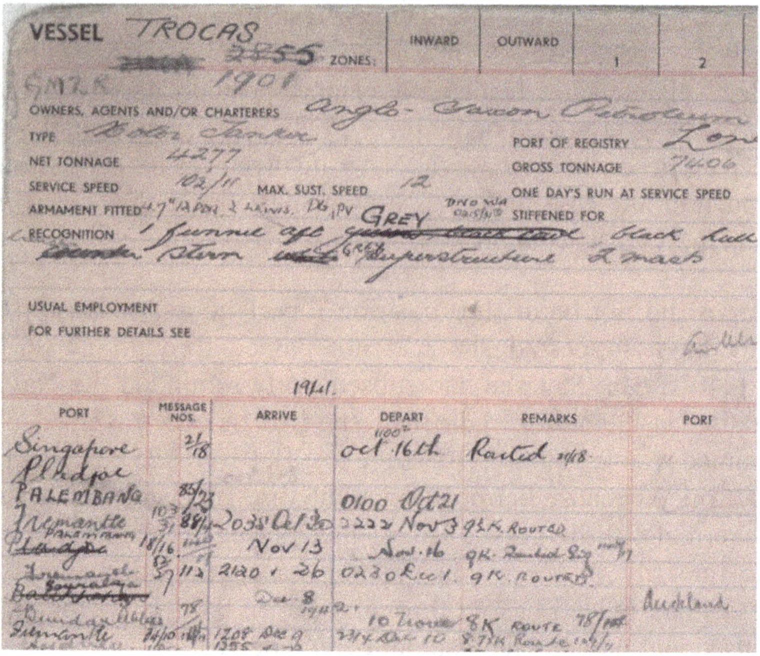
VESSEL TROCAS
2855 ZONES: | INWARD | OUTWARD | 1 | 2
GMZK 1901
OWNERS, AGENTS AND/OR CHARTERERS Anglo-Saxon Petroleum
TYPE Motor Tanker
PORT OF REGISTRY Lon
NET TONNAGE 4277
GROSS TONNAGE 7406
SERVICE SPEED 10½/11 MAX. SUST. SPEED 12
ONE DAY'S RUN AT SERVICE SPEED
ARMAMENT FITTED
STIFFENED FOR
GREY
RECOGNITION 1 funnel aft black hull
Stern superstructure 2 masts
USUAL EMPLOYMENT
FOR FURTHER DETAILS SEE

1941.

PORT	MESSAGE NOS.	ARRIVE	DEPART	REMARKS	PORT
Singapore	2/18		1100 oct 16th	Routed 2/18	
Palembang			0100 Oct 21		
Fremantle	103/31	2038 Oct 30	2222 Nov 3	93K Routed	
	18/16	Nov 13	Nov 16		
	57/112	2120 - 26	0230	9K Routed	
		Dec 8			Auckland
Fremantle		1208 Dec 9	2314 Dec 10	8K Route	

Movement Card for MV *Trocas* in 1941

[Pink cards are for British ships]

To this day, the general public have taken for granted the *Trocas* rescue position stated by C-in-C China on 24 November 1941, but this position is now highly questionable. That the tanker had not rescued survivors in position 24°06'S, 111°40'E can be further established below.

Drift analysis, in conjunction with the weather conditions prevailing at the time, produces the following outcomes:

As a rule, wind currents act at an angle of 30° to the left of the downwind direction for latitudes south of 10°S (30° to the right, north of latitude 10°N) and the velocity of the wind current created is equal to 3.6% of the average wind speed. All objects drift with an additional leeway factor, according to the type of wreckage. However, floating items and other debris do not always drift down-wind in exactly the same direction.

The leeway of any floating object is related linearly to wind speed and direction, but modelling from Australia's National Search and Rescue Council has established that both the shape and the exposed portion of the object are also factors that contribute to the direction and rate of drift. In the southern hemisphere, NATSAR Leeway Tables (2017 edition) specify that rubber rafts drift at a divergence angle of about 24° either from the left or right of the wind direction, and drifting objects recovered by the search vessels, for example, the swamped Carley float and the partly submerged lifebelts, take a path 10° right or left of the wind direction, as shown below.

NATSAR components of drift, sea current, wind current and leeway distances, including divergence angles that are specific to the HMAS *Sydney* disaster are shown hereunder:

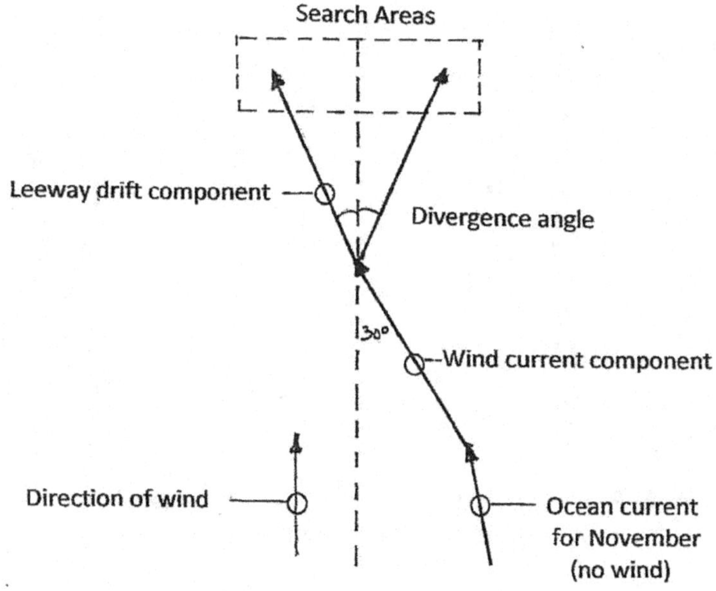

Components of Drift

In order to assist finding the wreck sites of the *Kormoran* and *Sydney* from the known positions of where the rafts and retrieved objects were found, expert advice on the weather conditions prevailing at the time was provided to the search team by the Bureau of Meteorology in February 2008. This involved hind-casting the wind speed and direction from two locations on longitude 111°E between latitudes 24.1°S and 26.5°S for the period of 18–28 November 1941. Hind-casting from barometric reports of the time by BOM experts is said to have largely contributed to finding the wreck sites. The results of the report are for 19–28 November, the period encompassing the drift of all debris found from the two sunken ships. The table also shows the pressure gradients and the associated strength of the winds for that period (**FSF.011.0022_R**).

Wind Hindcast (Two Locations)														
		Location 26.5S 111.0 E						24.1S 111.0E (2.4 degrees north)						
Date	Time	LAPS		Pressure Gradient		QuickScat		LAPS		Pressure Gradient		QuickScat		
19/11/1941	9pm	150	18	**160**	**18**	160	18	150	19	**160**	**19**	160	20	
20/11/1941	9am	150	16	**150**	**16**	150	17	160	15	**150**	**17**	150	18	
20/11/1941	9pm	170	17	**160**	**16**	170	14	170	17	**160**	**18**	180	18	
21/11/1941	9am	175	13	**170**	**17**	170	15	175	14	**170**	**18**	160	16	
21/11/1941	9pm	205	17	**165**	**17**	200	18	205	18	**165**	**18**	200	18	
22/11/1941	9am	175	16	**150**	**17**	180	12	175	17	**150**	**18**	180	17	
22/11/1941	9pm	165	18	**145**	**20**	170	17	165	18	**145**	**22**	170	17	
23/11/1941	9am	145	26	**140**	**22**	160	24	145	24	**140**	**23**	140	26	
23/11/1941	9pm	150	27	**150**	**25**	160	25	150	27	**150**	**27**	160	25	
24/11/1941	9am	140	21	**170**	**24**	150	23	150	21	**170**	**25**	150	23	
24/11/1941	9pm	160	21	**185**	**23**	160	23	160	22	**190**	**23**	160	23	
25/11/1941	9am	165	20	**200**	**19**	150	17	165	21	**210**	**20**	150	17	
25/11/1941	9pm	190	18	**205**	**18**	150	17	190	19	**210**	**18**	150	19	
26/11/1941	9am	240	10	**215**	**18**	180	14	240	12	**225**	**17**	160	15	
26/11/1941	9pm	280	13	**250**	**13**	150	8	280	13	**230**	**11**	150	8	
27/11/1941	9am	290	12	**280**	**12**	240	13	290	12	**250**	**10**	230	10	
27/11/1941	9pm	205	10	**230**	**11**	190	13	205	11	**200**	**12**	190	13	
28/11/1941	9am	160	20	**150**	**15**	160	19	160	22	**150**	**18**	160	22	

BOM Average Pressure Gradients and Wind Velocities for 19-28 November 1941 from the two locations

Leeway Target Class				Leeway Speed		Divergence
Category	Sub Categories	Primary Leeway Descriptors	Secondary Leeway Descriptors	Multiplier	Modifier (kt)	Angle (deg)
PIW				0.011	0.07	30
	Vertical			0.005	0.07	18
	Sitting			0.012	0.00	18
	Horizontal	Survival Suit		0.014	0.10	30
		Scuba Suit		0.007	0.08	30
		Deceased		0.015	0.08	30
Survival Craft	Maritime Life Rafts			0.042	0.03	28
		No Ballast Systems	no canopy, no drogue	0.057	0.21	24
			no canopy, w/ drogue	0.044	-0.20	28
			canopy, no drogue	0.037	0.11	24
			canopy, w/ drogue	0.030	0.00	28
		Shallow Ballast Systems and Canopy		0.029	0.00	22
			no drogue	0.032	-0.02	22
			with drogue	0.025	0.01	22
			Capsized	0.017	-0.10	8
		Deep Ballast Systems & Canopies	(See Table I-2 for Levels 4-6)	0.030	0.02	13
	Other Maritime Survival Craft	life capsule		0.038	-0.08	22
		USCG Sea Rescue Kit		0.025	-0.04	7
	Aviation Life Rafts	no ballast, w/canopy Evac/ Slide	4-6 person, w/o drogue	0.037	0.11	24
			46-person	0.028	-0.01	15
Person-Powered Craft	Sea Kayak	W/ Person on aft deck		0.011	0.24	15
	Surf board	w/ person		0.020	0.00	15
	Windsurfer	w/ person and mast & sail in water		0.023	0.10	12
Sailing Vessels	Mono-hull	Full Keel	Deep Draft	0.030	0.00	48
		Fin Keel	Shoal Draft	0.040	0.00	48
Power Vessels	Skiffs	Flat Bottom	Boston whaler	0.034	0.04	22
		V-hull	Std. Configuration.	0.030	0.08	15
			Swamped	0.017	0.00	15
	Sport Boats	Cuddy Cabin	Modified V-hull	0.069	-0.08	19
	Sport Fisher	Center Console	Open cockpit	0.060	-0.09	22
Power Vessels	Commercial Fishing Vessels			0.037	0.02	48
		Sampans		0.040	0.00	48
		Side-stern Trawler		0.042	0.00	48
		Longliners		0.037	0.00	48
		Junk		0.027	0.10	48
		Gill-netter	w/rear reel	0.040	0.01	33
	Coastal Freighter			0.028	0.00	48
Boating Debris	F/V debris			0.020	0.00	10
	Bait/wharf box holds a cubic meter of ice			0.013	0.27	31
		lightly loaded		0.026	0.18	15
		fully loaded		0.016	0.16	33

NATSAR Leeway speed and direction values for various drifting objects

From the two locations, the approximate average wind velocity and direction (in bold) for the rubber rafts having embarked from the *Kormoran* at say 2000H on 19 November is interpreted thus:

> *Aquitania* raft to 24°35'S, 110°57'E at 0630H/23: Av wind direction (from) **157°**, speed 18K.
>
> *Trocas* raft to (suspected) 24°06'S, 110°40'E at 1500H/23: **154°**, 19K.
>
> *Trocas* raft (C-in- C China) to 24°06'S, 111°40'E at 1500H/24: 154°, 19K.
>
> [Note the change of wind direction and velocity increase from 2100/22 to 2100/24]

South of latitude 10°S, NATSAR Leeway Tables, which nominate a (maximum) 24° divergence angle for rafts left or right of the wind direction, confirm the *Aquitania* raft had drifted northerly 19° to the right of the wind in approx. 82 hours to position 24°35'S, 110°57'E at 0630H/23 (94nm at a rate of 1.14 knots). The leeway distance (direct) for this raft is equivalent to 6% of wind speed. Similarly, the *Trocas* raft suspected to have drifted to position 24°06'S, 110°40'E had drifted by wind in nearly the same direction for 91 hours (109nm at an increased rate of 1.33 knots), but due to the change in wind direction (145°) and speed (25 knots) on 23 November, it had (as expected) drifted further west for 16nm at 1.75 knots to its position at 1500H/23. In this case the leeward direction and velocities equate to approximately 7% of average wind speed.

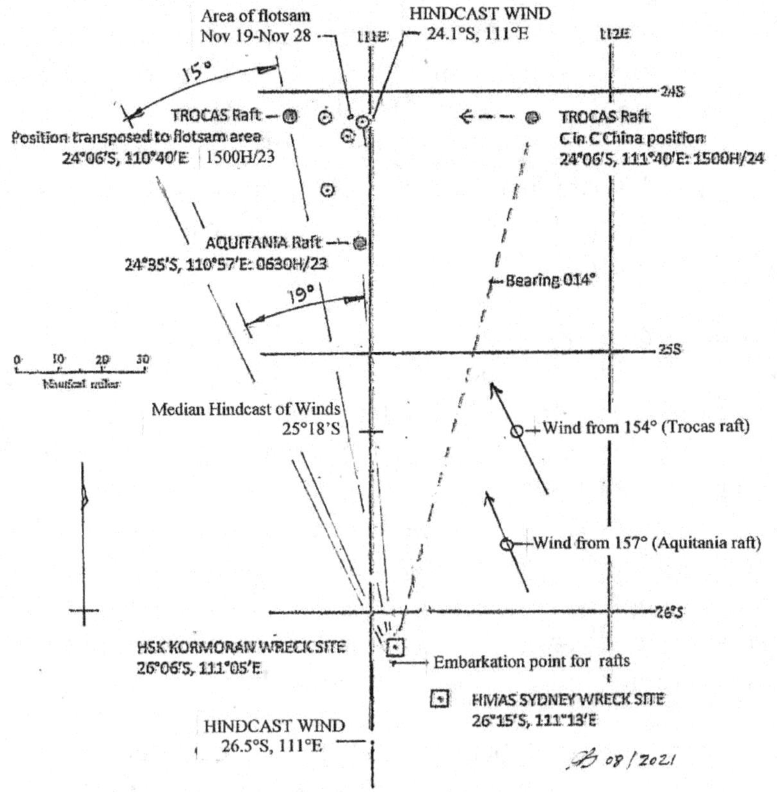

Leeway Speed and Direction of Rafts (H hours)

Claimed to have been found by *Trocas* at 1500H on 24 November in position 24°06'S 111°40'E, this raft had drifted contrary to the *Aquitania* raft, far in excess of 24° specified by NATSAR – to the right, about 36° from the average wind direction. And despite the strong winds of up to 27 knots experienced throughout 23 and 24 November, this raft had seemingly drifted by wind for 128nm in 115 hours at an average speed of 1.11 knots, approximately the same rate as the *Aquitania* raft.

Moreover, if the *Trocas* raft had otherwise drifted independently of the *Aquitania* raft to its position at 24°06'S, 111°40'E, average winds from 179° and 209° (24° either side of the drift line) were required to satisfy the claim by C-in-C China. But that as no such average winds persisted from these directions, the claimed position cannot be countenanced on the basis that average winds from 154° (BOM) were experienced from 2000H/19 to 1500H/24.

That the *Trocas* raft had drifted faster than the *Aquitania* raft was most likely due to the superior buoyancy and hence higher profile of the raft above the water which, in turn, captured an increase in the amount of wind. Alternatively, the *Aquitania* rubber raft had been less pressurised when launched, or for some reason it had lost some of its inflated pressure while drifting. Also, tethered to this raft was a much smaller raft carrying supplies, which may have impeded its progress. It is also possible that a type of sea anchor had been deployed by the occupants in order to reduce leeway drift.

That both rafts had been launched at about 2000H/19, it is highly unlikely that one of the two had been affected, for example, by eddy currents, known to be caused these days by the strong opposing Leeuwin Current, which was much weaker in November 1941. And given that the rafts are propelled by wind (of which the current is a component), they take a down-wind path, providing an opposing current from another direction is not stronger than the combined wind current.

Average wind directions and velocities for the rafts from 2000H/19 to 1500H/23 generally accord with those established by BOM (154° and 19 knots), and are well within the error margins. And due to the relatively small variation in wind direction of only 3°, drift distances in the above diagram are presumed to be in a direct line to the positions of recovery.

In the case of the drifting objects and debris to which NATSAR have assigned a divergence angle of 10° either side of the wind, the average BOM wind direction and velocity for the period 2000/19 to 0900/28 is assessed as 179°, speed 18 knots. But due to wind variations, the objects had drifted NW and then NE to their respective recovery positions. This means they had moved well in excess of the direct distance – at least 10% or more. As a result, these objects are calculated to have moved in average 15 knot winds along a drift line of 172°, thereby establishing that they had drifted to the left of the wind.

Drift distance for individual objects is established from the NATSAR Leeway equation:

W wind (kts) = D distance(nm)
T time (hrs) [0.036 (wind current) + m (wreckage type)]

Based on NATSAR Leeway Tables and by expert assessments of BOM pressure gradients and wind velocities for the period 19–23 November 1941, it has been demonstrated that the *Trocas* raft had drifted by wind current to position 24°06'S 110°40'E. Thus, the claim by C-in-C China that the raft was found in position 24°06'S 111°40'E after drifting for 117 hours is therefore not credible.

Again, based on the speed and schedule sailed by *Trocas*, the fallacy of the claimed position is evident, as follows:

It is known for certain that *Trocas* had departed Pladjoe at a particular time on 16 November. From this port, early morning sailing departures (z time) after sunrise were common for laden fuel tankers during the period of high tides. For instance, in 1941, individual movement cards show that the Dutch tanker *Saidja* had departed at 0300z on 27 September and at 0001z on 19 November, and her sister ship *Sardena* at 0500z on 27

September. Previously, *Trocas* had departed Palembang at 0100z (*0800 local time) on 21 October.
*NEI local time = GMT (z time) +7 hours

With tidal predictions in mind, the above schedules enabled piloted vessels to navigate the shallow Musi River from Palembang and Pladjoe unhindered for 50nm to the outer bar on the Bangka Strait while high tides persisted throughout the journey. Due to the shallow sand bars downstream and the speed of the tide (approx. 9 knots), this river is navigable by laden ships only at high tides. And because of the almost constant five-hour phase difference between the tide in the Java Sea and the tide near Palembang, all vessels are able to negotiate the river within six hours or so with the assistance of the fast-flowing tide.

Siltation and tidal surges can be hazardous when transiting the river to the Java Sea at night, but navigating the river in daylight hours was much less of a risk. When fully loaded with fuel, *Trocas* increased her draught considerably, thus increasing the possibility of her running aground. So at the very least, the tanker should not have departed after 1200 local time (0500z), otherwise she would not have reached the open sea by nightfall.

From the Musi River to Sunda Strait (via Bangka Strait) during the inter-monsoon period of November, winds and currents are variable and generally quite weak. And on entry to the Indian Ocean southwards, the southerly speed of *Trocas* was only likely to have been minimally affected by the east-west cross-current. But as a result of coastal water upheaval south of Java, the tanker may well have been assisted in its progress.

Overall, *Trocas* should not have been unduly affected by the sea and wind conditions and should have closely maintained her scheduled speed of 9 knots to a location approximately 300nm south of Sunda Strait where the northward-flowing Westralian Current merges with westward-flowing South

Equatorial Current. But south of this location near Christmas Island, the tanker would then have been impeded almost head-on by the Westralian Current.

Trocas did not sail directly to Fremantle, but if she had been routed west away from the normal shipping lane through Way Point 14°S, 110°E as the DNOWA had suspected (course 171°) and have sailed to the reported position (24°06'S, 111°40'E), the tanker would have sailed approximately 1,570nm from Palembang. At 9 knots per hour, this equates to about 175 hours sailing time (7 days, 7 hours), which means that *Trocas* had departed Palembang early on 16 November and arrived at the rescue position in the afternoon of 23 November (local time).

On the other hand, it was impossible for *Trocas* to have travelled at the designated speed for an additional 24 hours (total 199 hours), because in this instance the tanker would have departed Palembang at 0200z on 15 November and have arrived at the rescue position at 0700z/24 at an average speed of only 7.9 knots. This timetable does not accord with her movement card as *Trocas* is recorded as sailing from Palembang on 16 November.

There is one other method of testing the veracity of the position of *Trocas* at 1500H (0700z) on 23 November:

According to the *Trocas* movement card, the tanker did not sail along the normal direct route along the shipping lane to the reported rescue site. In fact, she had departed from the Shell Oil Refinery at Pladjoe on 16 November and is recorded as having arrived at Fremantle at 2120z on 27 November (0520H/28). And in order to evade possible enemy presence during transit to Fremantle, C-in-C China had notified *Trocas* that she had been routed west away from the main shipping lane via Way Point 15°S, 106°E at the allocated speed of 9 knots. Meanwhile, SWACH in Fremantle were unsure of her exact whereabouts.

Two messages (below) received by the ACNB from C-in-C China on 24 November were meant to confirm the notion that *Trocas* had picked up the Germans in position 24°06'S, 111°40'E and had taken a westerly route to avoid enemy shipping. The first (at 0816z) expressed the position of the rescue in numerals only, whereas the second message sent six hours later is explicitly worded and spells out the coordinates of the rescue position – this, to emphasise there is no mistaking the precise location. Also attached is confirmation from C-in -C that the tanker should have been in this position.

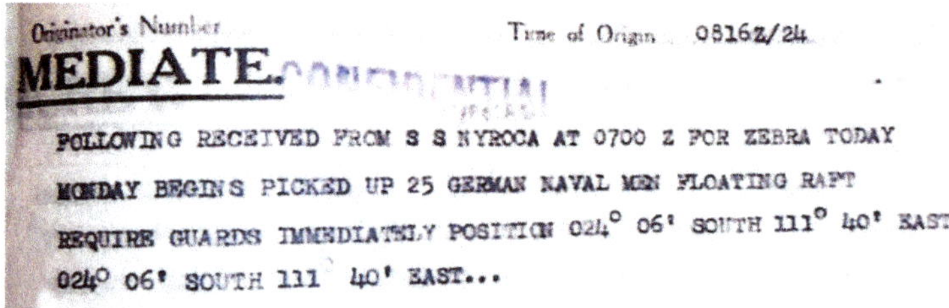
Originator's Number Time of Origin 0816z/24

MEDIATE.

FOLLOWING RECEIVED FROM S S NYROCA AT 0700 Z FOR ZEBRA TODAY MONDAY BEGINS PICKED UP 25 GERMAN NAVAL MEN FLOATING RAFT REQUIRE GUARDS IMMEDIATELY POSITION 024° 06' SOUTH 111° 40' EAST 024° 06' SOUTH 111 40' EAST...

Message 0816z/24

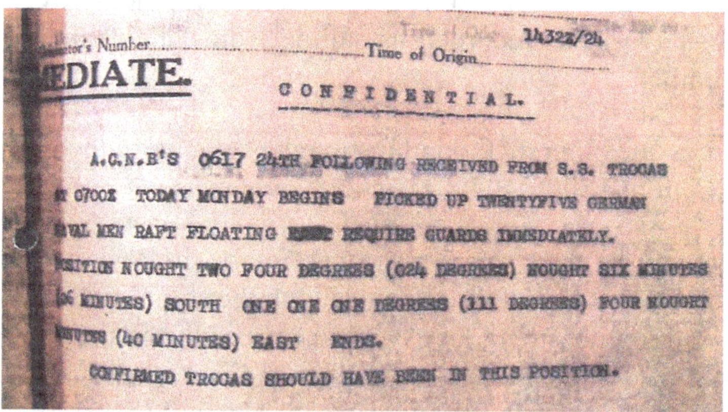
...tor's Number Time of Origin 1432z/24

EDIATE.

CONFIDENTIAL.

A.C.N.B'S 0617 24TH FOLLOWING RECEIVED FROM S.S. TROCAS AT 0700Z TODAY MONDAY BEGINS PICKED UP TWENTYFIVE GERMAN NAVAL MEN RAFT FLOATING [illegible] REQUIRE GUARDS IMMEDIATELY. POSITION NOUGHT TWO FOUR DEGREES (024 DEGREES) NOUGHT SIX MINUTES (06 MINUTES) SOUTH ONE ONE ONE DEGREES (111 DEGREES) FOUR NOUGHT MINUTES (40 MINUTES) EAST ENDS.

CONFIRMED TROCAS SHOULD HAVE BEEN IN THIS POSITION.

Message 1432z/24

Trocas should certainly have been in the vicinity of the said rescue position on the proviso that she had sailed from Sunda Strait direct to Fremantle (course 160°T). But this was not the case because her movement card shows that the tanker had been routed away from this shipping lane on 17 November (message 140/17). Unbeknown to the DNO in Fremantle, *Trocas* was thought to have been re-routed to sail through the way point allocated to *Largs Bay.* But this route (course 171°) from the way point is deemed unlikely due to the fact that no visual sighting of the vessel from the claimed rescue position had been made by the search aircraft on 25 November. In both cases, it follows that China Station had subsequently informed the Naval Board of the tanker's movements and SIM positions (from which the Vessels in Area is constructed), but they had not notified SWACH at that stage.

While SWACH had believed that messages 0816z/24 and 1432z/24 had been genuine, the movement of *Trocas* had indeed been mysterious, particularly the direct route which would have placed the tanker in danger of possible attack by enemy shipping. It is for this reason only that the DNOWA had suspected that the tanker may have been scheduled (by China Station) to sail east of the shipping lane via Way Point 14°S, 110°E. In his report on the search for survivors, words of ambivalence by DNO Captain Farquhar-Smith in his report on 10 December: ...'it was not known whether she [*Trocas*] would proceed direct to Fremantle or follow her proper [designated] route' **(NAA MP1049/5)**. It appears from this statement that the DNOWA had been uncertain as to the exact route at the time.

That the vessel was believed to have finally sailed east of the shipping lane is seemingly confirmed by the SWACHs MMS Plotting Sheet **(NAA MP 1049/5)**, which shows her course, together with the Dutch tanker *Saidja* (which had departed Palembang at 0200z on 19 November), plotted at the reported rescue position 24°06'S, 111°40'E. SWACH had therefore presumed that *Trocas* had recently been routed east of the shipping lane because this accounted for the claimed rescue position. This is why SWACH had anticipated her being near position 27°05'S, 112°10'E at 0400z (1200H) on 25 November (course 171°). Besides, *Bramora, Largs Bay* and many other vessels had sailed through the aforesaid way point and along a similar route.

In early 2009, however, the RANs Naval Faculty at HMAS *Watson* advised the Commission of Inquiry that at 0700z (1500H) on 19 November, *Trocas* had been situated 900nm from position 25°54'S, 111°20'E, the point at which the *Sydney* first sighted the *Kormoran* **(RAN.002.0142).** This position is shown plotted by the RAN west of the general shipping lane at approx. 11°52'S, 105°37'E **(RAN.002.0174)**. It reveals (via back-plotting) that the tanker had sailed 705nm from Palembang at the prescribed speed of 9 knots and had departed from there at about 0001z on 16 November. And given that the Naval Faculty had access to all information on *Trocas*'s proper schedule in their deliberations, including her movement card details, way point and SIM messages, the position calculated by the RAN is therefore the best assessment possible.

In order to arrive at position 11°52'S, 105°37'E, the Naval Faculty had made its assessment based on a known way point allocated to the tanker while en route to Fremantle – this, at 15°S, 106°E. This way point of *Trocas* at 0700z/19 is some 820nm from the claimed rescue position, said to have been reached at 0700z on 24 November, and as such, the tanker had travelled at an average of only 6.8 knots for 120 hours, well below her prescribed speed of 9 knots. But after taking into account the prevailing currents and wind speeds in the area and that there is no evidence of an engine malfunction, such a slow speed cannot be justified and is thus highly questionable. The only explanation for this is that *Trocas* had actually arrived in position 24°06'S, 111°40'E, a day earlier – at 0700z on 23 November. This meant that the tanker had averaged a respectable 8.5 knots against the current for 96 hours to the claimed rescue position.

However, of interest, Way Point 15°S, 106°E is most defining. This position accurately establishes the 'proper' route taken by *Trocas* and the significance of the position from which the tanker made its approach on Fremantle. In this respect, the way point and the tanker's given position of 29°18'S, 112°36'E, are intrinsically related – course 157°. Thus, *Trocas* had been instructed by C-in-C China to sail west of the shipping lane through the above way point and the tanker had therefore been expected to berth at Fremantle on the evening of 25 November (z time). On her previous journey, *Trocas* had sailed from Palembang at 0100z on 21 October and arrived at Fremantle at 2035z/30 within a similar timeframe.

In sailing west of the direct route, the tanker had not been scheduled to pass anywhere near position 24°06'S, 111°40'E. In fact, she had been due to pass 35nm west of position 24°06'S, 110°40'E. And that she had rescued survivors in this position could only have been possible if she had been diverted from her course, and such a diversion could only have been ordered by C-in-C China. After being directed to traverse the vicinity of the *Aquitania* rescue made nine hours earlier, *Trocas* had discovered the German raft in position **24°06'S, 110°40'E** at 0700z on 23 November.

The remarkable achievement that *Trocas* had stumbled across the raft just nine hours after *Aquitania* had rescued German survivors in close proximity can now be seen as extremely doubtful. And it questions the truthfulness of the evidence given by Captain Gibbons (master of the *Aquitania*) in not reporting his rescue for a further 74 hours after the incident. Perhaps some of the scepticism and adverse comments by senior RAN officers attached to the report (written by Commodore Muirhead-Gould, RN) are now vindicated **(RAN.039.0004)**.

There is, however, compelling evidence that the Naval Board had known about the track taken by *Trocas* and other vessels en route to Fremantle. The best example is on examination of the Naval Faculty's Appendix J **(RAN.002.0174)**, wherein *Bramora* (in lieu of *Trocas*) had been mistakenly placed on course 157°T in position 19°18'S, 107°54'E. – this, at the time the *Sydney* had sighted the *Kormoran.* But her actual position from ships intelligence messages shows *Bramora* situated some 160nm east of this position and on course from her allocated Way Point 13°S, 109°E **(RAN.002.0164)**.

Despite persistent requests for information from the Naval Board, complicity by C-in-C China in directing the *Sydney* to her eventual fate was to result in a lengthy delay of some 24 hours before informing the Naval Board of the rescue. During this time and for the ensuing nine hours, the whereabouts of the tanker had been completely unknown to SWACH.

Trocas had subsequently confirmed the rescue in the false position (message 1735z/24), but her whereabouts was not established until she radioed her actual position 26°47'S, 112°13'E to VIN Radio (Geraldton) at 0400z (noon local time) on 25 November while the concerted air search to locate the vessel was in progress. In fact, SWACH had not heard from *Trocas* for 21 hours since C-in-C China had reported the rescue at 0700z/24, but on account of the actual rescue made at 0700z/23, in reality, her movements had been unknown to SWACH for some 45 hours.

Due to the fact that *Trocas* could not be located by air on her track from the reported rescue position or elsewhere within the search area, she could only have sailed in a direction away from the rescue area during the night of 23 November and in the early morning of 24 November. After all, the tanker was believed to have been en route to Fremantle, but as the vessel could no longer have remained anywhere south of 24°06'S in case it was to be sighted by air and/or by another vessel, C-in-C China therefore had no option other than to order *Trocas* out of the search area. As a consequence, message 0816z/24 ultimately ensured that sea and air searches would be initially concentrated in the false vicinity of 24°06’S, 111°40’E.

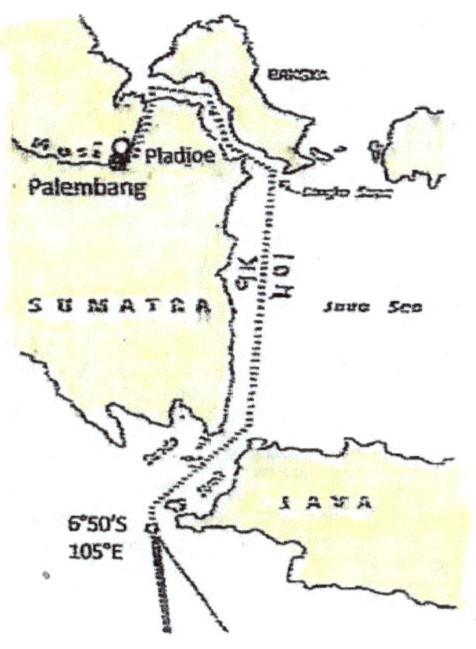

Route of *Trocas*: Pladjoe to Sunda Strait

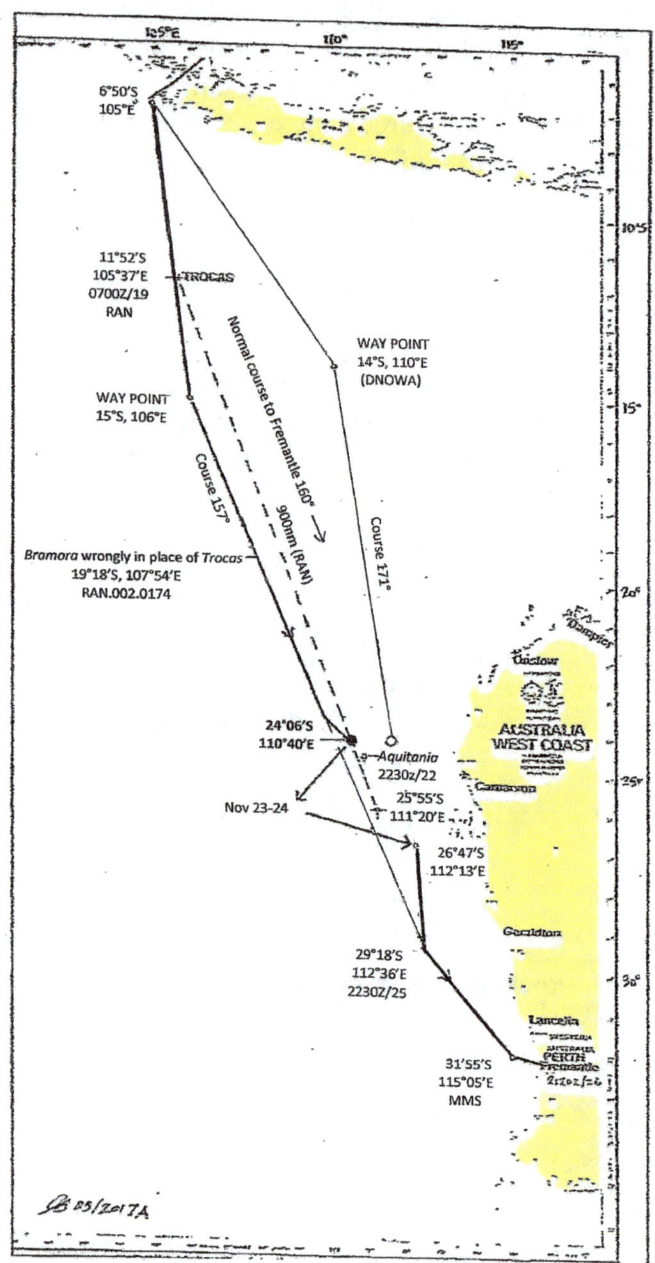

Route taken by *Trocas* from Sunda Strait to Fremantle

Of note in the above diagram is the rather precise bearing (157°) from Way Point 15°S, 106°E to position 29°18'S, 112°36'E. Obvious is the fact that considering *Bramora* had been inadvertently shown on course 157°, it follows that the RANs Naval Faculty must have identified the way point and the significance of the *Trocas/Wyrallah* rendezvous position.

The re-emergence of *Trocas* from outside the search area to position 26°47'S, 112°13'E at 1200H on 25 November, as shown on the MMS plot, gave SWACH the perception that the tanker had sailed direct from her reported rescue position at 0700z/24. But this position does not suggest there was any urgency for the requested soldiers to be taken on board to guard the prisoners, after all, it was expected that *Trocas* would have sailed direct for Fremantle at the best speed it could manage so that guards could be embarked at the earliest time possible.

The arrangement for *Wyrallah* to meet with *Trocas* in position 29°18'S, 112°36'E at 2230z/25 must have seemed odd for those at SWACH (message 1045z/25). Instead of sailing direct, her master, Captain Bryant, had chosen to rendezvous at this relatively out-of-the-way position because it was from this point that the tanker had originally intended to divert from course 157° towards Fremantle. The oiler got to the rendezvous from position 26°47'S, 112°13'E at a leisurely 8.2 knots, but for *Wyrallah* the sailing distance from Fremantle was much longer than necessary. After the two vessels had met, *Wyrallah* proceeded northward to the search area and **Trocas* (with the armed guard on board) continued on to Fremantle and arrived at 2120z on 26 November (0520H/27). On this final leg of 235nm, the tanker had dramatically increased her speed to an average 10.2 knots.

**Trocas* was designed to carry a full load of crude oil in her tanks, but as the specific weight of refined products, such as petroleum, diesel oil and aviation spirits is heavier than crude, she needed one or more tanks to be kept empty in order to maintain stability and not exceed her maximum draft. The Germans that were picked up on their raft were reportedly accommodated in one of these vacant tanks. [There were no oil refineries anywhere in Australia until 1949.]

The real expectation was that *Trocas* would have made every effort to take the shortest possible route direct to Fremantle. Instead, the tanker had travelled further than was necessary to rendezvous with *Wyrallah* and had shown no desire to close Fremantle at all possible speed. She had decided to meet at the position originally intended while on course 157°, but suspiciously offshore from her expected approach to Fremantle (some 50nm west of the direct route), which meant that the tanker was extremely unlikely to have been spotted by the ships that were heading to the search area.

The rendezvous position would certainly have been perplexing for those at SWACH conducting the search, but in the final analysis *Trocas* did have capacity for greater speed, which would have resulted in an earlier meeting with *Wyrallah*. This is demonstrated by the tanker achieving well above her allocated speed on her final leg to Fremantle.

Summary of the main points:

- The position of *Trocas* at 0700z on 19 November (approx. 11°52'S, 105°37'E) has been duly plotted by the RANs Naval Faculty. This had meant the tanker had departed Palembang at about 0001z on 16 November.
- *Trocas* had been re-scheduled to sail from the Sunda Strait to Fremantle via Way Point 15°S, 106°E. The validity of this position is beyond doubt because it accurately establishes her intended course (157°) to position 29°18'S, 112°36'E.
- During transit on course 157°, *Trocas* had been diverted by C-in-C China to the area where survivors had been rescued

by *Aquitania* and in the process of being re-directed the tanker had discovered the German raft in position **24°06'S, 110°40'E** at 0700z on 23 November.

- Consequent upon finding the raft, *Trocas* did not report her whereabouts for 45 hours. She had remained well clear of the search area while awaiting further instructions from China Station.
- After appearing in position 26°47'S, 112°13'E at 0400z/25, *Trocas* did not sail directly to Fremantle, as expected. She made slow progress and met with *Wyrallah* some 50nm west of the direct route in position 29°18'S, 112°36'E, the position from which the tanker had originally planned to make her approach on Fremantle.

It has been established beyond doubt that the rescue took place in position 24°06'S, 110°40'E. This position has also been verified by drift analysis using BOM pressure gradients and wind speeds. The claim by C-in-C China that the rescue occurred on 24 November at 0700z in position 24°06'S, 111°40'E, therefore, has no validity whatsoever.

....

Alliances inherently display a sense of cooperation among the partners. But this was not the case during the search for HMAS *Sydney* and survivors. It had been fraught with misleading and wrongful information, and given that survival in the sea can depend on just a matter of hours, the search in the fictitious position, which became the focal point for the search, had been a thorough waste of time for all concerned.

Sea and air searchers had been effectively sent on a wild goose chase and it was not until the evening of 27 November when the search vessels traversed the area where other drifting objects were found. But if C-in-C China had reported the true position of *Trocas* 24 hours earlier on 23 November, there is reason to believe that some survivors from the *Sydney* may have possibly been saved.

It is also beyond doubt that C-in-C China had known about the *Trocas* rescue well before the Naval Board had requested information on the *Sydney* at 1533z (2333H) on 23 November, details of which were not released to the Naval Board for a further 16 hours. The misleading information came at a time when the Naval Board were desperate for any information that could account for why the *Sydney* could not be contacted. But that *Trocas* had been informed of the *Aquitania* rescue, accounts for the tanker being in the vicinity on 23 November, as witnessed by Edgar Emerich.

Had *Trocas* not found survivors, the Naval Board would have not been aware of the *Aquitania* rescue and of the *Sydney*'s suspected involvement in a battle for many days until the troopship eventually sent a message by light to the Wilsons Promontory Signals Station at 0400z on 27 November. Further enquires by the Naval Board had led China Station to disclose beforehand that *Trocas* had made the rescue in a false position at a false time. Clearly, China Station had intentionally decided not to reveal the true position immediately.

That *Trocas* had revealed her noon position on 25 November did not appear to overly concern those at SWACH, even though air searches could not locate the tanker along her suspected course of 171°. However, they could be assured that the tanker had probably made the rescue at 1500H on 24 November in the reported position because she appeared to have travelled the required distance to the rendezvous with *Wyrallah* and within the timeframe and approximate speed allocated, albeit slower than expected.

Most concerning, however, is that given the *Kormoran* wreck site position has since been identified, basic drift analysis in

2008 by the RAN from NATSAR Leeway Tables should have made known to them the false position espoused by C-in-C China, as there had been ample opportunity to test the veracity of the position from way points and coded SIM messages. Therefore, it must have been clearly evident to the inquiry that *Trocas* would have reached latitude 24°06'S from 11°49'S, 105°36'E (via 15°S, 106°E) at her designated speed on 23 November, not on 24 November.

Finally, an Australian War Memorial publication in 2012, *Treasures from a Century of Collecting*, reveals the date *Trocas* discovered the German raft.

> As *Sydney* had been maintaining radio silence and was not expected into port for several days, it took some time to realise that something was wrong. It was not until 23 November that a group of German sailors was discovered adrift on a raft in the Indian Ocean. The sailors were from *Kormoran*, and told of an engagement that had resulted in the sinking of their own ship and serious damage to the *Sydney*, which had steamed over the horizon, badly damaged and on fire. An exhaustive search was launched, but it failed to find *Sydney* or any survivors from her crew. The only item apparently from *Sydney* was an empty life raft, of a type known as a Carley float, found by HMAS *Heros*. On 27 November Prime Minister John Curtin informed a shocked nation that *Sydney* was presumed lost.

AWM Publication, p327

Footnote: Captain Bryant's role in the *Trocas* affair had its foreseeable repercussions:

When the tanker had sailed from Fremantle on 1 December bound for Balikpapan it was to be his last voyage as master of the *Trocas*. He was transferred at Sourabaya on 8 December to the Singapore-based Royal Fleet Auxiliary tanker *Polshannon*, presumably to ensure that he could not be questioned further on the part he and C-in-C China played in secreting details of the rescue. [*Aquitania*'s Captain Gibbons (Royal Navy Reserve Officer) had been likewise transferred to another troopship] At the outbreak of war in the Pacific, *Trocas* ceased operations from Palembang and was re-assigned to transport crude oil from the Persian Gulf.

According to the Royal Fleet Auxiliary Historical Society, while under the command of Captain Thomas, RFA *Polshannon* sailed from Pladjoe in Palembang at 0700 hours on 2 February 1942, but at 1200 hours the ship grounded in the Musi River downstream (near Payung Island) after the pilot purportedly gave the wrong order to the helmsman. However, successful attempts were made to refloat the ship using her engines and by pumping fuel overboard. This was typical of the hazard faced by *Trocas* when negotiating the Musi River channel.

A week later, RFA *Polshannon* was attacked by Japanese dive bombers. Two bombs hit the ship and fearing that the cargo of aviation fuel and petrol could explode, the order was given to abandon ship. The fleet tanker was beached and later sank and some of the crew were rescued by HMS *Bulan*. As a result of the attack, Captain Thomas, the first officer, the third engineer officer and Captain Samuel Bryant, previously master of the *Trocas*, were hospitalised. [Bryant was not a Royal Naval officer or Naval Reserve officer]

❑ ❑ ❑

FABRICATION

The large British troopship *Aquitania* had sailed in restricted waters from Singapore on 19 November to Sunda Strait at the maximum allowable speed of 18 knots (as prescribed for large ships, such as the *Queen Mary* and *Queen Elizabeth*), and thence against the current at approx. 20.6 knots to position 24°35'S, 110°57'E where survivors had been rescued at 2200z on 22 November. It follows that the troopship had departed Singapore at approx. 0500z on 19 November (1230 local time). This particular route in the Indian Ocean along the shipping lane (course 162°) also meant that the planned track of the vessel had been due to pass within 6nm west of the rescue position and approx. 12nm east of 25°54'S, 111°20'E, the position where HMAS *Sydney* encountered *Kormoran* at 0900z on 19 November.

According to her Captain George Gibbons, after picking up the German survivors, *Aquitania* had then arrived off Cape Leeuwin at 0500z on 24 November, a further 660nm from the rescue position. This meant that Gibbons had increased the speed of his ship to an average 21.2 knots, most likely in order to maintain his schedule after stopping to retrieve survivors. Her voyage to Cape Otway had been at 21.4 knots (current-assisted) and her arrival in Sydney (against the current) at 0430z/28 had been accomplished at an overall average 20.85 knots from Sunda Strait. This average speed meant that *Aquitania* had been allocated a speed of 21 knots for the 3,774nm journey from Sunda Strait to Sydney Harbour.

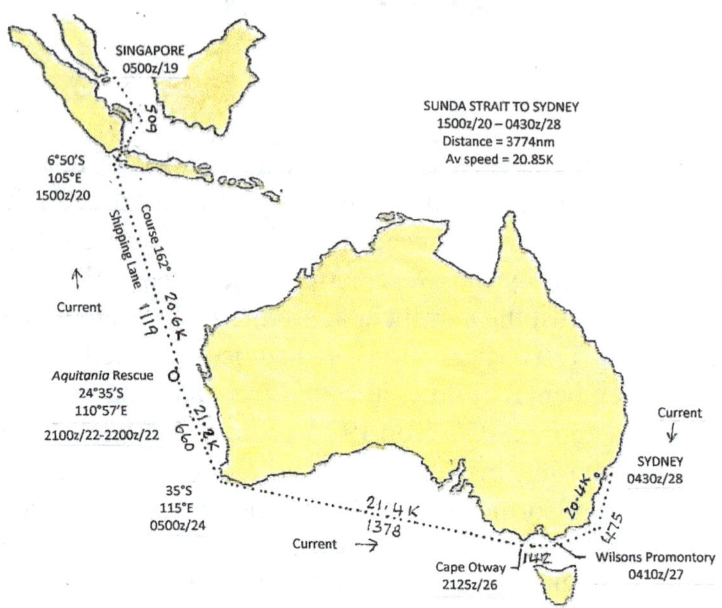

***Aquitania* schedule and track from Singapore to Sydney**

In sailing against or with the current the fluctuations in speed are seen as no less than an attempt by Gibbons to meet his scheduled average speed to Sydney. In fact, the *Aquitania* had arrived off Sydney Heads only about one hour behind her expected 0330z ETA (message, 0945z/20). However, due to delays in piloting vessels from Sydney Heads to her berth, the movement card shows she arrived in Sydney Harbour at 0430z on 28 November.

Such a large troopship was considered a potential enemy target, but the fact that Gibbons had violated his instructions not to stop mid-ocean (save for an engine malfunction), inevitably raises speculation that C-in-C China and/or Admiralty had sanctioned his actions. In the normal course of events and in order to avoid endangering his ship, it was just a matter of reporting the discovery of survivors so that a rescue could be mounted.

On 2 December 1941, the naval officer in charge of Sydney Harbour, CDRE Gerard Muirhead-Gould, interviewed CAPT Gibbons and forwarded his report to the Naval Board, explaining to VADM Royle and CMDR Durnford the reasons which guided the Master of *Aquitania*, CAPT Gibbons, in not reporting by WT the recovery of enemy survivors and not closing Rottnest Port War Signals Station to render her presence by visual signals **(NAA.039.0004)**:

> Captain Gibbons stated that at the time he picked up the survivors (at 2200z on 22nd November 1941), he had received no WT messages of any sort indicating that an action had taken place, or that any ship was overdue, or that there was any anxiety from a naval point of view. There were no signals about the action received in *Aquitania* until long afterwards. GBMS [British Merchant Ship] messages are received and dealt with correctly in *Aquitania*.
>
> The survivors were picked up at 6 am local time on Sunday morning, 23rd November 1941. They were turned over to the staff captain for interrogation. The *Aquitania* [then] proceeded on her voyage. No search was made for other rafts or wreckage as Captain Gibbons 'did not know what else there might be about' (meaning that another raider might be in the vicinity).
>
> It was not until nearly noon (local time) that Captain Gibbons read the results of the interrogation of the prisoners and realised that there had been an action and he says in his own words: 'It never dawned on me that there was anything wrong with the cruiser. I thought: 'Well she has sunk this German ship, and the Navy knows about it, and they have it in their scheme of things, and they know what they are going to do'.
>
> Captain Gibbons referred to CAMSI [a directive from the Admiralty] and said that he felt bound by CAMSI 63 because: 'There had been no distress signals, no enemy action signals, no raider, no submarine, no aircraft signals or anything hostile that I could clear myself with for

breaking wireless silence. I felt that I was bound by CAMSI 63 – Restriction on the use of W/T. Furthermore, I had no reason to suppose that anything out of the ordinary had happened, beyond the vital fact that a cruiser had sunk an enemy raider'.

The results of the interrogation did not convey to Captain Gibbons that the cruiser had been badly hit. He knew she had been hit and two Germans had seen fire on the cruiser; they did not say the cruiser was on fire. He had no reason to suppose the cruiser had been burnt out.

Captain Gibbons proceeded on his voyage and then gave some consideration to taking his prisoners into Fremantle, or at least, closing Rottnest and making a report. He knew, however, that the raider had carried mines and did not believe the Germans' story that none had been laid. He thought that Rottnest was a very likely mineable area. He still had it fixed in his mind that the cruiser would have made a report if she wanted to, and that the naval authorities must know all about the action, and that therefore he would not be justified in diverging from his route and taking his ship into a dangerous area.

The Leeuwin was rounded at 0500z on 24th November 1941. At 1706z on 24th November 1941, the ship was in position 35°30'S, 119°E (approximately). By this time, he had received a number of WT messages as follows: at 1157z 24th November from ACNB to *Trocas* (TOR 1434z), at 1052z from ACNB to *Trocas* (TOR 1531z), at 1214z from ACNB to *Hermion* (TOR 1625z) and at 1700z from *Trocas* (TOR 1706z). None of these was addressed to *Aquitania* and *Aquitania* was not included in any messages received. [TOR = Time Of Receipt]

Message 1052z/24 from ACNB to *Trocas* and *Trocas* reply (received 1706z) at once gave Captain Gibbons cause for anxiety. Up to this moment, he had been convinced that the naval authorities knew all about everything – now he suddenly realised that something was wrong and that he could have provided valuable information some 36 hours earlier. But *Trocas* in message 1706z/24 had given Navy as much information as Captain Gibbons himself possessed, and he decided therefore, still to maintain wireless silence. 'These two signals gave me some cause for anxiety whether the Naval Board knew as much as I had supposed. By this time, I knew that anything I could say would be too late, because I then knew that the Navy knew as much as I could tell them from information from the survivors. I couldn't tell the Navy anything that *Trocas* hadn't told them, except that I had some survivors too and the position I had picked them up'.

However, on receipt of messages 0848z/25 from district naval officer, Western Australia to *Trocas* and 1144z/25 and 1226z/25 from Naval Board to *Trocas* at 1732z on 25th November 1941, he realised that lack of information was more than he had supposed and after discussion with the staff captain of *Aquitania,* decided to break WT silence to pass in what information he had. Adelaide Radio was then called at intervals of about two minutes on 550kcs from 1938z/25 to 2155z/25 but no answer was received. Melbourne Radio was called instead a few times during this period and one call was made on 24 metres for Sydney Radio (VIS). No reply was received from either of these two stations. Adelaide Radio had been heard working some time before calls were made but not for at least half an hour before calls were commenced. Melbourne Radio was heard working during the period calls were made but Sydney Radio had not heard at all during the day. The ship was in approximate position 37°00'S, 133°00'E at 2100z/25.

In view of the difficulty of establishing communication, Captain Gibbons gave orders to cease calling and after one call had been made for any British man-o'-war at 2202z/25, calling was discontinued. The message it was intended to pass was eventually passed through Wilsons Promontory War Signal Station.

Mr Parsons, senior wireless operator, said that he was quite certain that the correct adjustments to the transmitter had been made. He had not attempted to tune by wavemeter during these transmissions and it had been impossible to get a cut on his receiver to check the frequency of the transmitter since it was swamped by his own transmissions. The main aerial had been damaged while in Sydney before this particular voyage and had been cut down as a result. However, a wireless inspector had visited the ship at Wellington before the ship left on this voyage and had re-checked the adjustments for the cut-down aerial.

Captain Gibbons made his visual signal to Wilsons Promontory in order to let the authorities at Sydney know that he had prisoner survivors. He knew there was always a visual (Lloyds) station there.

Muirhead-Gould appended he was satisfied that during the investigation, Captain Gibbons gave him every possible assistance and that he was, throughout, perfectly frank and sincere in all his statements, but at no stage did the Commission of Inquiry address the truthfulness of the report. And in response to the allegation that *Aquitania* had reported the recovery of German survivors on 27 November, the Commission of Inquiry accepted that the investigation led by Muirhead-Gould had fully justified the actions taken by Gibbons.

Gerard Muirhead-Gould (1889-1945)

Muirhead-Gould's report is unconvincing in many respects. For instance, notwithstanding that Gibbons had stopped to retrieve survivors by contravening his orders and had risked his ship to attack, initial interrogations had revealed that a battle had taken place and the cruiser was on fire; yet, he (Gibbons) 'had no reason to suppose that anything out of the ordinary had happened'? Gibbons had concluded that the Navy (presumably) knew all about it. Comments attached to the report by senior naval personnel at Navy Office also add to the scepticism and dubious conduct of Gibbons.

At face value, the report falls short of justifying the actions taken by Gibbons. For example, if he thought the Navy knew all about the engagement, it also never dawned on him why other ships and aircraft were not searching the area for survivors where a battle had occurred three days beforehand. He most certainly did not realise that he might have been the first to discover that a battle had taken place. And from the information given by the survivors (the cruiser was on fire), Gibbons had reason to suspect that something serious may have happened to the cruiser. These deliberations gave him just cause to break radio silence, as well as to report the likelihood of further seamen to be rescued.

Furthermore, if Gibbons felt it necessary not to break radio silence, his first opportunity to report the rescue was to send a signal by light to Rottnest Port War Signal Station, yet due to the possibility of the area being mined he thought it too dangerous so he sailed onwards. If entering Fremantle's shallow Gage Roads (though *Aquitania* was equipped with paravanes and degaussing) it could be dangerous, but not so in the deeper waters west of Rottnest Island. Besides, it was no more hazardous than the waters in Bass Strait (average depth 60m), especially on the inshore approach to Wilsons Promontory.

Gibbons had also been convinced that naval authorities knew all about everything up until *Trocas* had reported finding more survivors and after further receipt of signals he decided to break radio silence, claiming that Adelaide Radio and Melbourne Radio were called on 550kcs and Sydney Radio on a wavelength of 24 metres, but no response had been forthcoming. That no answer had been received from these three stations is incredulous, not just because *Aquitania* was unable to transmit effectively to the coastal stations, it inferred that his vessel had difficulty or was incapable of sending a signal to C-in-C China, announcing that survivors had been rescued early on 23 November (local time).

Written comments on the Muirhead-Gould report from those at Navy Office also convey a sense of disbelief. For example: 'Had interrogation of the survivors been complete, the plight of the cruiser would have been apparent.' And on the question of whether *Aquitania* should have diverted to Rottnest PWSS: 'They [Gibbons] could have asked for local craft [from Fremantle] to meet in deeper waters.' And in response to Gibbons's statement that he couldn't tell the Navy anything that *Trocas* hadn't told them: 'Why not? It would have confirmed the *Trocas* story.' A final comment on establishing contact with RAN coastal stations: 'It is understood these stations (Adelaide, Melbourne and Sydney) are constantly manned.'

Given that Gibbons had last tried to communicate with the coastal stations at approx. 2200z/25, he did not again attempt to establish contact before sending his message to Wilsons Promontory. By then, *Aquitania* had sailed some 500nm from position 37°S, 133°E. Obviously, he was in no hurry to send his message.

Although the tenor of Muirhead-Gould's report was not very persuasive, it had the full support of Admiral Royle: 'I think my reactions would have been the same as the captain of the *Aquitania*', he said **(NAA.039.0001)**. Nevertheless, the fact that Muirhead-Gould (and Royle) had absolved Captain Gibbons of such an inordinate delay in not reporting the rescue of survivors for four days or so has all the appearance of collusiveness.

However, above all, it is the sailing schedule of *Trocas* that confounds the report by Muirhead-Gould. The very fact that *Trocas* had been sent to the area where *Aquitania* had found survivors establishes that the report had no validity whatsoever. *Aquitania* had indeed contacted China Station, and in giving the precise position of the rescue, *Trocas* had then been informed. Soon afterwards the tanker had diverted from her proper course where she had found more survivors on a raft and picked them up on 23 November.

Royal Navy Reserve Officer Gibbons had the task of explaining why he had not informed the RAN about the rescue sooner than later. Notwithstanding that he had given tenuous reasons for not notifying Rottnest PWSS that he had stopped to retrieve German survivors, the only avenue available to him to explain protracted efforts to contact coastal stations was to put forth that *Aquitania* had experienced transmission problems. Gibbons was also aware that such problems at the time could not be proved or disproved by RAN authorities.

But while it is not known whether Gibbons was cognisant of the *Trocas* rescue in advance, or whether he had received any further messages from C-in-C China while in Australian waters, the real purpose was to delay for as long as possible news that he had made the rescue in position 24°35'S, 110°57'E. This meant that the search by the RAN for further survivors would be concentrated some 50nm north-east of the rescue position at 24°06'S, 111°40'E – the false position espoused by C-in-C China.

❑ ❑ ❑

FALSE ASSESSMENTS

When two ships meet at sea in battle, the victor is usually the one with the most powerful weapons. But this was not the case when the cruiser HMAS *Sydney* and the raider HSK *Kormoran* met in battle. A single torpedo and accurate gunfire were decisive in sealing the fate of the superior cruiser.

The proposition that the *Sydney* had been struck by one of two torpedoes fired by the *Kormoran* during the opening phase of the battle has been written into naval history, most recently by the 2009 Commission of Inquiry findings – this, despite divided opinion held within senior naval ranks at the time and consensus from the German survivors that three torpedoes had been initially launched at the cruiser.

Examination of naval reports, interrogation notes and German action reports not only establishes the number of torpedoes fired and the circumstances in which they had been fired, it reveals the tactics employed by the opposing commanders and the measures taken by the Navy in a quest to explain the action soon after the battle.

There will always be conjecture on some aspects of the battle, even by those who most ardently support the findings. For example, this may be due to conclusions not having been properly assessed and others may be satisfied that the images of the wreck sites generally confirm the testimonies made by the Germans. This analysis examines the scope of evidence and scrutinises the Commission of Inquiry, which supported the Navy's first attempt to explain the action between the two protagonists.

At the start of the war, German torpedoes were either straight-running or could be programmed to make one 45° turn immediately after leaving the tube. As the war progressed, U-boats were being forced to launch their torpedoes under more disadvantageous conditions. Thus, the need for a more effective convoy weapon became increasingly urgent and this ultimately led to the development of more sophisticated pattern-running torpedoes.

The raider HSK *Kormoran* was equipped with six torpedo tubes for use against HMAS *Sydney*. On each side there were three tubes – one twin battery above-water tubes just below main deck-level and one underwater (submarine) tube 3.5 metres below the waterline. These tubes were located in separate torpedo rooms below deck, one above the other and forward of the main superstructure. A hatch for suppling torpedoes serviced both facilities and a storage room for torpedo supply of U-boats was located further towards the bow of the raider.

Each torpedo room contained the required amount of torpedoes that would likely have been used in a battle and because they were closely situated near the tubes they were available for ease of reload. Normally, the underwater torpedo room stored magnetic mines for tube-launching in shallow waters up to 30 metres in depth. All tubes were serviced regularly and kept loaded at all times.

G7a torpedoes available in December 1940 at the time *Kormoran* departed Germany could be individually gyro-guided to turn 45° left or right after launching, but older-type G7v torpedoes used in WW1 (the forerunner of the G7a) were reputed to be straight-running. These were also suitable for use in the above-water twin batteries mounted on each side of the vessel, but unlike the underwater torpedoes it was not necessary to set the gyro angle because the tubes could be aimed and swung on to the target. And in the case of the raider's fixed underwater tube angled 35° abaft the beam, earlier version torpedoes were ideally suited for targeting an enemy vessel positioned opposite or on the starboard quarter, but the ship was required to be manoeuvred to align the target.

Coupled with the firing of the underwater torpedo was for the *Kormoran* to have been stationary or at least moving at a speed of less than 3 knots to fire it off. But during the action, most of the raider crewmen only seemed mindful that both vessels were travelling at a similar speed at the start of the action. No meaningful speed was ever espoused by crewmen during interrogations. At the very least, they should have realised whether their ship had slowed considerably or not when the action was about to unfold.

When first interrogated, the *Kormoran*'s Captain Detmers himself quoted that the cruiser had ordered his vessel to 'stop', but this rather incautious remark was never to be repeated by him, because at the time it was not known whether there were any *Sydney* survivors. However, the stop-order is not without foundation because several other crewmen had witnessed the same event, evidence of which is in casual conversations and also in their diaries.

A report was sent to the Admiralty in March 1941 to explain the reasons for the demise of the *Sydney,* which found that **two torpedoes** had been fired at the *Sydney* during the first phase of the battle – one struck forward and the other missed the bow. Likewise, in the 1950s, George Hermon Gill, commissioned to write the history of the RAN, came to the same conclusion. This scenario also found favour with the Commission of Inquiry, even though the Navy were aware of the existence of an underwater tube on each side of the raider.

The secret tube was definitely not a point for discussion among *Kormoran* survivors, particularly during interrogations. To do so may have led the Navy to suspect that it had been illegally fired before Detmers had announced the raider's nationality or by raising her battle emblem. It is for this reason that the three-torpedo scenario did not have much candid support during the interrogations.

When they left their burning ship, those rescued by the troopship *Aquitania* and the tanker *Trocas* had thought about 100 crewmen, most of them officers, were still on board when the raider exploded. As they had not seen other survivors during their ordeal, they were therefore unaware of the fate of their fellow crewmen. At the time, they had reason to consider themselves as possibly the only survivors fortunate to be rescued.

Those 25 survivors rescued by *Trocas* (none of them officers), who were first to give evidence on the action, were keen to discuss the action in detail in casual conversations for it had not been revealed to them that others had been subsequently rescued. LEUT AC Baume's rescue ship reported that the men seemed to agree that their ship fired **three torpedoes**, one of which hit the cruiser. But at the time it probably did not occur to them the seriousness of their allegation that three torpedoes had been launched, the implication being that the underwater torpedo had been fired off beforehand in defiance of the rules of international sea warfare. And when it became known that 315 officers and men had been rescued, the substance of their story was not repeated during formal interrogations held a week or so later. Most were reluctant to converse at all, preferring to remain silent on the issue. Thus, the initial casual conversations and the formal interrogations had yielded different results.

In a report made by LEUT JA Taplin on 30 November, the 72 survivors rescued by the *Yandra,* who were considered not to have been influenced by their officers, claimed that '...

when the cruiser was on her port quarter (sic) the raider fired **a** [single] **torpedo** which struck the cruiser forward'. However, if the cruiser's port tubes were trained on the raider (as the narrative suggests) and due to the fact that a torpedo had struck the *Sydney*'s port side, then it must be taken that the torpedo could only have been fired from the raider's starboard side, ostensibly from the underwater tube. In this case, the impression was that one tube had been fired, but they had not been prepared to declare from where it had been launched. The report also contained (independent) evidence from captured Chinese crewman Shu Ah Fah. He stated that '**three torpedoes** were fired in succession at the cruiser'. If this was the case, it was possible that the single underwater torpedo had struck the cruiser and the other two had missed. But his report was to be subsequently classified by the RAN as 'discredited'.

In an interview by LCDR Rycroft on his arrival at Carnarvon aboard the *Centaur* on 27 November with 62 other survivors, the *Kormoran*'s Captain Detmers merely stated that 'the raider's torpedo hit forward'. Although he did not specify how many were fired, he implied that the cruiser had been hit with a single torpedo. Again, he stated: 'We had good luck, **our torpedo hit him forward'** – inferring a single and only torpedo.

In summing up his report, Rycroft noted that these men, including those 103 who came ashore north of Carnarvon, had been obviously instructed by their officers to give incorrect answers. Thus, their comments on the action had been considered unreliable, so all prisoners were sent by road and ship to Fremantle before their formal interrogations began at Swanbourne (for officers) and Harvey (crewmen).

Another report on 29 November by Captain Farncomb in Sydney on the interrogation of the 26 survivors rescued by the *Aquitania* did not initially indicate the number of torpedoes fired during the opening phase of the battle, though the raider had obtained at least one hit with a torpedo under the *Sydney*'s forecastle. However, Farncomb's second report on 1 December stated that 'No. 41 (*Kormoran*) **fired three torpedoes**, of which one hit forward'.

Among those survivors willing to talk about torpedoes, the consensus was: Of the three torpedoes fired (one below-water and two in a battery above-water), one torpedo had hit the cruiser. Alternatively, some had said the raider had fired a single (below-water) torpedo which hit. As this last scenario was consistent with evidence given by most survivors rescued by *Trocas*, *Yandra* and *Aquitania*, the Navy had reason to suspect that the underwater torpedo may have been launched in advance of Detmers's declaration. Furthermore, it is noted that from all the comments on the action thus far, not one of these men (except for Detmers) rescued at sea had indicated that just two torpedoes had been fired at the cruiser.

As a result of interrogations in Fremantle on 28 November, it was reported by RADM Crace that the *Kormoran* was armed with only two torpedo tubes and that the *Sydney* had been hit forward by a torpedo early in the action. This he amended on 30 November in reporting that 'the raider was believed to have fired **three torpedoes**, one of which hit under *Sydney*'s forecastle'.

Also, on 30 November, a report on the interrogation of survivors rescued by the *Koolinda* contrasted with the above observations. CMDR Emile Dechaineux described it as coming from 'various sources', and of the 31 rescued it is believed to have been based on the evidence of five unknown survivors. This report supports previous evidence that the *Sydney* gave chase, ordering *Kormoran* to stop, but Dechaineux also found that '**K fired two torpedoes** from her starboard tubes'. It was believed one of these torpedoes hit and that a third torpedo had been fired afterwards during the second phase of the action when the cruiser was on the raider's port beam.

CMDR Emile Dechaineux (1902–1944) in 1943

It was not known at the time whether he (Dechaineux) had been aware of the fact that the raider possessed three torpedo tubes on the starboard side. He may have been influenced by the earlier report on 28 November from RADM Crace, who had mistakenly advised that the *Kormoran* was armed with only two torpedo tubes. Also, his assessment that two torpedoes had been fired during the first phase of the action and that a third torpedo had been fired later during the second phase does not accord with the overwhelming evidence that three torpedoes had been fired when the action began. That at least one other torpedo had been fired at the cruiser during the battle is not disputed (as discussed later).

However, due to the fact that the report of 30 November acknowledges that *Kormoran* had been ordered to stop, Dechaineux did not contemplate the ideal opportunity that then existed for Detmers to have launched the covert underwater torpedo on the starboard side facing the cruiser. Moreover, it would have been an anathema for him not to have used his ace weapon, for which it had been specifically designed.

At his interrogation on 1 December, CAPT Detmers re-quoted a similar scenario on the opening phase of the battle – this, at the time when the search for *Sydney* survivors had been officially abandoned. In order to clarify his statement at Carnarvon, he added: **'the raider (*Kormoran*) fired two torpedoes, one of which missed and the other hitting about 20 metres from the bow'.**

Despite contrary evidence from his crewmen rescued earlier, he had belatedly given the impression to his captors that not one but two torpedoes from the twin battery above-water tubes had been fired at the *Sydney.*

Detmers must have thought he was on safe ground in making this statement. That no *Sydney* survivors had been found, it could not be verified. But he had yet to effectively rule out the use of the underwater torpedo, which could only be launched at slow speed, but his stop-order statement had signified that he had obeyed signals from the *Sydney* and therefore the raider was presumed to have been moving slowly or making minimum headway to the action site.

He must have been then comforted by the fact that his Yeoman of Signals, Erich Ahlbach, had subsequently stated that the 'cruiser did not signal proceed nor stop'. Finally, in his interrogation on 7 December, Detmers re-worded his previous statement but with the same connotation: **'I torpedoed her, one of my torpedoes struck near the forward funnel'.**

At his last interrogation, Detmers provided what can be regarded as a damning admission after the cruiser had signalled for the identity of his ship. He stated that he was then 'uninterrupted by signals from the *Sydney* for half an hour'. In fact, it was during this half-hour period that Burnett had been instructed to routinely check on the whereabouts, bona fides and secret letters assigned to the so-called *Straat Malakka*, while being instructed to stop at the prescribed safety distance of 14,000 yards (approx. 7 miles) for an unidentified vessel.

Naval authorities did not appear to have been swayed by Detmers's latest disclosure because from the results of the interrogation reports there was little to doubt that at least one torpedo had hit the *Sydney.* However, they began to equivocate on the issue of whether two or three torpedoes had been fired at the start of the action. For example, the Naval Board's assessment to Admiralty on 7 December did not mention how many torpedoes had been fired, and in a summary on 18 December, Naval Intelligence was only of the view that the cruiser had been hit by single torpedo.

The question of whether the raider's crewmen had seen two or three torpedoes fired during the first phase of the action has never been satisfactorily explained by the Navy or by the inquiry, but that evidence given by Detmers and a few others that only two torpedoes had been fired has been influential in an historical context – in G Hermon Gill's history of the RAN and in the 2008 Commission of Inquiry Report. Strangely, even though senior naval personnel had identified that three torpedoes had been fired, the Naval Board did not entertain that view. They preferred to accept alternative evidence from those few *Kormoran* survivors who had asserted that one of the two above-water torpedoes had struck the *Sydney*.

Foremost is the apparent reluctance by the Navy to press for details on the underwater tubes during the interrogation process. For example, when questioned on 2 December 1941, Torpedo Officer Joachim Greter simply said 'he did not want to provide information about his battle station'. And on 9 December, Chief Torpedo Mechanic Edmund Schmidt spoke only about the above-water torpedo tubes in saying that 'only two torpedoes were fired at the cruiser' – this, after many other fellow crewmen had claimed that three were fired, but he was not questioned further and nor was Greter.

Notwithstanding the consensus among ordinary crewmen that three torpedoes had been fired, the Naval Board had reached a turning point by mid-December 1941. This rather sudden shift towards a belief in the two-torpedo scenario had been largely based on the evidence of Detmers, Bunjes and Ahlbach. But that the Admiralty in London desired that the RAN provide a report on the action on completion of the interrogations, it was imperative a report be forwarded as soon as possible.

On completion of the interrogation process, CMDR Dechaineux drafted an interim report to Admiralty. His report is said to have encompassed all of the evidencc accumulated, inclusive of summaries of the action written by senior naval officers. He prefaced the action thus: **'... Detmers and other prisoners have frankly told the story, and there is every reason to believe the authenticity of their story'**. He also concluded that very early in the action, **'the raider fired two torpedoes, one from above water and one from the submerged torpedo tube; one of these hit the Sydney...'**.

Dechaineux had made a completely different assessment in taking into account reports by senior naval officers, but his report on the single-torpedo scenario did not make sense in regard to the alleged speed of the vessels. Earlier he had conceded that the raider had been ordered to stop, but later Ahlbach had given evidence that the *Sydney* had made no 'stop' signal and that the raider had been travelling at an undiminished rate of 14–15 knots when the battle began – meaning, that the *Sydney* was also moving at a similar speed.

Intriguingly, the letter attached to his report from the district naval officer in WA (he had supervised the interrogations) had identified statements made by POWs that were considered to be of more interest than others. However, it is not known whether Dechaineux had based his report on this advice. His report was sent to the director of Naval Intelligence for final study and approval **(NAA MP1049/5, 2026/19/6)**.

Dechaineux did not doubt the authenticity of his report, but it seems inconceivable that he had presented a story on the action that was incompatible. For instance, the proposition that the raider had been travelling at 15 knots can in no way be compatible with a torpedo launched from the underwater tube because it could not be fired off if the vessel exceeded 3 knots. And that he had assessed that the raider had not been ordered to at least slow, compounds the ineptitude of his report.

As it stood, Dechaineux's report was typical of the discordant views held by senior naval officers at the time. Thus, an independent report to the Admiralty, seemingly free of naval influence, was thought the best solution for the director of Naval Intelligence, CMDR Rupert Long. Frank Burgess Eldridge, a lecturer at the nearby Naval College in Melbourne (who also wrote its history), was appointed by the DNI to prepare the final report on behalf of the Naval Board. It was sent to the Admiralty on 12 February 1942. [See Addenda.]

F B Eldridge

In summarising all the material to date, Eldridge concluded (similar to Dechaineux) that the story of the action **'was frankly told by Captain Detmers and others, and the story as told seems to ring true...'**. But in his report, he quoted Detmers almost verbatim in preference to others: **'...the raider had fired two torpedoes, one of which struck the Sydney forward about 20 metres from the bow...'**. He had also assessed (from Ahlbach) that the *Sydney* **'did not order the raider to stop'**. These two statements were eventually to have far-reaching consequences, both from the point of view of Detmers's conduct and in regard to Captain Burnett's culpability.

Eldridge had placed an intense belief in the word of Detmers, but on the key element in his statement that the raider had been ordered to stop he preferred to take the word of signaller Ahlbach (and others un-named) that the *Kormoran* had not stopped. And because the raider had presumably turned away and had increased its speed to 15 knots on sighting the cruiser, he took it that she had maintained that speed all the way to the action site – over 20 miles distant. Eldridge could thus justify ruling out the use of the below-water tube, despite the evidence of those interrogated. Hence, in quoting Detmers, he concluded that two above-water torpedoes had been fired, one of which had struck the *Sydney*. This was enough for Eldridge to conclude that a third torpedo from underwater could not have been launched at such a speed. However, an overall assessment from the bulk of the crewmen would have placed a completely different complexion on the opening phase of the battle.

He (Eldridge) had written his report only a few months after the battle and from whatever information had been given to him by the Navy and by the director of Naval Intelligence, but that he was not privy to subsequent action reports and diaries written later by the Germans, it is not surprising his assessment of the second phase of the action is demonstrably astray. For example, after the cruiser had launched her torpedoes unsuccessfully at the *Kormoran*, he had assessed that a torpedo fired by the raider about the same time had also missed its mark. In fact, this torpedo had been fired at the *Sydney* much later – this, at the extreme distance of approximately 7,000 metres.

Considering that Eldridge had made no mention of evidence given by prisoners said to have been segregated on board *Trocas, Aquitania, Koolinda, Centaur* and *Yandra*, as well as in associated reports from senior naval officers, the interrogation notes given to him from those 62 prisoners from *Centaur* and from those rescued on the beach north of Carnarvon had undoubtedly taken precedence in his conclusions on the action.

This group, who had not been segregated at all times, had been taken to Swanbourne and Harvey for formal interrogations, but ordinary crewmen had been reluctant to discuss *Kormoran*'s torpedoes, whereas some of the officers had spoken more freely and had given naval authorities the distinct impression that one of two torpedoes fired had struck the *Sydney*. On this evidence alone, Eldridge had deduced that these torpedoes had come from the twin above-water tubes.

His report is claimed to have been compiled from a mass of material, but casual comments by crewmen immediately after the action had been excluded from consideration, including reports made by senior naval officers at the time. These deficiencies mean that the information supplied to outsider Eldridge had been inadequate for the purpose of establishing the report's truth or otherwise, even though the Naval Board had all the information at their disposal to decide for themselves.

Eldridge could reliably ascertain the worth of the information given, albeit, unknown to him, selective. He had given his perception of the action in the form of a complete report on the loss of the *Sydney* in good faith, but he could not explain why the *Sydney* had come so close to the raider. Unfortunately, his deliberations on the action (which was normally the imprimatur of the Naval Board), are now known not to have encompassed all of the evidence gathered. The basis of the report to Admiralty stated: **'it came from** [only] **those POWs, whose evidence** [in the opinion of the Navy] **proved most useful'.** In fact, Eldridge had based his complete story on the evidence given by only a dozen or so of the more than 300 POWs and on the action he quoted just Detmers, Ahlbach and Bunjes **(Admiralty File 199/736).**

Much of his scenario, particularly in reference to the firing of two torpedoes featured in the ensuing German battle summaries and action reports. It was exactly the outcome the Germans wanted because the proposition that only two torpedoes had been fired while the vessel made 15 knots, effectively absolved them from any allegations that the underwater torpedo had played any part in the action.

The Germans also gave prominence to the two-torpedo scenario in various personal diaries that were later confiscated at the POW camp in Victoria. Of course, in the end the Eldridge story of the battle became cemented in G Hermon Gill's history of the RAN and synonymous with the findings made by the 2009 Commission of Inquiry report.

In returning to Petty Officer Erich Ahlbach [Yeoman of Signals (his counterpart being the cruiser's James Tyldsley)], whose duty (he was also on the bridge) was to decipher signals from the distant *Sydney* as accurately as possible using his powerful telescope and to interpret their exact meaning so that Detmers could devise his tactics accordingly, there could not have been a difference of opinion on the stop order during the lead-up to the battle. Clearly, the order was either issued or not. The most obvious conclusion to be drawn is that even though the prisoner groups had been segregated during the interrogation process, Ahlbach had been driven to deny Detmers slip-of-the-tongue stop-order statement in order to convey the story that only two torpedoes from the above-water tubes had been fired while moving at speed, effectively negating the overpowering evidence that a third torpedo had been fired beforehand.

Frankly, Ahlbach and Detmers had not been credible witnesses to the action. For example, Detmers had stated that when the *Sydney* was approximately abeam she asked by flags and flashing, 'Where bound?' The *Kormoran* answered, 'Batavia', and the cruiser then proceeded to ask for the secret letters **(NAA B6121, 164M)**. In contrast, after having given the name of his vessel, from 7 miles away according to Ahlbach, Detmers said he signalled, 'Batavia' in answer to its destination. Thus, there is no doubt that this signalling had occurred much earlier, approx. half an hour after sighting the cruiser **(*The Raider Kormoran*, p140)**.

The signalling distance for the request of the name of the vessel quoted by Ahlbach is plausible, but Detmers's assertion that the destination had been asked for while abeam of the cruiser is not. After all, it was incumbent for Burnett to have signalled for the secret letters assigned to the *Straat Malakka* after learning the name of the vessel, but that the vessel had already turned away from her northerly course, supports Ahlbach's story that her curious destination had been requested from a distance. Detmers had wrongly affirmed that the secret letters had first been requested while the vessels were close abeam. Therefore, the assertion that the *Sydney* had thereby asked for the secret letters as justification for the action to begin, is completely discredited. Detmers and Ahlbach had not described in sequence the events before the action began.

In assessing whether two or three torpedoes had been fired initially (professed to be type G7a or G7v torpedoes), those Germans in a position to observe the torpedoes at their action stations could not have failed to see the number of tracks produced by these wake-producing torpedoes. This is why the majority of crewmen had conceded the tell-tale wake of three torpedoes.

Typical wake of a G7a torpedo

The Eldridge Report had given the impression that the *Sydney* had closed steadily on the raider without completing the identification procedures and that Burnett had been negligent in doing so. Likewise, in a message to the Admiralty and other naval stations, the Naval Board had already made the assessment that the captain of the *Sydney* had been deceived and had 'placed himself in tactically unsound position'. But on 18 March 1942, a final statement from the chief of Naval Staff went even further in accusing Burnett of being 24 hours late in arriving at the rendezvous position and had taken a risk in getting so close to the raider. They had surmised that he had therefore not followed his orders. From this point onwards, the Navy considered Burnett fully accountable for the disaster.

In holding Burnett responsible, Eldridge had based his assessment of the action wholly on the evidence of a few officers, surmising that the *Kormoran* had opened fire at close range because Detmers could not reply to a demand for the secret letters – this, despite Burnett carrying out the correct Admiralty challenge and identification procedures from a safe distance. But Detmers was not familiar with Admiralty instructions, which specifically demanded that the secret letters be requested at 14,000 yards (7 miles) soon after the vessel had given her name. And that the secret letters were required to be solicited at the prescribed safety distance, further demonstrates the absurdity of his claim that the cruiser's demand for the *Straat Malakka*'s secret call sign while both vessels were about 1,000m apart, gave him cause to commence the action.

Like Dechaineux, Eldridge had reasoned from Detmers's account of the action that the raider had opened fire because the secret letters could not be supplied when close up, a claim also put forward by another fellow officer, Bunjes. But evidence from Ernst Hildenbrand partly dispels that notion. During extensive interrogations on 1 December (his battle station had been on the starboard aft 150mm gun), he testified that the raider had opened fire when the cruiser had asked for the secret challenge. That he had been supposedly kept segregated with 23 of his other shipmates and had no contact with other prisoner groups, suggests that it was Detmers's prerogative to make that announcement, not only to his officers on the bridge, but Hildenbrand said it was also repeated to all gun crews over the intercom while at their battle stations. However, in no way does it mean that the cruiser's request for the secret letters at the start of the action has any validity.

There are many instances where Burnett had successfully challenged and identified allied merchant vessels during his time in command of escorting ships to Singapore, but it was only on this last occasion involving a secret call-sign registered vessel that he was accused of not following the procedures laid down. But the fact that the disguised vessel identified as the *Straat Malakka* was not listed on the *Sydney*'s VAI as being in the area, it had turned away inappropriately and had not shown her silhouette in accordance with Admiralty procedures while trying to avoid the pursuing cruiser and showed all the characteristics of a suspicious vessel. Dutch merchant ships simply did not act this way when confronted by a British cruiser. Burnett therefore had good reason to believe he was in pursuit of an enemy vessel, not just because of her evasive actions, but due to the fact that allied vessels allocated with a secret call-sign did not hurriedly signal by flag at a distance of 7nm because the flag was too distant to be read with any certainty. This would necessitate the vessel coming closer in order to read the flag signals. The modern diesel vessel ahead had signalled completely out of character by flag.

Moreover, after having obtained the name of the suspicious vessel at the safe distance recommended in the Admiralty orders, it was then incumbent for Burnett to signal for the secret letters. But from this point on, Burnett is accused of acting completely out of order – he had not signalled for the secret letters from a safe distance, and in order to read the raider's flags, the *Sydney* had been drawn closer and closer to her quarry, eventually requesting them from a distance of some 900 metres. However, though Eldridge made these same points in referring to Detmers's story, it does not follow that Burnett did not ask for the secret letters from a distance, and nor does it follow that the *Kormoran* opened fire because Detmers could not reply to the secret letters that were said to have been sent at the last moment.

Burnett had ample opportunity to assess the bona fides of the *Straat Malakka* as the *Sydney* drew closer. At first, though obstructed by the sun, her evasive action had alerted Burnett to the possibility that it was an enemy ship, and when the raider had given the name of the so-called *Straat Malakka* from a distance, its visual appearance meant it was in all probability not the real name of the vessel. But there would have been no mistake close-up away from the sun, because the vessel definitely did not possess the typical physical features of the supposed Dutch merchantman shown in the identification handbook. By then, was he positive he was dealing with an enemy vessel, which also looked remarkably like the photo of Raider G issued to him as recently as the previous month.

Nevertheless, whether or not the raider had replied correctly to Burnett's request for the secret letters from a distance, he had drawn closer in order to board the vessel, in accordance with Admiralty's instructions recently issued to him. This action was also necessary to ensure that the claimed identity of the vessel had been *indemnified. Finally, that Burnett had disobeyed his orders or had forgotten to request the secret letters after identifying the so-called *Straat Malakka*, had not been proven conclusively by Eldridge due to the complete absence of survivors from the *Sydney.*

*Indemnification was not a license to approach and board the suspicious vessel without prior notification. This would only have occurred after the enemy vessel had complied with a stop order and that Burnett had signalled his intention to board. Anti-scuttling measures, a task in which Burnett's crew had been expertly trained, would also be carried out.

As noted in the 1999 Parliamentary Report: **'To say that Captain Burnett did not follow orders is simplistic'.** The latest instructions given to him were: **'if any suspicion exists, the ship should be boarded'.** That such action would also be undertaken in conjunction with Admiralty Message 771A (anti-scuttling measures) is by far the most plausible reason for Burnett's decision to close on the raider.

But these instructions were to prove Burnett's downfall for they did not distinguish between boarding suspected enemy merchant vessels and heavily armed raiders. Nevertheless, Eldridge had only to consider the selection of interrogation reports given to him by the Navy in his deliberations, none of which had obviously suggested that the cruiser had closed in order to board the raider. On the other hand, preliminary discussions with survivors such as Lensch and Ortmann reveal that a boarding party had been assembled and was about to set off for the raider when it suddenly opened fire.

Again, the Commission of Inquiry found that the *Sydney* had been drawn persuasively closer in order to read the raider's flag signals, which had been supposedly fumbled and concealed from view (according to Ahlbach and others). It was in this context that the inquiry found that Burnett had continued to close on the raider in order to read the flags, had not carried out the full identification, recognition and challenge procedures, and therefore he had not followed his orders.

The 'boarding' proposition had not been seriously contemplated by Eldridge, despite evidence from Engineer Rudolf Lensch that the raider had been ordered to stop and that the cruiser had lowered a boat, presumably to board the raider. That a survivor had admitted the raider had opened fire in response to the act of boarding, seemingly rendered void the excuse that Detmers took immediate action because he could not supply the secret letters. Nevertheless, the inquiry disregarded Lensch's evidence and chose the simplistic scenario in holding Burnett personally responsible for the loss of the cruiser.

Lensch gave more detail than any other survivor, most of which proved to be accurate. He also correctly asserted that throughout the battle, a total of four torpedoes were fired at the cruiser, three in the first phase of the action and one later at a distance of 7,000 metres. In the opinion of his interrogator: 'any information gathered from this man would be reliable' **(NAA B6121, 164M)**.

Regardless of distance, it is beyond doubt that the *Sydney* had signalled *Kormoran* to supply the secret letters (IIKP) because Detmers and Ahlbach had nominated the correct inner letters (IK) of the cruiser during interrogations. But their story on the action, which relied on the premise that the cruiser was completely unsuspicious of the raider, required a good explanation as to why the raider had suddenly opened fire.

In his first formal interview, Detmers quoted: **'Cruiser made signal NNP** [NNJ]**, didn't understand, didn't answer. Cruiser signalled stop, and ordered raider by searchlight in plain language to give secret call. Didn't know so had to fight'... range was** [then] **somewhat more than a mile'** (Chief Signaller Ahlbach said 7 miles). Unknown to Detmers, he had correctly described the identification and challenge procedures to be issued at a safe distance of 7 miles. Obviously, Burnett had indeed followed the orders laid down. However, Detmers's real intention had been to convey the story that the secret call was asked for at a distance of about 1 mile, which had also been attested beforehand by SUB LEUT Bunjes.

Much had been made by the Navy of the segregation of POWs, but the folly of separating large groups of prisoners was always likely to lead to collusive agreements among individuals whenever they got together, and in case of the

Kormoran officers, 23 of whom were accommodated together at Swanbourne, those who could give details of the action in good English (such as Bunjes) offered the interrogators the most compelling explanation. But comments from Navigator Henri Meyer also gave tacit support to the Admiralty's identification procedures. He said, **'Parley took place – hoist your signal letters – gave name of Dutch ship,** [then] **asked for secret signal. *Kormoran* did not reply.'** Although he did not indicate the signalling distance, in defiance of Detmers, Bunjes and Ahlbach (all of whom had conveyed the story of inefficient signalling by the raider), Meyer said that **'no trick was used to bring the cruiser nearer'.**

Navigator Meyer (he was present on the bridge) had given a completely different picture to what Detmers and Ahlbach had said at a distance. In addition to asking for the name of the vessel and secret signal, it was incumbent upon Burnett to also ask for the destination and the last port of call, but more importantly, a nonreply to the secret signal would have meant that the *Straat Malakka* was not what it was claimed to be. Detmers's ship, therefore, had no choice but to submit to the nominal speed the cruiser had signalled. The game of bluff had come to an end, but the crew were none the wiser about the flag signal which meant the raider would obey further instructions from the cruiser. Burnett had invoked Admiralty orders, which instructed that an enemy ship which had been identified was to proceed slowly while the arresting ship determined whether it was armed or unarmed.

Although most of the crewmen had been noncommittal on what caused the sudden action, they did supply some fleeting but unqualified comments at Harvey POW Camp on 4 December, some in support of the Eldridge Report, some not. At no stage had the interrogators pursued the actual speed of the vessels when the action began. Some had maintained that both had been travelling at 15 knots at the time. However, Torpedo

Officer LEUT Fritz Skeries had made an inadvertent comment which was not taken up. In describing the torpedo strike and that another had passed forward of the cruiser, he added: **'The cruiser was nearly motionless'** [at the time] **(NAA B6121, 164M).** Thus, that the *Sydney* had been virtually stopped could not have been due to the torpedo strike, reducing her speed suddenly from 15 knots to zero. Skeries statement per se, therefore, refers to the cruiser being torpedoed while stationary. In this instance, it is inconceivable that it was not due to the underwater torpedo being fired off.

On 12 October 1945, more than three years after Eldridge wrote his report amid concerns that a plausible explanation of the action and rescue efforts mounted by the Navy be provided to the Australian public, the intelligence flag officer in Fremantle, LCDR Rycroft, recommended to Rupert Long, director of Naval Intelligence, that a report prepared by WRANS Third Officer Mollie Westhoven would best suit this purpose. Westhoven, who had been seconded to the Shipping Plotting Office in Fremantle, had summarised the original interrogation notes, but unlike Eldridge, who had made his own assessments, no limitations had been placed on her. She had concluded that the *Kormoran* survivors agreed that **three torpedoes** had been fired at the cruiser, one of which had hit **(NAA B6121 165P)** – this, in contrast to the Eldridge Report which had previously subscribed to the two-torpedo scenario.

In writing her report, Westhoven was able to portray an almost complete picture of the action from the interrogation notes. However, in view of the diverse and contrasting evidence from the German survivors, she had been compelled to place a caveat on her report. In her assessment of the various stories told, she cautioned: **'how far their** [the German] **accounts varied from the truth, however, is something that would be almost impossible to establish...'**. [See Addenda] On the other hand, Eldridge had confidently quoted the (selected) accounts of Detmers, Bunjes and Ahlbach in his report that had not been a sincere assessment of the action which was, according to him, frankly told.

Within a week, the director of Naval Intelligence formally rejected the idea of publishing Westhoven's account on the basis that her analysis would still not be accepted by some people as being absolute confirmation of the loss of the *Sydney*. But more to the point, as the Naval Board had already explained the action to the Admiralty in the Eldridge Report, the RAN should not be seen to be confusing the issue nearly four years later. And besides, Westhoven's account describing that three torpedoes had been fired, would have meant that the underwater torpedo had been suspected of being launched (illegally) before the action started, thus undermining the Navy's censure of Burnett.

DNI CMDR Rupert Long had obviously considered it inadvisable to open up a can of worms. The Naval Board were committed to the Eldridge story (which had been accepted by the Admiralty), and they had held Burnett responsible for the loss of the cruiser because, according to them, he had inexplicably closed on the raider and had not carried out the full identification and challenge procedures. Thus, Long ensured that Westhoven's report remained unpublished.

Much comment has been made on the German action reports in the moments before the action began, for example, whether the engine of the aircraft on board the *Sydney* had been turned off (1942 and 1947 reports) or the cruiser's engines had stopped (1945 Report). The latter report, which does not refer to the aircraft, simply refers to the cruiser having stopped her engines due to her being stationary (Skeries). It is for this reason that FRUMEL had solved the parameters of the action (see cryptogram) and that the cruiser had slowed sufficiently to stop, Burnett's aim being to board the raider to once and for all confirm it was an enemy ship. This is much more likely to be correct because all three translations of the action reports follow on by describing that the cruiser or he, Burnett, seemed to Detmers to be completely unsuspicious.

Again, to suggest that Burnett would have been unsuspecting because the cruiser's engine had been turned off while the cruiser had been sailing along at, say, 14–15 knots as translated in the 1945 Action Report is not credible and makes no sense. It only makes sense if the cruiser was about to slow down and stop. And if the aircraft's engine had been running while extended on the catapult (1942 and 1947 ARs), it was normal procedure to turn it off when the cruiser had closed on the raider and retract the aircraft amidships should the *Sydney* have contemplated opening fire – this, to prevent damage to it from the percussion of the 6-inch guns. The term 'unsuspecting' is therefore valid in the context that the cruiser per se had stopped.

F	L G M O T O R A B
aircraft	engine off
Gegner stellt Flgz.	Motor ab,
enemy turns aircraft	engine off
S T E L L T	M O T O R A B
Cruiser stops	engines
Ist also völlig	ahnungslos
[He] is thus quite	unsuspecting
A L S O V O E L L I G	A H N U N G S L O S D A H E R
therefore completely	unsuspecting thereupon at
B E F E L E N T T A	R N E N
(1 7) 3 0 Order: off disguise	
1 7 3 0 B E F E H L E N T T A	R N E N
1 7 3 0 Order: off disguise	
E N T T A	R N E N X
1730 identity declared	
	K R I E G S F L A G G E
	battle flag at the mainmast
H O L L X F L A G G E N I E D	E R K R I E G S F L A G G E
strike Dutch flag	German colours
A M G R O S S M A S T W E H T	K L A R A U S
flies clear	
G R O S S M A C T W E H T	K L A R A U S X
clearly shown	

Action Report: 'Enemy Stops Engines' (COI.005.0011).

Translated Action Reports – 1942 version (green) 1947 (blue) 1945 (red) Evidence from survivors that the aircraft's engine had been turned off is not disputed.

However, in his book, Detmers attempts to qualify what his action reports had meant. He specifically refers to the Walrus seaplane's engines being shut down on the catapult. And in view of his concern that the seaplane would ultimately fly over his vessel, the reconnaissance observer was bound to recognise the raider as an auxiliary cruiser because his guns had already been hydraulically placed in position, both forward and aft. But as no such speed as 14–15 knots can be substantiated, as evidenced in the confined parameters of the battle site (see in the following chapter), it must be taken that his translation refers to his opponent, the enemy cruiser (German: 'gegner'), as per the 1947 Action Report (shown in blue).

Also, in his book, **(*The Raider Kormoran*, p142),** Detmers recounts that his eyes were glued to the bearing's compass, and as soon as he saw the enemy had practically come to a standstill (the enemy's bearing had been constant while moving at an indeterminate speed), he gave the order to de-camouflage. This does not necessarily mean that the raider had been completely stationary, rather, both vessels had been travelling at the same speed, albeit 'slow' (as stated by officer von Goesseln), and that shortly afterwards Detmers had witnessed from the bearing compass that the cruiser had almost come to a standstill. As the raider could not react to stop at the same time, this means that the raider had moved slightly ahead before stopping to launch the underwater torpedo at the cruiser.

The action reports are crafted to show in sequence that the rules for engagement had been observed. For example, each report describes the German ensign as being raised before de-camouflaging had taken place. However, the 1945 translation disclosing that the crew were then ordered to stand by with guns and torpedoes and that Detmers had given orders for all weapons to open fire, refers to (except for the smaller guns) only the main armament capable of targeting the cruiser opposite – four of the six 150mm guns (the other two were in the firing lee), one 3.7cm gun (mounted near the bridge), the large machine guns and all three starboard torpedo tubes (one underwater). Apart from the initial onslaught of the guns, the relevance of this is related to the fact that if one torpedo had struck the cruiser and the other two had missed, then three torpedoes had been launched, and as a consequence, the raider must have been moving at three knots or less to launch the underwater torpedo.

In keeping with Detmers's two-torpedo scenario, the action reports purport to indicate that because the *Sydney* had been moving at approximately 14 knots when targeted and that his compass reading had showed the cruiser at a 'standstill', then the *Kormoran* was also doing 14 knots. However, as previously mentioned, gunnery officer Skeries had witnessed that the cruiser was nearly motionless when torpedoed, and gunner Ernst Hildenbrand had said that after the cruiser was hit by the torpedo, it then gained 'fair speed' before turning and taking position astern. Yet notwithstanding the above witness accounts, the Navy has continued to assert that both the cruiser and the raider had been travelling 14 knots when the battle began. The solution as to whether the two above-water torpedoes had been fired is established analytically below.

When the cruiser had dropped slowly astern, two of the action reports describe: **Two torpedoes, inclination 90°, speed 14 knots** (cruiser). This had given the impression that the *Sydney* had been targeted by only the two above-water torpedoes while both vessels were moving at the speed nominated. However, the action report of 1945 that Detmers had escaped with resolves the question in its message (in red letters). In his bid to silence the cruiser's guns, he had quite rightly given the order to target the stem (bow) and stern with each of his above-water tubes in order to silence or at least minimize retaliation from the four turrets (turrets A and B were located forward of the bridge and C and D were at the aft end of the cruiser). See below. But as the above-water torpedoes had been partially disabled on their mounts, as described later in this chapter, both torpedoes had instead passed in front of the bow.

G E I T F S time 6 sec[onds] E N T T A R N Z E I T 6 S time taken to reveal identity 6 sec[onds] E N T T A R N Z E I T F S time taken to reveal identity 6 seconds.	K R I E G S F L A G G E battle flag E C E K X
A M G R O S M A S T W E H T flies clear at the main mast X A R T L X F E U E R E R A U Order to stand by with guns and torpedoes	K L A R A U S B N I S X T O R P E D O W A F F E
S C H I E S S	G E G N E R enemy [drops] Gegner sackt Enemy drops E R L X G E G N E R S A C K T Enemy falls
A C H T E R A U astern achteraus. astern L A N G S A M A C H T E R A U slowly astern	S T O R P M I T L A G E 2 torpedoes on inclination 2 Torp. mit Lage 2 torpedoes on Inclination S X T O R P X L A G E 2 torpedoes Position
F A H R T 9 0 speed 14 90, Gegnerfahrt 14. 90 enemy speed 14 F A H R T 8 0 speed 14	 A B K O M M P U N K T B U G point of aim stem
D A S U at the same time Dazu at the same time H E C K D A Z U L A N G S A M stern at the same time turned slowly	A U F G E D R E H T alter to 2 6 0 auf 2 6 0 gedreht. alter to 2 6 0 A U F to 260

COI.005.0012

Statements made on the exact number of guns fired are for some observers difficult to determine from the realms of fact and fiction. Nevertheless, a simple assessment can be made from the sequence of salvoes described in the action reports. As a general guide, most 150mm naval guns of WWI vintage could fire at a comfortable rate of four rounds per minute – one shell (salvo) every 15 seconds.

But according to ex-president of the Kormoran Association, Ludwig Ernst who, under the direction of gunnery officer

Skeries, gave the orders to the gun crews during the action, the raider's guns fired more often – about every 10 seconds during the action. This quicker rate was said to be due to the intense practise by the gun crews and he made it clear that they did not fire full salvoes and that each gun fired a salvo at a particular target as soon as it was ready. Also, the guns could be fired before the above-water torpedoes were fired because these torpedoes had to be de-camouflaged, pointed outwards and then aimed at the *Sydney*.

Given that Ernst is correct about the rate of firing and if according to the action reports the *Sydney* was hit by a torpedo after 8–10 individual salvoes **(COI.005.0015)**, then after allowing for minimum of *15 seconds to de-camouflage and fire the guns, each of the four guns had therefore fired at least twice (eight individual salvoes) in a space of 25 seconds (35 seconds for 12 salvoes). Consequently, a torpedo from the above-water tube, which took *32 seconds to deploy, could not have struck the cruiser 900 metres away because at 40 knots a type G7a torpedo took a minimum of *45 seconds to run this distance. This running time, plus the extra time required for deployment means that from the moment the de-camouflage order had been given it could take an above-water torpedo *77 seconds to strike the target. At 10-second intervals, up to 28 separate salvoes could have been fired within this period.

*Assessment by Defence Dept experts **(DSTO.003.0157)**.

Detmers recounted an even faster rate of fire. According to him **(*The Raider Kormoran*, p143)**, 'the first shot [one salvo] was fired from our leading gun within six seconds of the order to de-camouflage. Four seconds later, the other three went into action scoring direct hits on the cruiser's bridge and control tower. Then we fired eight salvoes with six seconds between each salvo' – this, before the torpedo hit. At this rate, two salvoes had been fired from each gun within 10 seconds and thereafter each gun had fired twice within a space of 12 seconds. This equates to a total of 10 salvoes fired in approximately 22 seconds from the order to de-camouflage. In this time, the above-water torpedoes would not have left their tubes. At Detmers's rate of fire, up to 46 single salvoes would have been fired in 77 seconds, but according to the action reports only 8 or 9 had been fired before one of the above-water torpedoes had struck the cruiser.

In order to portray the 1942 and 1947 action reports with some accuracy in his book, Detmers, who had since realised that more than 8–10 individual salvoes were required to have been fired within the time the torpedo took to reach the cruiser, had shrewdly quoted 'eight salvoes with six seconds between each salvo'. This was supposed to have meant that 8 (individual) salvoes had been fired in 48 seconds and it also meant that up to 36 single salvoes had been fired in 58 seconds from the order to de-camouflage to when the torpedo struck the cruiser 77 seconds later. Detmers did not nominate the deployment time for the torpedoes, but that 36 had struck in 58 seconds is not feasible because by this time the torpedoes would be still about 400 metres short of the *Sydney*. As can be gauged from his timing, up to 48 individual salvoes were required to have been fired before an above-water torpedo could have struck the cruiser.

Each of the instances described above negates any prospect of the above-water torpedoes striking the *Sydney* in the time required for them to be launched and run the distance while both vessels were moving at 14 knots. On the other hand, the underwater torpedo from the stationary raider launched before the de-camouflage order had been given could run the distance in 45 seconds. A witness statement from Hermann Ortmann, an assistant loader on no. 4 gun, also corroborated the rate of fire given by Ludwig Ernst **(SUBM.007.0003)**.

Sydney's AA Guns were not manned at all! Both ships were almost stationary and a small boat (cutter) was being swung out! Then I was told to run around to the camouflage screen and be ready to release it, but as I was about to go around to operate the release handle No 4 gun fired it's first salvo, Gun No 3 did the same thing! To operate the leaver was now impossible. I had to lie on my back and kick it with my feet, then it dropped away. The screen had been damaged by the blast from the gun or the shell clipping it! Suddenly there was a huge explosion and a wall of water rose up against the side of the Sydney, forward of her bridge. Then all of our guns commenced firing. Only one torpedo was fired at the Sydney. Our No 4 gun fired continuously for about 10 minutes (one shell fired every 10 seconds, that's 10 x 6 =60 shells) at the Sydney's port side, then we came around to the Sydney's starboard side and did the same thing for another 10 minutes.

Evidence from Herman Ortmann

Note: The raider had sailed to the cruiser's starboard side when the *Sydney* had turned sharply to port

[See chapter on The Action]

Ortmann (by then a South Australian resident) explained on his own volition that both vessels were almost stationary when the action began, the underwater torpedo striking the cruiser after only two salvoes had been fired. Based on his stated rate of fire and that of Ernst, the result is that an underwater torpedo had struck the cruiser about 30 seconds after the de-camouflage order had been given, and as a consequence, Detmers had ordered the torpedo to be launched well before he had raised the battle ensign and had given the order to de-camouflage.

Understandably, the explicit details Ortmann gave, especially on the use of the raider's secret underwater weapon had not been expressed by other survivors during formal interrogations held nearly 80 years ago. But now there is no shortage of evidence to substantiate his story, particularly from those crewmen who had been interviewed by journalist David Kennedy on audio tape in the mid-1990s. **[CORR.003.0056, SUBM.006.0057 and SUBM.009.0053]**

It is clear from the action reports that only two torpedoes had been fired from the above-water tubes and these were estimated by the RAN to have taken some time to deploy after the order to de-camouflage – this, well after the *Kormoran*'s guns had opened fire and in full view from the *Sydney*. And considering that the torpedoes took 45 seconds (presumably a G7a torpedo) to run to the target 900 metres away, Detmers could not have relied on them because by then the cruiser's guns could have instantly obliterated the raider which had 300 mines on board. The only realistic solution to his predicament was to launch the covert underwater torpedo beforehand, as described below:

Given that the vessels had been almost opposite each other and parallel (course 250°) but with the *Kormoran* a 'bit ahead' of the *Sydney* (gunners Hildenbrand and Buttner), most certainly the cruiser could have been struck from the tube angled 35° abaft the beam with a straight-running torpedo. In the case that both vessels were stationary, the torpedo would have hit the cruiser at an inclination of approx. 80°, at the time the *Kormoran* had changed course from 250° to 260°, as described in the action reports. In the instance both vessels had been moving very slowly, say at one knot, the torpedo would deviate from the tube about 10 degrees away from the target and strike the cruiser at an inclination of 70°. That the torpedo had indeed struck the cruiser within the ambit of 70–80° is evidenced by DSTO (Defence Department) expert analysts in their report to the Commission of Inquiry.

The act of launching the underwater torpedo without being detected was not a problem due to the fact that the Germans used the piston method of ejection from the submerged tube, which prevented the tell-tale sign of compressed air escaping when launching the torpedo. However, apart from the fact that the wake of a G7a or its predecessor the G7v torpedo could be easily observed and could be detected on acoustics equipment on board the cruiser, the noise of its engine and propellers could also be clearly heard downwind by those on the bridge of the cruiser while it was in transit. Again, in order to lessen the prospect of the cruiser taking avoiding action, it was imperative for the underwater torpedo to be launched in advance and as deep as necessary before the German battle ensign had been raised.

Detmers had also assessed that both above-water torpedoes targeting the stem and stern **(COI.005.0012)** would have impacted, should the cruiser remained stationary; however, he could not risk deploying one aimed at the stern in case the cruiser had in the meantime accelerated away upon detecting the torpedoes. The only sensible tactic if the cruiser had moved forward was to target the stem (bow) of the cruiser with both torpedoes, these inclined at an angle in order to achieve the maximum explosive power and destruction at any point along the hull of the cruiser. But when these displaced torpedoes were eventually released, both passed in front of the bow due to the *Sydney* having remained almost stationary **(COI.005.0015)**. This intention is shown in the translated 1945 Action Report (in red).

While almost stopped, Detmers was required to swing his vessel to port at the required angle for the underwater torpedo to achieve maximum impact. This was the method used when *Kormoran* disposed of the stationary freighter *Craftsman* in April 1941 in the Atlantic Ocean. A survivor later told his captors at the POW camp that the raider had turned unobtrusively just before the action began and that very few of his fellow crewmen had noticed.

Precise timing of the underwater torpedo attack was crucial for Detmers. His tactic of launching it before he had declared his identity while being targeted by the *Sydney*'s main armament appears to have been the only way for *Kormoran* to have survived a battle with the much superior cruiser. That the raider carried hundreds of mines, de-camouflaging and then waiting for at least 30 seconds to train and fire the above-water torpedoes was a recipe for disaster. But although Detmers could not have placed total reliance on his torpedoes, his timing in launching the covert torpedo in advance of his declaration undoubtedly led to his survival and the ultimate fate of the *Sydney.*

During internment in the POW camps in Victoria, a number of *Kormoran* survivors compiled personal diaries (in German) of the action between the two vessels. These diary entries were of a similar format and generally accorded with the action reports produced earlier. However, in a departure from the two-torpedo scenario in these reports, a description of the action seized from Officer Herbert Bretschneider detailed a much different picture.

A military intelligence translation of his diary in 1945 revealed that during the first phase of the action the above-water tubes had been displaced (probably due to vibration from the incessant firing of the guns), and as a consequence **two dud torpedoes** had been discharged. These two torpedoes had missed their target, meaning that the resultant explosion on *Sydney*'s bow could only have been caused by the underwater torpedo. Another independent translation by journalist Alan Leslie clearly supported this scenario, both of which are shown below.

hopeless task from the beginning for our fire fighting equipment is destroyed and will not produce water.

Our torpedo tubes have been displaced, both starboard tubes have emitted two dud torpedoes.

On the Cruiser there is a tremendous explosion, she has completely disappeared in a black fog, and as the smoke clears we can observe that her bows are slowly sinking.

Over our decks the cry goes up "Hurray she sinks", but this joyous cry was premature. Though she is deeper in the water and seemed totally destroyed forward turret C continues to fire. Slowly she moves astern and her fire grows weaker. Suddenly a discernable shock is felt on the Kormoran, from all ventilators leading to the engine room pours black fumes, obviously one of our oil binkers has been hit.

PAGE 4

Original extract by Military Intelligence of Bretschneider's proposed book on the voyage of the Raider *Kormoran*

(Underlined by persons unknown)

We attempt to quell the rapidly spreading fire on our own ship but, from the beginning, it is a hopeless task as our firefighting equipment is destroyed, or at least so badly damaged that it will not deliver water.

Our torpedo tubes are also displaced, both tubes having failed to fire on the last two attempts.

Yonder, there is a tremendous explosion. The cruiser completely disappears in a black fog, and, as it slowly clears, we can see that she is down by the bows.

Over our decks, the cry goes up, "Hurrah, she sinks," but this jubilant outcry is premature for, although she is deeper in the water

News Article by Leslie, Oct 1945

The Army explained the circumstances of finding Bretschneider's diary:

'Our intelligence staff have for the past 3 years been trying to gain information as to what did happen to the cruiser *Sydney.* They [the Germans] have never at any time given us any information that was of any importance as to the silence of the cruiser. After 3 years of searching for this information, it was not until the 28th February 1945 that after searching Lieutenant Commander Bretschneider's room that we got this information from a book that he started to write on his life on the raider *Kormoran* that we now know what happened.'

Consequent upon receiving the Army and Leslie translations of the battle, the Navy proceeded to construct a complete picture of the voyage of the *Kormoran*, with particular reference to the action. They produced a composite rewrite of the battle from the translations provided by the Army and from Leslie. Except for some re-phrasing, the Navy did not depart from the thrust of both translations. It is structured below as a mirror copy of the original FRUMEL translations **(NAA File B6121,165K)**.

Now we sustain a hit, the poop deck with the officers' quarters is hit and burns. The engines have also sustained a hit. The cruiser is now also afire in several places. We now attempt to quell the quickly gaining fire, but it is a hopeless task from the beginning for our fire fighting equipment is destroyedand will not produce water. Also the torpedo tubes have been displaced and both starboard torpedo tubes have emitted dud torpedoes. On the cruiser there is a tremendous explosion. The cruiser has completely disappeared in black smoke. As the smoke clears we can observe that her bows are slowly sinking.

Over our decks the cry goes up, "Hurrah, she sinks", but this joyous outcry was premature. Though she is deeper in the water and seemed totally destroyed forward turret "C" continues to fire. Slowly she moves astern and her fire grows weaker. Suddenly a discernible

Composite narrative by the RAN

Although almost every other aspect of the battle accorded with the Army translations, but intriguingly the Navy later made one major change to the text in substituting **deadly** (todliche) **torpedoes** in lieu of **dud** (wertlose) **torpedoes** – this, clearly in order to convey that the two above-water torpedoes had been fired, one of which struck the *Sydney* in the explosion that followed. See below.

The cruiser was now afire in several places. We now attempt to quell the rapidly spreading fire, but it was a hopeless task fr the beginning as our fire-fighting apparatus is destroyed and woul not produce water. The torpedo tubes were also put into use by us, both starboard tubes fired two deadly torpedoes.

Over yonder there was a tremendous explosion. The cruiser co pletely disappeared in a black fog and, as it slowly cleared, we could see that she was settling slowly by the bows. Over our dec the cry went up, "Hurrah, she sinks," but this joyous outcry was premature, for although she is deeper in the water and seemed total destroyed forward, her "C" turret continued firing. Slowly she drifted astern and her firing became weaker.

NAA File B6121, 165K

Understandably, the action reports do not mention the launching of the underwater torpedo because to do so would of course convey the impression that Detmers may have acted illegally according to the rules of sea warfare. But that his 1945 report by FRUMEL indicating that one torpedo had hit and the other two had missed the cruiser, clearly establishes that three torpedoes had been fired at the outset. This is further confirmed in Bretschneider's diary wherein the two above-water torpedoes had been displaced (or were dud), and therefore the subsequent explosion had been caused by the underwater torpedo. There can be no other explanation.

What is most apparent is that the Navy did not produce a translation of their own. This is borne out by the fact that the translations of Bretschneider's German text have been repeated ad nauseam almost word-for-word by the Navy throughout the eight-page document that I possess. The translation to 'deadly torpedoes', was the only major change made and this could only have been approved by senior naval officers at the time.

All torpedoes have the potential to be deadly, but in practice they are described as such if they are seen to hit the assigned target and explode. In the terminology expressed, it does not follow that because two deadly torpedoes were fired, one or both hit the target. Rather, this is an assumption due to the explosion that followed. As a consequence, it therefore does not rule out that a third torpedo had caused the explosion.

Bretschneider produced another diary which formed the basis of many other accounts that were to follow. Those of officers Diebitsch, von Malapert and Bunjes, each re-established the two-torpedo scenario. These were seized in 1947 on arrival back in Germany. Translated by the Admiralty, they all contained a similar pattern of events regarding the action in describing that only two torpedoes had been fired.

After having the German accounts translated and assessed, Australian Naval Intelligence concluded that because no new information has resulted from translations carried out on the documents, they (the repatriated Germans) had confirmed the previous information held. Thus, the value of Bretschneider's diary account revealing that the raider had initially fired three torpedoes had been classified as seemingly of little importance to the Navy. But in reality, his diary account had been intentionally covered up.

In stark contrast to other diaries modelled on the 1942 and 1947 action reports, many of which were later confiscated in the POW camp, Bretschneider's account plainly meant that three torpedoes had been fired. And it tallied with the encoded diary found on Detmers in January 1945 after escaping from his POW camp. Translated by FRUMEL in 1945, it also revealed that three torpedoes had been fired – **a single** [underwater] **torpedo hit the bow of the cruiser and two** [above-water] **torpedoes passed short of the bow.**

This translation also verifies the order of firing. Firstly, the underwater torpedo (ostensibly before de-camouflaging), followed later by the displaced above-water torpedoes (which took much longer to deploy), both of which not surprisingly missed. The relevant extracts of all three loosely translated action reports are shown translated below.

B E I U N S E R E E About our Schuss. Bel unserer About our E T W A B E I At about	R H B I S A O S A L F E T O R P 8th to 10th salvo torpedo 8 bls 1o. Salve Torp. 8th to 10th salvo torpedo H B I S J S A L V E T O R P X 7th to 9th salvo torpedo fired
T R E F F E R F O R K A N T E hit at front of Treffer Vorkante hit at front of T R E F F E R V O R K A N T E Hits on bow	T U R M A B T O R P A turret 2nd torpedo Turm A. 2 Torp. A turret 2nd torpedo T U R M X B T O R P X turret Two torpedoes
G E H T E B E N just misses geht eben just misses K U R Z passed short	F O R M B U G F O R B E I the bow vorm Bug vorbel. the bow V O R M B U G V O R B E I of bow.

COI.005.0015

Detmers's 1945 translated diary account had revealed for the first time that the underwater torpedo had been launched and for this to have occurred the raider was required to have obeyed the stop order signal issued for boarding. This diary had seemingly confirmed Detmers's original statement on the stop order, but most certainly those made by, for example, Hermann Ortmann (in Carnarvon), Rudolf Lensch (on board *Trocas*) and by Emile

Dechaineux (in his report of 30 November). However, the Navy took no subsequent action on these disclosures, which all suggest that Burnett had conformed to Admiralty measures in *stopping prior to boarding the raider. This further conjures a desire by the Naval Board to have already decided on Burnett's guilt.

*In those days, launches, cutters and whalers were not sturdy, being fabricated in timber or marine plywood, i.e., the ship would always stop to lower these boats to prevent damage to them.

Nowadays those hulls are made of steel, which doesn't involve stopping to lower the boats.

The recapture of Detmers and his encoded diary revealing the firing of three torpedoes must have been of grave concern for him should it have been translated. But amazingly he was not required to explain why he had now changed his story. He was never to be held to account for this glaring contradiction that a single (underwater) torpedo hit on the bow and two torpedoes passed short of the bow. So, in order to avoid possible repercussions should an inquiry be instituted, a third action report was produced in 1947 – this, consistent with the 1942 version in describing the two-torpedo scenario. These two reports were to serve Detmers favourably. They now form the basis of the Navy's history of the action.

The Navy's perception that only two torpedoes had been fired in the opening phase of the battle continues until this day, despite contrary evidence from Bretschneider. Detmers's translated diary and the more recent audio-taped admissions from ex-*Kormoran* survivors revealed that the underwater torpedo had been fired from the raider's starboard side.

As a result of this disclosure, the 1997 Parliamentary Inquiry into the loss of HMAS *Sydney* found that the *Kormoran*'s underwater torpedo played a major role in the defeat of the *Sydney*. And in order to reach this finding, this inquiry not only took into account the weight of evidence that three torpedoes had been fired, it also had good reason to believe (from the recent taped recordings) that the underwater torpedo per se was responsible for the ultimate fate of the cruiser. However, although this Senate Inquiry could not explain Burnett's approach on the raider, it stopped short of holding him responsible for the loss of the cruiser. On the other hand, the 2009 Commission of Inquiry held him completely accountable.

The Commission of Inquiry also found that the observable damage to *Sydney* (from the wreck site images) was consistent with the German assertion that *Kormoran* fired two torpedoes from her above-water starboard mounts, one of the torpedoes striking *Sydney* about 20 metres from the bow near A turret causing the ship to rise then fall, when in fact, the observable damage confirms only that one torpedo had hit **(COI Report Vol 2 p370)**.

This finding is questionable in two respects. Firstly, it disregards entirely the fact that soon after the action, most survivors had agreed that three torpedoes had been fired. After all, the Eldridge Report had been based on the evidence of only a few (Detmers, Bunjes and Ahlbach) and/or from diaries and reports on the action written by officers years after the battle and whose writings had been expected to be seized when searched (as was the case). Secondly, it is impossible to assert that the 'observable damage' had been due to one of two torpedoes striking the *Sydney*. Plainly, that one torpedo had struck the cruiser does not signify how many torpedoes had been fired off, or from whence they came.

Detmers was confident of not being captured after his meticulously planned escape (but if so, his diary would prove too difficult to translate), and that he was not asked to explain why he had suddenly changed his story on the action, is a measure of the RAN's then commitment to the Eldridge Report that was sent to the Admiralty four years earlier. It was therefore remiss of the Commission of Inquiry not to have seriously considered whether the FRUMEL translation had been the more genuine account of the opening phase of the action.

According to many of the German survivors and the action reports, soon after being struck by a torpedo, the *Sydney* turned to port in order to target the *Kormoran* with her starboard battery of four torpedoes, which had survived the initial onslaught from the raider. During this manoeuvre, she had crossed the path of the raider, which had shortly afterwards changed course to 240° in order to maximise targeting the cruiser. The *Sydney* had already unleashed her torpedoes at the *Kormoran* (without striking) during the initial phase of the action and continued at slow speed in a southerly direction. But she was then exposed to the raider's port-side guns and three torpedo tubes (two above-water tubes and one submerged). From German summaries on this phase of the action, the raider is said to have slowed to a stop due to a raging fire in the engine room as a result of gunfire from the cruiser earlier in the action. At this stage, the reports convey that only one torpedo had been fired at the cruiser at the extreme range of 7,000 metres.

Although the action reports do not specify from which tubes this torpedo had been launched, it is recorded as having been fired at the *Sydney* to hit at an inclination (angle) of from 80 to 110°. If so, given that the cruiser was at such an extreme distance on a southerly course at slow speed, and regardless of whether the raider had fired the torpedo directly in line with the target (or with a guidance angle setting), the torpedo could not have struck the cruiser at such an angle because the angle of inclination in both cases is demonstrably acute. These inclinations could only have been achieved in the case that the cruiser, for example, had been zigzagging to avoid torpedoes, or by having temporarily broadened her silhouette by adopting are more westerly course during her slow progress southwards. But regardless of the circumstances and due to the loss of his engines, Detmers was unable to manoeuvre the raider to accurately target the cruiser with the port underwater torpedo tube. 'Hope' had been forsaken for accuracy.

Again, the common theme throughout is that the German survivors carefully avoided mentioning the underwater tubes. In fact, when they were interrogated most do not account for their very existence. But in describing the second phase of the action, the action reports referring to a port-side torpedo being fired at the cruiser at 1800G hours (7,000 metres away), has been translated variously as 'single' and 'own' torpedo, without nominating the tube from whence it was launched, only that it was said by Wilhelm Bunjes to have been shot from the port-side tube.

In stating that a total of four torpedoes had been fired at the cruiser, and considering that his fellow crewmen had told of three torpedoes fired during the first phase of the action, Rudolf Lensch had heard that the port (underwater) torpedo had indeed been fired off at approximately 1800G (7pm WST) in the direction of the *Sydney*. Less persuasive is that only one of the two above-water torpedoes from the twin tube was most unlikely to be fired off due to the onboard threat of fires in the torpedo room.

Although the twin port-side above-water torpedoes are not mentioned in the reports, they were probably fired off as evidenced in a report by *Kormoran* aviation officer Heinfied Ahl. He stated that 'due to the possibility of the fire spreading to the [stowed] mines and torpedoes, the port torpedoes were launched at the *Sydney*, though meanwhile she was out of range'. He also infers that the starboard underwater torpedo was not in danger in its tube due to it earlier being fired off.

In his interview in 2008, Ludwig Ernst stated that the underwater torpedoes were not used in the battle with the *Sydney*. But he further confused the issue by saying that 'LEUT Greter [Torpedo Officer] fired the underwater torpedoes when laying the scuttling charges' – a statement referring to the firing of both underwater tubes. If so, Greter's action adds to Ernst's muddled version of events because in 1999 he claimed Detmers had sent him to fire off the starboard underwater torpedo, not the port torpedo as well. This assertion had been in response to the Parliamentary Inquiry finding that the underwater torpedo played a major role in the defeat of the *Sydney*. Both claims appear to have been motivated in denial of the underwater torpedoes being used at all against the cruiser.

The proposition that all three starboard-side torpedoes had been fired in the general direction of the *Sydney* during the initial phase of the action is clearly established. Evidence from engineer Lensch that a total of four torpedoes had been fired, means that three torpedoes had been fired initially and the port underwater torpedo had been fired off at the distant cruiser later in the action (as stated by Bunjes). In any case, if Detmers had genuine concern that the fire on board his ship could have reached the port above-water tubes, it is conceivable that all three had been launched in the general direction of the cruiser with little prospect of them striking their target, which by then was more than 7,000 metres distant.

A background summary, including the censure of Captain Burnett, is briefly summarised chronologically below:

- 24–28 November 1941: From casual conversations held with *Kormoran* survivors, the earliest reports from senior naval officers had established that three torpedoes had been fired at the cruiser in the first phase of action (LEUTs Taplin, Baume and CAPT Farncomb). This included the underwater torpedo. Only Detmers had stated that two torpedoes had been launched, but he said (on 1 December) the raider had been ordered to stop at a distance.

- 29 November: CMDR Dechaineux concluded (from an unknown source) that two torpedoes had been launched, though he had conceded that the *Kormoran* had been ordered to stop. During interrogations, Ahlbach testified that the raider had not stopped. Detmers (he did not elaborate on the stop order) again raised the two-torpedo scenario which had the support of Bunjes.

- 15 December: Dechaineux's interim report on the action was sent to the DNI for approval. He made the point that the story of the action was 'frankly' told by Detmers, concluding that two torpedoes, one from above-water and one from the submerged tube had been fired while moving at 15 knots, and that no stop order had been given. His report attempted to encompass the diverse opinions held by the Navy, but it was not considered plausible because the underwater torpedo could not be launched if the raider had been moving so fast.

- 23 December: In messages from the Naval Board to the Admiralty, CAPT Burnett is understood to have been deceived by placing the cruiser in a vulnerable position while both vessels were travelling at 15 knots (according to the Dechaineux report). The Naval Board had assessed (from Detmers, Ahlbach and Bunjes) that Burnett had not followed his orders by not signalling the demand for the secret letters from a distance, but did so at the last moment. The Naval Board had thus laid the foundation for Burnett's guilt in claiming that he had not adhered to the correct identification and challenge procedures.

- 12 February 1942: Eldridge was given the job of assessing the material and his conclusions were sent to the Admiralty as promised. But CMDR Long restricted him to evidence from a small number of survivors. In his report he again quoted the words of Dechaineux that Detmers had frankly told the story of the action. However, in assessing (from Detmers) that both vessels had been moving at 15 knots and that two torpedoes had been fired, he deleted all reference to using the submerged torpedo. He had assessed the story of the action largely from the evidence of Detmers, Ahlbach and Bunjes, and ruled out earlier reports submitted by senior naval officers.

- 1942: The first action report generally reflects the Eldridge Report on the action, except that the speed of the vessels is nominated as 14 knots in lieu of 15 knots. Point of aim: bow and stern. Two torpedoes had been fired from the twin battery and one hit at the front of A turret, the other just missed the bow – both torpedoes presumed to have been fired from the above-water tubes, which had operated normally. The assumption here is that *Kormoran* had been moving too fast to launch underwater torpedo.

- January 1945: The action report found on Detmers after his failed escape attempt placed a completely different complexion on the action. Translated by FRUMEL later that year, Detmers revealed the first torpedo had struck the bow of the cruiser and the other two passed short of the bow – original point of aim for each torpedo – stem and stern. This disclosure meant that in order to fire off all three starboard torpedoes, the *Kormoran* had to be almost stationary to launch the underwater torpedo, but the content of his diary account was not questioned by his captors.

- 28 February 1945: Bretschneider's diary likewise revealed the story of the action for he had been given the task of recording the entire voyage of the *Kormoran*. Translated by Army Intelligence, it showed that three torpedoes had been launched. It was obvious that the underwater torpedo had struck the stationary *Sydney* and those from above-water had been displaced and were described as 'dud'. Both had missed their target. And later in re-typing the Army translation, the Navy substituted in lieu the word 'deadly' in order to account for one of the above-water torpedoes exploding on the bow of the *Sydney*.

- 12 October 1945: Intelligence Officer Rycroft forwarded the Westhoven report to the DNI. From her report it had been established that three torpedoes had been fired, one of these striking the cruiser. The *Kormoran* had thus been assessed as stationary in order to launch the underwater torpedo. Within a week or so the report had been rejected by the DNI in preference to the scenario put forward by Eldridge in 1942.

- 28 February 1947: On arrival back in Germany, British naval personnel confiscated the action reports written by *Kormoran* officers on their return to Germany, as well as individual diaries that had been prepared by various crewmen. All of these contained descriptions of the action modelled on the 1942 Action Report, which had seemingly satisfied international law.

Note: During his time as a POW, Detmers had been concerned about possible court proceedings against him over his role in the battle **(*The Raider Kormoran*, p202)**. Interestingly, by the time he returned home to Germany, one of his raider commander counterparts, Hellmut von Ruckteschell, commander of the commerce raiders *Widder* and *Michel*, had been convicted by a British military court of naval-related war crimes.

- In 1957, naval officer George Hermon Gill completed writing the volumes of the history of the RAN in WW2. He had started this project in 1944 with access to all the records held by Naval Intelligence. His take on the action was not unlike those of Eldridge and DNI Rupert Long in countenancing that the *Kormoran* had fired two torpedoes while the ships were steaming parallel at 14 knots. One of the above-water torpedoes hit the *Sydney* abreast of her forward turrets.

- Mid-1990s: Interviews recorded with several ex-*Kormoran* crewmen revealed that three torpedoes had been launched from the stationary raider and that only the underwater torpedo had struck the cruiser.
- March 1999: A Parliamentary Inquiry concluded that a strong case can be made that the *Kormoran*'s underwater torpedo played a major role in the defeat of the *Sydney*.
- 12 August 2009: The Commission of Inquiry into the loss of HMAS *Sydney* broadly found in favour of the Eldridge/Gill scenario in asserting both vessels had been sailing at 14–15 knots when two above-water torpedoes had been launched at the cruiser, one of which hit the cruiser forward. The inquiry also held Captain Burnett responsible for the loss of the cruiser, alleging he had not followed his orders.
- March 2016: The cryptogram showing the coordinates associated with the planned and final bearing of the raider's course to Shark Bay had been solved mathematically.

The above chronology demonstrates the Navy's intransigence at every turn of events over a period of almost 80 years. In a haste to provide details for the Admiralty, the Navy's stance on the action has not changed one iota and now that the wreck site images are available, the claim by the Commission of Inquiry that the observable damage confirms the German account is plainly misleading. Rather, it shows a concerted desire to maintain support for the Navy's original conclusions reached by Eldridge shortly after the action – this, based on the evidence of a few and with the full support of the director of Naval Intelligence at the time.

As a consequence of the resolve by the Navy to countenance select anecdotal narratives on the action and despite overwhelming evidence to the contrary, the proposition that the cruiser had been struck by one of two torpedoes has been firmly entrenched in the minds of the public. This has misled the public into believing that both vessels had been sailing at 14–15 knots when the action began, meaning Burnett had been taken by surprise.

Now that ex-*Kormoran* crewmen have come forward to participate in taped interviews, Detmers's account is found to be blatantly misleading. Comments such as: '... the starboard underwater torpedo was fired first while at slow speed... the guns opened fire when the torpedo hit and... the torpedo was already zipping through the water as the flaps opened', has forever dispelled the myth that the underwater torpedo had not played a major role in the action.

The genesis for the Navy's story on the action relied on anecdotal evidence from a few select witnesses. But on testing the veracity of their story, the naval assessment based on complete trust in Detmers's story is found to have prevailed over contrary evidence by ordinary crewmen. The Navy has therefore failed to substantiate their case, as described below:

Amid pressure from the Admiralty to provide details on the battle, Eldridge, under the influence of the director of Naval Intelligence, based his report on statements from a few prisoners that were said to be 'most useful'. His skewed portrayal of the battle, in particular, that the story of the battle had been frankly told by Detmers and that both vessels had been proceeding at 14–15 knots before the action began, conveyed the false impression that Burnett had acted irresponsibly.

As with G Hermon Gill, the Commission of Inquiry relied too much on the evidence given by those who supported Detmers's story, for example, that officers such as Greter, Messerschmidt and Diebitsch agreed with the action report scenario indicated that Detmers had probably told the truth, thus dismissing contrary evidence from ordinary crewmen who said that the raider and the cruiser were stopped at the moment the battle began and that three torpedoes had been launched.

The Cole Inquiry is also at odds with the Admiralty's message received by the Naval Board on 28 November. In its assessment, the survivors rescued by the British tanker *Trocas* had revealed that three torpedoes were fired by the raider, one of which was thought to have hit. The message also advised that *Kormoran*'s armament consisted of two above-water and one submerged torpedo tube on each side, and it was generally considered that with few exceptions, survivors spoke the truth.

In an unmotivated quest to tell the truth by revealing the first shot in the action came from underwater, rank and file crewmen have clearly refuted Detmers's story on the opening phase of the battle. However, there was little argument by survivors who witnessed the ensuing gun battle, which is seemingly corroborated by the seabed images of the *Sydney*'s wreck site and which led the Commission of Inquiry to claim that the Germans had told the truth. But these images only show the accumulated damage to the Sydney – they do not identify the origin of the torpedo that struck her, or of the timing and sequence of events during the battle.

A submission to the inquiry showing photographic evidence of the angled starboard underwater tube of the type and configuration used on *Kormoran* had been concealed from viewing in the Commission of Inquiry report. Whether by design or not, the detail is indistinct and as a result, not shown in proper perspective. The dark image merely represents a torpedo tube per se, not the angled tube from which the raider's first shot from underwater determined the outcome of the battle. [Original photo supplied to journalist David Kennedy by ex-German intelligence officer Charles Noack of the angled torpedo tube on the raider *Komet*] See below.

SUBM.009.0055
Photo (left) has been reproduced from the original (right)

Blind acceptance of the Eldridge Report, Gill's history of the RAN and the German action reports of 1942 and 1947 and total disregard of reports by senior naval officers, the Bretschneider translation, the 1945 encoded diary and the Westhoven Report, has resulted in a humiliating failure on the part of the Navy to portray a plausible account of the action.

And in failing to heed the more recent taped evidence from those witnesses who had kept secret the systematic firing of the torpedoes, the Commission of Inquiry findings have compounded the mistakes of the past. This is clearly evident in the statements quoted. These quotes also confirm earlier suspicion by the Admiralty that the *Kormoran* had opened fire with an underwater torpedo before declaring herself **(PRO File 199/736)**.

But the greatest failure of all is that the Navy and the Commission of Inquiry have never thoroughly examined the accuracy of the story told by Detmers. On this issue alone, researchers have been consistently derided in favour of a status quo position, first put forward by Eldridge and then by Gill and with the full cooperation of the director of Naval Intelligence.

The role played by the DNI in this affair is obviously highly questionable, and in a quest to establish the facts, he sought the opinion of a so-called 'independent' analyst in preference to a serving naval officer. That he had effectively placed restrictions on Eldridge's analysis in order to arrive at the desired result, led to the false assessment of the action. It is therefore a sad indictment that the general thrust of the Eldridge Report has been upheld by the Navy for about 80 years, and now by the Commission of Inquiry.

Kormoran survivors have recently set the record straight, yet the Commission of Inquiry continued to maintain that only two torpedoes had been launched during the initial action, and as a consequence, both vessels had been moving at a rate in excess of that required to launch the underwater torpedo. Both assertions are demonstrably astray and have no absolute validity. Again, overwhelming is the evidence that three torpedoes had been fired from the stationary *Kormoran* and that the underwater torpedo had struck the *Sydney* is now beyond doubt. And launching this torpedo before the *Kormoran*'s battle ensign had been raised proved to be the decisive factor in the final outcome.

It is not uncommon for civil and military proceedings to deliver wrongful findings such as in this case where immediate answers to a crime or a disaster are sought, but as new evidence emerges, initial findings are sometimes appealed and overturned. In the HMAS *Sydney* affair, however, the Navy have remained steadfast and have been relentless in promoting the false assessment of the action. The public have simply been misled.

Addenda

Eldridge Report (1942)

This story of the action has been largely assessed from comments by Commander Detmers, Chief Signaller Ahlbach, and Sub-Lieutenant Bunjes (shown highlighted).

The action between the *Sydney* and the raider was frankly told by the captain, Fregatten Kapitan **Detmers** and other prisoners, and the story as told seems to ring true, though there is no explanation on the surface as to why the *Sydney* came so close, or why she came so close before attempting to launch her aircraft.

At about 1600G/19 the raider in position approximately 26°S 111°E was proceeding northward at a speed of about 10 knots (14 knots according to Sub-Lieutenant **Bunjes**), when what at first appeared to be a sail was sighted by the lookout to the north on the starboard bow. [About N.N.E., according to Sub-Lieutenant **Bunjes.]** The stranger was soon identified as a cruiser and Commander **Detmers** immediately turned away into the sun (250°) and increased to full speed which he estimated at 15 knots. The cruiser had obviously sighted them for she, too, turned and came up on the starboard quarter at high speed, repeatedly making the signal by daylight lamp NNJ, for about half an hour, no reply being made by the *Kormoran* as the Commander was of the opinion that the use of a powerful signalling lamp would have betrayed his identity as he was at the time posing as the Dutch ship *Straat Malakka*, and merchant ships did not carry such lamps. In addition, he said, he did not understand what the signal NNJ meant.

Some time before the action was joined, *Kormoran* broadcast QQQQ 26 S, 111 E, *Straat Malakka*, and repeated it once. Pachmann, an operator, stated that this message was given twice, about 10 minutes before the action began. It is worthy of note that a QQ message was picked up by tug *Uco*, at about 1000 G.M.T. on 19 November, but the position and ship's name could not be read by the P.O. telegraphist in *Uco*. Geraldton also read a mutilated time and position message at 1005Z/19. No Q's were distinguished and when after 10 minutes there was no repetition, a message was sent out to ships asking if there was anything to report, but no reply was received.

At a distance of about 7 miles, *Sydney* made the signal by flashing 'Hoist your signal letters'. In reply, *Kormoran* hoisted PKQI (*Straat Malakka*) on the triatic stay between the foremast and the funnel, but the funnel prevented the message being clearly seen aboard the *Sydney*. When *Sydney* made the signal 'Hoist your signal letters clear', **Ahlbach**, the Yeoman of Signals, stated that he lengthened the halyard and drew it towards the starboard side. It is reasonable to suppose that this apparent inefficiency in signalling by the *Kormoran* was a 'ruse de guerre' in the hope that *Sydney* would close to investigate, for *Sydney*'s signal had to be repeated continuously before it was complied with.

Sydney came up with the *Kormoran* with all guns and torpedo tubes bearing, and when she was approximately abeam of the raider she asked by flags and flashing 'Where bound?' According to **Ahlbach**, this was spelt in English by flashing. *Kormoran* answered 'Batavia', and *Sydney* apparently made 'IK' which *Kormoran* could not understand as in the International Code this means, 'You should prepare for a cyclone, hurricane or typhoon', but which was in fact the two interior letters of the secret call sign 'Straat Malakka' (IIKP). To this, *Kormoran* made no reply. *Sydney* then made by flashing 'Show your secret sign'. Having no reply to this, the raider captain (**Detmers**) decided to fight, which up to this time he had tried to avoid doing. According to **Ahlbach**, *Sydney* did not order the raider to stop, and this statement is made by other prisoners, but Captain **Detmers** mentions an order to stop immediately before the signal by searchlight in plain language to give the secret call.

At about 1700G/19 when the two ships were proceeding on parallel courses in a westerly direction at approximately 15 knots, the *Sydney* being on the *Kormoran*'s starboard beam at a distance of 'somewhat more than a mile (Commander **Detmers**) (or at a distance of 1,200 or 1,500 metres according to other prisoners of war), *Kormoran* dropping her gun-concealing plates and hoisting the German flag, opened fire with four of her six 15-centimetre guns. [The particulars obtained by the military authorities upon further enquiry would reduce the range still further to about 1,100 metres.] The first salvo hit the *Sydney*'s bridge. Almost simultaneously, but probably just afterwards, *Sydney*'s first salvo went over, though Sub-Lieutenant **Bunjes** states that *Sydney*'s first salvo hit the raider amidships. Her second salvo found the raider's engine-room and fuel tanks and caused a fire. In the meantime, **the raider had fired two torpedoes, one of which struck the *Sydney* forward** (about 20 metres from the bow according to Commander **Detmers**, at the same time that a salvo struck her amidships. The *Sydney*'s forward turrets were apparently put out of action by the explosion caused by the torpedo, and the *Sydney*'s aircraft, which is reported to have been warming up at the time that the engagement began, was shot to pieces. The range was so close that prisoners stated that they could see men about the plane and an antiaircraft gunner stated that the A.A. guns were used against the cruiser so that her A.A. guns and torpedoes might not be used.

Sydney now altered course to port across stern of the raider and continued on a slightly diverging course from the raider. She must have been very close as some of the raider's crew thought that she was going to ram. According to **Ahlbach** (yeoman of signals) who was on the bridge of the *Kormoran*, *Sydney* turned about 90° to port, passed close under the stern of the *Kormoran* and maintained her course in a southerly direction. At this stage apparently, though a fire was raging and could not be put out because all fire-fighting appliances had been destroyed, *Kormoran*'s guns were all in action and one of her guns is stated to have fired 50 rounds while all guns fired a total of about 450 rounds. *Sydney*'s X and Y turrets were still in action. *Sydney* now fired four torpedoes which *Kormoran* turned to meet, and three passed ahead and one astern. A torpedo fired by the raider about the same time also missed its mark. Both ships were now on fire, *Sydney* being heavily afire amidships and on the bridge, and down by the bows about 6 feet. The raider's bridge had been hit but not put out of action, *Sydney*'s first hit had destroyed the radio and a large fire was burning in the engine room. Approximately half an hour after fire opened the action was over, *Kormoran* was stopped, *Sydney* proceeding in a south-easterly direction at a speed of about 5 knots...

Apart from Detmers, Alhach and Bunjes, other crewmen whose comments were considered 'most useful' in completing the 10-page report on aspects of the voyage of the *Kormoran*, included:

Otto Jurgensen (Petty Officer)
Paul Kobelt (Petty Officer)
Hans Koblitz (AA Gunner)
Adolph Kohls (Engineer)
Edmund Lipinski (Tailor)
Rudolf Lensch ((Engineer)
Hans Linke (Wireless Operator)
Albert Ruf (Aircraftsman)
Otto Wiseman (Seaman)

From ***History of the Royal Australian Navy*** **(1957)**

George Hermon Gill

On the afternoon of 19 November 1941, the German auxiliary cruiser *Kormoran* (Commander Theodor Detmers) was steaming on a north-easterly course off the coast of Western Australia, approximately 150 miles south-west of Carnarvon. Just before 4:00 pm, a warship was sighted and Commander Detmers turned the *Kormoran* west into the sun, increasing speed to 16.5 knots, the maximum available. A broken piston rod was soon to reduce this to 14 knots.

The approaching warship, the light cruiser HMAS *Sydney,* had sighted the *Kormoran* and increased speed to intercept her. She quickly began to overhaul the raider, approaching on a slightly converging course off the German's starboard quarter and flashing the signal NNJ ('You should make your signal letters') on her searchlight. It was not *Kormoran*'s business to fight warships except as a last resort, as her best hope for survival was to convince the *Sydney* that she was an innocent merchantman. If fighting became unavoidable, however, the raider was best served by luring her opponent as close as possible before revealing her concealed armament. To this end, when replying to *Sydney*'s signal, the raider's flag hoist was deliberately fumbled and then hoisted in a position where the flags would be obscured by the funnel and difficult to read. The *Sydney* repeatedly demanded that the signal be hoisted clear, and, when the *Kormoran* eventually complied, the letters PKQI could be discerned. This was the call-sign of the Dutch freighter *Straat Malakka*.

While this was taking place, the range was steadily closing. By 5:00 pm, the *Sydney* was off the *Kormoran*'s port quarter and drawing abeam to a position where the raider's armament could be used to maximum effect. Still hoping to pass as a Dutch ship *Straat Malakka*, the raider began to broadcast QQQQ ('suspicious ship sighted'). This message was received faintly, in garbled form, by the tug *Uco* and the wireless station at Geraldton, and, presumably, by the *Sydney*.

Sydney next signalled: 'Where bound?', to which the *Kormoran* replied: 'Batavia'. Captain Burnett must have been still suspicious as the Australian cruiser's next signal was 'IK'. To the Germans, this signal made no sense as, according to the code book, it meant 'You should prepare for a cyclone, hurricane or typhoon'. The letters were in fact the middle letters of the secret call sign of the real *Straat Malakka* (IIKP) and the correct response was to send the outer letters. This, of course, the *Kormoran* could not do.

It was 5:30 and the ships were steaming parallel on south-easterly courses at 14 knots, the Australian cruiser abeam of the raider at a range of 1,500 metres, a perfect target. The *Sydney*'s fate was sealed when she flashed to the *Kormoran*: 'Show your secret sign.' Detmers now had no choice but to fight. The *Kormoran* hoisted the German ensign, uncovered her armament and opened fire. Two ranging shots pitched short and over respectively then a full salvo hit, smashing into the *Sydney*'s bridge structure and director tower. Simultaneously, **the *Kormoran* fired two torpedoes.** Her automatic 2-centimetre anti-aircraft guns and rapid firing 3.7-centimetre anti-tank guns played onto the cruiser's bridge and also amidships, where the two port 4-inch guns of the secondary armament and the torpedo tubes were mounted.

The *Sydney* replied with a salvo from her 6-inch guns that tore over the *Kormoran*. However, the cruiser's forward turrets were knocked out by the raider's third and fourth salvoes; then the fifth caught the *Sydney*'s aircraft on the catapult, wrecking it and spreading burning fuel over the ship amidships. About this time the *Sydney*'s after-turrets came into action, firing in local control. Y turret fired two or three unsuccessful salvoes before falling silent but X turret opened a rapid and accurate fire which hit the *Kormoran* in the funnel, engine room and electrical installations, starting uncontrollable fires. Shortly after this, one of the raider's torpedoes hit the *Sydney* abreast her forward turrets. Within 5 minutes of the commencement of the action, both ships were mortally wounded.

The *Sydney*, down by the bow, turned sharply to port onto a southerly course as if to ram the *Kormoran* or to bring her starboard torpedo tubes to bear. She passed close astern, under fire from the raider's after-guns. At 5:45 pm, as the range opened, the cruiser fired her four starboard torpedoes at the raider, all of which narrowly missed astern. About the same time the *Kormoran*'s engines broke down.

As the *Sydney* struggled off to the south, she was hit repeatedly by the *Kormoran*'s port side guns and at 6:00 the raider fired a torpedo from her port underwater tube which missed. The *Kormoran* continued to fire at the *Sydney* until 6:25, by which time her own engine room was wrecked and uncontrollably ablaze...

Westhoven Report (1945)

HMAS *Sydney* departed Fremantle on the 11th of November 1941, escorting HT *Zealandia*. And that was the last voyage of this famous cruiser, because while on this job she was sunk by the German raider *Kormoran*. There were no survivors from this ill-fated engagement, and no trace of any wreckage was ever found despite an exhaustive search. Exact details of the fate of HMAS *Sydney* will probably never be known.

A complete story of the action has been built up from interrogation of survivors of the *Kormoran*. But despite a thorough examination of these men, they could not, or would not, throw any light on the actual sinking of HMAS *Sydney*. According to them, the last that was seen of *Sydney* was when she disappeared over the horizon at dusk, 19th November, burning fiercely. A chronological account of events of the days from 21 November to 29 November, gives an idea of how gradually the fate of HMAS *Sydney* was pieced together:

When HMAS *Sydney* left Fremantle, she was to escort HT *Zealandia* to rendezvous in the vicinity of Sunda Straits at 8 o'clock on the morning of 17 November. She was then to return to Fremantle. When she had not arrived on 21 November, a signal was sent to Navy Board, and on 23 November [in fact, 24 November] an air search was carried out from Rottnest. And from then on until 29 November, when the search was abandoned, ships of the Royal Australian Navy, Royal Netherlands Navy, the Merchant Navy, and allied aircraft scoured a wide area of the Indian Ocean.

On 23 November, HT *Aquitania* picked up 26 Germans on a raft. However, word was not received of this until PM on the 27. On the same day that *Aquitania* picked up these men, HMAS *Sydney* was urgently instructed to report her estimated time of arrival at Fremantle. The first definite news came on 24 November, when the British Tanker MV *Trocas* picked up 25 Germans from a floating raft in position 24 degrees 06 minutes south, 111 degrees 40 minutes east, which is approximately 150 miles north west of Carnarvon. They requested an armed guard. On the same day, six Hudsons carried out an air search to a depth of 300 miles, with negative result, however. On the same day, too, Group 53, composed of HMAS *Wyrallah*, HMAS *Yandra* and HMAS *Olive Cam* sailed from Fremantle. *Wyrallah* and *Yandra* with orders to intercept *Trocas* and search for any survivors, *Olive Cam* was instructed to search for survivors only. *Hermion*, *Pan Europe*, *Saidja*, *Herstein*, *Sunetta* and *Centaur*, all ships of the merchant navy, were instructed to pass through positions between 24 degrees south and 111 degrees east to search for survivors.

The next day brought more information of survivors from the *Kormoran*. An aircraft, in position 24 degrees 52 minutes south, 111 degrees 09 minutes east, reported a lifeboat, and *Herstein* was ordered to the position to locate it. Another aircraft reported two life boats a-shore about 45 miles north of Carnarvon and a RAAF land party left to contact the boat's crew. At the same time, the air search was continuing over an area 180 miles by 400 miles from Geraldton, north-west to a point beyond where the raft had been sighted. Seven Hudsons combed this area, while Wirraways searched the coast-line from Shark Bay to North West Cape. One Hudson searched a 60-mile square south-west of Dirk Hartog Island. MV *Trocas* reported her noon position and *Heros* received orders to intercept her and search for survivors. On the same day, RNNS *Tromp* left Tandjong Priok [Batavia], and joined in the search.

On 26 November came the first definite news of what had happened. That was when a naval guard with Paymaster Lieutenant A C Baume, RANR in charge boarded MV *Trocas*. From interrogation of the prisoners, it was discovered that on the 19th of November, *Kormoran* had engaged a cruiser of the Perth class with a name which they thought began with 'ST'. **The prisoners agreed that their ship had fired three torpedoes,** one of which hit the cruiser about amidships and put her controls out of action. They said that the cruiser had fired one salvo which set fire to the German ship, which was diesel driven. It was impossible to put the fire out, they said, and there was a terrific explosion after they had abandoned ship, and they estimated that about 100 men, including the majority of the officers, were still on board. The last they had seen of the *Sydney* was at dusk, when she was burning just for'rard of amidships.

From these men it was learnt that the *Kormoran*, commanded by Kapt Detmers, was an auxiliary cruiser of 9,000 tons with a complement of 400 men. She had been at sea since December 1940, and from Hamburg had gone to the Indian Ocean, where she had sunk 10 ships. The exact position of the action was also established on 26th November when Staff Officer Intelligence, Fremantle, interviewed the raider survivors at Carnarvon. These survivors gave the position of action as 26 degrees 30' south, 111 degrees east, and the time of engagement as 1700. Captain Detmers stated that the raider attack was a surprise. Another survivor said that the boats were rowing towards what they imagined was HMAS *Perth* in the hope of being picked up when the cruiser vanished over the horizon so rapidly that they believed it sunk.

On the same day that these statements were made, *Koolinda* picked up a lifeboat with 31 Germans in it, and *Centaur* took two lifeboats in tow, and proceeded to Carnarvon. The air and sea search continued. On 27th November, MV *Trocas* arrived in Fremantle with prisoners, and the real work of interrogation was begun by Naval Intelligence. From this interrogation, an almost complete picture of the action was obtained.

According to the German story, *Kormoran* was steering north when the lookout sighted a ship on the starboard bow steering south. This was about 1600 on the 19th. The raider altered her course to westward, thus bringing the cruiser onto the starboard quarter. The cruiser altered course westward and closed rapidly, challenging with her daylight lamp. The raider made no reply but opened fire when the cruiser was in comparatively short range of about 2,000 yards. The first shots from the raider hit the cruiser's bridge and started a fire. At that, the cruiser altered course to port, and the survivors stated that it appeared she intended to ram. She passed close under the stern of the raider and gradually drew astern, on the port side of the raider. By this time, the cruiser was heavily on fire, burning on the bridge and mid-ship section. The raider was also badly damaged and on fire in the engine room area. The action lasted about an hour and the raider abandoned ship about 1900 because they could not put the fire out. At this time the cruiser was seen to be still heavily on fire and shortly afterwards disappeared. No violent explosions on the cruiser were seen or heard by the raider. **They believed that three torpedoes were fired by the raider**, one of which is thought to have hit. The raider blew up at midnight.

It was also ascertained that the raider carried six 15-centimetre guns, 2-centimetre AA guns, un-mounted machine guns, two above-water and one submerged torpedo tube on each side. Additionally, it carried one seaplane of the Arado type, but this was stated to have been damaged and not flown for three months. About 150 to 200 mines were also carried, but none of these had been laid.

While this interrogation was being carried out, the search still continued. The air search went on, and one aircraft sighted a boat containing Germans. HMAS *Yandra* was directed to the position of this boat, and picked up 70 Germans and 2 Chinese. Interrogation of these survivors was carried out by the commanding officer, HMAS *Yandra*, and Surgeon Lieutenant Robertson, and information was gained about an interchange of signals between the two ships. According to one man, the cruiser was abaft the starboard beam of the raider at a distance of 1,300 yards. HMAS *Sydney* challenged the raider, who gave the false name of *Straat Malacca*, Dutch nationality. After an interchange and fumbling of signals to gain time, the raider was given the order to 'Proceed'. Immediately afterwards, however, she was requested to 'Hoist the secret signal'. This, of course, they were unable to do, so the captain ordered action.

During this time, the two ships were proceeding on parallel courses 1,300 yards apart, and all the cruiser's guns and port torpedo tubes which would bear were trained on the raider. At the order 'Action', the German flag was broken out and all the guns and tubes that would bear were trained and fired. Apparently, the raider fired first. Seconds later the cruiser fired, but her first salvo missed over. The raider's first salvo struck about 'B' turret and bridge and 'Y' turret. The German stated that all salvos appeared to hit, and the cruiser took considerable time to find gun-hitting range. Also on the 27th, *Centaur* arrived at Carnarvon with lifeboats in tow, and an aircraft reported sighting three pieces of white timber. Additionally, HMAS *Wyrallah* picked up a RAN-type life belt in position 24 degrees 22' south, 110 degrees 49' east.

The search continued the next day, and HMAS *Wyrallah* picked up a foreign lifebelt and two foreign-type Carley floats and one dead German in the vicinity of 24 degrees 10' south, 110 degrees 54' east. *Heros* picked up a RAN-type Carley float damaged by gunfire in position 24 degrees 07' south, 110 degrees 58' east. The air search continued, and a Catalina reported sighting a patch of oil 5 miles south-east of the position of the engagement. That was on 28th November, and on the next day, orders were received that the search was to cease on the conclusion of operations on the 29th, unless new sightings were reported or further intelligence received.

However, interrogation of prisoners continued at Fremantle. All the prisoners were segregated at Harvey Camp, and the examination was carried out by two teams, each consisting of a naval officer and two interpreters. The information required from this interrogation was – movements in the Indian Ocean between June and November, details of supply organisations, details of neutral ports used, strategic policy, tactical action when attacking merchant shipping, any ruse de guerre employed, information on other raiders and every possible item of information concerning the action and fate of the *Sydney* and her men.

To gain this information, indirect questioning was used so that the prisoners would not realise the purport of the answers they gave. The opening questions were arranged as follows: A – Where were you when the action started? B – What time did you leave the ship? C – How did you get away? D – Did you see the British cruiser? Thus, from this interrogation it was possible to get from the Germans an almost complete picture of the action.

How far their accounts varied from the truth, however, is something that it would be almost impossible to establish...

As a result of the decision by the director of Naval Intelligence, CMDR Long, the above account by WRANS Third Officer Westhoven was placed on a Naval Intelligence Division file where it remained unpublished.

❑ ❑ ❑

CONFINED PARAMETERS

'He's coming alongside.'

These were the words of Captain Detmers, according to his adjutant with him on the bridge, LEUT Heinz Messerschmidt. On the 19th of September 2004, he was interviewed by ABC TV's *Rewind* programme at the Maritime Museum in Hamburg, Germany, by journalist Christopher Zinn, undersea explorer David Mearns and author Peter Hore.

During the interview, Mearns asked this question when the ships were alongside and parallel: 'Were you moving still at 14 knots at this time?', to which Messerschmidt replied, **'No, no, it was slowlier'** (sic). He did not elaborate, but given that he used the term 'slowlier' he certainly meant that the *Kormoran* was moving much slower than the purported speed of 14 knots.

This exchange had taken place more than three years before the successful search for the *Sydney* had begun. Nevertheless, having been forewarned that the *Kormoran* had then been sailing at a lesser speed, David Mearns forged ahead regardless of Messerschmidt's statement and produced a diagram **(*The Search for the Sydney*, p229)**, which took into account that same constant 14-knot speed for one and a half hours to the battle site, whilst also correcting what he thought was the noon position by 'moving' the longitudinal coordinates to 111°E to 111°09.5'E, despite the fact that all three German action reports describe that the raider had crossed meridian 111°E at 26°34'S on her way north to Shark Bay. The result was that the diagram had seemingly reflected all three action reports, but alarmingly the known wreck site positions of the cruiser and raider could not be accounted for. In addition, the diagram by Mearns shows the speed of the *Sydney* initially at only

17 knots. In fact, the distance between the *Durban* 0400z/17 handover position (7°56'S, 104°40'E) and on sighting the raider (25°54'S, 111°20'E) at 0900z/19 is 1135nm over a period of 53 hours. Thus, an average speed of *21.5 knots (22K against the current) over this distance (for which permission had been granted from China Station), means this certainly had not been a chance encounter. Again, permission for this speed had been given by C-in-C. And considering that the Commission of Inquiry had made little effort to establish the relevant speed of the vessels after the ships had closed and that no worthwhile comments from ordinary crewmen had been helpful, nothing can be construed from the diagram.

*On her previous return journeys from Sunda Strait to Fremantle, the *Sydney* made 16–19 knots on two boilers. [Three were required for a speed of 21–22 knots)

Again, Peter Hore in his book (***Sydney Cipher and Search*, p249)** also painted a similar picture, though his diagram, which accounted for the wreck site positions, clearly expressed that both vessels were moving at approx. 14 knots. This effectively meant the raider, according to the action reports, had been sailing a course of 025° but had crossed meridian 111°E much further south near latitude 27°S. However, no such latitudinal coordinate had ever been stated by the Germans as being the point of crossing longitude 111°E.

What must be said is that the 14-knot scenario assumed by Mearns and Hore had been taken for granted ever since the RAN first notified the Admiralty of its findings in early 1942. This had been based on the innocence of Detmers's story and of course the use of the above-water torpedoes to mortally damage the cruiser – this, amazingly, after adequate notice of the enemy's intention to de-camouflage had been signalled by raising the battle flag, as stated in the action reports.

The indifference by Mearns and Hore to the words of Messerschmidt is typified by any meaning of the fair or foul findings of the Commission of Inquiry. Unperturbed, the inquiry adopted that same story which has stood forever in navy parlance. But Messerschmidt's response to the question posed by Mearns doesn't end there.

One of the first to give an account of the action was a group of German survivors from a rubber raft – there were no officers among them. After being rescued, they were interviewed on the *Aquitania* on 23 November 1941 by the RAN's LCDR Ron Bagley, who wrote to the inquiry **(CORR.002.0274_R)**:

```
They informed us that Sydney hove to about 1000 yards off and
broadside on.  She then lowered a whaler with intent to board
Kormoran.  At this point Kormoran lowered the merchant flag,
hoisted battle ensigns, dropped the flaps and opened fire with
guns and torpedoes, achieving what proved to be mortal hits.

Sydney, obviously at action stations, returned fire mortally
wounding Kormoran which commenced to abandon ship.  Sydney
recovered her whaler - I specifically asked this - and made
off on fire fore and aft.

These survivors saw no more of her.
```

CORR.002.2268_R and SUBM No. 92 (JSCFADT)

[Bagley subsequently realised that the 'whaler' had been mistaken for a cutter]

And during an interview with interpreter Lobstein at Carnarvon on 27 November, raider crewman on no. 4 gun, Hermann Ortmann, quoted first-hand the opening of the engagement in more detail:

'*Sydney* told us to stop, which we did or almost so; *Sydney* also more or less stopped...We fired first, with guns – flaps on guns 1, 2, 5, 6 had to be raised [hydraulically], but those on 3, 4 were dropped and the guns could be aimed in advance. Didn't hit with first salvo, probably hit with the 3rd...*Sydney* had people on deck...she replied after our second salvo at a range of about 1,100 yards, some of her

shells exploded. She was hit by our torpedo, which disabled her [A and B] turrets, the B [surely C] turret targeted us, but only 3-4 salvoes were fired. Sydney then turned 360° [180°] and withdrew. [The] action had lasted 25 minutes.'

During interrogations, Ortmann did not repeat that both vessels were stopped; rather, his duty was to support his captain's plea that both ships were sailing at around 14 knots when the cruiser was torpedoed. He certainly knew the consequences should he tell otherwise. Thereafter, he held that line in interviews in Australia, but shortly before he died he again told his story of the action to Graham Ward some 65 years after he made his first statement in Carnarvon:

"... Later I looked over the gun screen and saw that all of *Sydney*'s guns were pointed straight at us and just forward of the bridge several bakers were leaning on the handrail. With normal eyesight I could see them clearly. The *Sydney*'s AA guns were not manned at all. Both ships were almost stationary and a small boat was being swung out. Then I was told to run around to the camouflage screen and be ready to release it, but as I was about to go around to operate the release handle, no. 4 gun fired its first salvo, no. 3 gun did the same thing... suddenly there was a huge explosion and a wall of water rose up against the side of the *Sydney*, forward of her bridge. Then all of our guns commenced firing. Only one torpedo was fired at the *Sydney* ..."

SUBM.007.0003_R

Regardless of Ortmann's evidence, other survivors have stated their support for him. For example, the newly acquired evidence by journalist David Kennedy that radio-operator Hans Linke had come forward voice to his concerns that the *Sydney* was nearly stationary when torpedoed.

In yet another report by CMDR Emile Dechaineax on the 31st, survivors rescued by the State Ship *Koolinda,* the stop order, this time at a distance, is unmistakable:

Report by Commander Deschaineux:

The following is a summary of the evidence collected from various sources.

The Action:

1. The alarm was sounded in the "Kormoran" at 1600/19. At that time the "Sydney" appeared on the Northern horizon, distant about 15 miles. The "Kormoran" then turned to the Westward, and increased to full speed. The Sydney gave chase, ordering the K. to stop. The K. on purpose made a great display of endeavouring to reply and also to comply with the instructions from the "Sydney." It is

Under formal interrogation in Fremantle 1 December 1941, it was Detmers himself who had testified that the cruiser had signalled the stop order from a distance **(NAA.012.0326)**:

Fregatten Kapitan Anton Gunther Theodor DETMERS :

Aged 39; not married. An active Officer, entered the Naval Acadmey in 1921.

At four o'clock ship's time (1700H) on the 19th, sighted Cruiser and altered course from North to South-west (250°) increased to full speed - not allowed to tell speed. Cruiser "PERTH" class. Cruiser made signal "NNP"- didn't understand, didn't answer. Cruiser signalled "Stop", and ordered Raider by search light in plain language to give secret call. Didn't know so had to fight,

Detmers was of the same view as Ortmann that the raider had been ordered to stop, but whether at a distance or as a precursor to the action, he spoke of the former.

Not long after having told that the cruiser signalled stop, Detmers produced a report on the action arranged in chronological order. In view of what he had said when interrogated, he felt compelled to distance himself from his words, which in any case could be construed as the cruiser being torpedoed by the secret underwater tube at a distance or when the ships had closed. Furthermore, such deceit would have constituted a war crime as it would be suspected that the torpedo had been fired before Detmers had given the order to formally announce his nationality by raising the battle flag.

The first action report of 1942, which broadly reflected the reports of 1945 and 1947, mentions that the raider had (albeit at a reduced speed owing to one of the four engines breaking down), travelled at approx. 14 knots for one and a half hours until the action commenced, a distance of some 21nm. According to all these reports this scenario applied and that de-camouflaging of the raider took place at that speed.

This 1945 Action Report (Gefechtsbericht) and Engine Room Log **(NAA B6121, 165K and NAA B5823)** dated 15/7/45 (below) had been sent to Naval Intelligence shortly afterwards by FRUMEL who had translated Detmers's take on the action. [Refer also to series **COI.005.0006** for comparison of all three ARs.]

Translation of parts of diary of Captain Detmers regarding the "Sydney"-"Kormoran" Action D.15/7 185

SECRET

237

ACTION REPORT.

26.10.41 — Detached KULMERLAND. Drew away to westward to effect alterations to engines. Exchange of nos. 1 and 2 engines.

(four figures omitted) — Midday: sighted an American, turned away. Then effected alterations. Alterations completed by (four figures omitted). Trial run without trouble. Proceeded on agent's way, as still time before new moon. Intend to be off PERTH by then. Report of CORNWALL with convoy off Cape LEEUWIN course west. Altered course to NE in consequence. Intention: investigation of coast off SHARKS BAY.

Wednesday 19.11. — Course 25, Speed 11; 26.34 South, 111 East. SSE 3 to 4, Sea 3 medium swell from SW. Very clear.

1555 — Look out JANSEN reports sailing ship in sight on port bow, bearing approx. 20° true. Report corrected currently to 2 sailing ships, several vessels, 2 smoke clouds, apparently escort.
Alarm. Turned away to port on to 260. Full speed ahead.

1600 — Cruiser made out, identified as PERTH class, on course South. Course 250 into the sun. Approach of darkness not due before 1900. Producing large quantities of smoke ourselves. Engine room reports: No. 4 engine out of order. Speed therefore approx. 14 knots.

1605 — Cruiser turns towards; range over 150 hm. Approaches slowly making "NNJ" repeatedly on searchlight. Hoist signal for STRAAT. Appreciate situation and make decision.

1645 — No. 4 engine running again on 8 cylinders. Speed 14 maintained; at 80 hm ceased measurement with 3 metre rangefinder, for reasons of disguise, continued ranging with 1.35 metre rangefinder. Continual signalling. Cruiser approaches slowly on the starboard quarter showing narrow silhouette.

1700 — Report on 600 metres QQQ STRAAT EBFS. PERTH radio repeats and requests further report if necessary.

1715 — Cruiser draws away on starboard beam 90 hm distant.

1725 — Morse signal in (MAKS): HOIST YOUR SECRET CALL. Further delay can only make situation worse. (Cruiser) stops engines, thus has not the least suspicion. Therefore

1730 — Removal of disguise. Dutch flag struck, War flag flies clear from main mast. Time taken 6 seconds. Guns and torpedo given permission to fire. Enemy drops slowly astern.
2 torpedoes inclination 80, speed 14, point of aim bow and stern. Also slow alteration to 260 so as not to interfere with guns. First salvo single shot short, Gun Range 13. Second salvo. Third fourth fifth, up 400. About 4 seconds later scores hit on bridge and control position, followed immediately by full salvo from enemy, over no hits. Then approx. 2 salvoes at 5 second interval. Hit amidships, aircraft, bridge. Correction for deflection left between forward turrets. A/A MG's and starboard 3.7 effective against bridge, torpedo tubes and A/A armament. Up to fifth salvo no reply, then "C" turret well and fast. Hits in funnel and engine room. "D" turret only two or three salvoes, all of them over. "A" and "B" turrets no longer (firing). At about eighth or ninth salvo torpedo hit forward of "A" and "B" turrets. Torpedo passed short distance ahead. Stern almost completely submerged. Course 260 maintained since torpedo tubes not manned because of A/A MG fire.

\- 2 -

Enemy turns sharply towards. Course and speed maintained to get clear. Top of "B" turret flies overboard, further hits forward.

1735 approx. Enemy passes astern in unfavourable position for firing his torpedoes. Thick smoke caused by fire in engine room conceals enemy from the bridge. A/A Control Officer continues with stern armament range approx. 40 hm. Enemy's guns pointing to starboard. His A/A is not manned.

1745 approx. Turned away to port in order to destroy enemy completely. Shortly afterwards revolutions drop rapidly, no communication with engine room. Simultaneously four torpedo tracks. Hold course because questionable whether engines would make the turn and tracks deviate well astern. Course 240. (Torpedoes) pass short distance astern. Simultaneously engines break down. LENSCH reports engine room and all fire-extinguishing apparatus completely out of order. Order to try and get at least one engine working. From

1750 approx. Gunnery control working again from forward position with whole battery at 60 hm. SIDNEY course south slow speed. On fire from bridge to after funnel. Constant further hits.

1800 approx. Single torpedo at 70 hm inclination 80, speed 5. Miss astern.

1825 Guns check. Last range 90 hm. Shots 104 hm. relative bearing 225. Rounds fired approx. 500 base fuze, 50 nose fuze. Prepare to scuttle. Lower all boats and life-saving equipment. Impossible to reach engine room; satisfied myself personally of this. No. 2 electric installation working but useless. Enemy disappears from sight at approx. 160 hm. course approx. 150. Glare visible until about 2200 then occasional flickerings.

2100 approx. All life-saving apparatus lowered and cast off. Still 124 men on board including almost all officers. Such guns as are still working can thus be manned. Only small quantity of smoke in mine hold. Both boats from no. 2 hatch.

2330 approx. Both lowered, one with 59 (men). Explosive charge in port forward oil tank.

2355 Smoke increasing heavily on mining deck.

2400 Paid off. Touched off charge, last boat cast off.

oo35 Mines explode. Ship sinks rapidly stern first.

The action report above and the former and latter versions of 1942 and 1947 are constructed almost word for word. Nevertheless, there are a few dissimilarities, namely:

1700G: 'QQQ Straat EBFS' [E26S] appears incomplete. The complete QQQQ (RRRR) emergency signal from the raider for a suspicious ship should have read 'AAAEBFS' (111E,

26S), the same position as the other two ARs (to the nearest degree). It, therefore, seems as though Detmers himself had memorised the value of the longitude coordinate before he had escaped from the POW camp. Also, *Straat Malakka* at the time was referred to as the name of the *Kormoran* by the German naval war staff (Skl). Radio operator Hans Linke said the above position had been signalled twice. However, due to the signal from the raider having been received by the RAN maritime emergency station in Geraldton in the form of '7C 11115E', the longitude coordinate of the Q signal can be easily read as 111°15'E (course 025°) with the corresponding latitude 26°07'S **(NAA B6121, 165P)**. [Refer hereunder to cryptogram.]

1715G: 'Cruiser draws away on starboard beam 90Hm distant.' This is definitely incorrect. The other two ARs specify 9Hm (900 metres), not 9,000 metres. Besides, at such a distance (approx. 5nm) the cruiser would have been relatively safe from the raider's shellfire and torpedoes and she could have made use of the distance with her superior armament which was more effective than the enemy's. In any case, Detmers had known the exact distance by using his small rangefinder. This mistake had been made during translation of his diary.

1725G: This 1945 diary account of the action is the only one to mention the following: **'Morse signal in [MAKS]: HOIST YOUR SECRET CALL. Further delay** [by us] **can only make situation worse...'** This comment appears to be out of sequence because Admiralty demanded that this request for secret call-sign-registered ships (including the *Straat Malakka*) was to be carried out at a safe distance of 14,000yds, immediately after the name of the ship has been signalled. It is thus the only inclusion in the ARs which justifies Detmers's call for action, albeit he could not reply to the secret call from a distance.

'(Cruiser) stops engines, thus has not the least suspicion.' Given that the other two ARs refer to the aircraft (seaplane) engine being turned off (it was supposedly on the catapult ready to fly over the raider), the act of shutting the Walrus down put paid to sighting the armament of the errant vessel from the air. In this case, the German captain would have regarded the *Sydney* command as completely unsuspecting per se. However, Burnett would still have remained suspicious because the raider had not replied to the request for the secret call at a distance. Another reason for turning the plane's engine off is to prevent damage to the aircraft from the impact of the six-inch guns should they be given the order to fire on the raider, the normal process being to retract the catapult and aircraft amidships. And due to the fact that sunset was due in approximately half an hour it may have proved difficult to land on the rising seas and that the Walrus may not have been able to land at the nearest aerodrome at Carnarvon 150nm away at night. Also, given the cruiser was to have stopped her engines at a speed of some 14 knots she would eventually have been uncontrollable and have eventually swung side-on to the wind. The term 'least suspicion' by the Germans would also apply to the *Sydney* stopping or dramatically slowing from a much lesser speed in order to board the raider.

1730G:' '2 torpedoes, inclination 80, speed 14 [7.2m/s], **point of aim bow and stern...'** This appears to be valid, providing the tubes had been splayed at an angle of approx. 10° and the 40-knot G7a torpedo aimed at the bow had been fired off some 20 seconds before the torpedo aimed at the stern. In this case, the aim is to knock out all of the cruiser's turrets situated at the bow and stern. But that the other two ARs quote an inclination of 90 [degrees], it is obviously impossible for a straight-running torpedo from the above-water tubes to strike at that angle because the cruiser had already dropped slightly astern of the raider. For a straight-running torpedo,

Detmers would be required to turn his ship from course 250° to port (both ships had been parallel beforehand), practically stop, aim at the bow and fire off the torpedo. It would have conceivably struck the target at an inclination of 80°. And now that the raider had turned back to 260°, the point of aim for the guns had again been at the *Sydney*'s four turrets at the bow and stern.

'At about the eighth or ninth [salvo] torpedo hit forward of A and B turrets.' This may appear to be correct if referring to <u>full</u> salvoes (all four guns firing together) and the running time of the torpedo over 900m (43–45 seconds), but it does not account for the evidence given by Ortmann, Linke etc, and nor does it make sense of FRUMEL's translation: **'Torpedo fired, hits on bow... and two torpedoes passed short of bow...'** This does, however, support the fact that the bulk of the crew had stated that three torpedoes were fired and that the translation of officer Bretschneider's diary by Military Intelligence had confirmed that two torpedoes (which had been jammed on their mounts) must be rid of in case the return fire from the cruiser's guns were to have struck the twin above-water torpedo battery on the starboard side and explode.

1735G: 'Enemy's guns pointing to starboard.' It seems that Naval Intelligence fell in line with naval academic FB Eldridge's report in stating that X and Y turrets were still in action after the cruiser had altered course to port. However, it was FRUMEL who were correct in their translation in stating 'enemy guns trained to port' (so, too, the ARs of 1942 and 1947).

1800G: 'Single [underwater] **torpedo at 70Hm** [7,000m] **inclination 80, speed 5. Miss astern.'** An inclination of 80° is not possible for the position of the raider because she was then drifting north of the cruiser which was sailing away at some 5 knots. And due to the fact that in assessing the angle of the torpedo striking the hull (it is measured from the bow of the target), the cruiser would have been sailing almost due south at the time. It is noted that the other two ARs appear almost correct in nominating 110° (it appears closer to 130°), or else on this occasion Detmers had simply repeated the angle of inclination for the torpedo that had been initially fired off.

1825G: 'Guns check. Last range 90hm. Shots [at] **104hm** [gun range], **relative bearing 225.'** This description is typical for all ARs. Note: The relative angle of the cruiser is measured clockwise from the bow of the raider. Due to the SSE wind her bow had turned, and as a result was then pointing in the direction of approx. 250° at the time.

It should be borne in mind that the above excerpts explained and highlighted in the 1945 Action Report are to be read in conjunction with the battle, as described in the next chapter.

ENGINE ROOM LOG.

19.11.41 Speed 11 knots. Nos. 1 and 4 engines on propulsion, no. 3 engine on ship's supply. On watch Warrant Engineer LENSCH and two Stoker P.O.'s.

1555 Alarm. Order from bridge: All engines ready for maximum speed. No. 2 engine turned on to propulsion.

1600 All watches at action stations;
1st Watch working stations, Warrant Engineer NAGEL
2nd Watch at damage control stations, Warrant Engineer LENSCH
3rd Watch engine room action parties, Warrant Engineer MITZLAFF

1602 Report to bridge: Engines ready for maximum speed.

1604 Report to bridge: No. 4 engine out of order by reason of piston running hot, maximum speed therefore approx. 14 knots.
On the attempt to increase the load of the engines, No. 4 main engine became unserviceable owing to piston 7 running hot. The engine was stopped forthwith, the damaged piston slung, the connecting rod removed and the valve gear disconnected.

1635 approx. Engine could be put to propulsion again on 8 cylinders. Ship thus again ready for maximum speed.

1715 Damage control centre shifted from starboard gangway to port gangway, as being probably away from the firing.

1730 Order from bridge: Remove disguise.

1735 approx. Several hits in main engine room. One shell tore the forward tank bulkhead of the engine room badly open. A thick jet of burning fuel oil poured into the room, which was rapidly filled with opaque smoke. The main fire extinguisher pipe was punctured on either side of the engine room, at the same time the whole foam extinguisher plant which had been transferred to the starboard side went out of action. An explosion on the starboard side rendered the transformers unserviceable, thereby putting the electrical excitation for the main generators and propulsion motors out of action. The whole of the main engine installation was thus out of action.
Report to bridge: Engine installation unserviceable by enemy action, very heavy smoke, query may personnel leave engine room? Order from bridge: Leave engine room. By this time only No. 2 electric installation was in order. The attempt by the Chief Plumber to get pressure in the fire extinguisher pipe from the power unit in the propulsion motor room failed, as pressure dropped immediately in the damaged pipe.

1745 Senior Stoker on watch reports verbally to C.O. on the bridge. At this time the engines failed. C.O. orders to try and get one engine working at least. All attempts to penetrate into engine room failed. First Watchkeeping Officer passed order from C.O. by telephone from Damage Control Centre to Engineer Officer in Control position. Engineer Officer replied that the order could not be carried out and crew of control position, Engineer Officer (corrupt passage) two P.O.'s and two stewards were suffocating. Shortly afterwards control position ceased to report. First Watchkeeping Officer reported to C.O.: engine room finally out of action and no further communication with control position.
Attempts to save crew of control position failed. Only one P.O. Stoker P.O. HAHNERT, succeeded in escaping from the control position. He states he saw the control position watch killed by a sudden burst of fire while trying unsuccessfully to open the hatch of the splinter grating.

1825 Order from C.O. : All hands to abandon ship.

NAA B5823

Above is the engine-room log, the bulk of which describes the damage on board the raider *Kormoran.* It had been carefully crafted by Detmers to dovetail with his 1945 Action Report.

In 1943, a cryptogram, which appeared to have all the hallmarks of a cryptic message of importance, had been confiscated at the POW camp in Victoria. Whether it was designed by Petty Officer Heinz Kitsche or not (it was purportedly found in his possession), it is definitely of German origin, so there is little point in trying to establish a link between the individual letters and what the drawings typically represent.

Some researchers have linked it to the *Kormoran*'s LEUT Fritz Lizt (Doctor of Economics), who had sketched a series of events on his ordeal in the lifeboat while making landfall from the battle site. This drawing included the *Sydney* on fire, his lifeboat sailing to the coast at Red Bluff north of Carnarvon, the adjacent shoreline where the boat landed, an Australian man (possibly SGT Anderson who escorted the Germans to Carnarvon), the cave where the Leica camera, which supposedly had filmed the action, was purportedly buried and a stop-over for rest (probably at Quobba sheep station). And when asked what the sketches might mean, stenographer, H Kevin, who had been called in to assist Military Intelligence, had mistakenly thought the cave drawing represented shorthand characters indicating Japanese involvement. After all, it was impossible to believe at the time that an ordinary merchant ship disguised as a raider could have sunk a much superior warship by itself. It had never happened before.

NAA B6121, 165K

Army LEUT Jonathon Rowbotham, formerly of the Tatura POW camp, spent many years after the war trying to find a connection with the hiding place of the camera. He took notice of the comment made by Kevin in believing that the simple strokes in the cave drawing might reveal the location of where it was hidden in the cave after Henri Meyer's lifeboat (also carrying Dr Lizt) came ashore at Red Bluff. He, like many others, had tried in vain to solve the puzzle. He attempted to solve the cryptogram (below), which he believed had been sketched by Lizt, but he could not link it to the site of where the camera was buried.

The following is the cryptogram that Rowbotham had tried to solve. As with most cryptograms there is likely to be no correlation between the diagrams and the coded letters.

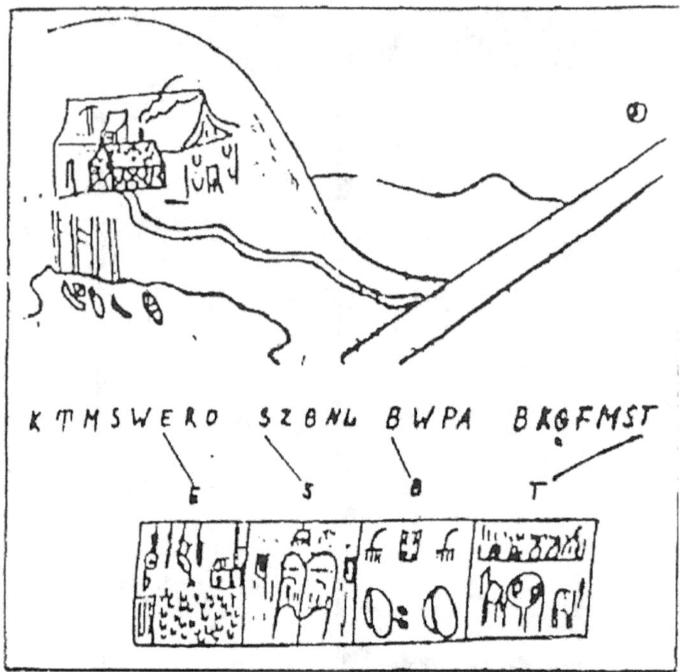

It is not too difficult to guess the meaning of the alpine scene where Eating (Ger = Essend), Sleeping (Schlafend), Bathing and Drinking were everyday occurrences (so too in the POW camp). However, in the English language the first two letters emphasized ostensibly mean E=East and S=South. If so, the other essential is a bearing (Bathing = Badend) and Drinking (Ger = Trink) was thought to represent time.

If we take, for example, the simple numbers allocated to the letters, as in AAAE, BFS (111E, 26S), where A=1, B=2 etc, the cryptogram can be solved thus:

E=KTMSWERO: E (East) = 11[20+13+19+23+5+18+15], i.e., E = 11[113] = 111°13'E.

Decoding: E is the key; then add up the letters as numerals (including E).

S=SZBNL: S (South) = 26[19+2+14+12], i.e., S = 26[47] = 26°47'S

Decoding: S is the key, but because S is the first letter the second letter (as a numeral) must be taken first; then add up the letters as numerals (including S).

B=BWPA: B (Bearing) =23 [2+16+1], i.e., B = 23[19], which could only be translated as 23.19°. Decoding: B is the key, but because B is the first letter, the second letter (as a numeral) must be taken first; then add-up the letters as numerals (including B).

T=BKGFMST: T (Time)=2[11+7+6+13+19+20]G, i.e., T=2[76]G = 2[1.16]G or 21.16G time. Decoding: T is the key. Add up the letters as numerals (including T). However, because G is underscored with a dot it is not applicable as a numeral.

In each case, the method of decoding is consistently applied.

The above coordinates 111°13'E, 26°47'S are unrepresentative of any of the raider's movements and they are not mentioned in casual conversations by crewmen or during formal interrogations. But they do refer to the general area of where the action purportedly took place and most certainly not ashore in the vicinity of Red Bluff. And considering that the bearing (23.19°) is precisely given in the cryptogram it must therefore be related to each latitudinal and longitudinal coordinates.

Specific coordinates have been stated in all three action reports, these being 111°E, 26°34'S, the position given by Detmers for the possible rescue of survivors. If, however, we draw a line through this point on a bearing of 23.19°, it reveals the corresponding coordinates, 26°47'S, 110°54'E and 26°07'S, 111°13'E. Obviously, whoever calculated the above angle had access to logarithmic tables in the POW camp to calculate the angle of the bearing and had expertly applied them.

The diagram below shows these same coordinates relative to course 23.19° drawn through 26°34'S, 111°E. Thus, it was this bearing (course) that had led to verifying the above coordinates and solving the cryptogram. Also, note that the person who devised the cryptogram had based his findings on the fact that at latitude 26°S he correctly indicated the distance between the longitude (54nm) and his calculations for the longitude distance at latitude 27°S had been based on 53.6nm, as was the custom in those days. All other part latitudes in between are proportional to 0.4nm for calculating an accurate course – this in 1943, well before the advent of automated global positioning (GPS).

In ascertaining the specific meaning of 21.16G, nowhere is it recorded that the German survivors spoke of this exact time. However, it can only refer to the time that *Kormoran* was being abandoned after Kohn's lifeboat had departed the stricken raider with a total of 46 men on board. Kitsche, Lizt and Meyer plus 54 others left soon after in another lifeboat to eventually come ashore at Red Bluff, north of the town of Carnarvon. Thus, in all probability it refers to the time Meyer's lifeboat departed the stricken raider.

Although *Kormoran*'s navigation has been independently validated, the Navy has asserted that it is not compelling enough to fundamentally challenge the Cole Commission of Inquiry findings. At the moment they just pass it off while obviously conceding the accuracy of the navigation. The mathematics cannot be disproved and they can only quote an inherent +/- 2nm error in astronavigation techniques for determining positions by sextant, inferring that the *Kormoran*'s navigator, Henri Meyer, may not have determined his positions correctly. Such a statement could be true if the *Kormoran* wreck site had not been identified, but now that this position has been surveyed beyond doubt, it demonstrates that the ship's navigator had also established the noon position (26°47'S, 110°54'E) rather accurately.

But regardless of any possible error factor, the point to be made is that Detmers's designated position 26°34'S, 111°E and course 23.19° are inseparable from position 26°07›S, 111°13'E, which represents the planned track of *Kormoran* and the positions through which the navigator thought the raider was travelling, positions that were either determined by accurate sextant observation, or alternatively by chance. Moreover, any adjustments made to the above positions would only result in unrealistic drift values to the *Kormoran*'s wreck-site position.

In order to identify the originator of the navigation, one must consider who had assessed the relative positions of the raider and her progress northwards. Surely, it was navigator Henri Meyer who had determined the position of the raider (26°47'S, 110°54'E) at 1200G time. He had assessed the solar noon position using sextant about 40 minutes before noon when the sun was most distant from earth (aphelion), this being achieved in accordance with the ships speed and course. But this is not to say that he had devised the cryptogram, only that others may have encoded these details and drawn the sketch shown above. Besides, Meyer as navigator of the *Kormoran* had known a great deal about navigation, so it must therefore be concluded that the course derived from the cryptogram had been the raider's intended course, as proposed by the captain who had briefed the ship's navigator and had devised a course to Shark Bay. But as to whether Lizt and/or Kitsche could have had a deep knowledge of navigation, is a matter of conjecture.

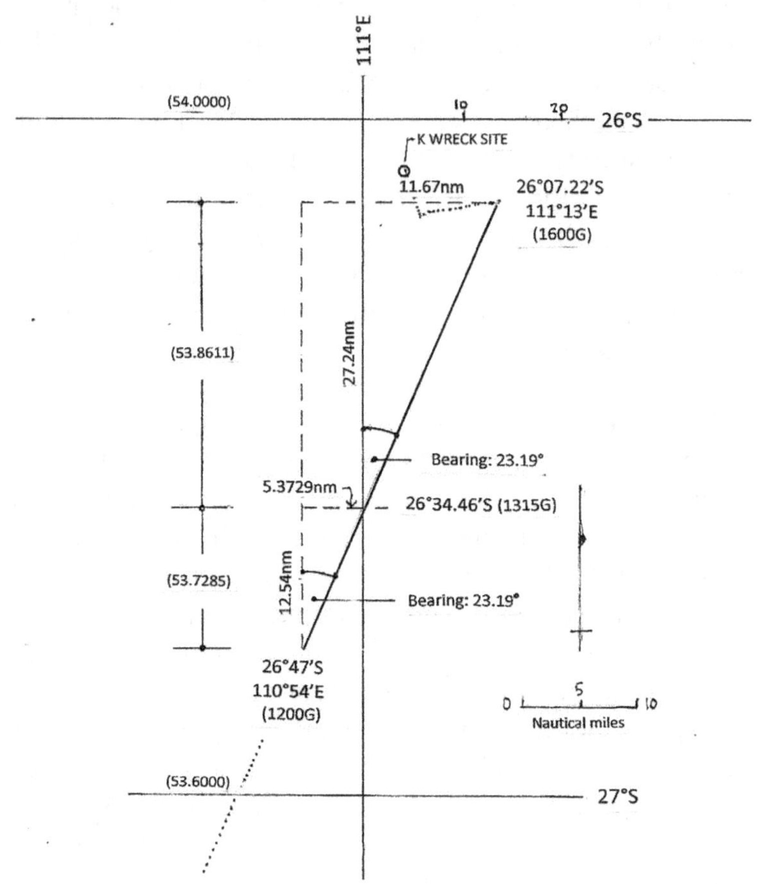

Considering the sheer accuracy of the bearing of the vessel crossing 111°E at 26°34'S and then sailing to 111°13'E, it confirms the turning point – just 0.22nm south of 26°07'S. In his book, *The Raider Kormoran*, Detmers had described that at 1500 hours (G time) on the 19th he checked his ship's course and therefore it must have come to his notice that his ship had crossed 111°E in the vicinity of 26°34'S (p137) – the same position specified in all action reports.

This bearing can be further corroborated. After he had checked the ship's course, Detmers had decided to carry on without change in direction until 2000 hours and then turn eastwards to lay his deadly anchored mines in the vicinity of Shark Bay, if the sea conditions permitted. An extension of bearing 23.19° would have meant that at 2000G his ship would have been almost opposite the northern tip of Dirk Hartog Island (Cape Inscription) and perfectly placed to lay his mines in the sea near the southern entrance to the Port of Carnarvon, adjacent to Naturaliste Channel, as shown below. And had Detmers ordered those mines to be laid it would have been potentially devastating for the predominantly state-owned ships plying the north-west and Kimberley Ports back and forth from Fremantle. [On entry to Carnarvon Port ships from the north enter the harbour via the Geographe Channel]

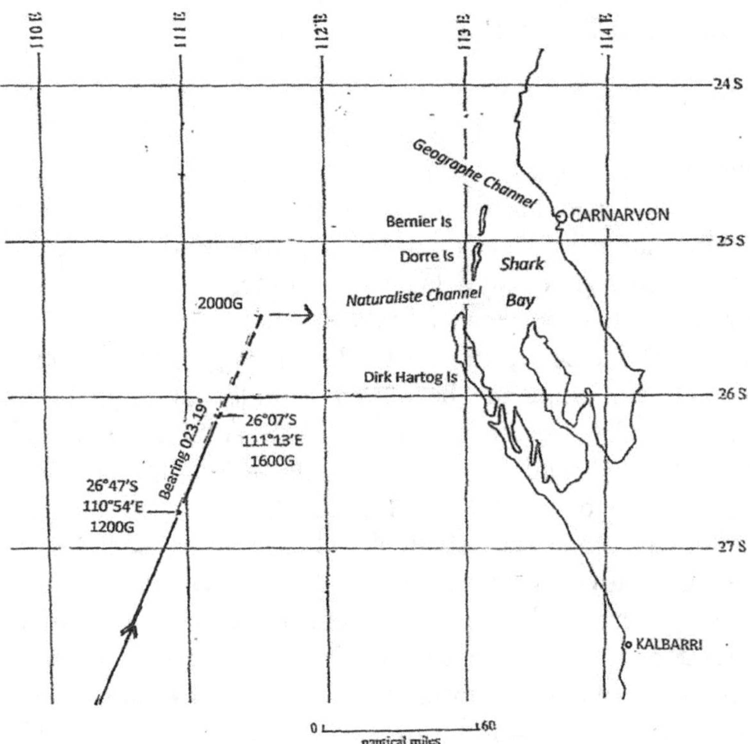

Proposed route to Shark Bay

Meyer's final course no doubt took into account the directional effect of the SW swell acting on the port side of the vessel, which according to Detmers, 'was hampered because of the barnacles and so on clinging to our bottom and sides'. Nevertheless, Meyer had calculated that the raider, which had the general assistance of the SW swell acting on the port side, must have veered at least 1.5nm east of the planned course in four hours to approx. 111°15'E and that his vessel had maintained its overall designated speed of speed of 11 knots from noon to 1600G (5pm WST). Furthermore, this position accounts for *Kormoran*'s engine room (log) speed to the turning point, thus confirming that the raider had sailed about 8 miles from the turning point (26°07'S, 111°15'E) to the battle site in one and a half hours (5pm – 6:30pm WST). This distance in no way represents 14–15 knots within the given time, as was stated by Eldridge and Gill in describing the action.

Detmers also mentions in his book (*The Raider Kormoran*) that the raider had made contact with Perth Radio in the suburb of Applecross, 'informing the world that we were being challenged by an unknown cruiser' (p141). But the Applecross station (manned by RAN personnel) was not in the business of relaying emergency signals sent from merchant ships because Geraldton Radio had been set aside for that purpose. Perth Radio had trouble detecting this particular message that was sent on an unknown frequency because the raider had signalled the full positional coordinates 111°E, 26°S. Applecross therefore would have advised *Straat Malakka* that the coordinates should be sent more precisely to Geraldton Radio on a frequency of 500kcs (the emergency channel). Thus, after consultation with navigator Meyer, who had supplied the exact turning point of where the cruiser had been sighted, it had been forwarded to Geraldton a few minutes later where the weak Q signal had been intercepted in the form of 7C 11115E **(NAA B6121, 165P)**. It was at this point of latitude (26°07'S) and longitude (111°15'E) while on her re-created course of 025° that the raider had turned away due to the presence of the 'unknown' vessel.

Note: Whole coordinates, such as 26°S, 111°E, represents an area of some 3,400 square nautical miles, whereas 26°07'S, 111°15'E theoretically pinpoints the area to the nearest square nautical mile and is the preferred format for tracking vessels. Also, considering that the Q signal had been sent to Geraldton, the south coordinate had been announced first by the raider in order to convey the English positional format, which all allied ships adhered to.

There is further confirmation of the route (25° bearing) of the raider between the hours of noon and 1600G when the raider had turned away. As from noon (1200G) the raider had travelled some 44nm at 11 knots in a north-easterly direction to position 26°07'S, 111°15'E – in simple mathematical terms the track could be simply determined from a right-angled triangle with sides 44.014nm x 39.78nm x 18.8368nm – this, on a course of 25.34°. See diagram below.

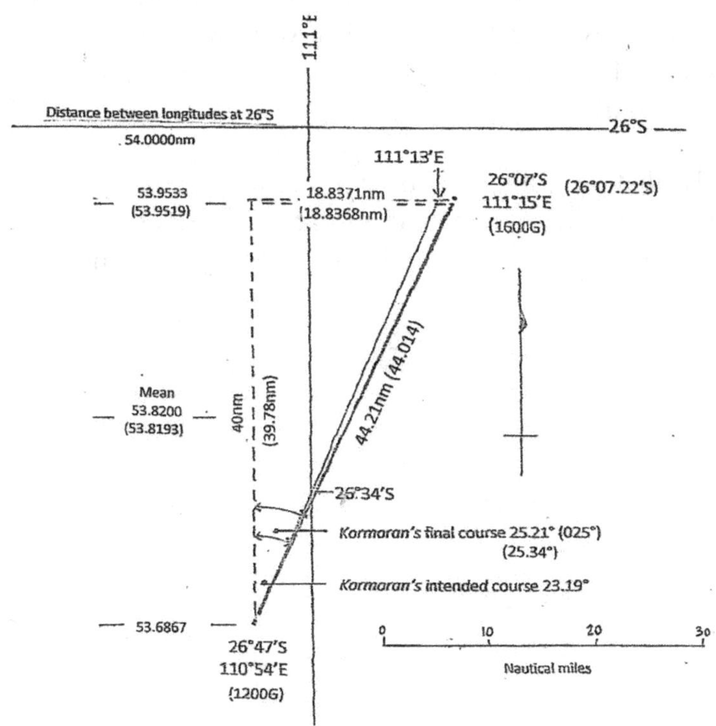

Final course established by Navigator Meyer

The above diagram confirms the findings by navigator Meyer – course 025°. But in the end, all the postulation from so-called experts and researchers had much ado about nothing. Each had tried to find and measure the track taken by the *Kormoran* for four hours at 11 knots between the hours of noon until she had turned away.

Some had said that the cryptogram would have led to re-discovering the lost camera, and some had concocted a weird version of their own. The inquiry was also impeded by virtue of the fact that the action reports per se contained information that somehow led the Navy into believing the *Sydney* had chased the *Kormoran* for one and a half hours and had taken absolutely no notice of the stop order issued by the cruiser. This is indeed evident in the Eldridge Report, CMDR Long's report and CMDR Gill's *History of the Royal Australian Navy.* But closest of all was the War Council's Advisory Committee on 28 November 1941 – this, after the *Sydney* had given chase - **she closed rapidly.**

Finally, that such a simplistic cryptogram could have escaped the attention of the Navy and military decoders to the point of being successfully deciphered is frankly beyond belief.

THE ACTION

After having established the precise navigational parameters, the story of the action becomes much clearer, whether it be from the action reports and Detmers's book, *The Raider Kormoran* (written in English) or from *Der Hilfskreuzer de die Sydney versenkte* (written in German), each are relative to the observations made. Preference is given to Detmers's diary found on him after escaping from the POW camp in Victoria in early 1945 as being more informative than the almost identical action reports of 1942 and 1947 and consequently much more likely to being closest to the truth. After all, it was meant to be a record of the engagement for German absorption.

Yet again, what is most significant is that all three action reports and Detmers's two books reveal the constant 14–15-knot speed of the raider, despite overwhelming evidence from Officer Heinz Messerschmidt and others that the raider was sailing much slower before the action began. This also includes an account provided by Nazi *Kormoran* officer Joachim von Gosseln in 1970, who stated: **'The *Sydney* is travelling along slowly on a parallel course some 1000 to 1500 yards away.'**

The foregoing is from Detmers's book, *The Raider Kormoran* (1959), 18 years after the incident, on how he remembered the interception, including his take on the phases of the action and aftermath. It is controversial to the extent that his recollections differ markedly from his original interrogation reports, the action reports and the words of many of his fellow officers and crew. An abridged account of his book reveals the following from page 136:

'It was November 19th, 1941, a beautiful day with warm sunshine. As is so often in the Indian Ocean the visibility was perfect. The

wind was south-south-east and had dropped to between Force 3 and 4. The sea had dropped too...a medium swell from the south-west. The Kormoran was proceeding at medium speed (approx. 11 knots) on her usual sweep and gradually approaching Shark Bay from the south-west. At 1500 hours (4pm WST) I checked the ship's course and decided to carry on without change until 20.00 hours and then turn eastwards...I went into the mess for some coffee.'

Kormoran had the general assistance of the SSE wind of approx. 18 knots on her foray to Shark Bay on 19 November. Any increase in speed would have been negated largely by the build-up of sea growth underneath the hull, bearing in mind that the SW swell had been incessant. A speed in the order of 11 knots is therefore considered appropriate. And again, while checking on the route to Shark Bay, Detmers couldn't help notice that his ship had earlier crossed 111°E at 26°34'S as he had planned and as evidenced in all three decrypted action reports **(Series COI.005.0006)**. See action report in previous chapter.

'At 15.55 hours [4.55pm WST] the alarm bells began to ring, and a moment or two later an orderly arrived to tell me a ship had been sighted ahead, probably a sailing vessel...The lookout in the foretop was revising his signals all the time, because in the shimmering light at the limit of visibility the contours changed continually. Before long we could see two sailing ships, then a number of vessels and behind them two clouds of smoke which probably came from an escort. I didn't care much for the outlook, so I turned away to port at 260° and ordered full speed ahead...'At first the air was quivering so in the heat that it was difficult to see anything, but then a typical cruiser shape began to come clear. It was one of three cruisers of the "Perth" class... (p137)

'I also turned to 250° and took up the most favourable shooting position available to me. I paid no further heed to the position

of the sun, because the smoke sent up by the simultaneous performance of all our engines was so visible, the enemy must have seen us...through the shimmering light, the cruiser turned towards signalling [the perplexing] "NNJ" [what ship?]. Soon afterwards no. 4 diesel engine broke down, limiting her speed to 14 knots'. (p138). Having understood the meaning of 'NNJ' they [we] signalled by flag, deliberately fumbling and obscuring the name of the vessel, but then hoisted the flags clear to reveal the name, Straat Malakka (p139). '...the real SM was about our size and shape, and it was certainly quite possible to take us for her. And we also knew she was somewhere around the Indian Ocean; but where exactly was another matter. *[She was currently in the port of Beira (Mozambique) at the time]* *It was hoped that this fellow [HMAS Sydney] didn't know either. By bad luck he might have left the ship behind in port. Or he might inquire by wireless; but at least he wasn't doing that, for my WT room reported that the enemy was maintaining wireless silence. The cruiser now morsed...and asked where we were bound for. Trusting to luck I replied "Batavia". But what I didn't understand was why he didn't signal me to heave to.'*

Admiralty instructions specifically demand that on sighting a suspicious ship the merchant ship turns away and increases to full speed and challenges by making her International Signal Letters either by flags or by international Morse (flashing) – this, whether the vessel had been issued with a secret call-sign or not. If issued with a secret call-sign, the warship then replies with the centre two letters of the merchant ships secret call-sign and the merchant ship replies with the first and last letters (**CAFO P336/41**). Thus, the proposition that Detmers had finally answered the request for 'NNJ' and had signalled the name *Straat Malakka* (signal letters 'PKQI') but had not requested the secret letters at that stage, differs markedly from Admiralty instructions, which the *Sydney*'s Captain Burnett was bound to follow.

Detmers clearly stated when first interrogated in 1941 the cruiser signalled 'NNP', which he didn't really understand as he hoisted the name of his vessel. The warship then signalled stop because his ship was not on the Vessels in Area Inventory (VAI). He was then ordered by searchlight in plain language to give the secret call **(NAA.012.0326)**. But given that the cruiser had signalled 'IK', the two centre letters of *Straat Malakka*'s secret call-sign ('IIKP') in accordance with Admiralty instructions, Burnett was then bound to have again signalled *stop because the merchantman could not reply to the inner secret letters. Undoubtedly Burnett would have been highly suspicious of the ship. If the vessel could not supply the secret letters assigned to the *Straat Malakka*, it could only be that the vessel's name is not what she had claimed to be. Besides, this ship was not on the twice-daily list of ships expected to be in the area and she did not possess the features of the silhouette shown, for example, in the Talbot-Booth handbook, which all British warships referred to.

*Enemy vessels were rarely stopped in mid-ocean unless sea conditions permitted, otherwise they experience uncontrollable drift if the wind is relatively strong. It is for this reason that they are told to go slowly.

Orders from the Admiralty also authorise that once a suspicious ship is ordered to stop they are presumed to be an enemy ship and told to continue on course at slow speed while the warship surveys the vessel and identifies whether it may be armed or unarmed. In the case of the *Kormoran* moving at 14 knots in difficult winds of Force 3–4, the term stopped implies she would dramatically lose speed when ordered to the extent that she would only just gain headway rather than be blown off her course. A reduced speed of 3 knots would not seem unreasonable in these circumstances.

After being intercepted and stopped, navigator Henri Meyer admitted under interrogation that a 'parley' took place. However, this term is rarely used in a discussion between two parties as it normally refers to an informal conference between enemies under truce to discuss terms, conditions of surrender, etc. But there is no evidence of Meyer's comment being questioned by the interrogating officers who, unbeknown to them, the cruiser had been sent by C-in-C China to intercept the suspected enemy vessel that had been detected by FEDO. As mentioned before, British Intelligence in Singapore had known the general whereabouts of the vessel being tracked by FEDO and therefore the order to stop or to reduce speed for a suspected warship was obligatory, otherwise the cruiser would have fired a shot across the raider's bow or have sunken the vessel. Yet Detmers flagrantly said in his book that he did not signal me to heave to and continued on at approx. 14 knots – regardless of the consequences. Furthermore, at such an undiminished speed the raider would have showed all the signs of being an enemy ship.

Submission by the raider therefore goes without saying, as the suspicious ship had been instructed to slow and remain on course while Captain Burnett assessed its likely armament prior to boarding and capturing the vessel, providing it was not heavily armed. Besides, it should be reminded that Captain Detmers and his chief signaller Erich Ahlbach were the only ones privy to messages actually sent by the so-called *Straat Malakka*.

Interrogating warships in 1941 kept a minimum distance of 6–7nm (12–14,000m) clear of a suspicious ship in case it was to suddenly open fire and cause damage, and as flag signals could only be read with great difficulty from this distance, the only sure means of signalling was by searchlight. So if Detmers had maintained that the warship signalled by using the searchlight, obviously the raider must have been too distant to use flag signals to announce the raider's name, secret letters and destination. It follows that the cruiser had closed the distance sufficiently to where the flags could be read.

Again, Detmers falsely replied he was bound for Batavia, and this had meant (from the original course he was sailing) that his ship had visited a port in Australia, but no record existed of her being there (the VAI showed she had not). Officers Messerschmidt and von Gosseln (they were both on the bridge) had agreed with Detmers that the reply to be sent via flag from the disguised *Straat Malakka* was from Batavia, destination, Lourenço Marques.

Detmers's book continues:

'At 5.35pm (WST) a message arrived on the bridge to the effect that no. 4 motor had been patched up and could run again minus one cylinder...I kept to the same speed of fourteen knots now in order not to awaken suspicions in the mind of my trustful enemy by any chance. The cruiser then approached slowly on the starboard quarter showing a narrow silhouette between 8 and 9 thousand yards away, and still coming closer....'we could see every detail clearly...In particular we could see that her four double turrets with their 6 inch guns and also the port torpedo battery were all directed at us...her eight [sic] anti-aircraft guns were not manned. So much the better. We knew that generally speaking the British did not man their anti-aircraft guns when there was no air alert. ...she came up steadily with an unchanging bow wave (p 140), still showing us the narrowest possible silhouette. She was obviously still curious about us and now she wanted to know what cargo we were carrying. I replied vaguely, "piece-goods".'

Detmers's book again pressed that his vessel had not been ordered to stop at the distance recommended by the Admiralty but merely continued on its way at 14 knots. It is also of interest that by definition the narrowest possible silhouette for the cruiser means that it had approached aft of the raider, as witnessed by Hermann Ortmann on no. 4 gun. Note also that the action reports describe the cruiser approaching *slowly and as either being on the raider's starboard quarter or port after-quarter.

*The cruiser had been making approx. 12 knots, the raider 3 knots. Closing speed = approx. 9 knots [See diagrams in this chapter.]

From a distance of some 4 miles the cruiser had already asked for the raider's destination, but for the raider to be asked what cargo she was carrying when the cruiser had closed further, conjures the belief that Captain Burnett had assessed the vessel as a large enemy minelayer, similar to the type used along the southern coast of Australia by the German Navy in 1940 – hence, the query on the cargo to which Detmers replied, 'piece-goods'. After all, when positioned aft of the raider Burnett should have clearly seen the outline of the twin mining doors at her stern and therefore he could be reliably assured that such vessels were generally lightly armed and no match for his cruiser.

'I now hoisted the Dutch flag to make the confusion still worse. I began to use my wireless sending out the Q signal, "QQQ Straat Malakka", and informing the world that we were being challenged by an unknown cruiser. Perth wireless station picked up my signals, acknowledged receipt...telling me to keep in touch...I could see that the enemy cruiser now had a plane on the catapult. The engine was probably warming up. At any moment it would be catapulted into the air; and once the observer spotted us from above he would recognise us at once for what we were, an auxiliary cruiser...But at least the enemy was something over three thousand yards away now, a beautiful shooting range. Would she slow down? Would she order us to heave to? Would she turn her broadside on us? And what should I do?...I wanted to bring every gun I had to bear at its maximum effectiveness in order to give me the biggest possible chance. So I let her come a bit closer still...For some time now we had been expecting a signal that would call our bluff, but so far nothing had come beyond almost casual queries which we had no difficulty in answering with some show of reason'. (p141)

The Perth wireless station Detmers referred to could only have been the long-range HF station situated in the Perth suburb of Applecross, which had wide coverage of the Indian Ocean approaches. [Likewise, her sister stations at La Perouse near Botany Bay and at Pennant Hills had long-range coverage of the Pacific Ocean for receiving and transmission.] However, many researchers insist that the Q signal had been sent only to the emergency station at Geraldton Radio VIN, but if it was monitored there on such a low frequency as 500kcs (wavelength 600m), by contacting this particular emergency station, Detmers was certainly not going to inform the world of the *Straat Malakka*'s predicament.

The inquiry had also thought that Navy Office Decode (NODECO) shown below, had been received on 27 November (the same day *Aquitania* announced the rescue of German survivors) by Geraldton Radio in the form of **QQQ *Straat Malakka* 111°E, 26°S, 1000 GMT,** or alternatively in the easily translated (numerated) coordinates AAAE, BFS. But what is most intriguing is that this same emergency Q signal had been detected by the tug *Uco* at approx 1803H and again at 1805H on 19 November. Unfortunately, however, the signals were unable to be read. This is most perplexing because in the first instance, Detmers and others had maintained that the message had been delivered only once in the above format, but radio operators Ernst Pachmann and Hans Linke said the message was sent out twice. Linke went even further when interrogated on 8 December 1941, and said both messages included the position 111°E, 26°S, although at the time he was bound to comply with the story his officers gave **(NAA B6121, 164M)**. Secondly, the NODECO message also states that Geraldton picked the Q signal in part, but with more precise coordinates and in a different form (see previous chapter for full meaning).

Providing the *NODECO message has been deciphered accurately, it can be concluded that the emergency QQQ signal had been initially sent from the raider in high frequency to the Perth station in Applecross at 1803H, indicating an approximate position. Besides, in this case it was not necessary to quote them more accurately in terms of the nearest mile because Detmers had now been resigned to his likely fate at the hands of the cruiser. An approximate position would have thus sufficed. Then, two minutes later, a Q signal to Geraldton pinpointing the coordinates of where the so-called enemy cruiser had been sighted – this, to the nearest nautical mile. It was wireless-operator Hans Linke who evidenced that the Q signal was to emphasise the vessel was the real *Straat Malakka.* He also described the simple position for the Q signal, presumably in medium frequency that was 'intended to be picked up in the Dutch East Indies' (and hence relayed to the British in Singapore). See below for the decrypted message.

*NODECO (Navy Office Decoding): Coastal and HF radio stations also sent messages to the Navy Office in this format.

IMPORTANT. NODECO-IMPORTANT-OPERATIONAL- S E C R E T .

2.53 27/11.

FOLLOWING NOW REPORTED.

ON 19/11 at 1000Z TUG. U.C.O. IN POSITION 2645S 11320E HEARD FAINT SIGNAL QQ REPEAT QQ REMAINDER UNINTELLIGIBLE AND AT 1005Z QQQQ REP AT QQQQ AND UNINTELLIGIBLE GROUP OF FIGURES BADLY MADE POSSIBLY CONTAINING FIGURES 110 FOLLOWED BY 1000 G.M.T. (H) I.C.W. NOTE STRENGTH 526 ESTIMATED BY OPERATOR WITHIN 300 MILES. GERALDTON RADIO REPORTS THAT AT 1005Z 19/11 THEY RECEIVED WEAK MESSAGE STRENGTH 2 BEGINS XXX UNINTELLIGIBLE THEN 7C 11115E 1000 G.M.T. ENDS. COULD NOT ESTIMATE DISTANCE. NO Q'S. DISTINGUISHED WAITED TWO MINUTES NO REPETITION. AT 1015Z 19/11 GERALDTON SENT OUT MESSAGE TO SHIPS ASKING IF ANYTHING TO REPORT BUT RECEIVED NO REPLY.

Distribution:

NAA B6121, 165P

In some respects, the 1945 Action Report makes sense in that the cruiser's engines were stopped, but to do so she would have found it most difficult to steer in Force 3 or 4 winds. Rather than stop completely, she had slowed from 12 knots to just gain headway. Suddenly, and due to the SE wind, which blew away from the raider, her engine noise could not be heard from a distance of 3,000 yards. It was as though her engines were stopped altogether. In any case and unknown to his crew, Detmers had been acutely aware that the Admiralty required confirmation that if his vessel was suspected to be an enemy ship, boarding the vessel was now the only sure means of identifying it, as well as its purpose for being there.

Again, the maximum effectiveness of every gun also meant that each hidden 150mm gun capable of firing to the starboard side should be trained in the same direction, otherwise each gun commander would be required to search for the target at the point of de-camouflage. Detmers or Gunnery Officer Skeries could only have given this order in advance, as described by Hermann Ortmann and Edmund Buttner.

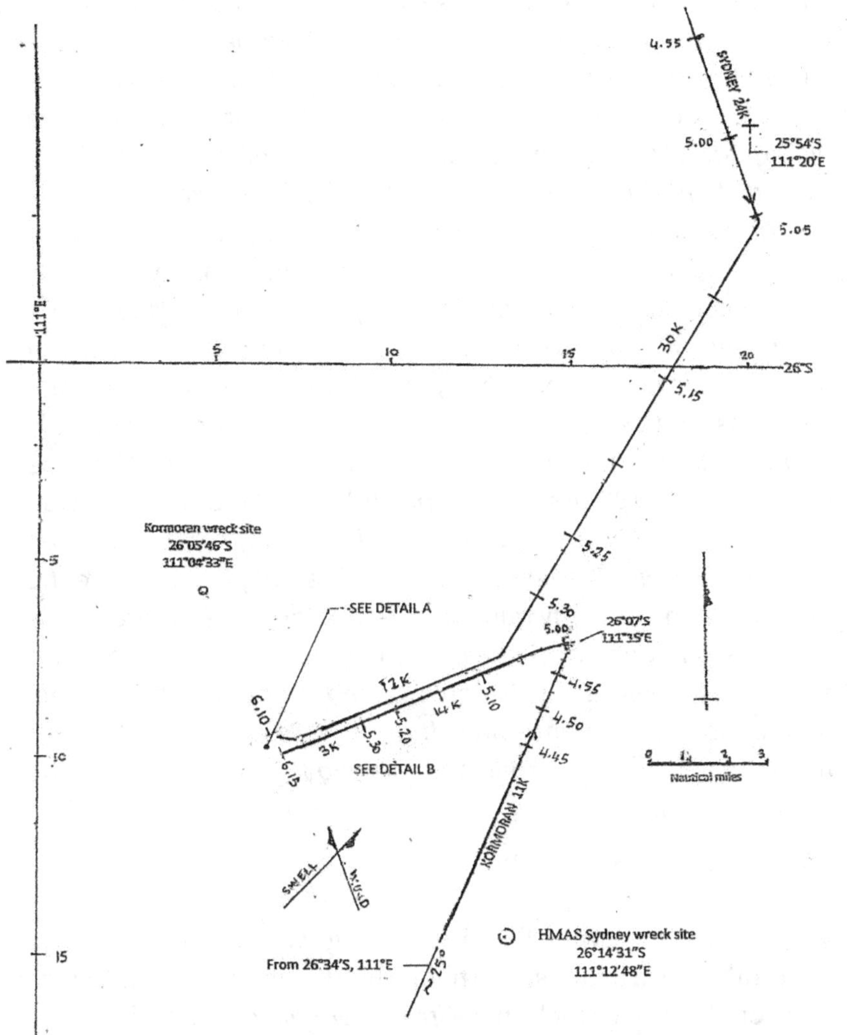

The Interception and Route to Battle Site

[Clock times indicated are WST (H hours)]

At just 3 knots along course 250°, the raider had to contend with the sea conditions to keep on track due to the SSE wind and SW swell acting on her port side. The site of the action is therefore most likely to have been located marginally north of her intended course.

*'The enemy had changed course a *point or two to starboard so that the cruiser's silhouette became a little broader... But at the same time she morsed, Give me your secret call! We had been expecting some such signal for about an hour...of course, we did not know the secret call sign...so much time had now been gained [fumbling with the signal flags] that she was broadside on and sailing a course parallel to that of the Kormoran at a reduced speed. The range was only one thousand yards now and we could see the cruiser's pantry-men in their white coats lining the rails to have a look at the supposed Dutchman... I needed no more time. My eyes were glued to the bearings compass, and as soon as I saw the enemy had come practically to a standstill I gave the order [to] de-camouflage!. The time was exactly 17.30 hours [6.30pm WST]. The Dutch flag was hauled down and the German naval war flag ran up...and as soon as my Chief Signalman reported War flag flying, I gave the order to open fire to my gunners and the torpedo batteries. The ship's rails folded down, the heavy camouflage covers fore and aft were whisked away, Hatches 2 and 4 opened up to reveal their guns, the 2cm anti-aircraft guns were raised, the torpedo flaps opened and all barrels and torpedo tubes swung on to the target' (p142).*

*One point = 11°15' (11.25°).

Again, Detmers was far from being well-acquainted with Admiralty instructions, particularly if she was a call-sign-registered ship (which the *Straat Malakka* was). Thus, to suggest the secret call was requested in Morse from the cruiser at only 1,000yds, the proposition has no validity whatsoever.

The account of those on deck of the raider, however, is seemingly accurate. According to an ex-crewman, who had parted company with the cruiser prior to this last voyage, the chief petty officer cooks on duty at the time were the only persons on board exempt from action stations. This being the case, either

Thomas Carey or Walter Schache had been the pantry-men who had taken a stroll on deck to view the supposed Dutch ship that had submitted to the cruiser. And while the cruiser's guns were directed at the raider there may have been one or more cooks peering at the vessel from the rails. And even though the AA guns were not manned, some of those persons so assigned would have been required to make preparations for boarding the raider.

Detmers had observed that the cruiser had virtually come to a standstill, his bearings compass showed his vessel was now slightly ahead, but more importantly his book had finally placated a number of his officers and crew by implying that the raider was making slow headway at the time (both ships had been parallel shortly beforehand). And by stating the cruiser had been sailing at 'a reduced speed' (on which he did not elaborate), he felt safe to use this term owing to her previous moderate to high speed.

The result was that the inquiry had mistakenly surmised that because both vessels were said to be moving at 14 knots and that the bearings compass was constant, both vessels had been travelling at that same speed, which is now shown to have been discredited by many crewmen, including Detmers's aide de camp, Heinz Messerschmidt. Besides, Detmers had admitted beforehand that the cruiser had been sailing parallel with the raider only 1,000yds away. Therefore, she must have been nearly opposite, albeit at a reduced speed. But his bearings compass would have been constant, meaning both vessels had been sailing at the same speed. Likewise, it did not occur to the inquiry that if the bearings compass was constant and regardless of the speed, then both vessels were moving at the same rate, or had stopped altogether.

'Within six seconds...the first shot was fired from our leading gun. Four seconds later the other three went into action,

scoring hits on the enemy's bridge and in his artillery control post. Immediately afterwards the enemy opened fire, too, with a full salvo. But it roared away harmlessly over us...Then we fired eight salvoes, with six seconds between each salvo, without any answering fire at all from the enemy...every shell we fired was a direct hit...our anti-aircraft guns peppered the upper deck and his torpedo batteries, and our army 3.7 anti-aircraft gun pumped shells into his bridge. Our own torpedoes were now discharged at the enemy, and to do so I had to turn to 260°...in order not to disturb our gunners. One of the first two torpedoes passed across the cruiser's bows, but the other hit her abaft Turret A. An enormous column of water shot into the air and her stern dipped into the water up to the flagstaff...Turrets C and D began to fire independently...D fired two or three salvoes...after that it ceased firing altogether. But Turret C... ripped through our funnel...but its next hit us amidships and set our engine-room on fire. Our own guns were continuing to fire rapidly...A motor cutter was hanging...over the side, the heavy turret deck of Turret B had been ...hurled overboard...The plane...on the catapult had been blown into the sea. Not a man could show his face, because of the fire of our machine guns, whilst our 3.7cm gun continued to pump shells into the bridge...Not a torpedo was fired at us.' (p143)

Hermann Ortmann on no. 4 gun and others have already explained the sequence of fire from the guns and the underwater torpedo launched well in advance of his declaration. In doing so, the raider had turned approximately 25° to port to fire off the underwater torpedo, as well as aligning all main guns on the target, which had been pre-aimed abeam when sailing parallel with the cruiser (course 250°). After firing the torpedo, the raider had turned slowly to starboard 260° on a slightly converging course with the cruiser. This manoeuvre Detmers considered essential for it enabled all starboard 150mm guns, in particular gun no. 3, which was soon to be blinded by the main superstructure, to now target the stationary cruiser for a much longer period than had he kept to his original course of 250° (see the layout of the raider's guns, below). And when the torpedo hit home destroying A and B turrets, the guns opened up, obliterating the cruiser's gunnery control centre and making it impossible for the immediate return of accurate fire from C and D turrets, causing them to be switched to local (individual) control. Shells from these turrets hit the raider several times, however, Turret C managed to hit the engine-room. The raider's manoeuvre to port and thence to starboard presented Detmers with a two-fold motive, as follows:

Firstly, such a manoeuvre to port 225° allowed for his straight-running torpedo from the underwater tube fixed at 35° abaft the beam to strike at 80°, as shown in Detail A below.

Secondly, by then returning to starboard 260° it enabled his 150mm guns to strike the port side of the cruiser also at an angle of 80°, the cruiser then being positioned directly in front of the raider, as evidenced by Edmund Buttner on no. 3 gun and Ernst Hildenbrand on no. 5 gun **(TRAN.010.0001_R, TRAN.006.0042_R)**. They both told of how the guns were given the elevation and angle via telephone to the respective gun commanders beforehand, well before the camouflage had been removed. A further slow manoeuvre to starboard 260° was executed so as not to upset the aiming of the guns as the raider slowly moved away. Thereafter, those aiming the guns at the target could do so with minimal movement.

Note: In his book (*Der Hilfskreuzer de die Sydney versenkte*) Detmers states that the two above-water torpedoes had been delivered by the 'steam out' method, which is dependent upon the speed of the attacker, regardless of the enemy's speed. In that respect, the same applies to the underwater torpedo in the case where both vessels are considered to be stationary.

Amongst Detmers's orders for raider activity there existed: **'Armed clashes with enemy forces or auxiliary ships are to be avoided. If, however, an encounter is unavoidable, every attempt to destroy the enemy by means of camouflage** [and] **by unexpected use of all weapons, should be made' (NAA B6121, 164N).** Hence, the secret underwater torpedo delivered accurately was to define the outcome of the battle.

Detmers was never going to give his enemy the advantage by either raising the battle flag or by de-camouflaging his weapons before the underwater torpedo had been due to hit. To do so would have made it so evident to the extent that the cruiser may have suddenly opened fire, possibly hitting the mine deck and obliterating the vessel. On the other hand, the process of de-camouflaging would not be perceptible from a distance of 900 metres or so.

Finally, it was Hans Linke who had succinctly put his case when he discussed the fixed underwater torpedo with journalist David Kennedy: 'You must turn the ship' [to align the target]. He further added, 'We had the ship in the position we needed to aim for and we discussed this [while] in captivity' **(PTE.006.0196)**. Likewise, the raider had turned back onto a bearing of 260°, the guns being pre-aimed on the starboard beam (Green 90°). In this case, the shells had struck at an inclination of 80°. [The angle of inclination is measured from the bow of the cruiser.]

'The enemy cruiser now turned towards us and passed behind our stern. It looked almost as though she was trying to ram us...and she no longer had any [capable] speed. I thought perhaps she was turning in order to bring her starboard tubes into action...But no torpedoes were discharged. As the battered cruiser came behind our stern she enjoyed a short respite...our forward guns were temporarily unsighted...for a while we had only two guns in action [Nos 5 and 6]. I kept to my course

[260°] in order to show the narrowest possible silhouette..., but [no torpedoes] came. A lot of smoke was now drifting...to starboard from the fire in the engine-room...He [gunnery officer Skeries] continued to direct fire...but he was getting no counter fire...and all the enemy's turrets seemed out of action, and their gun barrels were pointing helplessly away [to port]. The crews of our guns, 1, 3 and 4 used this enforced pause to cool down their barrels...But it was only a short pause and then all four guns were in action...guns Nos. 2, 3, 4 and 6. Guns Nos. 1 and 5 were now in our firing lee...'

Although hampered by a gaping hole caused by the torpedo strike on the port side approximately 20m from the bow, by then containing about 1,000 tonnes of seawater, the cruiser was able to gain 'fair' speed, according to Ernst Hildenbrand when interrogated **(NAA B6121, 164M)**. Besides, the only avenue of escape for the cruiser without sustaining even further damage from the raider's penetrating 150mm shellfire was to depart from the battle scene as quickly as possible and in a direction showing the narrowest of silhouettes.

With the bridge wiped out, second-in-charge CMDR Edmund Thruston in the after-control steering (his permanent action station), turned the cruiser sharply to port and within a few minutes had crossed the wake of the raider at a decent average speed of some 10 knots in an easterly direction that would present a narrow silhouette to the raider's aft no. 5 and no. 6 guns (nos. 1, 2, 3 and 4 were then in the firing lee).

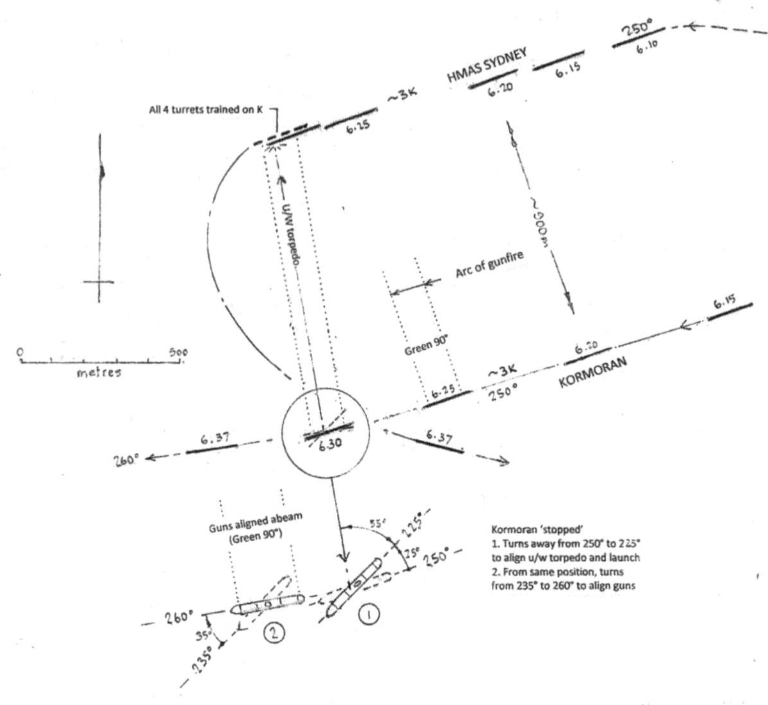

The Initial Assault (Detail 'A')

[All times showing the relative positions of the ships have been converted to WST (H hours)]

Having adopted this route and with the *Sydney* down by the bows it was short-lived owing to the incessant swell from the SW, which of course submersed the fore part of the ship even further with the added danger of her foundering or rolling over. A much safer course was therefore called for, which involved turning the ship to starboard into the wind to largely negate the constant swell, but she was soon exposed to further portside shellfire from guns Nos. 2, 3, 4 and 6 after the raider had turned to 240°. In the meantime, the cruiser had maintained her speed out to a distance of some *2.16nm (4,000m) from the raider.

Note: *The distance between the vessels had increased rapidly due to the raider going away in the opposite direction.

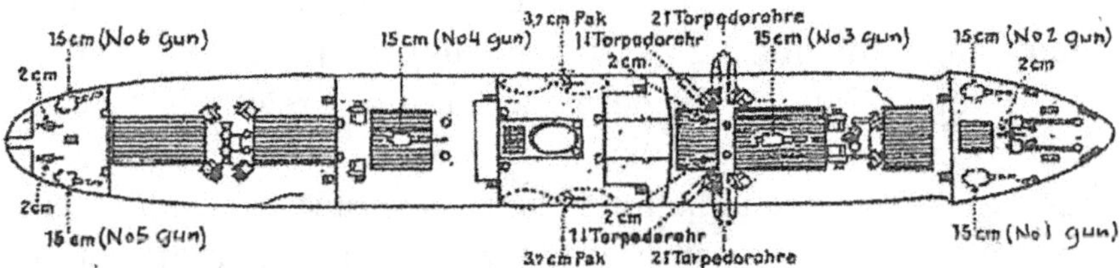

***Kormoran*'s Armament**

Nearly eight minutes later, the action reports showed the cruiser going south into the wind and slowing at a range of 3.24nm (6,000m) at an average speed of approx 8 knots. She had reduced her speed due to the intense strain levied on the keel from the damaged bow as she ploughed into the seas.

'At about 1800 hours [ARs quote 1745 (6.45pm WST)] I wanted to turn to port [240°] to run parallel with the enemy and finally destroy her...[but] the engine-room telegraph reported that the revolutions of both machines [two of four diesel engines] and contact with the engine-room had been broken. At that moment I saw the wake of four torpedoes discharged at us... made no changes to my course and they disappeared behind us. Immediately they had passed the whole ship shuddered from stem to stern owing to the failure of our engines....' (p 144)

From the moment the cruiser had turned sharply to port, the cruiser's C and D aft turrets had been silent with all guns now pointing away to port. And that only two of the raider's four engines had been operating, we finally learn from Detmers that she could only travel at a maximum rate of approx. 10 knots. He still held the upper hand with the vessel's gunnery at such a close range, there being no return fire from the cruiser. The raider had made no more than 5 knots in order to minimise the ever-increasing distance between the ships while not overly upsetting the gunnery. [3 engines = 11–14 knots, 4 engines = 15–18 knots]

Detmers had been unable to target the cruiser with his four guns while on course 260°. But to suggest in his book that at 1800 hours (7pm WST) he made the turn to 240° is akin to his vessel widening the distance for some 30 minutes whilst just two guns were in action against the cruiser, is contrary to reason and common sense. It is for this reason that the action reports nominate that the raider had turned to 240° as soon as practicable, no later than 1745G (6:45pm WST). Detmers could not otherwise have made use of his four port guns.

Having already been unable to cope with such a sustained speed as 5 knots due to the fire in the engine-room, at a distance of 3.78nm (7,000m) there had been a further reduction in average speed of the cruiser to 4 knots (approx 4.65K against the current in 19K winds) – this, compared to 5 knots as quoted by Detmers in his book and in the action reports.

One would have expected some embellishment in Detmers's book and in the action reports, and in this respect the statement that 'four torpedoes [were] discharged at us' is no exception. After all, the Germans were the only survivors of the battle and what they said is difficult to disprove. However, the underwater images showing the cruiser's starboard battery of four torpedoes consist of two in the four-bank torpedo battery, plus two in the debris field. On the other hand, only two torpedoes are shown in the port battery – the other two are not accounted for. But because Detmers had forgotten his earlier statement (it is not in his book) when he claimed (in Carnarvon) that two torpedoes were fired at the raider, these must represent the two that cannot be found and therefore if the Secretary of the Naval Board has correctly interpreted what Detmers meant, these torpedoes were obviously from the cruiser's port torpedo battery that were launched sometime during the initial phase of the action and before the cruiser had turned to port.

DEPARTMENT OF DEFENCE CO-ORDINATION.

Copy of OUTWARDS Teleprinter Message.

MOST SECRET

To: SECRETARY, DEPARTMENT OF THE NAVY

From: SECRETARY, NAVAL BOARD.

Date 23/11/41. Time of Despatch 1115 Hours No. M.2801

MOST SECRET. My M2799

Following for His Excellency the Governor-General, the Prime Minister, the Minister for the Navy, and Mr. Shedden.

The raider Captain confirms the previous reports with the addition that the action took place in latitude 26°, longitude 111°. He states that "SYDNEY'S" two torpedoes missed. The raider's torpedo hit forward and the salvo hit "SYDNEY" amidships. "SYDNEY" was badly on fire.

***Sydney*'s two torpedoes missed (NAA B6121, 165P)**

Wireless operator Hans Linke came out in support in his interview with David Kennedy: 'We found ourselves between two torpedoes. One passed in front [of the raider] and the other behind. We were in the middle, we were lucky' **(PTE.006.0196).**

Detmers recounts: *'In the meantime, our guns were keeping up their devastating fire...From the fore bridge to the stern mast the cruiser was now a mass of flame and she was moving forward only very slowly...so we sent a torpedo after her at about 8,000 yards, but it passed harmlessly behind her stern. At 18.25 hours [7:25pm WST] I gave the order to cease fire. By this time, the cruiser was over ten thousand yards distant; drifting rather than sailing...It was growing dark rapidly now, and she was gradually faded into the darkness, apparently making for Perth. Up until 21.00 hours [10:00pm WST] we could see the glow and then we saw the flames dart up even higher as though from an explosion... My aim now was to lower and launch as many of our boats as were still serviceable...Amidships the Kormoran was well alight...I opened the midships door into the engine-room, but billows of thick smoke rolled out and darting flames shot up...I got the door closed again...I was informed that the fire-fighting equipment in the engine-room had apparently been destroyed and that the whole starboard foam equipment was also out of action...There was no pressure in the damaged pipes...we concentrated on rescuing our comrades [in the engine-room], but unfortunately everything we tried failed.' (p 145)*

A torpedo fired from this distance (8,000yds) took at least six minutes running time for a 40-knot G7a torpedo. But Detmers insisted his underwater tubes were equipped with an older WW1 version, namely the 29-knot G7v, which (if used) was to cover the distance in nearly eight and a half minutes. Thus, due to the lead time necessary in both cases and regardless of the speeds shown, the inclinations stated in the action reports (80 and 110 deg) could not have been achieved by him in the forlorn hope of torpedoing the cruiser.

Unlike the action reports, Detmers's book fails to give an account of the distance between the ships after 7:25pm WST. He does, however, explain that between the hours of 6:50pm and 7:25pm, the cruiser was last seen at a distance of 9,000m (~10,000yds), meaning the *Sydney* had experienced a further reduction of speed from 5 knots to an average of approximately 2 knots (about 2.65K against the current) for that period.

The last separation distance of 160Hm (16,000m) from 7:25pm to just before 10:00pm recorded in the action reports showed the *Sydney* making very slow progress at an average speed of approx. 1.5 knots for that portion of time. Thereafter, a course of approx 150° (as witnessed by Detmers) would have been deemed appropriate to reach either Geraldton or Fremantle ports, or to the coordinates of where the cruiser sank to the seabed at 26°14'31"S, 111°12'48"E (see Detail B below).

The distances between the ships during each period gives a clear indication of the *Sydney* sailing at a progessively slower rate. She had lost her initial speed to the point where she could barely manage just over one knot (barely 2 knots against the current) by 10:00pm WST.

The action reports also describe the large fire on board the *Sydney* as having been visible until about 2200 hours (11:00pm WST), indicating that the fire had yet to be *quelled.

*Due to the fact that the cruiser was heading into the wind (which had increased in intensity), the fire was sure to have spread lengthwise below-decks and throughout the superstructure of the ship.

'...I had to make up my mind to sink the gallant Kormoran. Once I had taken this decision my only job was to save as many men as I could...I told off a party to watch the mine deck and report to me currently on the state of the temperature there. I hoped to have a few hours before the fire came too close to the mines to allow anyone to remain on board. Another point was that as long as the ship was still afloat in case another enemy happened to come up with us, perhaps attracted by the light of the flames...I didn't know whether the enemy had succeeded in sending off a wireless signal, though we had certainly heard nothing.' (p146)

*'Two motor-boats and a cutter were too damaged to float, and only one cutter was still seaworthy. But on deck there were four boats in which the crews of various [captured] ships had come aboard, and fortunately they had not been damaged. And in addition, there were four inflatable rubber dinghies and a number of small rescue rafts...All our rescue boats were now launched and manned. The wind had risen and was now blowing at *Force 5 or 6. The boats were straining at the lines...and the first rubber dinghy we had manned [carrying mostly wounded men] tore itself away and floated off into the darkness and [reportedly] capsized with the loss of 40 men...'*

*Force 5 (Beaufort scale) = 17–21k (29–38kph), Force 6 = 22–27k (39–49kph)

After having made a decision to scuttle the ship and save as many crew as possible, Detmers gave orders to his XO (CMDR Foerster) to lower all *boats and life-saving equipment that was on hand. Engineer Lensch and his assistant Fritz Noll reported it was impossible to get through to the engine-room (situated below the mine deck), which Detmers had personally inspected. The fire in there had been continually under suveillance.

*In this instance, the 'boats' referred to the three large inflatable rubber rafts, one of which capsized and was lost in over-turning with the wounded. Of the other two, which contained 25 and 26 ordinary crew (no officers), they were picked up some four days later by the British ships *Aquitania* and *Trocas* on 23 November. Of all the lifeboats, the rubber rafts were first to leave the striken *Kormoran*.

According to Detmers, no wireless signal from the cruiser had been detected by the raider, but considering the many frequencies that were required to be monitored he could not be sure that every frequency had been overheard. It must be remembered, however, that as C-in-C China had sent the cruiser to investigate a suspicious vessel, it follows that wireless contact with the *Sydney* had been essential to this exclusive Royal Navy operation.

Detmers revealed there were four lifeboats available that were undamaged. But his book and the action reports state that at approximately 2100 hours (10:00pm WST) some crewmen (134 in total) had left the raider in three lifeboats, two of which were under the command of Petty Officer Paul Kohn and Navigator Henri Meyer, had made it to the coast about 50 and 70 miles north of Carnarvon, respectively. One smaller boat containing 31 survivors under Petty Officer Hans Kuhl had been rescued by the State ship *Koolinda.* He had thus failed to account for the fourth lifeboat, which presumably he may have mistakenly counted, or that for some reason it was too risky to launch from the raider's deck.

Note: Meyer's lifeboat is suspected to have departed from the *Kormoran* at 2116G (cryptogram).

'At 2100 hours [10pm WST] the boats put off...and 120 men and almost all my officers assembled for the last time on board... There were two boats available for them in hatch no. 1... The derrick proved to be unusable and the boats had to be hauled out manually with rope and tackle...and at 2330 they were both safely launched, and the first of them pulled away. My fire-watching group reported that matters were rapidly getting worse on the mine deck...my explosives officer placing his charges by one of the oil bunkers...I gave the order to abandon ship, took charge of our war flag, and was last to leave my ship. It was just midnight. There were 62 men in my boat and only three oars...At 0010 hours [1:10am WST] precisely the explosive charges went up whilst we were still under her bows but on the lee side from the charge so that we came to no harm. I had four men pulling and pushing on each oar...to get as far away as we could before the mines went up. At 0035 [1:35am WST] there was a tremendous explosion and the whole stern and midships of the vessel turned into one gigantic sheet of flame...And a little after that a shower of small debris fell all around us...the Kormoran lifted her bows into the air and slipped back under the surface.' (p147)

The three lifeboats (with Kuhl, Kohn and Meyer in charge) had departed, leaving Detmers, the remaining officers and crewmen to save themselves by winching the two boats from the hatch before launching them, provisioning them, manning them and casting off, all within a period of two and a half hours. The first boat, commanded by Nazi officer von Gosseln, pulled away before the explosives had been set at approximately 2330G (12:30am 20 November, WST). Then Detmers's boat (supplied with only three oars) narrowly escaped being blown up just after midnight (G time), but fortunately his boat was on the lee side of the explosive charges.

The observations made in view of the restricted parameters of the action in Detmers's book and in conjunction with the action reports, have all the essential elements of the German story. But to even suggest that the raider ignored the ultimatum to stop is a falsity in the extreme. For 80 years, ignorance is not a defence, and we have constantly heard that very same story of both ships gradually closing at speed over a period of one and a half hours. But the fact that the *Kormoran* had sailed through coordinates 26°34'S, 111°E on her track to Shark Bay has been completely overlooked by the Commission of Inquiry, whose brief was to examine the evidence and not to accept carte blanche the words of Eldridge and Gill. And as to whether it was meant to be a long chase for an hour and a half, or a deliberate attempt to clear Detmers and level the blame at Burnett for his so-called carelessness in approaching the raider, the reader can adjudge accordingly.

Overall, the cruiser's ever-increasing distances from the raider in the given times means that the *Sydney* had slowed considerably, and given that she was visible to the Germans from the raider at approximately 2200G (11pm WST) while on course 150° and 9.7nm distant, she had ostensibly succumbed at the wreck site while drifting without power at approximately 1:00am on 20 November. [Some survivors gave evidence that they had last seen the cruiser at 2300G (12 midnight WST)]

NATSAR stipulate that no known floatable object follows the path of the wind, but large modern ships, such as commercial fishing vessels and coastal freighters, can diverge up to 48° left or right of the wind direction when drifting. Then what of the *Kormoran*'s pattern of drift?

This vessel had been recently re-supplied by the *Kulmerland* with fuel and other items, enough for at least six months' sailing, but in addition it carried heavy armaments in the form of shells, torpedoes and some 400 magnetic and anchor mines. As this load was not evenly distributed throughout the ship, search and rescue values for this type of ship (angle of divergence and leeway speed multiplier) are largely unknown.

However, compared to a modern coastal freighter stacked with containers, again, using the NATSAR formula previously specified, the added leeway speed in the diagram below, for winds of 18 knots during the 6.6 hours she remained afloat and for the distance of 4.7nm to the wreck site, the value of m (multiplier) for the wreckage type for the *Kormoran* is designated thus:

$$\text{Wind 18 (knots)} = \frac{\text{4.7nm (distance)}}{\text{6.6 (hours) } [0.036 + m]}$$

$$\text{i.e., } 4.276 + 118.8m = 4.700 \quad m = \frac{0.424}{118.8} = 0.003569$$

From the above result, it is apparent that the additional multiplier had little effect on the drift rate per hour on the raider, for she had drifted in 18-knot winds, marginally in excess of the value (18x0.036 = 0.648K/hr), to finally drift at a rate of 0.72K/hr (18x0.04), as shown in the NATSAR equation above.

There are obvious reasons for this, as exampled in the leeway chart for container ships. They have a multiplier of at least 0.028, but they are subjected to a lot more wind drift because they possess a much higher profile than a raider or any vessel of the 1940s vintage. Moreover, due to the extreme loads they carried as supply ships for U-boats, the raider had been hampered in its drift by the sheer weight of munitions on board. But more to the point, the fact that she carried hundreds of tons of mines situated towards the aft of the vessel had been the most telling factor, compared with the more evenly loaded container ship, which NATSAR specifies can drift at the widest angle of divergence.

Similarly, as HMAS *Sydney* has a lower profile than even the *Kormoran*, this ship is, however, regarded as uniformly loaded with munitions. As a result, the cruiser should not have gone much beyond the 3.6% limit of wind current drift, and by using the NATSAR formula above for a drift distance of 1.6nm for a duration of, say, two hours (as shown), we find that m = 0.0084 (more than twice that of the raider), which defines that particular type of wreckage. In this case, it is estimated that the angle of divergence is comparable with that of the raider, both of which had drifted roughly 24° to the right of the wind direction.

Rae Baynton further corroborates the time the *Sydney* sank:

While on duty at the switchboard at the Postmaster General's Office in Perth, she explained that on the night of 19 November 1941 she received a phone call from Geraldton PMG shortly before midnight (WST) indicating that HMAS *Sydney* was heading there after being badly shot up. If this was the case and her memory of this event is clear, no such record exists with the PMG at Perth or at Geraldton, both of which purportedly received the message but has obviously failed to release it. Nevertheless, Baynton's evidence supports the fact that the *Sydney* had drifted to and had sunk at the known position (26°14'31"S, 111°12'48"E) in the early hours of 20 November.

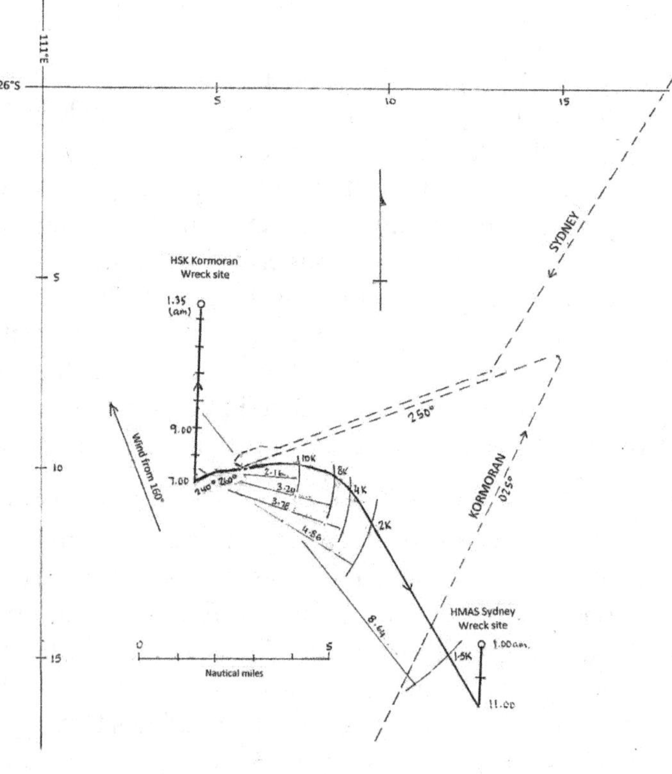

Detail 'B'

Note: The *Sydney*'s *total speed into the wind slows considerably the further the distance from the raider. [Times shown have been converted to WST (H hours)]

*For total speed, add 0.036 x 18 = 0.65K (wind current component in 18-knot winds)

Should Detmers have underestimated the direction of travel by the *Sydney* by a few degrees, then the cruiser would still have drifted to its known sinking position sometime in the early hours of the following day. In fact, the Royal Navy contend that the *Sydney* sank on the 20th, whereas the Royal Australian Navy subscribe to 19th November on their monuments of remembrance.

Another sure example offered by Detmers at approx. 7:25pm (WST) was the relative bearing of the cruiser at the time the raider was in the process of drifting. He estimated the bearing had been 225°, which demonstrates that a line drawn through the position of the ships at the time (180°) indicates that the raider had been positioned somewhat side-on to the angle of drift and that the bow faced in a north-westerly direction. Thereafter, the *Kormoran* had drifted northerly to the wreck site.

The real fallacy that Detmers had always portrayed has been the long-drawn-out sea chase of more than 20 miles, wherein the *Kormoran*, after being ordered to stop or slow down, had continued on at an undiminished speed until the ships were nearly opposite and thereby had torpedoed the *Sydney* from its starboard twin above-water tubes while at speed. This story, endorsed by the Commission of Inquiry, is demonstrably false in view of the confined parameters of the battle site. And that after it was realised, he had purportedly torpedoed the *Sydney* at 14–15 knots, Detmers had absolutely no further reason to blatantly mislead on any other aspects of the action. This is a measure of the inquiry's belief in the portrayal of his story; in fact, it was a tale of deceiving the naval authorities.

It had not been until all the distances between the *Sydney* and *Kormoran* have been assembled, has it been possible to piece together the final moments of both ships. But what is clear is that Detmers's book in company with the German action reports give a meaningful exposé on the interception, the action and most importantly the timing and sinking of both vessels, information that had already been made available to the Commission of Inquiry.

In many instances, the observations made by Detmers in his book have been cast by many researchers as invalid to the point of accusing him of wilfully presenting false information aimed at misleading the general public. On the contrary, his writings, whether they be from his book or from the action reports can be easily followed, showing an obvious decrease in the speed of the cruiser before it sunk to the seabed in waters over 2,000 metres deep.

❑ ❑ ❑

PRISONERS

Detmers and 62 other men left the stricken vessel in the last lifeboat to depart from the *Kormoran*. Administration officer Bretschneider, whose boat had been probably launched at 2116G with Meyer at the helm, had been 3–4,000 metres away when the mines blew up, which fits with the drift expected over a period of three hours. Lizt, in his diary of the voyage to the coast with Meyer, records that he met with von Gosseln's and Bunjes's boat early the next morning (20 November) before setting course towards the coast in a north-east direction. Kuhl's boat was not there and nor was Kohn's. Both had gone their separate ways.

Detmers recalled that they rowed throughout the night of 20 November as it was easy for the two boats to sail east to the coast because the night was cloudless and the stars were bright for navigation. In the morning, they inspected the sails, which had been made useless by the tropical sun, but blankets had been put into each boat and were hastily made into sails. Despite the high winds, the *iron lifeboats did not leak, but took in seawater over the gunwales.

*In those days, lifeboats were often sheathed in metal – usually steel or copper-alloy.

For the next few days, Detmers goes on to describe the lack of freeboard and the privations aboard his overcrowded lifeboat while sailing slowly towards land. The weather was hot and the water for drinking was running low, but he knew gradually the monotony and misery would corrode the morale of his men.

On Sunday, 23 November, they sighted the large British four-funnelled *Aquitania* about 5 miles away which, unbeknown to him, had earlier rescued 26 survivors from one of the two large rubber rafts. Detmers had identified her as an auxiliary cruiser because of the armament she carried, but his dehydrated crewmen wanted to attract the attention of the ex-liner by firing rocket signals. This he forbade in favour of hoping to be rescued by a neutral steamer and since now that his lifeboat was closer to the coast, there was the possibility of rescue where the shipping lanes merged. An aeroplane (piloted by FLT Rooke) appeared on Tuesday and where it circled distant northwards were the words on a sail: 'No Water'. It was the lifeboat commanded by von Gosseln that had departed from the *Kormoran* for the coast at about 2330G on 19 November.

Again, on Wednesday morning, a plane was sighted, but disappeared towards the coast, and as it became dark a ship was spotted so they fired red rockets into the air on account of their lack of drinking water. It was the ship MV *Centaur* (later to be sunk by I-177 after conversion to a hospital ship in 1943) commanded by CAPT Dark. He demanded that only the injured seamen could come aboard for fear that the Germans might take over his ship. Dark then ordered that two of his lifeboats be lowered and took them in tow to Carnarvon on the night of 26 November (see below). However, while on the way there the boats got flooded and afterwards the towrope parted.

MV *Centaur*

Rescue by MV *Centaur* (sunken German lifeboat behind)
Australian War Memorial

Detmers had often wondered about how the lifeboats and crew had fared in their quest for safety, whether they had managed to reach shore, whether they had been fortunate enough to be towed by a steamer, or whether they might still be adrift. And in considering their likely predicament, he would, at the earliest opportunity, give the position of the engagement so that a rescue could be mounted.

He was also concerned about the fate of the cruiser that had been shelled many times, but he was worried that she might have stayed afloat. If so, what would they have said about his conduct during the engagement? Such disquiet could easily lead to a court martial, he thought. This anxiety he could do without.

On the evening of 27 November, Detmers was ordered from his lifeboat to board the *Centaur*, which had arrived in Carnarvon Harbour alongside the long pier, meeting with the nine men the ship had originally taken aboard. Accompanied by his Number One (LEUT Foerster) and LCDR Rycroft from SWACH, he asked about the whereabouts of the *Sydney.* Rycroft replied she had been overdue in Fremantle, so after learning that the cruiser had not reached port, he surmised it had been sunk. Detmers next told Rycroft the position of the engagement had been at *111°E and 26°34'S. He had thus given a good starting point for the rescue of possible survivors from both vessels.

*The wind direction and current had changed from the south-east to west from 19 to 27 November (BOM). Nevertheless, he had given the position in good faith, the raider having crossed 111°E at the abovesaid latitude at approx. 1300G, albeit some 25nm south of the battle site. Again, the position of the *Kormoran* on its journey to Shark Bay is emphasised.

Meanwhile, Kohn's lifeboat had come ashore near Quobba station approx. 50 miles north of Carnarvon on the afternoon of 24 November and the next day Meyer's boat, about 20 miles further north, landed in the morning at Red Bluff on the coast. These two groups (103 crewmen) were put on trucks that took them to Carnarvon gaol where they were interrogated by naval officers from Perth.

Unknown to Detmers, a raft with 26 men on board had been rescued by the tanker *Trocas* while en route to Fremantle from Sumatra on the afternoon of 23 November, the same day as the *Aquitania* made its rescue. In addition, Kuhl's lifeboat containing 31 survivors had been picked up by the State ship *Koolinda* late in the afternoon of 26 November while en route to Fremantle and von Gosseln's overcrowded lifeboat (72 survivors) had been rescued by the patrol vessel HMAS *Yandra* at midday on 27 November and taken to Carnarvon.

MV *Koolinda*

HMAS *Yandra*

In all, out of a total of 398 men, 319 had been accounted for, including those 103 that landed on shore north of Carnarvon and the 62 crewmen in the boat commanded by Detmers. Except for the 26 taken to Sydney by the *Aquitania*, they were to find themselves prisoners of war in Western Australia. At Carnarvon gaol, the bulk of them (234), plus some officers, were to undergo questioning by the Navy. And while in Carnarvon, Detmers reminisces on his luck in seeking the most favourable position for opening the engagement and how the *Sydney* had sailed into his prepared trap, although he concedes that one lucky hit in the mine storage deck was all that was required to blow them out of the water in an instant. He again felt sure he would face an inquiry over this issue.

After a meal at the Carnarvon police station, Detmers and Forester were taken to Naval Headquarters and then the party set off in a motor column for Geraldton with the Western Command Headquarters' Garrison Brigade on its return journey to Perth. They stopped at the police station at Moora and finally at the Swanbourne Barracks, arriving on the afternoon of 29 November.

On 30 November, Naval Board member, CMDR Dechaineux, interviewed Detmers at Swanbourne. According to Detmers, they got on quite well together. Detmers showed him the course that the *Sydney* had sailed and described how the cruiser had sailed off after the first phase of the action, but at 2100 hours (10:00pm WST) he had seen no more of her. And when he asked how many of his boats had been picked up, Dechaineux replied that he thought eight, including the two large rubber rafts. Detmers had felt so grateful that most of his crew had been saved. The Swanbourne Barracks was to be his home for the next 14 days.

On Monday (1 December), all the remaining officers from the *Kormoran*, who had been taken from Carnarvon to Fremantle by ship, arrived at Swanbourne. At last, they were together again, but hundreds of ordinary crewmen, who supposedly had been kept segregated, had been sent to the POW camp near Harvey, 140km south of Perth. And for the next week or so formal interrogations were carried out amongst all the crewmen and officers.

Apart from Detmers stating in the three action reports that he was travelling at 14–15 knots for one and a half hours (Eldridge Report to Admiralty), the interrogations did not reveal any worthwhile evidence regarding the speed of the ships to the action site. And nor did the interrogators pursue the obvious question of speed of the vessels during the engagement in order to consider whether the above-water tubes or the below-water tube had been responsible for the torpedo strike on the *Sydney*. Except for Gunnery Officer Fritz Skeries, who had seen that the cruiser was nearly motionless (to launch the underwater torpedo), no one else supported him **(NAA.012.0498)**. They were circumspect, for they had all toed the line, possibly in fear of retribution from Detmers. It was not until the 1990s that Detmers's story was refuted by quite a number of ex-*Kormoran*ers of the likes of Linke, Abel, etc, who affirmed that the guns opened fire when the torpedo hit. This had been undoubtedly the key that had completely unravelled the story told by Detmers.

Further evidence, which clarifies some of the misconceptions and allays some concerns about other aspects of the action, has startling revelations in many cases. However, no limit had been placed upon the voyage of the *Kormoran*. In this respect, obfuscation was to be the order of the day when it came to giving individual evidence when interrogated. Such was the confusion it created for the naval officers and those who had the task to piece together the action itself.

The following select evidence given to the interrogators by officers and crewmen of the *Kormoran* are generally from file **NAA B6121, 164M** or otherwise they relate to the Commission of Inquiry Report entries:

Evidence was given by Officer Johannes Diebisch that the milk bottles with Japanese characters came from a German supply ship **(NAA.012.0501)**. His statement was further reinforced in Harvey by Paul Mahe who said this particular ship was not so big **(NAA.012.0526)**. He had thus identified the vessel as the supply ship *Alstertor* (4,000 tons) from Germany from which the *Kormoran* had been re-supplied in the Atlantic. The significance of this is that this *milk had not been supplied by a Japanese submarine as is so often claimed.

***Note:** The Tripartite Agreement of September 1940 had been amended to provide for an exchange of strategic and manufactured goods between Germany, Italy and Japan.

Others who testified **(NAA B6121, 164M)** said the milk was 'fresh, not preserved' (Hans Widder). Oscar Marwinski, Ernst Hildenbrand and Robert Brune were consistent in claiming that the milk came from Germany, and when the constituents of the unrefrigerated milk was analysed, the method of processing could not be determined by the Commonwealth analyst. This forerunner to the long-life milk was so different from the condensed milk produced in Australia at the time.

Diebisch also testified that he saw one torpedo from the raider strike the cruiser forward, their relative positions at the time being 90–100°. Thus, it was significant that the raider had been up to 10° forward of the cruiser (both ships being opposite and parallel beforehand). And no matter whether the torpedoes fired were from the deck tubes or from the underwater tube, each torpedo could be fired abaft the beam **(NAA.012.0502)**.

On that same day (4 December), CMDR Ramage interrogated Officer Wilhelm Brinkmann **(NAA.012.0500)**. When the ships were parallel Brinkmann had said the torpedo struck almost at right angles and he evidenced that only two torpedoes were fired by the cruiser at the raider in the second phase of the action – both of them missed (see previous chapter). He had left in the last lifeboat with his captain (the cruiser not then being visible) and last saw it at 11:00pm (midnight WST). Officer Skeries testified that he also saw the *Sydney* at midnight **(NAA.012.0498)**. Brinkman said he knew nothing of a parley between each ship, as witnessed by Navigator Henri Meyer because he was (unlike Meyer) not on the bridge at the time.

When he was interrogated on the evening of 9 December, Chief Signaller Erich Ahlbach said he sent flag signals over a distance of 7 miles to the cruiser in reply to the signal 'NNP' (hoist your signal letters), but the funnel prevented seeing the four letters 'PQKI' (*Straat Malakka*) due to the extreme distance, the ship being just visible to the cruiser over the horizon and he eventually drew the halyard clear to reveal the *Kormoran*'s disguised name. But he, like Detmers, was not to know the Admiralty instructions given to all British warships – that a secret call-sign-registered ship like the *Straat Malakka* (IIKP) be immediately required to identify herself, certainly not when the ships had closed to within 900 metres, but from the distance recommended by the Admiralty.

Ahlbach continued: 'When the cruiser came parallel, Detmers was asked where they were going?' – Ahlbach answered, 'Batavia' when asked by searchlight and by flags. 'Cruiser gave a two-flag signal [IK] they did not understand', meaning (internationally), have you suffered damage from a cyclone, typhoon or tempest? 'Then by flashlight, Show your secret sign. *Kormoran* did not answer. Then the fight began.' This description was the so-called theme that had sparked the confrontation between the two ships, as agreed to by the Commission of Inquiry.

Note: Had Detmers supplied the secret letters, the stern features of the raider (counter stern in the Talbot Booth identification handbook) contrasted with the cruiser stern as sighted, adding to Burnett's suspicion that the vessel was not what it had claimed and that the secret letters of the *Straat Malakka* may have been compromised. See sketch below.

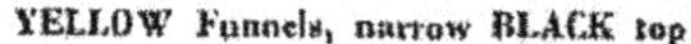
YELLOW Funnels, narrow BLACK top

80. STRAAT MALAKKA, STRAAT SOENDA.
Tonnage : 6,400 G., 3,900 N., 8,600 Dwt 14,900 Dwt
Dimensions : 455 62 28 *Draught* : 27·4.
Machinery : Oil engines, twin-screw, 1,240 N.H.P., 16¾ knots, 8,000 S.H.P.
Fuel Capacity : 1,143 tons.
Builders : Van der Giessen, 1939.
Cargo : 509,000 c.f. G., 488,000 c.f. B.
Complement : 12 passengers
Remarks : Single deckers with shelter deck

Talbot Booth sketch showing the counter stern

The chief signalman could not remember which ship opened fire first and he did not know whether the German flag went up before the Dutch flag came down. He only thought it was the former, though Ernst Hildenbrand on no. 3 gun witnessed that they (the raider) had opened fire sometime before the cruiser had fired **(NAA.012.0389)**.

Ahlbach's evidence also featured prominently in the Eldridge Report that was sent to the Admiralty a few months afterwards. His report detailed that inefficiency in continually signalling with the tangled halyard from a distance was akin to a 'ruse de guerre' and that the *Sydney* would have been brought closer to investigate what name and nationality was being flagged. But Ahlbach's story that the cruiser did not order the raider to stop or proceed excels all others, for he is effectively responsible for countenancing that the raider, regardless of the consequent likely action by the cruiser, ignored the order and continued on its merry way with the cruiser chasing her. Plainly, Eldridge had adopted that very same story of not at least slowing. He had also said the stop order had been evidenced by other prisoners when the ships had closed, but fellow crewman Heinz Schott had later subsequently torpedoed this assertion in his diary **(NAA B6121, 164M).**

19th Nov.41 - Wednesday - The day progressed as all the others without particular meaning until about 1600 hrs. We just came off watch and were eating when we heard that the lookout had sighted a ship but had not been able to recognise her. We were pleased to have another victim and prepared our "Mae Wests". Then the alarm went and in a few seconds made clear for action. The steamer had sighted us and was turning towards us. Our machines went full speed ahead but the other steamer was much faster and the distance increased quickly. We could see her on the horizon with the naked eye and then the "fellow" began to send messages ordering us to stop. One thing was certain we were up against an auxiliary cruiser or even a cruiser. Now we had enemy

Heinz Schott unmistakeably confirms Detmers's order to stop at a distance

When interrogated, Senior Petty Officer Paul Kohn, officer-in-charge of coding and who had commanded the lifeboat that came ashore at Quobba station, said the emergency Q signal was sent out once or twice, but did not know the content of the message(s) **(NAA.012.0138)**. Again, we have the situation wherein the Q signal had indeed been sent twice, but with different coordinates, the first being detected by the tug *Uco* and Perth Radio in stating the position of the suspicious ship in whole degrees (111°E, 26°S), and a couple of minutes later another detected by *Uco*, which Geraldton Radio also detected, but this time the distress signal was sent in the usual form at the point (coordinates) where the raider encountered the cruiser in the correctly written British format, 26°07'S, 111°15'E.

Edmund Schmidt, whose battle station was in the port (above-water) torpedo room, said his duty was to clear a torpedo for loading in case another one was required. This was standard practice, providing the torpedo room was adjacent and at the same level as the tubes, otherwise should another torpedo be required it involved hoisting or lowering the torpedo into the tube if reloading from a level surface was not possible. He also indicated that the two above-water torpedoes that were (eventually) fired were ready in their tubes **(NAA 012.0138)**.

Otto Jurgensen (assistant navigator) was on the bridge during the action. He saw the first shots from the raider and the torpedo which hit the cruiser. According to him, they had also put up extra masts on *Kormoran* to look like the passenger-cargo ship, *Straat Malakka*, their disguise for the past several months **(NAA.012.0101)**. On entering the Indian Ocean, the raider had previously been disguised as another ship, but the change in identity was necessary because Detmers had learnt that this vessel rarely operated in the western sector. Even in those early days rumours abounded that she was disguised as a Norwegian cargo vessel, then by far the biggest fleet of ships, worldwide.

At the end of the war, the *Kormoran*'s operational war diary had been translated by the Admiralty (it had been taken to Germany aboard the *Kulmerland* in October 1941), revealing that the raider had only two disguises while in the Indian Ocean – those of the Japanese ship, *Sakito Maru* and later, the *Straat Malakka* **(Admiralty file 1/18899)**. Although a number of researchers still disagree on the form of disguise, Otto Jurgensen at his interrogation had firmly stated that they had never used the Norwegian flag in order to conceal her identity.

In response to Captain Reinhard Richter's story about the action in May 1989, ex-crewman Johannes Schneider, a member of Gun no. 4, wrote that shortly before the action commenced the sides of the ship behind the four cannons (150nm guns) were lifted or lowered and the guns were put into position (trained) for firing. This is corroborated by Edmund Buttner (also on no. 4 gun) in his interview by the inquiry in Germany. The manoeuvre of turning the raider to starboard 260° (after firing off the underwater torpedo) resulted in the cruiser being directly in front of the guns. This had meant that little or no change in the direction of the gun had been necessary before opening fire **(COI.003.0003)**.

Again, in his interrogation, Buttner knew of only one torpedo that had been fired, but he also gave evidence that when his ship had been asked by signal and lamp for the port of departure, destination and cargo, he answered in an appropriately stalling manner **(NAA.012.0065)**.

Detmers had said his destination was Batavia and that he was carrying 'piece-goods' (which sounds very suspicious) and he could not be sure if the cruiser had seen his vessel turn away.

But in steering 250° (his original course had been 025° to Shark Bay) he interpreted the manoeuvre as a normal evasive action on encountering an enemy ship.

Detmers's and Schneider's notes on their interrogations differ markedly with those of LEUT Joachim von Gösseln, battle officer of the watch, who was on the bridge with Detmers. He wrote an article in 1970, in which he again said unequivocally that the raider had been sailing 'slowly' at 5:30pm (6:30pm WST) just before the action began. But in a letter to the inquiry in 2008 from the *Kormoran*'s Administrative Officer Heinz Messerschmidt in support of von Gösseln, (he had rebuked Detmers's claim) that the raider's destination had been the port of Batavia. Messerschmidt stated forthrightly that the ship was coming from Batavia and was going to *Lourenço Marques (now Maputo) in Mozambique, East Africa. He said that was the opinion that prevailed on the bridge at the time and that very signal was sent to the *Sydney* **(WIT.011.0208)**.

*Lourenco Marques lies approximately 2,000 miles due west of the action.

When confronted by the cruiser, Messerschmidt said they mentioned the name of the ship in the Q signal so that the enemy would believe that the ship was the *Straat Malakka.* After turning to starboard 260° he quoted Buttner (no. 3 gun) that the cruiser lay broadside directly in front of the four 150mm guns which had been previously aimed abeam. He does, however, subscribe to the two-torpedo scenario that was predicated on the fact that the fixed underwater torpedo was required to be aimed by the ship (as claimed by Hans Linke).

Messerschmidt also observed that the fore turrets (A and B) of the *Sydney* had been silenced by the torpedo hit and gunfire, but turrets C and D were in action spasmodically, one shell hitting no. 1 wireless room and injuring many and one (unexploded) shell penetrating the ammunition room and emerging on the port side. In the finish one hit the engine-room below the mine deck and caused the irreparable damage that resulted in the evacuation of the ship. At this stage, the *Kormoran* was making about 5 knots when two port torpedoes from the cruiser had missed their mark **(NAA B6121, 165P),** which readily conforms to evidence given by Engineer Rudolph Lensch during the action with the cruiser in disclosing that the speed of the raider was 'considerably reduced' **(NAA.012.0383)**].

SBLT Wilhelm Bunjes gave a rather convoluted assessment of the battle in his interrogation, but he was still quoted by Eldridge in the report to the Admiralty. Both had wrongly surmised that the raider had been making 14 knots (in fact, 11K) on its way north to Shark Bay. However, Bunjes's evidence was clearly awry in the rest of his report. He attested that one of the two torpedoes fired struck the cruiser at the same time as the

Sydney's first salvo hit the raider amidships, the second salvo piercing the engine-room and fuel tanks, which resulted in a raging fire. This statement had meant that the raider fired the two above-water torpedoes in full view of the cruiser and those aboard had observed the splashes as both torpedoes entered the sea.

Yet, the evidence is that one torpedo had struck the cruiser near the bow almost at right angles, which demonstrates that no evasive action had ever been contemplated, the cruiser being taken completely by surprise. This point from Bunjes alone renders the Eldridge Report null and void in legal terms. Similarly, no faith can be placed upon the almost identical and protracted drawn-out version of G Hermon Gill's *History of the Royal Australian Navy*, and likewise of the Commission of Inquiry report.

A number of ordinary crewmen interrogated corroborated the firing of the torpedo and guns **(NAA B6121, 164M)**. Comments such as 'we fired only one torpedo shot' (Wilhelm Schmitz), 'knows of only one torpedo fired' (Adolf Dornis), 'they dropped screens and fired' (Josef Pullman), 'guns were in holds covered and then raised by hydraulic press. [They] take 2-3 minutes to bring in position (holds opened by hand). They were already in position when action started, surrounded by camouflage' (Andreas Pattner), 'K removed screens and fired' (Georg Stich) and 'when torpedo was fired, ships stood parallel' (Johann Schneider). There is no doubt that these example comments from the crewmen demonstrate the fallibility of statements on the above-water torpedoes and guns made by Detmers and some of his officers.

And from the same file, evidence that flights over the coast occurred not long before the action took place – '[Arado] plane last used some weeks before fight' (Johann Schneider), 'last flight more than a month before fight' (Karl Kluger), 'aircraft made reconnaissance flights on Australian coast' (Willy Tummers) and 'last saw plane used in October. Flew for an hour out of sight' (Rolf Zupnke). Paul Kobelt agreed with Zupnke – both had said 'the last flight was in October' **(NAA B6121, 164M).**

Other appurtenant issues include the mines, the use of flags and transmissions made by the *Kormoran.* For example, interrogations had revealed that Paul Kobelt had observed that his ship 'had mostly round mines, but [there were] some long mines on board – about 6ft long and 21 inches in diameter.' He had thus aptly described these as TMB-type magnetic mines. Hans Kure was adamant that they used Dutch and Japanese flags but not American when spotted by ships or allied aircraft and Hubert Berghoff said 'I do not think we flew a foreign flag during any part of our journey.' Finally, telegraphist Willy Tummers: 'Twice a month [we] communicated with Germany.' He had thus verified that the raider had sent a message at least every two weeks on average, meaning that the FEDO station at Jandakot should have determined the *Kormoran*'s approximate position off the coast.

Only days after the interrogations had finished on 9 December, Detmers and some of his officers appeared before (in what he termed) a *Commission of Inquiry chaired by Rear Admiral (Crace), CMDR Dechaineax and another senior officer (probably DNO CAPT Farquhar-Smith). This was a matter of course in any naval disaster. The Court first heard from officers and by the time they came around to Detmers, he had nothing much to add to what the others had already said. In the end, the panel of senior officers had accepted his story in toto and the story was believed by Dechaineax (and Eldridge) to have been 'frankly told' to the extent that it rang true.

*A Commission or Court of Inquiry had apparently taken place in the SWACH building in Fremantle. The Court of Inquiry is so named in the layout produced by Mrs Mort, ex-secretary, DNOWA. [See next chapter.]

Detmers had subsequently learnt from Dechaineax that about 320 of his crew were saved – a loss of some 80 men and not one crewman from the cruiser's complement of 645 had survived the ordeal. Thus, one could be forgiven for accepting the lopsided views during the German interrogations due to the fact that not one person had survived from the cruiser. Some crewmen were below deck and did not contribute much, while others who were in a position to observe the action relied totally on their own recollections, be they honest or not. But one thing is certain – they were acutely aware of the truth that both ships were nearly stationary and not making 14–15 knots when asked by the cruiser for the secret letters. And when only 900 metres separated the ships, Detmers was conscious that his ship was about to be boarded.

On 13 December 1941, the German naval officers boarded the troopship MV *Duntroon* for the voyage to Melbourne (via Adelaide) and were then sent to Murchison in the State of Victoria, and finally to Dhurringile where the officers were housed. In the meantime, the ordinary crew and non-commissioned officers had journeyed from Perth by train across Australia to nearby Tatura and thence to the many POW camps, which in those days surrounded the town. They were to serve another six years at these places before being repatriated to Cuxhaven in Germany on the SS *Orontes.*

❑ ❑ ❑

HELD IN ABEYANCE

The Commission of Inquiry investigated the message forwarded by Squadron Leader Eric Cooper from Geraldton Aerodrome to RAAF Western Area Headquarters (WAHQ) in Perth. Some had believed it was a distress message from HMAS *Sydney* on 19 November 1941, as a result of her battle with the German raider HSK *Kormoran*. Justice Terence Cole, however, concluded that the events occurred on 4 December, not on 19 November, as recalled by SLDR Cooper.

This finding was based entirely on the message Cooper phoned to WAHQ that is shown to have been recorded on 4 December in the South Western Area Combined Headquarters (SWACH) logbook. However, Justice Cole had failed to adequately address the overall content of the message, in particular the distress signal component. Consequently, his findings and analyses raise some serious doubts.

In Cooper's signed statement of January 2002 **(Annexure 1)**, he explained that on the night of Wednesday, 19 November 1941, he was approached by FLGOFF Gerry Bogue, adjutant of No. 4 Service Flying Training School (No. 4 SFTS) in Geraldton, with notes he had made of a message he had received from CPL Dawson of RAAF, who with others in his company had heard plain Morse short-wave signals on a radio receiver at Geraldton's Esplanade Hostel that were possibly from HMAS *Sydney*. Cooper and Bogue composed a message from these notes, which Cooper then phoned to the signals clerk at RAAF headquarters (WAHQ) in Perth later that evening, requesting it be passed urgently to the Navy.

Years later after viewing the message from RAAF File AA1969/100, 2/18/INT at folio 12A, Cooper was astonished to find that the message was not a true account of the information that he had phoned to Perth. He says, 'In it I stressed that the signals received by CPL Dawson were in Morse code and that he and the other airman in attendance could read Morse'. And although the message did not mention that three ladies and another airman also heard the signals from the ordinary short-wave receiver, it included the word 'Aeradi', which Cooper did not mention. He had thus found that the text of the message he had phoned to WAHQ had borne a different wording.

Cooper appeared satisfied that the original notes in the same file at folio 11A, which had outlined the chronological sequence of events, were generally those that FLGOFF Bogue wrote down from CPL Dawson's phone call on 19 November and that this message was later passed on. But he emphatically denied that he sent his message on 4 December, as shown recorded in the SWACH logbook.

In consideration of the wide publicity given to the *Sydney*'s loss and to the search process, Cooper's initial and ongoing recollection of whether the message was sent before or after the battle with the raider *Kormoran* must have been indelible on his mind from the time he became aware that the cruiser became overdue in Fremantle.

Cooper's memory of the occasion cannot be so easily dismissed. He had taken a leading role in the air search for survivors and that the battle had taken place on 19 November, at the very least, he could not have failed to remember that he sent his message to WAHQ before the search began. It therefore seems an unlikely case of memory lapse due to his personal involvement in such a momentous event. This appears to be the case because when interviewed on a number of occasions, Cooper was being adamant that he sent the message on the night of the 19th, well before he got personally involved in the search.

In his report, Commissioner Cole did not dispute Cooper's claim that the signals were heard only in Morse. Nor did he address the specificity of the content – the apparent distress message, 'Call from Sea' and other indicators suggesting that efforts were being made to contact the vessel, possibly HMAS *Sydney*. Justice Cole preferred to accept verbatim the general content of all messages, which he noticed contained similar substance, emphasizing that the attached letters 'RT' (voice) discredited the notion that voice messages were received from the *Sydney* because the warship did not have the capacity to send voice signals over the horizon.

On the basis that the SWACH log records of 4 December contained almost identical information on both messages and that SLDR Cooper's message (12A) was addressed to Flying Officer Palmer who was on duty at SWACH on that day, the Commission concluded that the events did not occur on 19 November, as recalled some 60 years earlier by Cooper **(Annexure 2)**. Thus, the analysis by the inquiry was based primarily on the events having been recorded in the SWACH logbook on 4 December. The corollary was that the message did not relate to HMAS *Sydney*.

In order to further assess the merits of Cooper's message, the customary modes of long-distance transmissions and relay of messages in November 1941 are briefly examined below:

During 1941, Australia's civil communications system consisted of a conglomerate of commercial radio and telegraphy stations interspersed throughout the country and along the coastline that were primarily coordinated for military purposes, receiving and transmitting messages from within and overseas. The network comprised two powerful transmitter stations situated at Pennant Hills outside Sydney and at Applecross in Perth that were also both capable of receiving world-wide radio broadcasts for re-broadcasting internally and overseas via Radio Australia. Another powerful radio tower at the AWA control centre in central Sydney could be used for sending high-speed telegraphy.

The largest receiving station in the southern hemisphere was situated on the heights of La Perouse overlooking Botany Bay. From here, wireless traffic could be received from a network of stations throughout the world, including messages from ships in the Pacific and Indian Oceans and from the coastal radio stations around Australia. The RAN controlled two other high-frequency (HF) stations for contact with HM ships and for naval intelligence purposes, in Canberra at the Royal Australian Navy Wireless Transmitting Station (later named HMAS *Harman* in 1943) and in Darwin at HMAS *Melville* (later, HMAS *Coonawarra*). The RAN station at Darwin comprised three separate stations for transmitting, receiving and for high-frequency direction finding (HFDF). HMAS *Harman* and the long-range broadcasting and WT stations at Sydney and Perth were all capable of communicating with naval ships in Australian waters and overseas.

Melbourne was serviced by the high-frequency Beam wireless transmitting station near the town of Ballan. The receiving station at Rockbank was taken over by the RAN at the outbreak of war and later used in partnership with the United States (FRUMEL). Direct lines were established from the major radio stations to the closest naval intelligence, coding and operational centres, Area Combined Headquarters, RAAF and other military establishments. All intelligence information was channelled to the Naval Intelligence Division (NID) at Navy Office in Melbourne. Each of the major WT stations could communicate with one another and with other service establishments via high-speed telegraphy transmissions.

RAN intercept stations in Canberra and Darwin covering the Indian-Pacific region, linked to the Far East Combined Bureau (FECB) intelligence-gathering network in Singapore, were each supplemented by HFDF stations. Another separate HFDF station was located at Jandakot, between Perth and Fremantle. These three stations were complemented by those constructed and operating in Singapore, Canada and New Zealand, forming part of the Royal Navy's Far East Direction-finding Organisation (FEDO). In addition to the major intercept and transmitting stations, the communications network also comprised the interlinked RAN coastal stations, Aeradio stations operated by DCA, the Overland telegraph system and interstate phone services. By the outbreak of the war in the Pacific, the RAN had in place a formidable intercept organisation supported by a cryptographic bureau.

Cooper's message (marked 12A on RAAF Form A22 below) does not contain any identifying features, such as the time of receipt of the message, serial number, office date stamp, time of origin or time of reply. Such untimed and undated messages were liable to be wrongly inserted in the logbook and unfortunately in those days incoming messages were routinely written in pencil making them more prone to alteration in the logbook. Message 12A contains an opinion from Aeradio Geraldton, which gives the impression that part of the message was received in RT and not entirely in Morse.

Taken over phone by Signals Clerk [illegible] for 5 A.S.U. S/L Cooper Geraldton

MESSAGE FORM

24.50/metres:

Geraldton [illegible] is under the intense [illegible] from [illegible] Sydney.

R/T & morse | [illegible] (2140 H) (2335 H)

Calling during [illegible] till [illegible]

"Calling Darwin or Technical Telegraph operator" — "Call from Sea Sydney calling send Corres men on board" — "Calling Frazer D/F of Darwin" — "Cannot detect you" — "Singapore call Darwin" "This H M S Sydney calling message (is) received frequency satisfactory will put through morse" (at 2310 H) Col Dawson & Geraldton — Four stations transmitting in morse on same wavelength — "Sydney calling Darwin Distress sig — [illegible]"

S/L Cooper

Message 12A from SLDR Cooper to WAHQ

Note: Additions and comments in red pencil (circled), some post-dated from past tense to present tense.

Commissioner Cole found that the contents of the document made it clear that the message did not come from HMAS *Sydney.* He pointed out that the message is marked as sent in RT and Morse, and that the *Sydney* could not send RT. But because the message states it will be later put through in Morse it implies that the complete message was not received in Morse. However, he failed to elaborate on a number of other message components that would have helped in his analysis. There are nine components in the message:

(1) This notation, **for 5 ASO,** appears to be an attachment by WAHQ to the addressee for action – viz., (to) Area 5 (SWACH) **A**rea **S**enior **O**fficer (LCDR Philip Bailhache). Note the badly formed 'O' can be mistaken for a 'U'.

(2) The impression here is that as the complete message has come from sea on **24.5 metres**, it would have been unlikely for Dawson to have so accurately determined the wavelength from the radio receiver dial setting. But because his party at the Esplanade Hostel had more than likely tuned to Radio Australia, the only station available to listeners after 10:30pm in those days and which often broadcast at night on the 25-metre band in 1941, the approximate wavelength on the receiver dial should not have gone unnoticed.

(3) This note, **Taken over phone by Signals Clerk Western Area from S/L Cooper Geraldton** accords with Cooper's statement and was applied by the same person (same handwriting) who wrote down similar notes (refer Bogue's Message 11A, below). Significantly, it does not specify the time and date of arrival of the message.

(4) **Aeradio Geraldton** (is) **under** (the) **impression came** (coming) **from Aeradio Sydney**, suggests that Aeradio

Geraldton may have also heard the messages on 24.5 metres, and had then contacted WAHQ or SWACH. Alternatively, an opinion on Cooper's message had been obtained by WAHQ before phoning SWACH and that they had later sought an opinion after receiving Cooper's message. The handwriting accords with the rest of the message text. Note that the wording has been changed from past tense to present tense, giving the impression that the message was suddenly deemed urgent but dealt with at a later time.

(5) Cooper denied mentioning RT or **R/T & Morse**. He made it clear that all messages were heard by Dawson in Morse, but this inclusion appears to take into account that short-wave (voice) broadcasts were also heard on 24.5 metres and that according to Aeradio Geraldton the apparent distress message had emanated from Aeradio Sydney. But the fact that RT was only ever mentioned in Bogue's notes is indicative that the notation had been later applied. Consequently, the thrust of Cooper's message is portrayed differently.

(6) This component, **Mr Palmer (Bailash)**, is addressed for the action of FLGOFF Palmer (SWACH duty officer) and LCDR Philip Bailhache (SWACH Senior Naval Operations Officer). Had Bailhache applied the note then he has spelled his name incorrectly (with intent) and rather authoritatively. Alternatively, the message had been addressed to Palmer and Bailhache for action by their superior officers – CMDR Victor Ramage or CAPT Charles Farquhar-Smith.

(7) The **Call from sea** distress signal implies that the *Sydney* is urgently calling Darwin telegraph operator on 24.5 metres, briefly describing her predicament and requesting the transmission of a common wavelength carrier in order to establish contact by Morse, followed

by a call to DF Darwin for a bearing on the emitting signal and then requesting Singapore to call that station for a bearing on that emission. It appears that the signaller has been previously in contact with Singapore. Finally, the message in Morse is acknowledged by MS Sydney, which proceeds to send in Morse to the *Sydney*. This supports the notion that Aeradio Geraldton may have thought that the message had emanated from Aeradio Sydney at MS (Mascot). Alternatively, it was meant to signify an abbreviated 'HMAS' (MS Sydney appears as 'AS Sydney' in Bogue's message 11A).

(8) The word, **Aeradio,** appears to have been included after an opinion had been sought from Geraldton. It was not mentioned in Cooper's original message that he had phoned earlier to WAHQ. Aeradio Geraldton's assessment was that three other stations at the time were transmitting on about the same wavelength is further evidence that Message 12A contains additional information that was not supplied by Cooper or by Bogue.

(9) The message is clearly described as a distress signal, implying that *Sydney* had been calling Darwin to acknowledge the signal sent from **Struts Lykard** (Leichardt). And considering that 'Lykard/Leichardt' has two syllables that sound almost identical, it is highly likely that the name was misspelled when the message was taken down over the phone. This indifferent spelling by some observers is also believed to indicate that the signals had been possibly transmitted by one of the *Sydney*'s ordinary signalmen by the name of Terrence Lockard.

According to Cooper, Message 12A contains the general thrust of his message relayed to WAHQ, but it also includes other comments that had been apparently obtained from Aeradio Geraldton and attached, plus other alterations such as 'Leichardt' and those others marked in red pencil. Attention is again drawn to the fact that the wording has been changed from past tense to present tense, indicating that no action had been taken when the message had been originally received by SWACH, but it was later deemed appropriate to deal with it on the basis that the signals were being currently sent. It should also be said that with four stations transmitting in Morse on a similar wavelength, the commonly-used term 'frequency satisfactory' could have come from any other source, and therefore may not have been related to this particular signal.

The notion that some of the signals were sent in RT is probably based on the fact that Dawson was believed to have also heard the voice broadcasts from the short-wave receiver. It also appears that he interpreted the Morse-coded name as 'Leichardt' and that the name delivered verbally by Cooper was incorrectly written down by the RAAF signals clerk as 'Lykard'. The corrected version shown in Message 11A could therefore only have been applied to Message 12A **after** receipt of Bogue's notes. And if it was true that more than one station was transmitting in Morse, Dawson probably had trouble translating the word he described as 'Struts', indistinctly shown on Message 12A, but clearly shown on Message 11A. The word 'Leichardt' can be construed as a place or person's name, but the word 'Struts' may have been mistakenly interpreted as 'instruct'.

That the message was addressed to FLGOFF Palmer, who was the SWACH duty officer assigned on 4 December, does not automatically mean (as shown later) that the message was not received on 19 November. On balance and without regard to the opinion from Aeradio Geraldton, Cooper's Message 12A generally implies that the signals can be taken as having emanated from HMAS *Sydney*, but the order in which the messages were received, as shown hereunder in Message 11A, places a different complexion on Cooper's message.

Message 11A, seemingly dated 5 December outlining the sequence of messages provided by CPL Dawson, was obtained by

WAHQ by phone from FLGOFF Bogue at RAAF Geraldton and eventually sent to SWACH, the message being purportedly passed to FLGOFF Wesche at the Combined Operations Intelligence Centre (COIC) at SWACH by secraphone that same day.

The information received from Bogue via Dawson is of similar content to Cooper's message said to have been received on 19 November, and given that Cooper's message had been jointly composed from Bogue's notes, Message 11A can be described as being the 'parent' document because it includes information that Cooper says should have been shown on his Message 12A – notably, the personnel involved at the Esplanade Hostel and his claim that the signals were received only in Morse. See below.

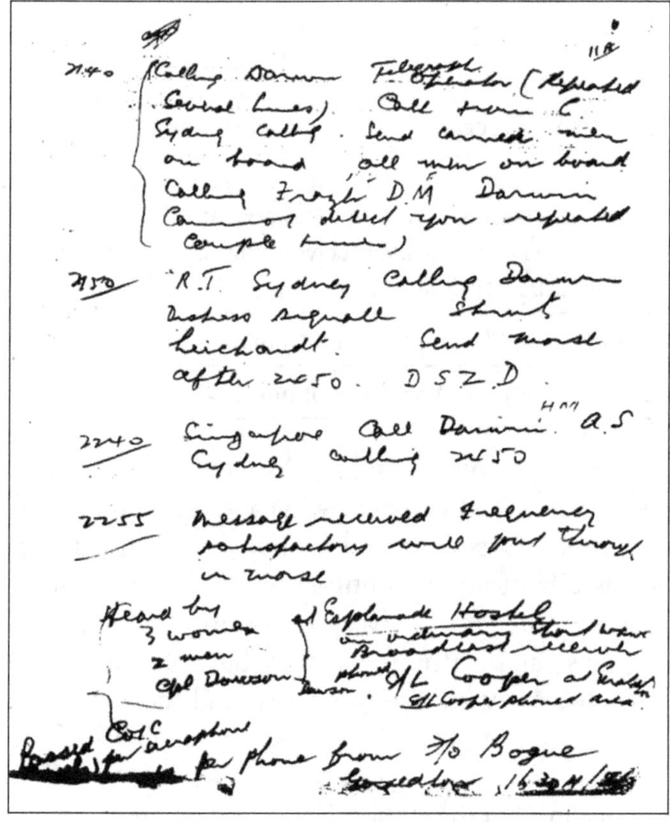

11A

2140 (Calling Darwin Telegraph Operator (Repeated several times). Call from C Sydney calling. Send cannot. men on board, all men on board. Calling Freight D.M. Darwin Cannot detect you repeated couple times)

2150 R.T. Sydney Calling Darwin distress signal Strait Leichardt. Send morse after 2050. DSZD.

2240 Singapore Call Darwin HMAS Sydney calling 2050

2255 message received frequency satisfactory will put through in morse

Heard by 3 women 2 men Cpl Dawson at Esplanade Hostel on ordinary short wave Broadcast receiver. Dawson phoned F/L Cooper at Geraldton. F/L Cooper phoned me.

Passed to COIC per secraphone [illegible] per phone from F/O Bogue Geraldton 1630 [illegible]

Bogue's message 11A received from CPL Dawson

Commissioner Cole concluded that the date of this message in the SWACH logbook on 5 December was further confirmation of the events not having occurred on 19 November and that this message was not a distress call from HMAS *Sydney*. The corollary is that Message 12A is also not a distress call. However, due to the distinct timing of the events, the components of Message 11A present a different perspective. The message consists of seven components, as shown below.

[a] 2140 Calling Darwin telegraph operator (repeated). Call from C. Sydney calling, send carrier, men on board, all men on board. Calling Frazer DM (DF) Darwin, cannot detect you (repeated twice)
[b] 2150 R.T Sydney calling Darwin Distress Signal Struts Leichardt. Send morse after 2450. DSZD
[c] 2240 Singapore call Darwin AS Sydney calling 2450
[d] 2255 Message received frequency satisfactory will put through in morse
[e] Heard by 3 women 2 men Cpl Dawson at Esplanade Hostel on ordinary short-wave broadcast receiver. Dawson phoned S/L Cooper at Geraldton. S/L Cooper phoned area
[f] per phone from F/O Bogue, Geraldton 1630/5
[g] Passed COIC (Wesche) per secraphone 1645/5

[a] This message implies that prior to 2140H a station in Sydney NSW had detected what was an apparent distress message in Morse from a vessel at sea. The message gives brief details of an unidentified vessel in apparent trouble. It has possibly lost power, is possibly sinking and/or is motionless and drifting. But they have not abandoned the vessel, the crew are still on board and they request that a carrier (wavelength 24.5m) be sent to enable contact to be made. The station in Sydney then proceeds to call ‘Frazer DF Darwin’, but the station is not immediately contactable.

The message suggests that the original distress message had been picked up by a station in Sydney that was capable of receiving high-frequency signals, for example, via the main receiving station at La Perouse. The signals heard in Morse by Dawson at 2140H were thus a repeat of the message by a Sydney transmission station capable of sending HF signals directly to Darwin. In 1941, such signals could be conveyed by the HF transmitting station at Pennant Hills and via the radio transmission tower at the AWA control centre in central Sydney. One of these stations was responsible for signalling Frazer (Fraser) HFDF station and the Darwin HF receiving station, which were both located at HMAS *Melville*.

[b] Ten minutes later, a station, designated as 'RT Sydney' tries to call Darwin again in Morse, drawing attention to the earlier distress signal and requesting 'Struts (sic) Leichardt' to send Morse after[wards] [on] 24.5 metres to [in the direction of] 'DSZD'.

That Dawson claimed that all signals were received in Morse effectively rules out the possibility of the transmission of a voice message. However, Aeradio stations equipped with RT (voice) transmitter/receivers could also send and receive localised high-frequency Morse signals for contact with aircraft. These messages and signals could be relayed to other Aeradio stations on 24.5 metres (12.2Mcs), but the transmitters were not powerful enough to send messages over long distances. [Aeradio WT and voice messages could generally be sent on frequency ranges of between 2Mcs and 20 Mcs.]

This particular message component appears to be a request to pass the message on from one station to another. But in this case, 'RT Sydney' most likely refers to the powerful transmission station at the AWA control centre, then simply known and referred to as the massive **R**adio **T**ower in central Sydney, used for transmissions by commercial radio stations pre-war, but then used exclusively by the armed services. This station does not appear to have been assigned a designated four-letter call sign in November 1941 for general use.

AWA Control Centre featuring the Radio Transmission Tower on York Street, Sydney

Completed in 1939, the radio tower facility ('RT Sydney') was in a shared arrangement.

Taken in context, the message describes the AWA station's efforts to contact or 'instruct' the 'Leichardt' station to relay the message to Fraser HFDF station (named after **Sir Bruce Fraser**, 4th Sealord and Controller of the Royal Navy) to send out Morse signals on 24.5 metres (12,245kcs) in order to make contact and thus determine the direction of the emitting signal. If so, the name 'Leichardt' has probably been mistaken for the receiving station at HMAS *Melville*, then situated south of Darwin on the coast and adjacent to **Reichardt** creek (shown below).

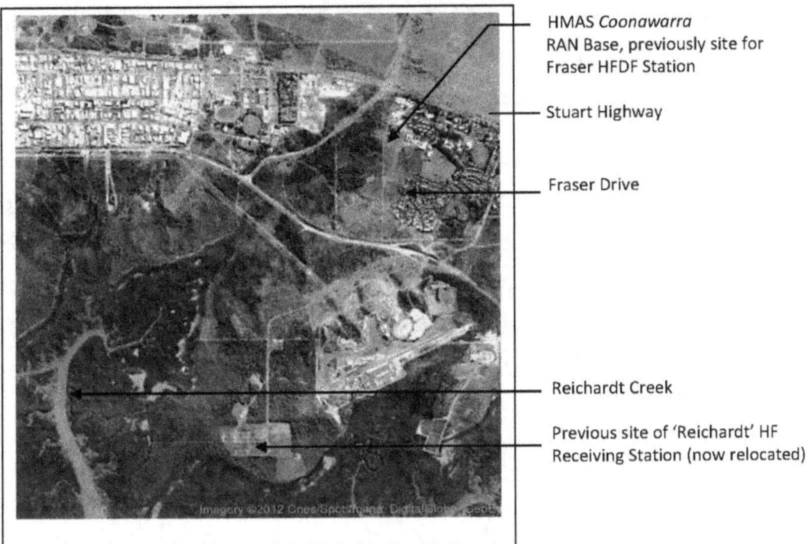

'DSZD' appears to be an abbreviation for **D**istress **S**ignal **Z**one (Area) **D**, the Australia Station sea area in which the *Sydney/Kormoran* battle took place. Although it is shown in abbreviated form in Bogue's notes taken over the phone, the full meaning may have been originally stated by Dawson. And it may also have been stated by Bogue in full, but abbreviated 'DSZD' when sent to WAHQ.

[c] After considerable elapse of time during which there was apparently no response from the Darwin (Reichardt) receiving station, the Sydney station calls Singapore to contact Darwin, indicating that **'(HM)AS *Sydney'*** is calling (or had called) on 24.5 metres.

The call from Sydney to Singapore requesting they contact Darwin would appear to be a routine call in the circumstance of Darwin not having been able to receive the messages over a period of time. Besides, high-frequency signals in the order of 25 metres designed for intercontinental WT traffic sent over only 3,000km at night from Sydney to Darwin would have proved difficult to intercept (see below). That this message refers to 'AS Sydney' can be taken to indicate that the cruiser had earlier signalled her identity and that the distress message was presumed to have emanated from that vessel.

[d] Darwin finally receives the (wake-up) call message via a signal in Morse on 24.5 metres from either of the stations in Sydney or Singapore and commenced to signal on the same wavelength hoping to make contact with the vessel in distress. Alternatively (as in Cooper's Message 12A), this could also have been an unrelated signal from another station.

[e] Cooper conveyed this same information to SWACH, but for some reason it was not included in his message.

[f] Bogue's message appears (at first glance) to have been obtained by phone at WAHQ on 5 December.

[g] The message appears to have been passed to FLGOFF Vern Wesche's COIC office at SWACH shortly afterwards.

Bogue's message contains elements that are not included in Cooper's original message. That words such as 'Leichardt' and 'RT' have been applied to Cooper's message indicate that Bogue's message was available to SWACH at the time Cooper's message was dealt with and recorded in the log on 4 December.

If in fact Cooper's message had been delivered to SWACH on 19 November, Wesche and other COIC officers accommodated there were likely to have been privy to its content – if they were on duty at the time. If so, Wesche should have been informed of any new developments. This would explain why Bogue's message was sent to him. But although his role in the Cooper/ Bogue messages is unclear, on face value there is nothing to suggest that he did not receive Bogue's message at SWACH on 5 December at 1645H, the day after Cooper's message had been purportedly dealt with.

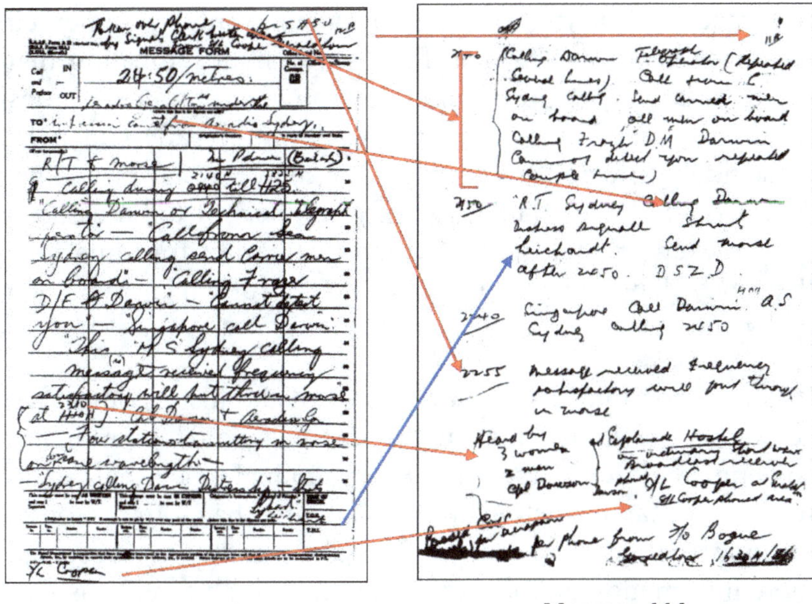

Message 12A Message 11A

The above messages show examples of similar handwriting, which indicates that the same person who took down Bogue's message also attached notes to Cooper's message. But the fact that message 11A carries the abbreviated 'RT' mentioned in the logbook on 4 December, demonstrates that Message 12A had been received by SWACH beforehand and thus could not have been obtained afterwards on 5 December. It has not been possible to identify the handwriting of the person at WAHQ who wrote down Bogue's Message 11A.

Given that the messages were heard by Dawson in Morse only, it could be argued that Aeradio Sydney had passed the Morse messages to Darwin and that Darwin then forwarded them on to the RAN receiving station at HMAS *Melville*. But the problem was that the messages were initially reliant on being relayed from Sydney to Darwin via a series of aeradio stations in northern Australia (e.g., via Brisbane, Cloncurry etc), which could conceivably account for the inordinate delay in contacting Darwin. This would account for the fragmented messages heard by Dawson for over an hour indicating that these relatively short-range low-powered transmissions (primarily used for communicating with aircraft) had been most likely affected by propagation and/or aerial problems. This would also explain why only snippets of the messages were picked up and the likelihood that earlier transmissions that may have been made before 2140H had remained undetected by Dawson.

It is also possible that the originator of the distress message could have initially transmitted the positional coordinates sometime before Dawson and his group had tuned their radio receiver to Radio Australia on the 25-metre band. In that case, the principal receiver station in Sydney may have received more information on the circumstances of the vessel's distress and even its approximate position, abbreviated 'DSZD'.

In short, Bogue's message 11A gives the general impression of a transmitting station in Sydney trying to alert the main receiving station at Darwin of the apparent distress signal heard earlier from sea and that attempts were being made to pass on the information, whereas, as previously mentioned, Cooper's Message 12A, which is derived from 11A and which is shown in different context and sequence, largely portrays that the signals were heard directly from the vessel in distress.

It is not surprising that attempts to pass on the messages to other stations proved difficult due to the high-frequency transmissions made at night. After all, it is well known that daytime HF short-wave frequencies in the order of 24.5 metres (12,245 kcs or 12.2 Mcs) are normally suitable for intercontinental communication, but they are generally unreliable for such short-range transmissions at night, for example, from Sydney to Darwin.

Propagation or 'skip' can become a problem as short-wave signals bounce off the ionosphere one or more times between the transmitter site and the receiver site, and that the ability of the ionosphere to reflect radio signals depends on sunspot activity and the time of day generally makes shortwave reception a hit-and-miss proposition. Thunderstorms, which are likely to frequent northern Australia, especially in the Darwin area also interfere badly with HF radio waves at night. Thus, in order to overcome these problems, lower frequencies in the order of 6–7Mcs have generally been found to be more suitable for night-time transmissions over long distances.

During daylight hours, high-frequency signals in the order of 24.5 metres emanating from the Indian Ocean should have been picked up by a number of stations, including for example, at Perth (Applecross), but in consideration of the unpredictability of such signals at night, it appears that only the main receiving station in Sydney at La Perouse had intercepted the original distress signals. Consequently, the follow-up transmissions to Darwin from the Sydney station on the same wavelength allowed for a much broader reception, thus making it possible for the signals to be heard on the short-wave receiver by Dawson in Geraldton.

The frailties of sending high-frequency signals at night over relatively short distances are further demonstrated by the frequencies used by HMAS *Sydney* if contact with the shore station at HMAS *Harman* was to have proved necessary. Given that the station monitored the *Sydney* on a daytime frequency of 12,330 kcs (24.33 metres) and on 6,610 kcs at night **(JSCDFAT p610)**, *Harman* may not have received the distress signal from the cruiser transmitted on 24.5 metres because the daytime frequency had not been monitored at night.

Due to the propagation characteristics of high-frequency signals, it is possible that other overseas HF receiving stations were capable of these intercepts. For example, there is evidence from Royal Navy's Admiral Bruce Fraser that signals from the *Sydney* were intercepted at the Kilindini station in Mombassa (later HMS *Alidina*), giving her position and stating that she was under attack **(JSCDFAT p4095)**. Although Commissioner Cole conceded it was improbable that Fraser would have invented such an account and despite the hit-and-miss issue of propagation, he agreed with Fraser's account on the basis that it was 'extremely likely that it [the signal] would have been heard by many other stations' **(COI Report Vol. 3, p160)**.

Most concerning, however, is that an alteration to Message 11A reveals that Bogue's message, purportedly obtained by SWACH on 5 December, was available at the time Cooper's message was dealt with in the log book on 4 December. The authenticity of the date appended to Bogue's message received at 1630H, therefore, requires examining.

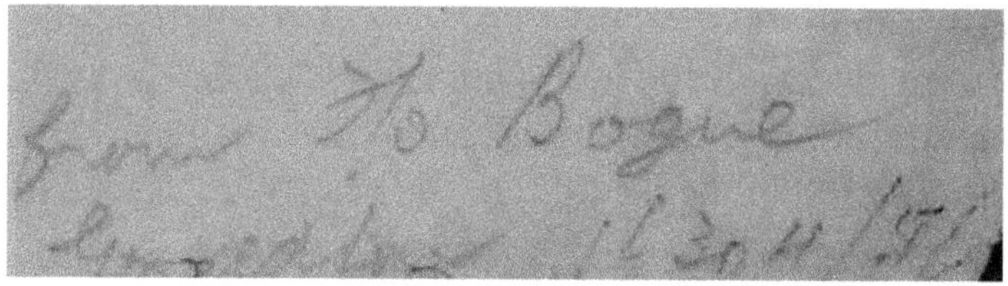

Enlargement of Extract from Message 11A

The original message showing the time and day appears to be 1630H/1/, which could only mean that it was dated on 1 December, i.e.,1630H/1/12. Clearly, the enlargement above shows that at some stage it has been changed to 5 December. The formation of the superimposed '5' does not match with that same figure shown elsewhere in the message (e.g., at 2150 and 2255 hours), suggesting that the alteration was most likely made by someone other than the message-taker. This alteration is not recent because copies of Message 11A obtained in the early 1990s contain this same alteration.

An enlargement of Bogue's message above appears to show it having been passed to FLGOFF Vern Wesche 15 minutes later at 1645H (not 1115H as read by Justice Cole). This is probably correct because the formation of the '5' appears in the same handwriting as the message-taker, meaning that Wesche had been actually informed four days after receipt of the message. Thus, given that SWACH had knowledge of Bogue's message on 1 December and that sudden action was taken on Cooper's message on 4 December, it shows that the entries in the SWACH logbook are highly irregular.

Enlargement of Message 11A (line 5)

Whoever took down Bogue's notes corrected the meaning of 'calling Frazer DM Darwin' by adding the notations 'B2' and 'F', as shown above in line 5. His opinion was that the signal would be to DF Darwin, not to DM Darwin because there was no such station. [Call-sign for Darwin Coastal Station = VID]

Bogue's notes to SWACH containing these annotations clarify the meaning of Frazer (Fraser) station. It had been realised that the station referred to was likely to be **Fraser HFDF station** at HMAS *Melville*, located south of Darwin, and afterwards referred to as HMAS *Coonawarra*.

In November 1941, each of the Western Area services headquarters was separately located with direct communication links with SWACH. The Army HQ operated from Beaufort Street in Perth, the Air Force HQ from ANA House in St Georges Terrace and the Navy HQ, including the offices of DNOWA, COIC and SWACH, from the Elder Building adjacent to the entrance of Victoria Quay in Fremantle.

Although SWACH was essentially a RAN affair, in order to facilitate the efficient coordination and collection of operational data for the Western Area commands, it was essential that SWACH be comprised of representatives of each of the Services. SWACH reported directly to the Central War Room (CWR) in Melbourne on operational matters and to COIC on important intelligence matters.

The SWACH offices on the corner of Phillimore and Cliff Streets, Fremantle included the operations room, plotting room, combined intelligence centre and the offices accommodating the district naval officer (DNO), CAPT Ian Farquhar-Smith and his deputy, A/CMDR Victor Ramage. A Court of Inquiry was also contained within the building where interrogation of German officers also took place. Operations personnel employed there during late 1941 included Senior Operations Officer LCDR P Bailhache, Staff Duty Officers LCDR J Ryrcoft and LCDR A Moir, RAAF Senior Operations Officer WCDR D McLean, SLDR L Daniel and FLT Roberts. During the Sydney crisis, the operations room was manned full-time on a rotational basis by FLGOFFs L Palmer, J Pigdon, L Prentis and I Way.

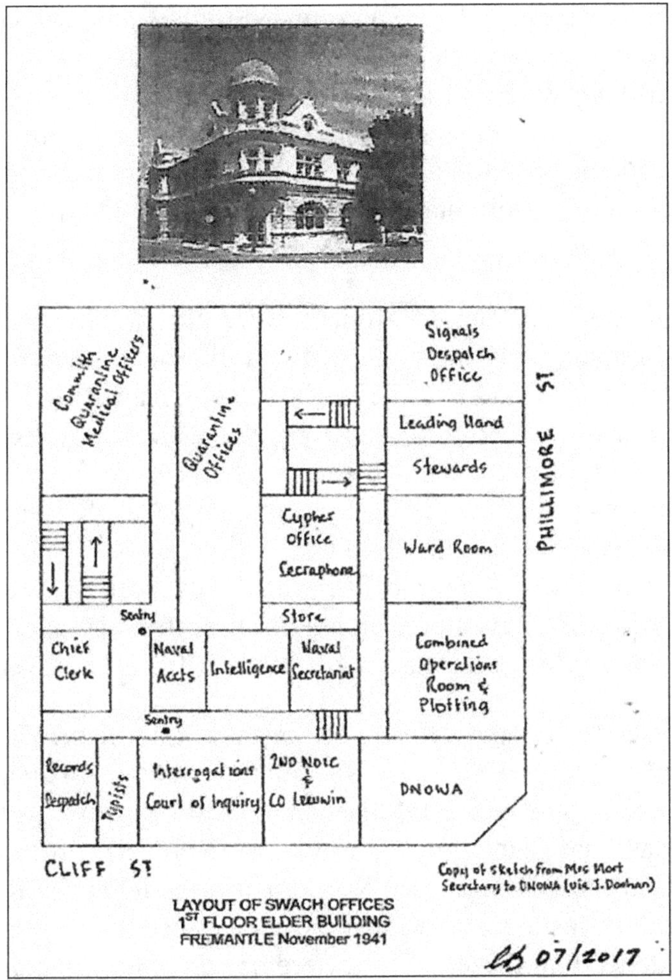

Layout of SWACH Offices in Fremantle

The 'Commission of Inquiry' that Detmers refers to in his book *(The Raider Kormoran)* was actually a Court of Inquiry. This inquiry at the time consisted of an admiral and two other officers, including a destroyer commander, which could be none other than the Naval Board's CMDR Dechaineux (ex-commander of the destroyer HMS *Vivacious* and *Eglington*). ADM Crace the only admiral in WA at the time, who obviously headed the inquiry and the most senior third member in charge of the interrogations, CAPT Farquhar-Smith. Detmers recounts that the members of the panel had a very good overall idea of what happened and there was no mention of any charges against Captain Detmers. He had then remained in Fremantle for a few days with his officers, who then boarded a ship that sailed to eastern states and by road to the POW camp in northern Victoria.

Several SWACH senior officers were for a period absent from Fremantle during the *Sydney*'s fateful return. On 18 November the DNO and his deputy, accompanied by Second Naval Member, CMDR J Durnford, were on nearby Rottnest Island inspecting the signal station. Their whereabouts on 19 November are unknown. On the same day, LCDR Bailhache and SWACH colleague WCDR McLean were airlifted to Geraldton. These senior officers had not been on duty at SWACH on 19 November. McLean's aircraft (A41-1) is listed as returned to Maylands airfield in Perth early on 21 November.

The absence of these officers around the time of the *Sydney/ Kormoran* battle has fuelled speculation that the *Sydney* had been directed to intercept an enemy vessel operating off the WA coast and that senior command were present to monitor signals at the WT station at Rottnest Island and at the RAN's Geraldton coastal station. It can be also argued that it was pure coincidence that these officers were absent from Fremantle at the time the sea battle was about to unfold.

The capacity for decisive action by senior officers at SWACH is supported by their respective service records, wherein each possessed a variety of good operational experience, but on this occasion it is evident that they were not all available as a team for crucial decision-making. Also, it is not known whether the decisions taken by SWACH could have been influenced by the Naval Board, in particular by CMDR Durnford, who was visiting Fremantle at the time.

SWACH did not report the cruiser's non-arrival on the 20th (she was due to return to port sometime in the afternoon or evening of that day). However, at 9:30am on 21 November, 39 hours after the battle, the DNO messaged the Naval Board that HMAS *Sydney* was overdue. Seventy hours later, SWACH made a search to locate the cruiser early on 24 November. But regardless of the possible reasons RAN gave for the cruiser's non-arrival and the fact that she had sent no signals, such an inordinate delay in mounting a full-scale search resulted in a reduction in the ability to rescue survivors should she have been engaged in battle or in danger of sinking.

Daily entries were inserted in the SWACH logbook in the narrative form of the messages and signals received by the assigned duty officer as directed, and they were normally recorded in order of receipt. Each duty officer was responsible for compiling the daily narrative entries in the logbook. However, in the period from 3 December to 6 December 1941, there is a noticeable departure from the normal practice of recording. The table below shows entries made by the assigned duty officers from 19 November to 7 December. Each duty officer can be identified throughout the SWACH logbook by their own distinctive handwriting.

DATE DUTY OFFICER(S) SWACH ENTRY BY:				
19 Nov Way/Pigdon Way Pigdon	20 Nov Prentis Prentis	21 Nov Pigdon/Way Pigdon/Way	22 Nov Palmer Palmer	23 Nov Way/Pigdon Way/Pigdon
24 Nov Prentis/Daniel/McLean Prentis/Daniel McLean	25 Nov Way/Daniel/McLean Way/McLean	26 Nov Palmer Palmer	27 Nov Daniel/Prentis Prentis	28 Nov Palmer/Prentis Prentis
29 Nov Prentis/Pigdon Prentis/Pigdon	30 Nov Way/Palmer Way/Palmer	1 Dec Palmer/Way/Pigdon Palmer/Way/Pigdon	2 Dec Pigdon/Prentis Prentis	3 Dec Pigdon/Way *Prentis
4 Dec Way/Palmer *** Prentis**	5 Dec Palmer/Pigdon *** Prentis**	6 Dec Pigdon/Prentis Prentis	7 Dec Prentis/Palmer Prentis	

Duty Officers – SWACH Logbook pp100-149

The table shows that FLGOFF Prentis was not on duty from 0830H/3 to 0830H/6, yet all SWACH log entries for the period are held over and subsequently recorded by him on 6 December. Prentis also recorded the entries for 7 December while FLGOFF Palmer was on duty. Thereafter, there is a resumption of normal recording by the assigned duty officer.

It appears that there was no urgency to log the messages at the time of receipt and they were left in abeyance for three days until Prentis resumed duty on 6 December. Obviously, this dubious practice could facilitate inadvertent inclusions and lead to false recording of the log narratives and order of events. But as there is no evidence of such systematic irregularity elsewhere in the SWACH log, it raises suspicion that the log entries for 3–6 December have been for some reason 'edited' and as a consequence sanctioned by the DNO and/or by assigned RAN duty operations officer at the time.

For instance, certain log narratives in the SWACH log hereunder on page 148 have been inserted selectively by SWACH, and therefore the sequence of events differ from Cooper's original message. Also, the narratives of Cooper's message, purportedly phoned to SWACH on 4 December and recorded by Prentis on 6 December, contain a number of extracts that do not convey the totality and thrust of the Cooper/Bogue messages. See hereunder.

Extract from SWACH Logbook 4 Dec, p148

Narratives by FLGOFF Prentis are reproduced in component form for clarity, below:

1520z: *W/A phoned message received from Geraldton = Geraldton heard a call on 24.50 metres possibly from HMAS *Sydney* and requested Pearce to call Darwin for bearing.

This narrative is not part of Cooper's original message which requests Singapore, not RAAF Pearce to call Darwin. It does not state whether it was picked up by the Geraldton coastal radio station or via WT at Geraldton Aeradio and considering there is no mention of the earlier 'men on board' message, it appears that this station had only picked up the signal that was also recorded in Bogue's message at 2240H. And that Geraldton requested Pearce to call (HFDF) Darwin for a bearing on the signal gives the impression that SWACH took prompt action to ascertain the source of the signal. The SWACH logbook does not record a reply from Pearce (Air Base).

*W/A = RAAF Western Area Headquarters (WAHQ)

1125z: Unrelated signal

1543z: Received following by telephone from W/A: S/L Cooper at Geraldton reports one of his operators listening on 24.5 metres heard R/T telephone signal calling Darwin or technical telegraph operator. Signals weak and operator thought it may be from HMAS *Sydney*. Later, Geraldton report strength of signal increasing.

This message, logged separately 23 minutes later, contains elements of Cooper's message and of Bogue's message. Some additional information, such as 'signals strength' that was not mentioned by Cooper or Bogue has been introduced. However, given that Cooper made it clear to WAHQ that the messages were received in plain Morse, it was not possible for Dawson to have heard the 'RT telephone' (voice) signal and furthermore, it was not possible that a 'technical telegraph (Morse) operator' could have heard a (modulated) RT telephone signal. The message is confusing, probably due to the *RT transcription from Bogue's message, but more perplexingly it also implies that Geraldton continued to monitor the signals that Dawson heard.

*The abbreviated form of 'RT' has several meanings:

Radio-telegraphy: telegraphy without using wires, i.e., wireless telegraphy, WT (voice)

Radio-telegraph: to telegraph by radio-telegraphy, i.e., by wireless (in Morse)

Radio-telegram:	a written message transmitted by radio-telegraphy
Radio-telephony:	to transmit and receive voice messages by radio, i.e., by wireless-telephony
Radio-telephone:	to telephone using radio-telephony, i e., a telephone signal transmitted in voice by radio-telephony (a wireless telephone)

From the definitions above, it can be concluded that 'wireless' is symptomatic of 'radio', each distinguished only by the mode of transmission. SWACH, therefore, correctly described the 'RT telephone' signals as voice messages, but it appears that they were misled by the opinion of Geraldton Aeradio in presuming that the signals had emanated from Aeradio Sydney in voice mode, some 3,000 miles away. In fact, in those days it was highly improbable for Aeradio stations to have transmitted over such a distance without relaying HF signals. Moreover, none of these stations could relay direct to Western Australia in November 1941. Geraldton Aeradio was thus correct that the signals came from Sydney, but in WT mode.

1545z On instructions from LCDR Moir, Naval Duty Staff Officer, signalled Darwin. Immediate = Establish watch on 24.5 metres immediately. Geraldton heard R/T signal calling Darwin or technical telegraph operator and thinks call possibly from Sydney = 1500z/4

Again, this narrative represents a combination of the Cooper and Bogue messages. It establishes that Operations Officer LCDR Moir was on duty at the time and that Senior Operations Officer Bailhache did not appear to take a leading role, even though Cooper's message had been addressed to him. There is no evidence in the SWACH logbook to suggest that he was on duty at the time.

In this narrative, Moir includes the beginning of Cooper's message, but he fails to include the central discourse of the distress signal, preferring to give Geraldton's impression that the signals were transmissions from Sydney to Darwin by RT. He recommends the only action to date – a watch on 24.5 metres by Darwin. This selective message appears to have been arranged so as not to convey the sense of a distress signal and the general thrust of the wording is designed to demonstrate the immediate action taken and the efficiency in dealing with it.

1555z: W/A phoned following received from SLR Cooper at Geraldton = Geraldton Aeradio opinion call coming from Sydney Aeradio on 25 metres. Following heard, Calling Darwin or technical telegraph operator from sea. Sydney calling, send carrier, men on board; calling Frazer D/F Darwin cannot detect you; Singapore call Darwin. This M.S.S. Sydney calling, message received frequency satisfactory, will put through **one more** [time]. Heard at 1510z.

Finally, the substance of Cooper's distress message is logged together with the opinion that Geraldton Aeradio thinks the call is coming from Sydney Aeradio. This entry is almost taken by SWACH verbatim from the message form. It is the only entry that suggests the *Sydney* could be in trouble. Note there is no mention of 'RT'. The 'MSS' Sydney notation has been probably mistaken for 'MS' as shown in Cooper's message, and the time of entry, 'Heard at 1510z' is misleading for it implies that the complete message was heard at that time, whereas the messages are shown to have been received over a period of some one and a half hours, the actual distress signal having been heard much earlier (at 2140H).

Cooper phoned only one message to WAHQ, yet it is odd that the SWACH log records a series of entries that are found to be extracts of his original message and those of Bogue's notes. These log entries also contain information not mentioned by Cooper and given that he emphasised that all signals were received in Morse, again, no mention is made of the mode of transmission in the SWACH log. In the last message SWACH referred to 'RT' to deliver the impression of voice signals emanating from a station in Sydney. Also, the above log entry carefully avoids any mention of WT by changing the wording on the Cooper/Bogue messages by inserting **'one more',** in lieu of **'in Morse'.** This mistake can only be explained if the wording had been misconstrued by FLGOFF Prentis when he wrote the log entries on 6 December.

Understandably, SWACH would have initially treated Cooper's message with a degree of apprehension due to the fact that the cruiser was shortly to arrive in Fremantle from routine escort duties and from the general area where enemy activity had not been recently reported. Under the circumstances it could not have been envisaged that she could have been in serious trouble, but at the very least they should have been alerted that the 'call from sea, men on board' message was synonymous with a vessel in distress. But the opportunity to prosecute Cooper's message of 19 November was not taken up until it was ultimately required to be dealt with after Bogue's message surfaced nearly 12 days later.

On 1 December, Prime Minister Curtin officially announced to the Australian public that the *Sydney* had been lost and there were no survivors, and therefore it could not have been seriously thought that the cruiser could have remained afloat for another two weeks and to then have sent a distress signal. As a consequence, SWACH could ill-afford to seriously investigate the issue of a distress signal from HMAS *Sydney* after her fate had been officially explained.

0930 Recd signal fm. Darwin : Your Z126 4/12 Station identified as P.H.B., Darwin & P.N.C., Sydney : telegram channel = 0230 Z/5.

SAT., DEC., 6th 41

The above extract is taken from the SWACH logbook on 5 December (p149):

0930z: Received signal from Darwin = Your Z126 4/12. Station identified as PMG Darwin & PMG Sydney telegram channel = 0230z/5

This narrative is in reply to LCDR Moir's signal sent to Darwin some hours earlier on 4 December, which stated, 'establish watch on 24.5 metres immediately, Geraldton heard an RT signal calling Darwin or technical telegraph operator and thinks call possibly from Sydney' – signalled at 2345H/4 (1545z).

The above reply implies that the PMG had been transmitting on 24.5 metres at the time indicated, but the message from Darwin does not mention the mode of transmission by the PMG. However, that Darwin identified that the signals were sent via a telegram channel between PMG Darwin and PMG Sydney is indicative that the message had been sent in common WT mode, and hence by Morse. A further message sent by SWACH to CWR on the following day helps to clarify:

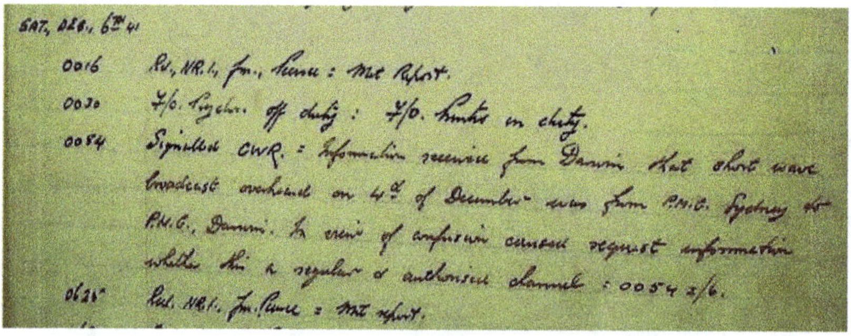

Extract from SWACH Logbook, 6 Dec, p149

0054z: Signalled CWR = Information received from Darwin that short wave broadcast overheard on 4th of December was from PMG Sydney to PMG Darwin. In view of confusion caused request information whether this is a regular or authorised channel = 0054z/6

SWACH had interpreted that the message heard had come from a 'short-wave broadcast'. Apparently, they were still of the opinion that the message heard in Geraldton was voice-broadcast (RT) by the PMG on a channel or band-width of 24.5 metres, thus vindicating the log narratives of 4 December. But considering Darwin had identified the signals as emanating from PMG Sydney to PMG Darwin on a telegram channel (WT), CWR therefore must have considered the matter closed because they did not reply to the SWACH query about whether the PMG used 24.5 metres as a regular channel or whether that particular wavelength was authorised to be used on this occasion.

The Sydney/Darwin telegraph link appears to have been well established by November 1941. In June 1938, the Lyons Government announced that Darwin would be developed as a large military base that would be linked strategically to Singapore. In addition to these preparations for possible enemy attack, it was anticipated that Darwin Post and Telegraph Office would become a focal communications centre should conflict occur.

Effective communication would not have been possible without direct links to Darwin with civil and naval authorities in the major capital cities. However, even though the technical facilities were available for maximum reliability in message transmission, the physical phenomena encountered in shortwave propagation and the fundamentals of telegraph communication remained problematical. In this respect, the SWACH log narratives of 5 and 6 December are canvassed in more detail below:

By definition, given that a 'channel' is a frequency band wide enough for one-way communication (the width of the channel tailored to suit the particular type of transmission), the Cooper/Bogue messages that were detected as having emanated on

24.5 metres and were again sent on that same wavelength, demonstrates that the messages heard by Dawson could only have emanated from a single source – from a WT transmitting station in Sydney to a receiving station in Darwin.

The signal to CWR at 0054z/6 stating that the messages were 'overheard' during the short-wave broadcast does not indicate either a Morse or voice transmission. But the message sent to Darwin by LCDR Moir does specify that Geraldton heard an 'RT signal' and because Dawson only heard Morse, it can only be concluded that the messages were in fact passed from Sydney to Darwin via a WT channel in Morse. And although there may be some doubt about the location of the station in Sydney from which the signals were transmitted, nevertheless, the reply from Darwin on 6 December identified the mode of transmission.

It was also desirable that the messages received on 24.5 metres should also be transmitted on the same wavelength in case further distress signals were to have been received, but for the PMG to have been transmitting at night on such a high frequency, a narrow band adjacent to the frequencies 11.6–12.1Mcs (wavelength 24.8m–25.8m) then often used by Radio Australia when broadcasting on 25 metres, would not have produced good reception and therefore was extremely unlikely to have been a regular or authorized channel.

Curiously, although this message appears in the CWR operations diary, CWR did not reply to the SWACH query about 'authorisation' or even acknowledge the signal. It follows that they may have previously been aware of the content of the distress signal. Also, it was well known that frequencies for civil transmissions, such as for PMG telegraph, were usually nominated in terms of wavelengths to allow for broader reception, whereas for military and naval signals, specific frequencies were more concise for the purpose.

PMG should not have been authorised to transmit on 24.5 metres at the time because such a frequency could have interfered with other transmitting organisations, each of which had been granted the conditional right to transmit on their prescribed frequency. In fact, during WW2, all of the various types of transmissions in Australia were strictly controlled by the allocation of dedicated frequencies and wavelengths, specifically to prevent signals interference from different sources. Besides, PMG transmissions on 24.5 metres could have affected naval communications, and if for example should it have been necessary for HMAS *Sydney* to contact the shore station at *Harman*, only two frequencies were set aside for the purpose (12330kcs during daytime and 6610kcs during the night-time). And as this daytime frequency equates to a wavelength of 24.33 metres, PMG transmissions on 24.5 metres (depending on bandwidth) could therefore adversely affect routine and/or emergency signals from the *Sydney.*

Given that the survivors on board the *Sydney* would have desperately tried every avenue to get signals out via a range of frequencies and various bandwidths in order to provide more scope for being detected, it would have been expedient for them to have signalled in short wave on 25 metres to a much wider short-wave listening audience, not just in Australia but overseas. Also, in those days it was common practice for telegraphy operators to listen in to various short-wave bands for entertainment during down-time at night when there was little or no telegraphic traffic.

Although receipt of HF transmissions at night were problematic, there was also the possibility that the signals could be intercepted worldwide during daylight hours by any of the Royal Navy's network of receiving stations, providing the signals were sent with sufficient power. However, in the case of the signals being sent on a reduced wattage due to damage sustained to the *Sydney*'s transmitting or aerial apparatus, it was still possible that signals could be received, for example by the closest Royal Navy station in Singapore and by almost any station in Australia.

In considering the destruction on board the *Sydney* after the battle and the certain loss of life and injury to crewmen, it would appear from the tenor of the 2140H (message 11A) that those capable of sending the signals may not have been experienced telegraphers. The distress message per se is poorly constructed and does not include positional coordinates, though it is conceded that this information may have been conveyed earlier and had remained undetected by the Sydney station. In the normal course of events, however, it cannot be ruled out that the WT operators on board the *Sydney* had tried sending on the alternative 6610kcs, but HMAS *Harman* could not be raised. No other receiving station should have been tuned to this frequency or wavelength.

What is most disconcerting about the message purportedly sent to SWACH on 5 December is that PMG Sydney is said to have got involved in the 'men on board' message, a message that was roundly conceived to be a naval matter, a distress signal from sea. In this respect, the veracity or otherwise of the message has never been explained, only that the reply from Darwin absolved SWACH from pursuing the matter any further. And in view of the fact that coastal stations, including the Sydney station at La Perouse, which was at that time under the control of the RAN, it is inconceivable that the distress message received at 2140H escaped the attention of naval authorities elsewhere in Australia.

In order to decide between the merits of Cooper's evidence and the findings made by Commission of Inquiry, it is necessary to examine the passage of the message at SWACH and the personnel who may have been involved. In both instances, there is only one common thread to work from – that the message phoned by Cooper to WAHQ is found recorded several times (in partial form) in the SWACH log on 4 December. Thus, the order in which Cooper's Message 12A was passed on requires examination to establish whether the message could have been sent on 19 November.

Commissioner Cole's proposition is predicated simply on his claim that Cooper's message was delivered to SWACH on 4 December by WAHQ, an immediate investigation was undertaken and the source of the signals were identified and recorded in the logbook on the following day. However, the referral on Cooper's message clearly indicates that it was addressed to Bailhache (5ASO). Duty officer Palmer, who was signed on for duty, did not record the events in the logbook and nor did Bailhache appear to be on duty to take any role in the subsequent enquiries that were made by RAN duty officer LCDR Moir. But the irregularities in the logbook are even more disturbing because the events that purportedly occurred on the night of 4 December were held over and recorded by FLGOFF Prentis after he signed on for duty at 0830H on 6 December.

The SWACH narratives that were derived from Cooper's single message and subsequently entered on 4 December at 1520z, 1543z and 1555z are strangely cast as though the messages were received separately and the necessary enquiries were made as the situation developed. Those entries at 1520z and 1555z indicate that WAHQ had been in touch with Geraldton Aeradio beforehand for an opinion on Cooper's message, which was subsequently written on the WAHQ message form, but it was not until 35 minutes later at 1555z that the crux of Cooper's message had been revealed.

Obviously, the original message had not been urgently passed on to SWACH as requested by Cooper and WAHQ had obtained an opinion from Geraldton Aeradio before phoning his complete message to SWACH. But that opinion was purely supposition, for there were insufficient grounds that the signals had emanated from the distant Sydney Aeradio. Another anomaly concerns the entry at 1520z implying that Geraldton also heard the signals that Dawson recorded, but then curiously requested Pearce to call DF Darwin for a bearing – well after the signal transmissions had ceased!

Duty officers at SWACH had gone through the motions of making the necessary enquiries, but they failed to record the totality of Cooper's message. And the fact that the distress signal was not mentioned in the signal to Darwin can only be described as a measure of trying to water-down the overall concern. But there had to be a simple explanation that would identify the source of the signal and that was provided by Darwin the following day in reply to LCDR Moir's signal made 30 minutes after the signals had purportedly ceased. Therefore, Darwin PMG did not hear any distress signal on 24.5 metres and could only enquire as to whether Sydney PMG had transmitted to Darwin between the hours of 2100 and 2300H on 4 December.

It was claimed that a number of stations were transmitting in Morse during these hours, and whilst it is conceded that other PMG transmissions could have been included in Cooper's message received at 2255H, there is no evidence or explanation provided in the SWACH log to conclude that Sydney or Darwin could have been involved in sending the distress-like signals received at 2140H. Moreover, the text of the message, particularly that recorded by Bogue, is quite unlike normal PMG jargon and considering that the original call came from sea, the claim that this particular signal had been identified as emanating from Aeradio Sydney can only be seen in the context of it having originated at sea and detected in Sydney – from a ship in distress. The remainder of the messages describes efforts to contact the station in Darwin in order to make contact with the vessel.

Entries recorded by FLGOFF Way until 1800H on 19 November refer to routine signals received from Pearce and thereafter the recording shows that only FLGOFF Pigdon was on duty on this day during the period when HMAS *Sydney* was in trouble and during which he recorded one unrelated message in the log. But unfortunately, it is not possible to identify the handwriting of Cooper's message received from WAHQ. It was certainly not that of Pigdon, or of Bailhache, and certainly not of other senior officers who were absent that day. Rather, Message 12A is actually the original message recorded by the WAHQ signals clerk in Perth, whereby a subsequent opinion from Geraldton Aeradio was obtained and other notations attached. In other words, Cooper's message had not been forwarded immediately to the Navy as he had requested. It is also curious that the complete message was logged in partial form and within designated timeframes that were not specified by Cooper.

Cooper's message sent late in the evening should have been regarded as a matter of high importance. However, the fact that the *Sydney* was shortly due back in Fremantle and that an explanation for the origin of the message had been subsequently obtained, it diffused the importance of the issue and reduced the urgency to further investigate the authenticity of the reported signals. This is not to suggest that it was the sole cause of the 15-day delay in recording these events in the logbook, but rather it is symptomatic of the reluctance to delve any further into the loss of HMAS *Sydney* until it had been formally dealt with by the prime minister.

If in fact Cooper's message had been forwarded promptly to the Navy by WAHQ, it should have been sent directly to the operations room or to the office of the district naval officer. However, such a message sent around midnight on 19 November was unlikely to have attracted the attention of DNO Farquhar-Smith until he resumed duty on the morning of the 20th at the earliest and not long before *Sydney*'s expected arrival

PM that same day. On the following day (providing he was available) he was therefore required to consciously decide on whether to make further enquiries or to take further action on the somewhat downgraded importance of the message assessed by Geraldton Aeradio, or to await the almost imminent arrival of HMAS *Sydney*. Nevertheless, that he did not consider it necessary to order an air search in the morning to confirm the cruiser's safety (it would have undoubtedly eased his conscience), is a measure of his opinion that the message did not relate to the cruiser.

Awareness of Cooper's message may not have been only confined to the DNO. After all, it would have been expected that the likely meaning of the message would have been canvassed and opinions sought amongst other senior officers such as CMDR Ramage and CMDR Durnford (if he was still available in Fremantle). But although there must have been some disquiet about the particular phrasing of the message received at 2140H, that should have been regarded at the very least as symptomatic of a vessel in distress, the weight of opinion and an overwhelming reliance must surely have been placed on the RAAF assessment that the signals had emanated from Aeradio Sydney. But in any event, the test by SWACH of whether their assessment was well-founded or not, would have been confirmed when HMAS *Sydney* had arrived within a matter of hours. And when she did not arrive, SWACH could not in all conscience have thereafter dealt with Cooper's message retrospectively.

As previously explained, senior SWACH naval staff were not available at the time to deal with the issue, which in any case had become downgraded as a matter of priority. It would have been inconceivable for them to think that HMAS *Sydney* could have been in serious trouble on her return from a routine escort in an area where enemy warships and U-boats were considered non-existent and where armed raiders if present were no match for the cruiser. It is mainly in this environment that examination of the likely passage of Message 12A and those involved in dealing with it are made.

By 4 December, the fate of *Sydney* had been well and truly established. Most would have thought there could not have been the remotest possibility that she had managed to stay afloat for three weeks and then to have sent a distress message. After all, the evidence gained from the German survivors and the positions of the retrieved rafts and flotsam all point to the general locale of the battle site, notwithstanding that a vessel as large as the *Sydney* could not have escaped detection during the expansive sea and air search.

Senior intelligence officers in WA were conspicuously active during *Sydney*'s return from escorting HMAT *Zealandia* to the Sunda Strait. The Port War Signals Station logbook records that on 18 November, Farquhar-Smith, Durnford and Ramage attended this short- wave receiving station on Rottnest Island on this day at noon when the *Sydney* was positioned about 1,000nm distant to the north.

The other inter-related event occurred the following day when intelligence officers McLean (RAAF), Bailhache (RAN) and Wolfenden (Army) flew to Geraldton, purportedly for regional inspections. At Geraldton they had surely been accompanied by WCDR Heffernan, commanding officer of No. 4 SFTS who, according to Cooper, was not at home late on 19 November when he and Bogue jointly composed the message that Cooper phoned to WAHQ. But at the very least, the gathering was an opportunity to celebrate Wolfenden's appointment on 20 November as commanding officer of Western Command in WA.

While McLean and Bailhache were in Geraldton on 19 November, the *Sydney* was less than 300nm away when the battle with *Kormoran* began, although their exact whereabouts were unknown. Whether they were privy to information of a possible interception by the *Sydney* is also unknown, but it is odd that they could not have been made aware of the Q signal received at 1800H/19 by the RAN-controlled Geraldton coastal radio facility. It appears that for some reason, the Q signal intercept from the *Straat Malakka (Kormoran)* was not initially taken seriously by the RAN and so it was deemed not important, even though it must have been regarded as a sign of enemy activity close to the coast, and which in any case should have been interpreted as a possible Allied vessel in distress. However, there is no record of follow-up discussions or of action taking place.

It is also hard to imagine that McLean, Bailhache and Heffernan had not been informed about the short-wave messages that were passed from Dawson to Bogue late on 19 November or even by the following morning prior to their departure from the Geraldton airfield on 21 November. Yet, as far as intelligence records are concerned, there is no evidence to suggest that these men were aware of or became involved with these signals at the time. But surely, the expectation was that Bogue, who was also the acting intelligence officer of No. 4 SFTS, would have at least sought an opinion on the source and nature of Dawson's message from the visiting SWACH officers.

Bogue's role in this whole episode is perplexing for he was clearly aware that the signals were received in Morse and that only Cooper phoned their response to Perth, yet the SWACH log entry at 1555z from WAHQ shows Cooper's message prefaced with an opinion from Geraldton Aeradio indicating that WAHQ had sought an opinion after the arrival of Cooper's message. Unknown to Cooper, Bogue must have subsequently made contact with WAHQ and forwarded that opinion.

All of these matters are further complicated by the fact that up-to-date COIC weekly summaries for December 1941 have not mentioned the Q signal that was sent by the raider. These reports routinely carried the latest HF and DF tracking information and it therefore raises the question of whether the COIC were cognizant of or had suspected the presence of an enemy vessel in the vicinity of the *Sydney*'s return path on 19 November.

The significance of the distress signals received at Geraldton at approx. 1800H on 19 November by the so-called *Straat Malakka* and by the tug *Uco* should have been immediately registered. It was extremely important that these signals were routinely reported at the time it had occurred because they were a sure sign of current or potential enemy activity in the area whether it was considered genuine or not, but there is no mention of the Q signals in the logbook. Curiously, Naval Intelligence had informed SWACH (via CWR) eight days later on 27 November. Thus, the decision to release this information was not automatically forthcoming and it did not feature in the context of the suspected loss of the *Sydney* until the *Aquitania* reported to Wilsons Promontory Signal Station on that same day, which had picked up German sailors four days previously.

However, given that the Q signal intercepts were of limited transmission range, naval intelligence in Fremantle should have expected that HMAS *Sydney* would also have picked up the signals that had emanated in the vicinity of her return track. And at no time did SWACH or even the Naval Board appear to correlate the timing of the 'call from sea' message and the emergency Q signals that had been detected by the RANs Geraldton coastal station only six hours earlier. Nowhere in the National Archives is it mentioned. Cooper's message should therefore have been taken more seriously because of a possible link with the Q signals. After all, the message was clearly marked 'Distress Signal' and its contents indicated that the call came from a vessel at sea.

The comforting factor for SWACH was that Cooper's message was construed to have emanated from Aeradio Sydney. But that Central War Room had been belatedly made aware of the Q signals held by SWACH on 27 November (message to CWR, 0630z/27), suggesting Geraldton radio had passed the distress message to SWACH well beforehand. Besides, SWACH had known about the distress signal detected by *Uco* when she berthed at Fremantle early on 21 November. This message should have immediately led them to suspect that the distress signals on 19 November were most likely to have been connected with Cooper's message. But that the Navy did not reveal the timing of the Q signals to CWR soon after it was known that *Trocas* had rescued survivors, resulting in an unwillingness to divulge to CWR Cooper's inter-related message received on 19 November.

It is also perplexing that the Navy hierarchy had reaffirmed that the *Sydney* could have been in the process of hunting for a suspected raider at a time when many observers had already conceded that she had been lost. Surely, concern that the *Sydney*'s fuel reserves after 13 days would have been severely depleted (she would have expended considerable fuel while returning at 23–24 knots), conjures a determination not to reveal the suspected loss of the cruiser. After all, a signal from the shore station at HMAS *Harman* and a (brief) acknowledgement in order that the enemy could not have obtained an accurate fix on the signal, was all that was required to conclude that the *Sydney* had been safe.

Although it is not possible to confirm that the RAN had been cognizant of the *Sydney*'s actual plight from signals and messages that have been made available from the archives, it does raise the possibility that more accurate positional signals may have been intercepted by navy telegrapher Crawford Young aboard the tug *Uco*, the vessel closest to the battle site. His son, David Young, stated that his father had received the last message(s) from the *Sydney* before she was destroyed in an action not far away, but due to a warning of possible submarine activity in the area, *Uco* had been ordered not to break radio silence **(JSCFADT p3029)**. Concern by SWACH that Young may have received the Q signals in more detail, was to result in him appearing before the DNOWA immediately after the *Uco* had arrived in Fremantle early on 21 November and shortly before Farquhar-Smith had informed the Naval Board that the *Sydney* had yet to arrive. As a consequence, Crawford Young had been promptly transferred to another ship.

Early on 21 November Farquhar-Smith ought to have been seriously concerned that the *Sydney* had not arrived in Fremantle, as he would have realised that finding and tracking an enemy vessel during the night of 19/20 November was an almost impossible task without radar. In these uncertain times, the Q signals were suddenly a stark reminder of possible raider activity in the Indian Ocean, reinforcing the Admiralty's view regarding the fate of *SG Embiricos* amid the background of intelligence reports of Japanese expansionism and preparations for war (COIS Weekly Summary25/26). Plainly, that the *Sydney* was so long overdue, it was indicative that something serious had occurred, and that she had not signalled meant that it was extremely unlikely that the cruiser had made contact with an enemy vessel, as the Naval Board had reason to suspect.

Although the RAN would have thought that an action with a raider per se could not have been responsible for the loss of the *Sydney*, in the worst-case-scenario that the *Sydney* had been sunk due to rapidly increasing IJN activities, the Navy should have been acutely aware that a total loss of the cruiser could only have been attributed to a torpedo attack rather than by gunfire from a surface vessel.

And considering that U-boats had not entered the Indian Ocean at that time, it must have occurred to the RAN that only a

Japanese or Vichy French submarine (as later suspected by the Admiralty) could have delivered a fatal blow to the *Sydney*. Even more to the point, although RAN did not know for sure whether German raiders and supply ships could have acted in concert with Axis submarines, the alliance between Germany and Japan meant it could never be completely ruled out.

Comments made by the ACNB regarding the *Sydney*'s non-arrival and that she was probably tracking a raider(s) was thus purely supposition, and that the cruiser had no means of tracking during the night unless her quarry had been sighted before nightfall, Burnett could only have employed his walrus seaplane to search a wide area the following day. If that search proved unsuccessful then the *Sydney* should have returned no more than a day later – on 21 November. In any case, if contact had been made and because the suspect vessel was not listed and plotted on the VAI, the cruiser would have routinely signalled to HMAS *Harman*. Besides, in November 1941 the VAI was regarded as 'an accurate tool'. Merchant ship arrivals and departures on Australia Station for Dutch and Norwegian vessels were fully reported. Only 2–3% of vessels (mostly from Japan) were not **(COI Report Vol 1, p246)**.

The DNO had been issued with the twice-daily coded VAI by the RANs Mercantile Movement Section. This information would normally have been plotted in the SWACH operations and plotting room and together with *Sydney*'s progress during her return from Sunda Strait, a complete picture of arrivals and departures on the eastern Indian Ocean approaches on 19 November would have been observed. And it should have been noted that certain vessels (including *Astora, Bramora* and *Largs Bay*) located near or approaching the vicinity in which the distress signal had emanated, could also have been in danger of attack. However, no raider warnings were ever issued.

Another reason offered by the DNO in his search report to the Naval Board on 11 December is similarly flawed. Farquhar-

Smith wrote that he had decided to carry out an air search early on 24 November because he had assumed that the *Sydney* had experienced engine trouble and the cruiser did not wish to break radio silence. This rather lame excuse is an admission that he had overlooked the prospect of an air search well before he had reported *Sydney*'s non-arrival about 70 hours earlier. At the very least, the extensive intervening timeframe should also have warned him that the cruiser may have stopped or had reduced speed dramatically, and in this circumstance he would have expected that the cruiser would have signalled its predicament, or alternatively he could have arranged for contact to have been made in order to avoid an unnecessary air search.

Summarizing the main points:

- That Message 12A is marked as having been received in RT and Morse is due to the fact Aeradio stations were known to have a dual transmission capability – by voice, and/or WT. As a consequence, the RT mode of transmission is misleading because the signals have not been found to have emanated from Aeradio Sydney.

- Message 11A can be regarded as the parent document from which 12A has been constructed. Essentially this message initially conveys the text of a distress message that was detected by La Perouse wireless station in Sydney, which had relayed it to RT Sydney, and thereafter it describes the attempts to contact Darwin in order to transfix the signal.

- Dawson did not hear the messages directly from the vessel in distress but indirectly in Morse from the transmitting station RT Sydney as the messages were being sent to Darwin at the times indicated in Bogue's notes.

- That La Perouse station had relayed the distress signal to RT Sydney for Darwin to assist indicated that an approximate direction and distance of the distress signal had been ascertained as emanating from Australia station in Zone D (shown as 'DSZD' on Message 11A). By early December 1941 SWACH were confident of the general location of the battle because the array of positions given by the Germans were all known to be within Zone D. In any case, SWACH should have recognised the meaning of this abbreviation as being the locale where the *Sydney* was expected to be from information given by the SWACH Plotting Room.

- SWACH should have been aware that except for naval ships and some very large liners and troop transports, only naval-equipped vessels were capable of transmitting HF signals on 24.5 metres. Merchant ships in distress or in imminent danger would usually call coastal stations on the international emergency 500kcs frequency (wavelength 600 metres).

- Given the fact that HMAS *Sydney* was known to have been in Western Australian waters on 19 November and considering that the distress message was sent on 24.5 metres (a frequency used by the *Sydney* for contact with *Harman* encompassing the 24/25m band), plus the fact that Q signals had been detected by Geraldton Radio earlier that evening, it is incredulous that SWACH could not have suspected that the 'call from sea' distress signal in Cooper's message may have involved HMAS *Sydney.*

- Bogue did not come out openly in support of Cooper. He apparently did not want to involve himself any further, and he neither confirmed nor denied the date of receipt of the message from Dawson. But Cooper's message, purportedly sent on 4 December, contains portions of Bogue's notes obtained on 5 December. Both messages contain the following elements:

    - Cooper's message has been altered (in red pencil) from past tense to present tense to give the impression that

SWACH were taking immediate action at the time it was received and entered in the logbook.

- Cooper's message contains notes identified as being in the same handwriting as the person who took down Bogue's notes.
- Cooper's message had been addressed to Bailash (sic), but he appeared to take no part in prosecuting the message.
- Cooper's message was held in abeyance and elements of it were eventually recorded in the SWACH log on 4 December.
- The Cooper/Bogue messages mention 'distress signal', the SWACH log does not.
- In Cooper's message, the reference to 'Lykard' has been noted as 'Leichardt', which had been taken from Bogue's notes.
- Bogue's notes were originally written down on 1 December at 1630H and signed off again (fraudulently) on 5 December.

- Commissioner Cole failed to address any of the above issues, nevertheless at the very least he should have noted that the SWACH log entries of 4 December were delayed and recorded on 6 December when FLGOFF Prentis came on duty. And considering that Cooper's message and the log entries for this day contain so many elements of Bogue's message, plainly, SWACH could not have taken action on Cooper's message without being in possession of Bogue's notes.

- The failure to deal with Cooper's message on 19 November can be attributed to a combination of factors – the fact that senior SWACH officers were unavailable and that SWACH were satisfied the signals had emanated from Aeradio Sydney. They could not have imagined that HMAS *Sydney* could have been in trouble on her return voyage was due to the fact that the cruiser was scheduled to arrive shortly in

Fremantle on the afternoon of the following day. This was probably the main reason why SWACH was reluctant to take action on Cooper's message on 19 November.

- SWACH became aware of the seriousness of their decision not to have fully investigated Cooper's message after WAHQ received Bogue's notes via telephone from Geraldton on 1 December. Bogue had supplied these notes as a result of a request by Air Commodore De La Rue, RAAF Commanding Officer Western Area, for information on all matters relating to HMAS *Sydney* and the air search so that a complete appraisal of RAAF operations and performance could be undertaken. Consequently, this new information required WAHQ and SWACH to deal with the totality of both messages in the days ahead.
- Prime Minister Curtin's announcement to the press on the fate of the *Sydney* on 3 December, officially notifying the public and giving a detailed account of the action, gave the greenlight for SWACH to take action on Cooper's message. All regular log entries were withheld for three days for the purpose of inserting in the log an explanation for Cooper's Message 12A and with regard to Message 11A.
- On 4 December, SWACH decided to address the issue by inserting their response to Cooper's message in the logbook in a series of entries to give the impression of the matter being urgently addressed and as though it was happening at the times indicated by Cooper. However, the sequence given to the SWACH log entries are demonstrably flawed. They were initially couched as though Geraldton Radio was the first to have detected the signals, followed by excerpts of Cooper's message, falsely indicating RT telephone signals as the source of the signals. But telephone signals were not mentioned in either of the Cooper/Bogue messages. Besides, such signals could not have been detected by short-wave radio in Morse and that each of the four logbook entries

carefully avoids any mention of the words 'distress signal', clearly, we are finally left with the false impression that the signals had emanated from Sydney to Darwin via a normal telephone conversation on an unusual and unauthorised high frequency of 24.5 metres.

- The 'call from sea, send carrier, all men on board' distress message Morse signals, totally unrelated and unexplained in terms of PMG activities, did not originally emanate from Sydney. However, this is not to say that PMG and/or AWA may have been monitored by the RAN in Darwin and that the PMG may have been transmitting at the time.
- SWACH had no intention of acting on Cooper's message until advised of Bogue's message by WAHQ. That details of the battle had become known and that routine Court of Inquiry proceedings into the *Sydney* disaster were likely to have been instigated soon afterwards, SWACH arranged for the embroidered narratives, together with elements of Bogue's notes to be inserted in the logbook on 4 December.
- Provision was made to insert the log entries at the required times by withholding the logbook recordings of all incoming and outgoing signals and messages from 3 December until 6 December, each of these signal narratives being required to be numbered and placed in order for ease of recording at a later time. The log narratives for 4 and 5 December were recorded by FLGOFF Prentis, who was not on duty during this period and therefore was probably indifferent to the circumstances surrounding the recording of the narratives.
- SWACH could not have prosecuted the Cooper message without the cooperation of their counterparts in Darwin at Admiralty House. A plausible reply from Darwin was all that was required to put the matter to rest and that no action appears to have been taken against RAN and RAAF officers implicated at Fremantle, raising the question of who else may have been privy to the content of the Cooper/

Bogue messages. For example, the RAN should have been cognizant of the signals received at the main receiving station under their control at La Perouse in Sydney. But in a matter of weeks, the beginning of the war in the Pacific rapidly overtook the relative importance of the *Sydney* disaster.

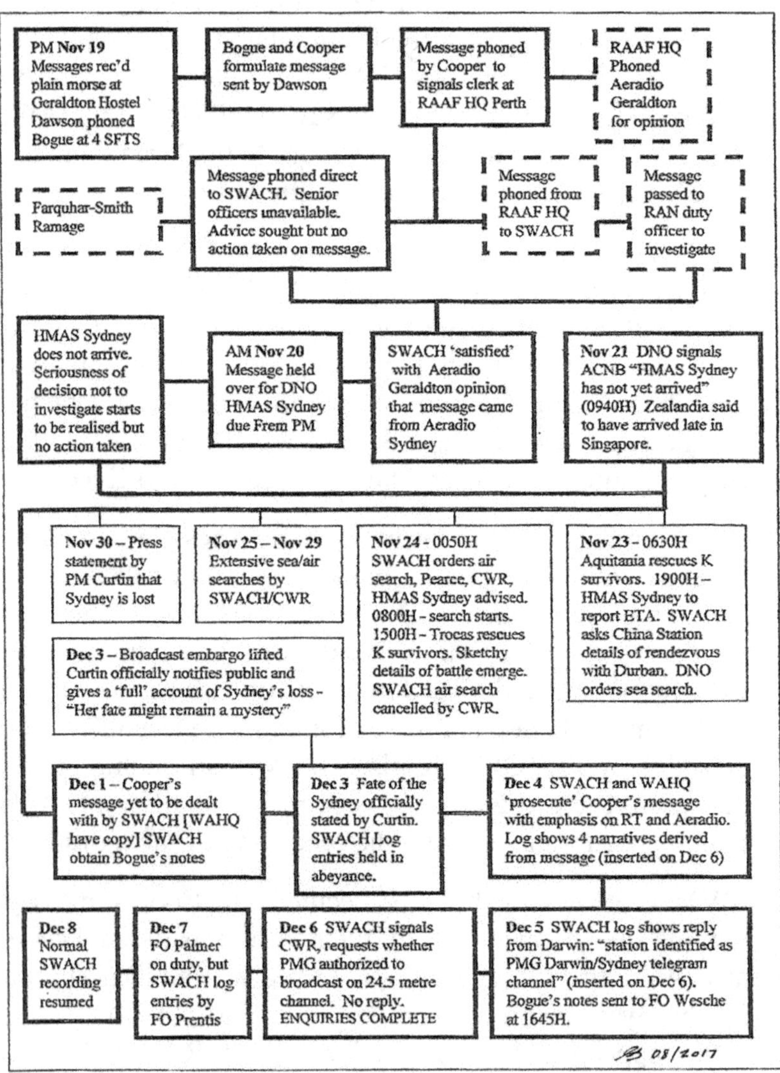

Time-line Diagram: 19 November – 5 December

Much of this controversy is embodied in the proposition that the signals were heard by CPL Dawson variously in both RT and Morse, as shown appended on Cooper's message. However, conceding that HMAS *Sydney* did not have the capacity to send distant HF voice signals, obviously the 'call from sea' distress message heard at 2140H did not come directly from HMAS *Sydney*, rather it was heard by Dawson in Morse on his short-wave receiver as it was being transmitted in Morse from Sydney to Darwin. And due to the unsuitable night- time frequency of the wavelength of 24.5 metres, he heard intermittent Morse signals of several efforts by the Sydney station trying to contact Darwin in order to ascertain a positional fix on the signal.

SLDR Cooper's affidavit emphasises that Message 12A was not a true account of what he sent. He stressed that the signals were all received by Dawson in Morse. But Commissioner Cole could only offer, '...that to say in a message that it will later be put through in Morse implies that the message was not in Morse'. But in consideration of Bogue's notes at 2150H that an earlier request had already been made for Darwin to signal in Morse, the latter response (at 2255H) is clearly an acknowledgement of that original request.

Cooper's claim that his message was not a true account is absolute, because even from a superficial viewpoint it is obvious that the opinion from Geraldton has been added, the message has been re-worded to reflect the currency of the situation and it contains elements of Bogue's notes received by WAHQ on 1 December. Plainly, these additional notes, which include 'RT' and the word 'Leichardt', indicate that Cooper's message could not have been seriously dealt with by SWACH while the event was occurring three days later on 4 December. Above all, the act of post-dating Message 11A from 1 December to 5 December, including those additional notes contained in the SWACH narratives of 4 December, clearly establish that Bogue's original message could not have been received at any day afterwards.

SWACH had been negligent in not taking immediate action on 19 November because the message heard at 2140H on 24.5 metres, albeit incomplete, was consistent with a vessel with HF transmission capability, ostensibly a naval vessel in distress. And that the *Sydney* station had sought Darwin to provide a positional fix, further indicates that they had thought the vessel to be situated somewhere off the West Australian coast in the vicinity of Australia Station Area D.

Again, in his findings Commissioner Cole found the events occurred on 4 December, not on 19 November. He cites the logbook entries and he cited that because Message 12A bears the name FLGOFF Palmer, who was duty officer on 4 December but not on 19 November, it demonstrates conclusively that the events recorded in messages 11A and 12A occurred on 4 December. In fact, Palmer was also on duty and made entries in the logbook during duty shifts on 22, 26, 28, 30 November and 1 December – the day Bogue's notes were obtained by WAHQ. But it was during his period as duty officer on 4 December from 0830H to 0915H on 5 December that SWACH decided to prosecute Cooper's message, together with information taken from Bogue's notes.

That no action was taken on Cooper's message after it was phoned from WAHQ to SWACH late on 19 November until 4 December indicates RAAF/RAN complicity in the matter – in the following order:

- On receipt of Bogue's notes on 1 December, WAHQ notified SWACH because the notes contained similar substance to Cooper's message, of which they had the original copy that had been previously phoned to them on 19 November. SWACH could then ill-afford to disregard Cooper's message.
- Cooper's original message (with RAAF comments attached) and Bogue's notes were then conveyed from WAHQ to

SWACH. The logbook details of 3 December confirm that the narratives were held in abeyance to allow for the 'processing' of Cooper's message at the most suitable time.

- Cooper's message (marked for the attention of Palmer and Bailhache, together with information from Bogue's notes was prosecuted late on 4 December – with the full cooperation of WAHQ.
- Both the Cooper and Bogue messages were then returned to WAHQ and filed.

The role of the enigmatic LCDR Bailhache, who was given the responsibility of dealing with Cooper's message, is unclear. That it was naval duty staff officer LCDR Moir who took a leading hand in prosecuting Cooper's message does not mean that Bailhache was not on duty with Palmer on 4 December. As senior officer at SWACH in managing operations, Bailhache ostensibly played a supervising role, and as area senior officer, he became inextricably involved in the affair on 4 December.

Findings made by Commissioner Cole have been made on a purely superficial basis and without thorough investigation. In contrast, this analysis has identified many inconsistencies and dubious actions in efforts to exonerate SWACH officers of prior knowledge of the Cooper and Bogue messages. Failure to act immediately on Cooper's message and the fact that the RAAF possessed a copy that had not been immediately dealt with by SWACH, led to a concerted attempt by SWACH and WAHQ to later explain the content of Cooper's message.

The extent of cognizance by the naval hierarchy in the affair is unknown, but should a formal Court of Inquiry on the subject have been held, it is highly likely that these dubious practices by SWACH would have been exposed. But what is most disconcerting about establishing the truth of the matter is that other RAN signal station logbooks for the period are not available to conclusively test the veracity or otherwise of Cooper's Message 12A once and for all. And given that Dawson at the Geraldton hostel probably only picked up snippets of the overall messages sent by the Sydney station, a fuller text may have been recorded in the signal logs then held elsewhere, for example, at ACH Darwin and at the RAN-controlled coastal station in Sydney at La Perouse.

RAAF personnel who were involved in prosecuting Cooper's message appear to have had more than a passing interest in the *Sydney/Kormoran* affair. It appears that the SWACH logbook, Cooper's Message 11A and Bogue's Message 12A (RAAF file AA/1969/100, 2/18 INT) were saved for a reason. Originally, the logbook was held by either an ex-SWACH duty officer or possibly by the COIC's Vern Wesche (who later became a lawyer) at the Bull Creek retirement estate and later by the National Archives at Victoria Park in Perth, and finally by the National Archives in Canberra. [RAAF Bull Creek will neither confirm nor deny Wesche's presence there.]

However, without the addition of Cooper's message and Bogue's notes from which the narratives in the logbook of 4 December 1941 were fabricated, this assessment and the historical significance of the Geraldton messages would not have been possible.

Annexures

Annexure 1

Signed statement by EW Cooper:

1. During November 1941, I was Squadron Leader Eric Cooper, Chief Flying Instructor of No. 4 Service Flying Training School (No. 4, SFTS) RAAF Geraldton, West Australia.

2. On the night of Wednesday, 19th November 1941, I was the senior officer present at the above unit when the adjutant of that unit, Flying Officer Gerry Bogue, came to me with detailed notes he had made of a telephone conversation he had just received from an RAAF Corporal Dawson.

3. Apparently, Corporal Dawson with another airman was in the lounge of the Esplanade Hostel in Marine Terrace Geraldton with three ladies listening into a commercial short-wave radio broadcast when he heard transmissions in Morse code which he and the other airman could read and he made notes of them.

4. Corporal Dawson then telephoned the station duty officer that night who was Flying Officer Bogue, who was also the intelligence officer as well as adjutant of No. 4 SFTS, and relayed this information to him.

5. As the station commander was not at his home and could not be contacted, Flying Officer Bogue and I then jointly composed a message from his notes to enable me to pass the information to R.AA.F Headquarters, Western Area in Perth.

6. Later that night, I telephoned HQWA and was answered by a clerk in Signals Section. I carefully dictated my message to that signals clerk and requested that its contacts be passed urgently to the Navy.

7. I subsequently took part in the Avro Anson air searches for lifeboats and rafts from Geraldton, Carnarvon and Onslow resulting from the battle between HMAS *Sydney* and a German raider.

8. Many years later in 1991 in the home of Dr Ted Strachan (former Medical Officer RAAF Pearce during World War Two) in his presence and that of John McArthur and Malcolm Barker and sighted Enclosure 12A of RAAF Headquarters, Western Area file 2/18/INT which purported to be a record of the message I passed to the HQWA signals clerk. I was astonished and perplexed because it was not a true account of that message. In it, I stressed that the signals received by Cpl. Dawson were in Morse code and that he and the other airman could read Morse. Also, they and three ladies heard the signals from an ordinary short-wave receiver at the Esplanade Hostel in Geraldton. This does not appear on Enclosure 12A. The word Aeradi does appear, which I did not mention.

9. It is only recently that I have sighted photocopies of page 148 of the South Western Australia Combined Headquarters (SWACH) logbook and pages 40 and 41 of the 3rd Edition of Richard Summerell's Guide No. 3, *The Sinking of HMAS Sydney*, A guide to Commonwealth Records and more specifically the footnotes on those pages 40 and 41.

10. The chronological sequence of events on page 41 could only have been provided by Flying Officer Bogue from the notes he wrote down from Cpl. Dawson's telephone call on the night of 19th November 1941. I kept no record of his notes. It is obvious from the written comment at the bottom of page 41 that it was Flg Off Bogue who passed this message by secraphone to someone (name blacked out) at 1630H hours on Friday, 5th December 1941.

11. I emphatically deny that I telephoned any messages about HMAS *Sydney* to RAAF Headquarters Western Area on the 4th or 5th December 1941 as recorded on page 148 of the SWACH logbook and referred to in the footnotes on pages 40 and 41 of Richard Summerrell's 3rd Edition of Guide No. 3. Once I had passed my message to the HQWA Signals Clerk late in the evening of Wednesday, 19th November, I considered the matter closed.

EW Cooper (signed)
3/1/2002

Annexure 2

Commission of Inquiry Analysis:

Re: the document referred to as 'Enclosure 12A'. The pencil notes at the top of the page read, 'Taken over phone by Signals Clerk Western Area from S/L Cooper Geraldton' and below that, 'Aeradio Geraldton is under the impression coming from Aeradio Sydney'.

There can be no doubt this note on the message form is a record of the events referred to in the SWACH log for December 1941. That is clear from the following:

- Both record a message received from SQNLDR Cooper.
- Both record the 'opinion' or 'impression' that the message of Geraldton Aeradio is coming from Sydney Aeradio.
- Both record the message to have been heard on 24.50 metres.
- Both record the following words being heard:
  'Calling Darwin or technical telegraph operator'
  'Call from sea'
  'Sydney calling send carrier men on board'
  'Calling Frazer D/F Darwin'
  'Cannot detect you'
  'Singapore call Darwin'
  'This MSS (MS) Sydney calling'
  'Message received frequency satisfactory will put thru in morse'
  Heard 'at 1510z' (equates to 2310H)

The SWACH log is a continuous log, and it is clear that the events recorded occurred on 4 December 1941, not 19 November 1941, as SQNLDR Cooper recalled some 60 years later.

It is said that at the Esplanade Hostel, Geraldton, were CPL Dawson, another airman and three women. They were listening to a short-wave radio broadcast when they heard transmissions in Morse code. CPL Dawson and the other airman were able to read the Morse message. It is said they made notes of what they heard, but those notes have never been discovered. CPL Dawson is said to have telephoned FLGOFF Bogue and told him of this event. FLGOFF Bogue who, according to SQNLDR Cooper, made 'detailed notes' of his telephone conversation with CPL Dawson. FLGOFF Bogue's notes appear to be in accord with the document shown.

The following is of note:

- The note bears the name of FLGOFF Bogue.
- The first entry, at 2140, is in substance the same as that recorded in the 'message form', being 'Enclosure 2A' referred to by SQNLDR Cooper.
- Each of Enclosure 12A and FLGOFF Bogue's notes records:
  'Distress signal starts Leichhardt'
  'Singapore call Darwin'
  'Message received frequency satisfactory will put through in Morse'
  It is apparent that both documents relate to the events recorded in the SWACH log on 4 December 1941.

The contents of the documents make it clear that the messages heard and recorded did not come from SYDNEY. Both documents refer to 'putting through' the message in Morse, SQNLDR Cooper's note stating 'RT & morse'. If there was a message in 'RT' it could not have come from SYDNEY because she had no capacity to transmit. Further, to suggest that SYDNEY would send a distress call in 'RT'—even if she had had the capacity to do so—and say she would later send the same distress message in Morse, makes no sense. To say in a message that it will later be put through in Morse implies that that message was not in Morse. If it was a message in 'RT' it did not come from SYDNEY, as she could not send such a message.

There is one other piece of evidence that demonstrates conclusively that the events recorded in the two handwritten documents occurred not on 19 November 1941 but on 4 December 1941, as the SWACH log records. The 'message form' written by SQNLDR Cooper bears the name 'Palmer'. FLGOFF Palmer was one of the shift supervisors at SWACH. On 19 November 1941, he went off duty at 0830H; he resumed duty at 0830H on 22 November 1941. On 4 December 1941, he replaced FLGOFF Way on duty at 0830H and was on duty all that day. The 'message form' note refers to him, so the events occurred while he was on duty—on 4 December 1941.

Added to the foregoing are two entries at the foot of the notes of FLGOFF Bogue. The first appears to read, 'Passed COIC (Wesche) per secraphone 1115 H/5/12' and the second reads, 'Per phone from F.O. Bogue Geraldton, 1630 H/5'.30. These entries are confirmatory of the events recorded as having occurred on 4 December 1941, not 19 November 1941.

Whatever message CPL Dawson and his friends heard in the Esplanade Hostel, Geraldton, which was conveyed to FLGOFF Bogue, who conveyed it to SQNLDR Cooper, who conveyed it to SWACH, which recorded it in its log, four things are clearly established:

- The events occurred on 4 December 1941, not 19 November 1941.
- The message was not a distress call from SYDNEY.
- Contemporaneous investigation established that the messages were from the Post Master General in Sydney to PMG Darwin.
- HMAS *SYDNEY* did not have the capacity to send voice messages over the horizon.

From the above finding there is little doubt that Commissioner Cole had placed his reliance on the word-for-word content in the SWACH logbook. He had solicited this safety net as a means of rejecting the word of Cooper and without even investigating whether the logbook had been an accurate account of what occurred.

❑ ❑ ❑

IDENTIFIED

HMAS *Sydney* suddenly lost buoyancy and succumbed a few hours after her battle with HSK *Kormoran* on 19 November 1941. It was thought the extensive damage, flooding and fires on board the ship had caused this to happen, according to the Commission of Inquiry.

However, a claim made by a so-called eyewitness after the war, purportedly by an ex-crewman of the *Kormoran*, asserted that a Japanese submarine was responsible for the death of the *Sydney*. The inquiry examined this claim and concluded that this person could not have witnessed such an event because he was found not to have been a member of the crew and therefore his story could not be believed.

No absolute evidence of third party involvement was found, but in the process the inquiry made no attempt to positively identify the person who made the claim. Thus, a more detailed examination of this matter has cast doubt on the inquiry finding.

This matter relates to an extraordinary claim made by Pastor Ivan Wittwer in the late 1990s in which he described an eyewitness account of the battle by an employee of the Snowy Mountains Hydro-Electric Authority. He had asserted that in 1951, Gerhard Heinz Grossmann, supposedly an ex-*Kormoran* crewman, had given him details of the *Sydney/Kormoran* battle. But on examination of his memory 46 years after the event, the inquiry found that his story could not be substantiated because the employee Wittwer had identified had, in addition to not being a crewman of the raider, had not come to work in Australia after the war.

In his statutory declaration, Wittwer said the witness he initially referred to as Gerhard had been a gunnery officer on board the raider *Kormoran.* Elsewhere in his statement he referred to him as Heinz. In order to apply to emigrate from Germany to Australia he was told that Heinz had assumed the name of his brother, Waldemar Heinz Grossmann, who had been killed on the Russian Front. If so, such an alias would have seemed plausible because of the SMHEA policy not to employ German servicemen who had fought against Australians or her Allies.

Grossmann claimed that the *Sydney* approached to within 7 miles of the *Kormoran*, signalled her identity and then closed to within 4 miles before asking for the secret call sign. The two ships then fired simultaneously, and shortly afterwards, two torpedoes fired from a Japanese submarine hit the *Sydney* broadside on from a range of two and a half miles.

This observation seems credible because the cruiser had stopped the vessel at the recommended distance of about 7 miles and then sailed to a distance required to read *Kormoran*'s flag signals (approx. 4 miles). It also suggests that the *Sydney*'s Captain Burnett had followed the standard Admiralty procedures for challenging suspicious ships, and so it appears that this particular statement by Heinz Grossmann possibly has an element of truth.

But other aspects of Grossmann's story of the battle are not so accurate. For example, he said that the battle began at a distance of some 4 miles and that the *Sydney* was hit by torpedoes fired from a Japanese submarine more than 2 miles away, whereas, in fact it is now known that the battle started between the *Sydney* and *Kormoran* at a range of about half a mile. On the other hand, his observation that the cruiser had retreated from the battle and stayed afloat for a number of hours does not exclude the presence of a nearby submarine delivering the final blow. And although reconstructed Japanese records do not mention submarines in the Indian Ocean at that time, it cannot be completely ruled out that the cruiser had been given the coup de grace some hours after the battle.

Grossmann's claim is also odd because the Germans had stated unequivocally that they alone were responsible for torpedoing the cruiser and they have emphatically denied any Japanese involvement. If they have taken the credit for sinking the *Sydney* (some being awarded Iron Crosses for the feat), then this new claim 10 years after the event can only be described as an attempt by Wittwer to set the record straight. And in the absence of precise pre-war Japanese submarine movements, such as from logbooks, there may yet be some truth in the claim made by Heinz.

However, despite the claim, the inquiry found there were no Japanese submarines in the Indian Ocean in November 1941. In fact, Japanese records do not specify pre-war operational matters or the whereabouts of submarines at any particular time. They are mainly listed in terms of assignment and deployment to areas and bases for war operations against US and British forces. Thus, pre-war operations and the patrols of the 60 or so IJN submarines are mostly unknown in Japanese archives, despite attempts by historians to confirm a complete absence of them in the Indian Ocean in 1941. It is in this context that Wittwer's story on Japanese submarine presence should be assessed.

Evidence that submarines could not have acted in concert with the *Kormoran* due to the Axis powers not having recognition procedures in place in 1941 may seem pertinent. Generally, reciprocal procedures for signalling were required in order for vessels to exact a rendezvous. In the case of the *Kormoran*, a rendezvous for the purpose of refuelling a submarine could conceivably have been arranged in Japan via a message from the German naval attaché in Tokyo to the German supply ship

Kulmerland, which had refuelled the raider three weeks before the battle.

One of the roles of the raider was to refuel and re-arm U-boats. But in the case of refuelling a Japanese submarine, common procedures and logistics would have posed difficulties. Even so, a pre-arranged rendezvous with a submarine could have accounted for the raider's rather uneventful and prolonged presence off the Western Australian coast in early November 1941.

The inquiry also found that the *Sydney* lost buoyancy and rolled over without warning, trapping the crew below deck. This meant that those who had survived the battle had no time to launch any lifesaving apparatus and the crew did not foresee any immediate danger of the cruiser sinking and did not prepare themselves for survival in the worst case scenario. A theoretic view has therefore been based on the incessant flooding of the warship as a result of damage sustained during the battle, a rather simplistic finding that requires closer examination:

Firstly, the *Sydney* had been badly damaged and was dangerously low in the water, but even without serviceable lifeboats and rafts, it beggars belief that those on board (possibly 100 or more, including wounded) would not have prepared for such an emergency. Suitable timber materials from the ship were available at hand to keep them afloat. Besides, as they could not hope to rely on plugging all the shell holes to stop the inflow of seawater, preparations to abandon ship must have been uppermost in their minds. And any sign of instability should have been detected well in advance.

Secondly, from most German reports the cruiser was aglow and evidently still afloat three to four hours after the battle, but she had made off south easterly only 8nm from the battle site in all that time, at an average 2 knots. According to the Germans, the *Sydney* left the battle scene at moderate speed and it appears as though she had slowed considerably thereafter and had drifted at the mercy of the wind and sea to her final position. While drifting without power she could have succumbed at any moment, but in the meantime the surviving crew had time to prepare to abandon the increasingly unstable ship because by then there was little hope that she would stay afloat.

Thirdly, on leaving the ship with whatever life-supporting flotation they could gather, survivors would have drifted approximately18° to the left or right of the SSE wind, and if deceased a drift of 30° (NATSAR) – this, on a much wider path than the debris and rafts. There is reason to believe that some of those wearing lifebelts would have survived even without food and water to be rescued within a week or so, unless they had met with foul play by the German survivors or by third party involvement.

Note: A small RAN Carley float (similar to a rubber raft) carrying a decomposed occupant had come ashore on Christmas Island on 6 February 1942, 1,000nm north of the *Sydney* battle site.

In order to explain the fact that there were no survivors from the *Sydney*, the inquiry settled on a scenario free of any suggestion of third party involvement. In other words, the cruiser had lost buoyancy and sank suddenly taking all the survivors with her. But that experienced sailors did not take the necessary measures and initiatives to abandon the cruiser beforehand, this proposition is, frankly, absurd. A complete absence of Japanese submarines in the Indian Ocean in November 1941, therefore, cannot be ruled out.

Note: In the case of a submarine sinking the *Sydney*, the use of a torpedo should not have been considered necessary due to the fact that the explosion could have been seen and heard over long distances by other shipping that may have been in the vicinity. Instead, the mortally damaged cruiser could have been easily disposed of by gunfire from the submarine's deck gun.

Ivan Wittwer described Heinz Grossmann as a con man who had worked himself into a position as representative of all Germans working at SMHEA. But the inquiry produced evidence from immigration records that showed Heinrich Grossmann as the person employed at SMHEA in 1951 **(NAA.111.0056)**. He was also the Workers' Union representative of all German employees and a troublemaker to boot. Thus, it could be argued that Heinz and Heinrich were the same person.

According to immigration records, Heinrich had arrived in Australia on 25 June 1951, which was in marked contrast to Wittwer's firm statement that the meeting with Heinz first occurred beforehand – on 13 May of that year. This led the inquiry to conclude that Heinz (or Gerhard) was an imposter. Heinrich was not the same person because his record showed that he had not arrived in Australia until well after Wittwer's initial meeting with Heinz had taken place. But the inquiry had made no allowance for error by Wittwer in stating the date of this meeting, despite the fact that he had recalled the events some 46 years ago.

The information given by Grossmann to Wittwer at the first meeting was given again to an arranged meeting with ASIO in the presence of SMHEAs Chief Engineer, William Hudson. But the inquiry could not countenance that this meeting had actually taken place, partly on the basis that there was no ASIO record of the meeting and that it was improbable in the extreme that the CEO would have accompanied the person pretending to be Gerhard or Heinz to such an interview. In fact, another six reasons were given as to why Pastor Wittwer's account was considered to be a fabrication and many extraneous issues put forward were also ridiculed by the inquiry **(COI Report, Vol 3, pp195–6)**.

ASIO neither confirmed nor denied that Wittwer's Heinz Grossmann may have been interviewed, though he was a person of interest as an absconder from SMHEA and a suspected member of the Communist Building Workers Union. These observations appear to have been taken into consideration by the inquiry to a certain degree, but curiously it found that even if Wittwer's account was a true rendering of what was said and occurred, it provided no basis for finding that a Japanese submarine was involved in the sinking of HMAS *Sydney*. In summary, Wittwer's story may have some credence, except for his story of the submarine. Obviously, such a finding is simply based on the belief that all pre-war Japanese submarine movements have been accurately determined by post-war recollections of (surviving) Japanese naval officers – an almost impossible task.

In dismissing the account of Gerhard (Heinz) Grossmann, the inquiry did not contemplate that Wittwer may not have correctly recalled his name, because by the late 1990s Gerhardt Grossmann was known to have been one of the *Kormoran* crewmen rescued by the *Aquitania*, so it appeared that Wittwer had referred to him. But the name Heinz should have alerted the inquiry to the fact that it is the shortened version of Heinrich. Nevertheless, in its attempts to discredit Wittwer on the basis of the (mistaken) Gerhard identity, the inquiry went to great lengths to produce a raft of evidence to prove that this person did not migrate to Australia after the war. However, no attempt was made to positively identify Heinrich who appeared to have an intimate knowledge of the *Kormoran* and her battle with the *Sydney*.

Heinrich Grossmann's identity is shown on the Department of Immigration form for aliens entering Australia. This form (below) shows that he was born in Posen (now Poznan in Poland) on 26 October 1906 and had enlisted to work for SMHEA. Although it is not known whether he had engaged in military service during the war, in order to apply successfully to enter Australia as a German emigrant in 1951, Heinrich's only prospect for work was to demonstrate that he had met the conditions of entry into Australia, viz., he had not fought against

Australian forces. Sympathetic consideration for prospective workers at SMHEA was also given to those who were Jews and to those Germans who had been interned in prison camps.

Aliens Act 1947.

The information to be given is required in accordance with the Aliens Act and Regulations, from aliens (non-British persons) over sixteen years of age entering the Commonwealth.

Name of Ship or Identification Marks of Aircraft.	Date of Landing.	Port of Landing.
M/S SKAUBRYN	[illegible]	MELBOURNE

Name G R O S S M A N N / Heinrich
(Surname in Block Letters.) (Christian or other names.)
Previous name or alias (if any) ---
Intended Address in Australia ~~c/o Immigration Depart, Canberra~~
S.M.H.E.A. N.S.W.
Nationality German Previous Nationality (if any) ---
Birthplace Town or City Posen, Country Germany — Date of Birth 26, October 06 Sex m
Height 172 cm feet inches. Build Colour of Eyes blue
Colour of Hair Marks nil
Passport or Certificate of Identity No. 0606641
Date of Issue March, 27,51 Place of Issue Berlin/Germany
How long do you intend to stay in Australia? indifinitely
Name and address of nearest relative, friend or business connection in Australia .. nil
State number of Landing Permit or particulars of document authorizing admission to Australia ---
If previously resident in Australia state—(1) Port of departure ---
(2) Date of departure ---
State whether married, single, widowed or divorced
Occupation or Profession Electro.Fitter
Intended occupation in Australia Emigrant
Details of accompanying wife or husband and accompanying children under the age of sixteen years—

This information is required only from aliens who are entering Australia for more than 60 consecutive days.

	Name.	Sex.	Birthplace.	Date of Birth.
Wife/husband				
Children				

NOTED FOR SECURITY

Signature of Alien.

For official use only.

Certificate of Registration No. 61315 issued
State if Form RA5 issued
Remarks

DEPARTMENT OF IMMIGRATION
Place 2 5 JUN 1951
Date
Electorate

Signature of Issuing Officer.

For instructions concerning the completion of this form see back hereof.

NAA.111.0056

Posen (later Poznan) was a German enclave in Poland. The city had been devastated in 1939 by the Germans and again in 1945 by the Soviets. Few, if any, archival and church records survived. But whether Heinrich's birthplace is true or not, he auspiciously nominated Posen because the city, like Warsaw, lay in complete ruin. It would thus have been a difficult task for the German authorities to confirm his status as a prospective German emigrant. Similar doubts were also expressed by the Immigration Department in the ASIO Field Officers report and comments in regard to a number of German SMHEA workers reasoned that the information supplied by them in Berlin, including birth dates, 'cannot be reconciled in all cases'.

However, the inquiry made the mistake of overlooking the fact that apart from Gerhard, the list of *Kormoran* POWs included yet another Grossmann. This crewman, known as Heinz, had been listed variously as Grossmann, Grossmaas and Grossmass. Heinz's surname is spelt 'Grossmann' in the POW list provided by Detmers **(COI.004.0163)**, whereas it is shown as 'Grossmaas' on the Nominal Roll of *Kormoran* crewmen who arrived at Murchison Camp No. 13 on 20 December 1941 and as POW 42229 'Grossmass' in the National Archives and POW camp register. Only Gerhard's surname is consistently shown spelt as Grossmann. See below.

55. " " " Pona
56. " " " Ziegler
57. " " " Bindemann
58. " " " Vahley
59. " " " Grossmann
60. " " " Stich
61. " " " Schnur
62. " " " Jentsch
63. " " " Winter
64. " " " Albers
65. " " " Menzel
66. " " " Zahn
67. " " " Hausen
68. Mtr. Gefr. Schiefler
69. Mtr. Gefr. Fend
70. " " Rönchen
71. " " Hofmann, A.
72. " " Zoppeck
73. " " Schröder,J.
74. " " Erb
75. " " Frank
76. " " Ortmann
77. " " Dolatowski
78. " " Wendroth
79. " " Dornis
80. " " Meyer, H.
81. " " Grossmann
82. " " Elmecker
83. " " Wiermann

COI.004.0163

Gerhard Grossmann (59), Heinz Grossmann (81)

42227	WARNECKE Henry
42228	KUGLER Karl, Albert, Gustav
42229	GROSSMASS Heinz
42230	KLOS Joseph

Murchison Camp POW List

Heinz Grossmass 42229

Of the three, Grossmann's age was the biggest difference. Gerhard and Heinz were much younger. In 1951, Heinz (b. 1922) and Gerhard (b. 1917) were 29 and 34 years old, respectively. Heinrich, purportedly born in Posen in 1906, was 44 years old.

But his photo attached to his entry permit by Immigration attests to a man in his mid-forties. Thus, Gerhard and Heinz seemed much too young to have posed as Heinrich. In any case, German archival and family records show that Gerhard, whose given names were Gerhard Willi (not Gerhard Heinz), lived in East Germany and did not go to Australia after the war.

A.A. Form A.111A.
(Introduced September, 1939)
(Revised December, 1941)

AUSTRALIAN MILITARY FORCES

GERMAN

Report No. PG.1181

REPORT ON ~~INTERNEE~~ **PRISONER OF WAR**

FOR INFORMATION OF

International Bureaux of Relief and Information

ITEM	DETAIL	REMARKS
1	Identification Number	PWGA. 42229
2	Name (Surname)	GROSSMASS
3	(Other Names)	Heinz
4	Nationality	German
5	Date of Birth	22.7.1922.
6	Place of Birth	Bochum
7	Regimental Number	
8	Place of Capture	At sea.
9	Date of Capture	27.11.1941.
10	Place of Internment	Murchison, Victoria
11	Rank	A.B.
12	Unit	Navy
13	Surname (Father)	GROSSMASS
14	Name of Mother	PLEWZINSKI, Emilie
15	REMARKS:	

Next-of-kin: (Father) Heinrich GROSSMASS,
Bochum-Hordel,
Rochlinghauser Str. 47.

Date – 2 MAR 1942

A. R. Heighway Captain,
Officer in Charge, Prisoners of War Information Bureau.

Heinz Grossmass POW

National Archives information on POW Heinz Grossmass reveals that he was born in Bochum (near Essen) in West Germany. Surprisingly, his father's name was Heinrich, who lived in Bochum-Hordel at Rochlinghaussen Str. 47. But although his wartime address was in Bochum, it is still possible that Heinrich was born in Posen, Poland, circa 1906. His wife, Emilie Plewzinski (probably spelt Plucinski) was obviously Polish. As in Germany, the name Grossmann was common in this Prussian enclave where most of its inhabitants had been deported or exterminated during WW2.

Grossmann was regarded primarily as a Jewish name in Germany and in many cases during the war, measures were taken to change the Grossmann family name, for example, to Grossmass or similar, to avoid being arrested. However, Grossmass is not a German surname. It is a derivation of the Dutch name of Grossmaas.

As SMHEA's Heinrich Grossmann had expressed considerable knowledge about the *Kormoran*, there is only one person who could have supplied this information – it came from his son, Heinz Grossmann (aka Grossmass/Grossmaas). It is likely that he had been stationed on one of *Kormoran*'s guns, but he was not an officer. Together with Hermann Ortmann and Bill Elmecker, he is suspected of being a member of the aft no. 5 gun crew. All three of them are listed close together as Division 1 crewmen.

During internment at the POW camps, several photographs were taken of the German prisoners. They reveal that the two Grossmanns on board the raider certainly did not look alike, as shown below.

Murchison, Australia, 6 March 1945. Group of German prisoners of war interned at No. 6 Labour Detachment, No. 13 POW Group. Back row, left to right: 41296 Haug, 42295 Koenig, **42104 Gerhard Grossmann** (including insert), 42107 Froehlich. Front row: 42347 Backhausen, 41315 Albers, 42224 Berghoff, 42321 Weissflog. Note: The number is an assigned POW number.

Nagambi, Australia, 1 December 1943. Group of German prisoners of war interned at Graytown POW Camp. Back row, left to right: 42170 Eilers, 42377 Otte, 147 Jentsch, 42360 Wegener, 42254 Hauske, 42403 Rolf, 42286 Winter. Front row: 42258 Ellerbrock, 42240 Lorenz, 42208 Reinicke, **42229 Heinz Grossmass** (see also insert), 42153 Koenig.

Heinrich Grossmann in 1951
b. circa 1906
(NAA.111.0056)

Heinz Grossmann
(aka Grossmass, Grossmaas)
POW in 1943, b. 1922

Gerhard Willi Grossmann
in 1950
b. 1917

Heinz was probably a member of the gun crew which gave cause for Heinrich to masquerade as a gunnery officer. But by far the most convincing factor is the photographic resemblance of them – like father and son (see above). The age difference, however, requires an explanation:

Due to the almost complete destruction of records in Posen during the war, Heinrich was at liberty to nominate his birthday. He chose 26.10.1906, but this does not appear to be correct. At just 44 years of age in 1951, he was unlikely to have been only 15 or 16 years older than his son Heinz and considering that his photo also attests to a man in his latter 40s, there is reason to believe that he may have been closer to 48 years old (born in 1903).

Heinrich was the oldest of the SMHEC workers who left Bremerhaven in May 1951 to work at SMHEA, but he would not have been considered for employment if found to be over the maximum age of 45 years. And given there was no way that the German authorities in Berlin could have checked on Heinrich's bona fides, in the process of applying to emigrate he was at liberty to also change his name from Grossmass or Grossmaas back to Grossmann.

His decision to leave Germany for Australia was made probably because Bochum city and its steel industry had been almost completely destroyed by the RAF in 1943. This city had borne the brunt of the Ruhr bombings. It was completely in ruins from fires caused by incendiary bombs and because Heinrich lived in central Bochum (Bochum-Hordel) he had probably lost his home. The fate of his wife Emilie is unknown, as is the whereabouts of his son Heinz. However, he obviously had good reason to seek a better life and remuneration in Australia than he could get in Bochum or elsewhere in devastated Germany.

Due to the fact that Grossmann had openly claimed to represent all German migrants working for SMHEA, it should have been plainly evident to the inquiry that the person referred to by Wittwer as Gerhard Heinz Grossmann was the same person identified as Heinrich Grossmann. This is verified in both Wittwer's affidavit and in the ASIO Field Officers report into German migrants. Instead, this issue became convoluted to the extent that the inquiry dismissed Wittwer's statement partly on the basis that because he did not remember Grossmann's precise given name, it therefore followed that the story told by the so-called Gerhard had no foundation. Gerhard had at no time entered Australia.

Wittwer correctly identified Heinz (otherwise known as Heinrich), but he had been influenced by others who had advised him that Gerhard Grossmann was most likely the person who had told him the story for it was apparent to them that Gerhard was the only Grossmann on board the *Kormoran*. The link to Gerhard was ostensibly made from his interview at Sydney in 1941 by CAPT Farncomb (after being rescued by *Aquitania*) from information that was available in the 1980s, in which he stated that the battle was deemed to have begun from a distance of some 10 kilometres. Heinrich (Heinz) gave a comparable distance of 7 miles.

Now that Heinrich has been identified, Wittwer's naming of Waldemar becomes much clearer. Considering that we know for a fact that Heinrich applied for emigration under his own name, Waldemar could only have been his brother – uncle of Heinz. Thus, Waldemar may have been resident with Heinrich's family at the given address in Bochum-Hordel, but he too may have been born in Posen and quite possibly may have served on the Russian Front.

Much of this controversy has stemmed from the fact that Heinrich Grossmann had arrived in Australia in late June 1951, well before Wittwer's claimed meeting with Heinrich in May of that year. But it is now obvious that the first meeting with Heinz could not have occurred before July 1951 at the earliest.

Understandably, Wittwer's recollection after 46 years was far from perfect. Heinrich did not apply for immigration using Waldemar's name; he was probably making the point to Wittwer that he had not fought on the Russian Front, and therefore preference should be given to him for work at SMHEA. And given that the name Gerhardt was an assumption by Wittwer, instead of trying to recall the name, Wittwer should have got the list of personnel from SMHEC in order to verify Grossmann's first name. It is conceded that he would have done so for the inquiry had his death not intervened.

That a submarine could have been responsible for the eventual fate of the *Sydney* in delivering the coup de grace cannot be discounted and the claim of third party involvement should have been taken more seriously by the inquiry, due simply to the fact that reconstructed records showing pre-war disposition of Japanese submarines are unreliable. Orders and dates for assignment and deployment for war operations do not constitute reliable records per se for the whereabouts of submarines pre-war.

Heinrich Grossmann's time in Australia was apparently short-lived. He had come under the surveillance of ASIO, whose primary concern in those days was to keep an eye on suspected communists. He took a leading role in the Building Workers Union because the German migrant workers were extremely discontented with their living and working conditions. They claimed to have migrated to Australia under false promises. For example, overtime payments had been abolished, and so they were willing to accept any form of politics that would assist their cause, though they were inherently anti-communists. While the latter may suggest that Heinrich had genuine sympathy for the Soviet cause, he also came under notice for his anti-British sentiments and was therefore considered by ASIO to be a security risk.

Deportation of undesirables was common in those days, but curiously there is no record of Heinrich's extradition. His actions and behaviour suggest that he became disillusioned and unpopular, maybe, as a means of being deported. In fact, ASIO had been handed a two-fold motive to deport him – that being a combination of his suspected communist beliefs and his revelation about Japanese submarine involvement in the demise of the *Sydney*, whether it was thought to be true or not. And that he had no family in Australia to follow up on his well-being and whereabouts, it is conceivable that he met with an untimely death. After all, deportation back to Germany would not have necessarily prevented Heinrich from again giving his account of what could have turned out to be a nightmare for German authorities.

Finally, the Commission of Inquiry has arisen a great deal of fuss over this story in a manner which has unfairly characterised Wittwer to the extent that he was believed to have fabricated his account in order to bolster the reputation of Captain Burnett. This analysis has shown otherwise.

❑ ❑ ❑

LED ASTRAY

The Commission of Inquiry had asserted that even though Captain Burnett had known that no ship was expected to be in the area, he had failed to carry out the correct identification and challenge procedures in the process of overhauling the raider, he had not recognised the danger the innocent looking vessel posed as he drew the cruiser close abeam while both ships were travelling at some 14 knots and he was taken by surprise as his vessel was struck by one of two above-water torpedoes. This is indeed a simplistic scenario in the extreme. These same assertions came as no surprise as this was also the scenario that was initiated by some top-ranking RAN officers in early December 1941.

The genesis of this assertion originally stemmed from the assessment of the action made partly by CMDR Emile Dechaineux and then expanded by teacher Frank Eldridge and Rupert Long, director of Naval Intelligence, in their official report to Admiralty. The latter had cast aspersions on Burnett as being an incompetent commander. Obvious is the conclusion that Burnett had been careless in approaching the raider and had not followed his orders.

But this is not the actions of a man who, during escorting troopships to and from the Sunda Strait, was renowned for challenging and identifying merchant ships at a distance as attested by an ex-crewman **(WIT.001.0001).** Burnett had been (as later revealed was known to Rupert Long) directed by C-in-C China to intercept a suspected enemy vessel, a Royal Navy operation that had been initiated exclusively while the *Sydney* was under China Station command.

Burnett's option was to sink the so-called *Straat Malakka* because it could not reply to the secret letters from any distance, but his motive for closing the suspicious vessel and with all main armament trained was to board and capture it. However, in order to board the vessel, Burnett was required to bring his ship in close in accordance with the latest Admiralty directive to circumvent scuttling, a suicidal position and a recipe for disaster should he be dealing with a heavily armed raider. But whether he had been directed by C-in-C China to board the vessel or he had made the decision himself, the fate of the *Sydney* had been already sealed.

Today, very little has changed in Navy parlance on Burnett's perceived guilt and throughout the years much has been written attributing his responsibility for the loss of the *Sydney*. But there is quantitative evidence that demonstrates Australian Naval Intelligence had been cognisant of the approximate position of the *Kormoran* when sighted by the cruiser. In this regard, George Hermon Gill's portrayal of the engagement is remarkable for the accuracy of the position he gave some 60 years ago.

In Gill's history of the RAN, he wrote: 'On the afternoon of 19 November 1941 the German auxiliary cruiser *Kormoran* was steaming on a north-easterly course off the coast of Western Australia, **approximately 150 miles south west of Carnarvon**. Just before 4:00 pm [G time] a warship was sighted and Commander Detmers turned the *Kormoran* west into the sun...'

In fact, the distance from Carnarvon (24°53'S, 113°39'E) to the established turning point (26°07'S, 111°15'E) of *Kormoran* is almost exactly 150 nautical miles – 149.76nm to be precise. A quote of this distance is indicative that naval intelligence may have already established the turning point from the course sailed by the raider (025°) via 26°34'S, 111°E to longitude 111° 15'E (received in full by Geraldton Radio). Gill had certainly not been referring to the distance from Carnarvon to Detmers's claimed battle site at 26°34'S, 111°E, more than 175nm distant.

George Hermon Gill (1895–1973)

Knowingly or unknowingly, Gill had established *Kormoran*'s precise turning point at 4:00pm G time (5pm WST) on 19 November, but at the moment the action began he falsely assumed that both vessels were moving at 14 knots, as stated in the action reports. Although it was impossible for him to independently substantiate this speed and had he known at the time that the *Kormoran* had sunk only about 10 miles from her turning point in position 26°06'S, 111°05'E, he would have concluded that Burnett had ordered the raider to stop well before the action began. Obviously, the raider could not have maintained a speed of 14 knots for one and a half hours over a distance of some 10 miles.

CMDR Long had given Gill access to all NID files for writing the history of the battle, but one might ask how much did other branches of the RAN know in respect to the position of the engagement and Burnett's directive from Singapore? Surely, there must have been some disquiet amongst other naval personnel, but apart from comments made by naval officers on the actions of the master of the *Aquitania*, there is no substantial evidence in naval records that suggests otherwise. It is truly extraordinary that not one adverse official comment from serving officers in 1941 or since has arisen from the Eldridge-Long report and Gill's history of events. Rupert Long thus appears to have exercised complete control over the *Sydney* affair. His record speaks for itself:

CMDR Long's superiors thought of him as free of deceit and some even described him as perfectly reserved and candid, but because his job in NID was secretive, his behaviour tended to be somewhat erratic. He also had a tendency to lead astray those he chose to work with, such as Eldridge. As head of Naval Intelligence, he exercised his control over naval matters, but his task in intelligence meant that he worked fervently with his allied cousins. This gave Rupert Long exceptional powers, even to the extent of the Naval Board. However, he was also able to skilfully manage those who served him in the RAN at NID.

CMDR Rupert Long (1899–1960)

Long worked closely with his counterparts in London and elsewhere. He was the main contact in Australia for MI5 and MI6 and he was in Singapore on 17 November when the *Sydney*, while under the command of C-in-C China, had been sent to intercept a suspected enemy vessel, and on 19 November when the cruiser and the raider met in battle. He left there on 21 November on the day DNOWA declared the *Sydney* overdue, returning to Australia on 27 November. By this time, he is claimed to have heard only an outline of events on the loss of the *Sydney*. Royal Navy involvement could not also have escaped the attention of Australia's Chief of Naval Staff, the Naval Board's Admiral Royle. After all, it was incumbent for Royle to fall in behind matters, especially those that were Royal Navy-related.

During Rupert Long's time in Singapore, he attended a secret conference at the behest of the Far East Combined Bureau with representatives of other allied intelligence services, but as with many other intelligence matters in the Far East in 1941–42, these discussions are shrouded in secrecy. Due to the very nature of his work with British intelligence, he was firstly loyal to the British Empire. It is therefore beyond belief that British naval intelligence had not made him aware that the cruiser had met with the troopship *Largs Bay* before being despatched at high speed. Besides, it was just a matter of time before he found out because Long's role was subservient but integral to the success of the British naval intelligence global network as a whole. Distrust and secrets not shared was a dangerous combination that could jeopardise the firm relationships already established with his counterparts. This alone is reason for Long to have been made aware of the circumstances of the loss of the *Sydney*, well before he returned to Australia on 27 November.

In adopting Detmers's story, Rupert Long had made a concerted effort to hide the fact that the *Sydney* had been under the direction of C-in-C China while on Australia station. And in order to rule out any complicity in the *Sydney/Kormoran* interception, he felt compelled to portray the story as an accidental encounter. It was this approach that was to forever dismiss any suggestion of involvement by the Royal Navy and/or by the Naval Board in Australia.

Rupert Long was also involved in the British secret intelligence services, but as close liaison with Australian naval intelligence was considered obligatory for this spy network, he was conceivably privy to the names of individuals who may have been involved in secreting the actions of C-in-C China. For instance, the identity of those involved in the *Aquitania* affair, and those who kept secret the false rescue position of the tanker *Trocas*.

The role played by Rupert Long in providing details on the action to the Admiralty is most intriguing. Initial reports from senior naval officers on the *Sydney* disaster had not impressed him. His take on the action was influenced solely on evidence gained during the interrogations, especially that from CAPT Detmers. He disregarded the final report by CMDR Dechaineux, and in a haste to report to the Admiralty after the completion of interrogations, he sought the views of an outsider – teacher F B Eldridge. Long manipulated Eldridge by providing him with select interrogation notes from which to make his assessment. Modelled on Detmers's evidence, the Eldridge Report was ultimately to become entrenched in RAN folklore.

Towards the end of the war, Rupert Long made a thorough search for information regarding the loss of the *Sydney*, gathering information and investigating government departments that may have access to information that had to be kept secret. He was also responsible for the destruction of many naval files in 1945, the year in which he wrote the letter that ended any hope of revealing to the public the true circumstances of the *Sydney/Kormoran* action. This was the end of the story about the *Sydney* as far as Long and the RAN were concerned. However, it is strange that while he said there were a number of reasons a full analysis could not be published, he avoided any explanation of just what those reasons might be.

Rupert Long's dilemma was that the weight of evidence from the German survivors had led senior naval officers to report that the *Kormoran* had fired three torpedoes at the *Sydney* and at least one had hit. Three torpedoes meant that the raider had launched the underwater torpedo including both above-water torpedoes and had been virtually stopped when the action began. But in his interim report to the Admiralty (which required Long's approval beforehand), Dechaineux had wrongly surmised that two torpedoes had been launched (one above and one below water), but this did not change the scenario of the raider having stopped before the action commenced.

Any final report on the action which concluded that Burnett had ordered the raider to stop and that the underwater torpedo had been involved in the action, should have inevitably led to suspicion that it had been launched before the raider had raised her battle ensign. This, in turn, meant that Detmers may have breached the rules of warfare and that an illegal act had been committed. A full Court of Inquiry was the only way to get to the bottom of the matter, but that was something Long could not avoid, as it might have exposed Detmers's guilt and his original claim that the *Kormoran* had, in fact, dramatically reduced her speed. But fortunately for him the presiding officers ruled in favour of Detmers.

In order to satisfy the Admiralty, who must have been generally cognisant of the role China Station played in the *Sydney* disaster, it was essential that Long portray that the cruiser had accidentally come across a vessel that Burnett had not ordered to stop, the corollary being that both vessels had been proceeding at speed when the cruiser had been torpedoed and that Burnett had carelessly approached the raider. And because he had not stopped the vessel at a distance in accordance with Admiralty instructions, he could be accused of not following his orders.

But the solution to Long's predicament was there in the interrogation notes on the action – Detmers's statement. This he gave to Eldridge, together with the notes of Ahlbach, Bunjes and a few others, on which to base his final report, a report seemingly free of naval influence that Long had said had been independently assessed from all the available evidence. Thus, the customary Court of Inquiry into the disaster was a fait accompli due to the evidence of these three officers (named above), who had frankly told the story of the action, so much so the Naval Board and Long's NID would not disagree with their findings.

The proceedings of the top-secret conference of Secret Service personnel attended by Long in Singapore have not been released, nor have any of the British intelligence papers on the Far East during 1941 and 1942. But most curious also is the fact that VADM Guy Royle had gone to Singapore in early December (before interrogations had been completed), purportedly to confer with the Royal Navy's ADM Phillips. He did not return to Australia until mid-December. While Royle was away, CMDR Dechaineux had been entrusted with preparing a report on the loss of HMAS *Sydney*. Naval Board member CMDR John Durnford (also from the Royal Navy) undertook the acting role of Chief of Naval Staff. His views on the *Sydney* affair did not appear to be unlike those expressed by Long and Royle.

ADM Guy Royle (1885–1954)

The Rupert Long/Guy Royle relationship was very close throughout WW2, both of whom were privy to FEDO intercepts. Darwin HFDF station intercepts were sent straight to Long's NID office in Melbourne for decryption. They were not for general circulation amongst the naval hierarchy, most of them being retained and issued on a need-to-know basis. But in the case of the *Sydney* having sent emergency signals on 19 November, it beggars belief that Darwin HFDF station and/or

Jandakot station did not intercept signals from *Kormoran* that Long would have got to have known about on his return from Singapore.

As Rupert Long had died in 1960, his enduring friend, G Hermon Gill, had begun to write Long's history of his life, and when Gill died in 1973, Long's manuscript (written by Gill) had been unfinished. Long's character was not straightforward, as described by Barbara Winter in her book, *The Intrigue Master*. Secrecy was the nature of his work in the intelligence business. His role was seemingly one of complete autonomy and answerable to no one. However, he had the necessary guile and was regarded as a saviour for his work in NID during WW2.

Knowledge of the action is not likely to have been restricted to Rupert Long's naval colleagues and members of the Naval Board. Notwithstanding the message sent from Geraldton to Fremantle on the night of 19 November suggesting the *Sydney* was in trouble, the District Naval Officer in Fremantle, CAPT Charles Farquhar-Smith had further reason for concern about the safety of HMAS *Sydney*. He had requested a brief response (an acknowledgement from the cruiser) to the message he had sent via WT at 0431z on 20 November, but no reply had been received.

DNOWA Charles Farquhar-Smith (1888–1968), circa 1914

This message (which bore a wrongly quoted reference) appears to be related to a message sent earlier to the cruiser on 14 November, notifying Burnett that some of his crewmen would be sent to *Cerberus* for further training. MV *Duntroon* had arrived at Fremantle and was considered suitable for this purpose. It was important for Burnett to be informed of her time of departure to Adelaide. See below.

To [illegible] "SYDNEY" (R) N.B. 311.

From D.N.O. W.A.

Method of Transmission [illegible] P/L. CODE. CONF. CODE. CYP. PL. N. CYPHER A.

Date and Time Sent 20/11/'41.

Date and Time Received 20/11/'41.

Originator's Number Time of Origin 0431Z/20.

SECRET.

N.B. 0748 31ST OCTOBER "DUNTROON" IS ONLY SUITABLE SHIP AND WILL SAIL FOR ADELAIDE AT APPROXIMATELY 1600Z 21ST.

Message marked (R)

When maintaining radio silence, naval vessels generally did not acknowledge messages unless the sender specifically requested one. However, for operational messages marked (R) an initial non-response meant that the message was required to be repeated again by the sender, if not, several times. Thus, Farquhar-Smith had cause for genuine concern for the cruiser early in the afternoon of 20 November.

A non-response to the message may have signified to Farquhar-Smith a malfunction with the WT receivers and/or aerials on board the *Sydney*, but as there were three WT offices on board, each connected with separate truncations to the main aerials, a complete shut-down of the system was unlikely to have occurred. Another scenario was that the cruiser had been mechanically disabled and possibly adrift and not able to fully power her WT equipment. The worst case scenario was that the *Sydney* had engaged an enemy ship that had damaged her wireless apparatus. However, the necessary repairs to her WT equipment and jury-rigging of her aerials should have been promptly accomplished, but that no response had been received may have indicated irreparable damage, possibly of catastrophic proportions.

As time went by without any response, DNOWA Farquhar-Smith, amid suspicion that something drastic might have happened to the *Sydney*, signalled the Naval Board on the morning of 21 November that the cruiser had not yet arrived. But the Naval Board still appeared unconcerned and thereafter for the next two days it was thought the *Sydney* may have been delayed because it was possible that she may have been hunting for an enemy vessel while under *radio silence, even though the DNO had been cognizant of the fact that the cruiser had repeatedly failed to acknowledge his message.

*Radio silence is absurd in reference to naval vessels of the early 1940s. The stability of equipment in those days was different from the circuits of today. A cold set could not be turned on for an immediate transmitting or tuning in. Except for radar equipment, shutting down WT transmitters and receivers over short periods was of no real worth. But in idling mode, their performance depended on the temperature of the cabinet, valves and surrounding humidity. In this respect, the term 'strict radio silence' is a misnomer.

Radio sets in idling mode were capable of being operated for transmitting or receiving at any time. Even if not transmitting, HFDF stations were able to track emissions of enemy radio sets, in particular Morse sets, sometimes up to 100 nautical miles away (as in the case of the *Kormoran*), depending on atmospheric and ionosphere fluctuations. In order to control these errant emissions, disconnecting the aerial was the only solution.

The *Sydney/Kormoran* battle had taken place at a time when Second Naval Board Member John Durnford was visiting Fremantle supposedly to inspect naval facilities. He and his colleague, DNO Charles Farquhar-Smith, had something in common. Durnford and Farquhar-Smith had served with the Royal Navy in WWI and both had been appointed Second Naval Member (the latter from 1933 to 1935). Farquhar-Smith had previously undertaken the duties of the director of Naval Intelligence, but by the age of 50 he was regarded by his superiors as lacking initiative, tact and judgement. Nevertheless, it must have been considered desirable that he be informed of the Royal Navy operation that had unfolded in waters under his jurisdiction.

The message specifically sent to the *Sydney* at 12:31pm on 20 November under the auspice of the DNO would no doubt have alerted senior officers under his command, particularly CMDR Victor Ramage and LCDR Philip Bailhache, of the non-response from the cruiser. They would surely have been concerned about her plight simply because the DNOs message had not been acknowledged. And when it became evident that the *Sydney* could not be contacted in the ensuing days, conceivably other personnel at SWACH had been aware, including those from the RAAF. It is also true of employees at Navy Office in Melbourne, particularly those involved in decoding messages sent from Singapore to the Naval Board.

It is not known what discussions (if any) had taken place between DNOWA and the Naval Board during the following days, however, cause for concern at SWACH that the *Sydney* was overdue generated rumours among the public that the cruiser was missing. On 23 November, Farquhar-Smith reported that *Zealandia* had arrived in Singapore a day late on 21 November, and at 1854H that same day the Naval Board belatedly signalled the *Sydney* to report her ETA Fremantle. Complete silence from the cruiser prompted a second request shortly afterwards at 2236H to again provide her ETA. Thus, four days after the battle had occurred and nearly three days after her expected ETA Fremantle, the Naval Board had confirmed the cruiser could not be contacted. On the other hand, some naval personnel at SWACH had most likely known since midday on 20 November.

Suspicion by Farquhar-Smith (and SWACH) that *Trocas* had been discretely diverted from her 'proper route' is contained in his letter summing-up the search for the *Sydney.* After being given an assurance that *Trocas* had informed him on 25 November that she was following her proper route and that *Wyrallah* would intercept the tanker early next morning, he and others at SWACH ought to have known from the VAI plot that *Trocas* was due to have passed some 80nm west of the claimed rescue position on 23 November, approximately 24 hours earlier. See extract from his letter, below.

3. As TROCAS had asked for the assistance of an armed guard, and as it was not known whether she would proceed direct to Fremantle or follow her proper route, YANDRA was sent direct to TROCAS' last position, while WYRALLAH was told to follow up TROCAS' route reversed. OLIVE CAM and HEROS were told to proceed close to the coast as far as Geraldton, so that they could be given further instructions as they passed Geraldton Radio. During the day TROCAS indicated that she was following her proper route, and WYRALLAH was given instructions so that she would intercept TROCAS in the early morning of Wednesday 26th. The guard was duly placed on board TROCAS, and the position on board reported as

NAA MP1049/5

Again we have the situation when SWACH officers were initially privy to a strange claim from C-in-C China about the location of a rescue, but the nominated position became questionable when sea and air searches for the *Trocas* proved negative. And when the tanker had not been sighted on its way from the claimed rescue position to Fremantle, it reinforced that frame of mind. But when *Trocas* had signalled she had been sailing her proper route, the falsity of the claimed rescue position became apparent to SWACH because it made no sense for the tanker to have been diverted 80nm west and then have resumed her proper course. And rather than sailing direct to Fremantle from position 24°06'S, 110°40'E, the tanker had travelled a much further distance via 29°18'S, 112°36'E. But although the positional claim by C-in-C China went unchallenged, those at SWACH must have been acutely aware that *Trocas* had been diverted from her proper course and sent to the claimed rescue position, a sure sign that the Royal Navy had falsified the given position.

The other intriguing factor was that the SWACH log narrative (p110) supposedly pin-pointing the position of *Trocas* at 1200H/25 had been supported by direction-finding. But because this position (26°47'S, 112°13'E) is shown on the MMS plot **(NAA.042.0009)**, SWACH had presumed that the tanker had sailed directly from the claimed rescue position of 24°06'S, 111°40'E. However, DF tracking by the Jandakot station would not have clearly distinguished between the bearing on her proper course and the course shown on the MMS plot. Therefore, SWACH had accepted without foundation the general accuracy of FEDO's Jandakot direction-finding, which had supported but had not verified the position. But even more intriguingly, as Jandakot was controlled by the RN in Singapore, FEDO had given the impression to SWACH that *Trocas* had sailed directly from the claimed rescue position en route to the interception position arranged with *Wyrallah.*

Others definitely had first-hand knowledge of HMAS *Sydney* meeting with the *Largs Bay* just two days before the fateful encounter. Apart from those on board the vessels (including witness Lindsay Drake) the master of the troopship and many of his crew had been conscious of the cruiser's presence, but curiously this is not mentioned in naval archives. Nor could the rendezvous have escaped the attention of the departing Dutch warship escorts and commanders de Meester (*Tromp*) and Lagaay (*van Nes*). It is therefore inconceivable that the Dutch C-in-C NEI, Admiral Helfrich, had not also been informed of the cruiser's rendezvous with *Largs Bay*.

Admiral Conrad Helfrich, CZM (1886–1962)
C-in-C NEI

The extent to which NEI intelligence had been made aware of Royal Navy involvement should also have also been known to LCDR Vincent Kennedy, NIDs Dutch liaison officer in Batavia. He is known to have been recalled to Australia, because he and his counterpart, NEIs CMDR G B Salm, together with CMDR Long, attended Navy Office in Melbourne at the time when the search for the *Sydney* was in progress. Salm and Director of Operations, CMDR Dechaineux, were then sent to Fremantle to interrogate *Kormoran* survivors, the latter reporting to CMDR Long, whose take on the action became the basis of the final report to the Admiralty.

Long's influence was indelible. Whether justifiable or not, he had an intense belief in Detmers's story. But it was Dechaineux who first wrote that the story of the action was frankly told by Detmers. The term 'frankly' was then repeated by Eldridge in his report, though Gill's explanation of the battle in the history of the RAN was essentially the same but more simplistic. Unlike Eldridge, Gill refrained from qualifying the action by not mentioning from whence or from whom he had sourced his information.

CMDR Long was also comforted by the fact that C-in-C China, VADM Sir Geoffrey Layton, had full confidence in his colleague, CAPT John Collins, previously commander of HMAS *Sydney*, who in June 1941 was appointed assistant chief of staff to Layton in Singapore. His immediate task was to plan for the employment of Allied air and naval forces. He established a good rapport with Layton but was disappointed when ADM Sir Tom Phillips relieved him. Then in January 1942, Collins became Commodore commanding China Force, which consisted of RN and RAN cruisers and destroyers based in Batavia. Like Long, Collins's term in Singapore under Layton during the *Sydney* crisis and his knowledge of Layton's role in directing the cruiser, is beyond doubt.

Admiral Geoffrey Layton (1884–1964)
C-in-C China Station

John Collins (1899–1989)
Previous Commander HMAS *Sydney*

On his arrival at Fremantle in March 1942 after the fall of Singapore, Collins became the most senior naval officer in Western Australia, replacing DNO Farquhar-Smith. Intriguingly, except for LCDR Rycroft, SWACH senior naval officers, including Ramage and Bailhache, had been transferred to other duties. WCDR and Senior RAAF Operations Officer McLean had been appointed to HQ Pearce as commanding officer. He had taken a coordinating role in the air search for *Sydney* and *Kormoran* survivors at WAHQ and SWACH.

Collins's command had been effectively replaced by new arrivals that were not privy to the suspicious movements of *Trocas* and the fact that HMAS *Sydney* had not acknowledged the DNOWA's message. But CMRE Collins term as DNOWA was short-lived. In August 1943 he took command of the heavy cruiser *Shropshire* (a replacement for the sunken HMAS *Canberra*), and was later appointed commander of the Australian Naval Squadron with HMAS *Australia* as its flagship.

The replacement of Farquhar-Smith and his senior colleagues had been at the behest of Chief of Naval Staff and First Naval Member ADM Royle who, together with CMDR Durnford, had been seconded from the Royal Navy in 1941. As first and second naval member of the Naval Board, they both served the RAN throughout the *Sydney* crisis and they controlled naval staffing at all RAN establishments. In addition, CDRE Muirhead-Gould, RN, had been appointed in 1941 to the key post of naval officer-in-charge of Sydney. These appointments were to result in the RAN being heavily influenced by decisions made by Royal Navy officers.

On reversion to the RN to take up duties at the Admiralty, CMDR Durnford, RN, was succeeded by CDRE George Moore, RAN, as second naval member of the Australian Commonwealth Naval Board (ACNB) in June 1942. He served the Naval Board until November 1944 when Moore succeeded Muirhead-Gould as NOIC Sydney. Promoted to rear admiral, Moore was made acting first naval member in August 1945 due to the illness of VADM Hamilton, RN, who had replaced ADM Royle in June that year. George Moore thus became the first Australian to command the Royal Australian Navy. So in February 1948, Hamilton retired and thereafter the RAN controlled its own destiny, free of Royal Navy influence.

❑ ❑ ❑

EPILOGUE

Fact-finding is a process of finding the truth. There is no substitute, the only alternative being to interpret a story from a wide range of individual testimonies, an impossible task should there be conflicting or inconsistent evidence.

Such was the case with the Commission of Inquiry in 2009 when considering the German survivors' evidence – evidence that varied greatly. Nonetheless, it was on this basis that the engagement between the *Sydney* and *Kormoran* on the 19th of November 1941, has been interpreted by the inquiry. It has been unfortunate that no independent fact-finding has ever been presented to the Australian public – facts that may well have disproved some of the German accounts.

The Commission of Inquiry findings have indeed been based largely on the word of senior *Kormoran* officers. This very same outcome had been similarly expressed in the past by naval academic Frank Eldridge, first in his report of the action to the Admiralty in 1942 and later by author George H Gill (*The History of the Royal Australian Navy*) in 1957, in manifesting the story of the action, which seemingly put it beyond doubt. However, the conclusions reached also failed to encompass any form of fact-finding, including the weight of evidence that would have made the inquiry's findings more decisive.

Despite these failings, the Report based its findings on a so-called alternative method of fact-finding that was said, '... **analysed in an impartial manner all the evidence available from the German survivors who were able to see the encounter, with a view to determining whether their accounts should be accepted as an accurate statement of what occurred'.** This method was also said to be described as a normal function for a tribunal to determine the facts, but unfortunately it did not depend on consistency being found in the contemporary assessments made by those senior RAN officers who had separately interrogated each survivor. And nor did the inquiry consider those who did not witness the encounter that was frequently discussed in the POW camps that they could have any idea of the way the battle unfolded, well after the interrogations had ceased.

The conclusions reached by the inquiry took into consideration whether the assessment of the engagement so derived accorded with the interrogating officers, together with the empirical (observable) evidence available from the wreckage sites of the *Sydney* and *Kormoran.* But due to the diverse evidence from survivors, it was impossible to clearly establish the facts. In its final deliberations, the inquiry had merely based its story of the engagement on Detmers's account and those of his officers who supported his take on the action. No real fact-finding had been undertaken in the process of determining the way in which the action began.

Many of the conclusions reached by the inquiry were claimed to be consistent with the German statements in describing the events before and after the action. However, there was a noticeable lack of agreement on the sequence of events. For example, several German survivors were adamant that the distant cruiser had signalled the raider to stop or reduce speed and that both vessels had been almost stationary before the action commenced, vindicating that Burnett had been aware he had been dealing with a suspected enemy vessel – the very vessel he had been sent to investigate. These points alone rendered the inquiry's judgement highly questionable.

Some of the findings by the Commission of Inquiry can be aptly described as befitting the category of doubt and although evidence by certain *Kormoran* officers is claimed to have been consistent with those found in the interrogation statements, observations from other crewmen interviewed had been totally disregarded, including from those crewmen who later came forward in taped interviews to clarify the firing of the underwater and above-water torpedoes.

The inquiry also had the opportunity to test the veracity of the German accounts. It had at its disposal a means of finding the facts. For example, a witness statement, revealing that HMAS *Sydney* had met with the troopship MV *Largs Bay*; shipping movement card details, SIM positions and way points for the ships, including that of the oiler MV *Trocas.* However, bland acceptance by the Naval Board for the reasons why HMT *Aquitania* failed to immediately report the rescue of survivors hindered the inquiry's judgement on the facts and the role played by C-in-C China.

A simple analysis of the movement of each of the abovementioned vessels would have suggested that there was something seriously wrong with the story told by certain German survivors. For instance, how could it be that Burnett had considered the raider to be friendly while steadily and incautiously closing in on the vessel when in fact he had been sent at high speed to intercept a suspicious vessel that was not on the daily list of vessels expected in Australian waters. Would he have not signalled the raider to stop at a distance for identification in accordance with Admiralty instructions and have considered the vessel suspicious at all times? What else seemed wrong?

According to her movement card, as from 21 November, *Largs Bay,* the first vessel to pass near the battle site, had not met her scheduled allocated average speed from Singapore to Sydney. This ship had been unaccountably delayed in the Indian Ocean for a lengthy period, culminating in her very late arrival (10 hours) at Wilsons Promontory in Victoria, yet no suitable alternate explanation has ever been forthcoming.

Trocas had also rescued survivors on the day before it was announced by C-in-C China – this, in a completely different position. Thereafter the vessel could not be contacted, her whereabouts unknown for two days. It was not until she finally arranged to meet with a RAN ship at a pre-determined position to take on board an armed guard that her actual course could be identified from her allocated way point (15°S, 106°E). This was the 'proper' course that DNOWA had referred to and had complained about, but the way point coordinates had not been passed on to SWACH by the Naval Board via the Central War Room. C-in-C China's role in diverting *Trocas* while en route therefore should have been considered suspicious by those conducting the search.

Just three factors – the *Sydney*'s rendezvous with *Largs Bay* and subsequent high speed to intercept *Kormoran*, the untimely schedule and the mysterious movement of *Trocas*, all indicate that C-in-C China had been cognisant of the engagement and the general location of the battle site. Not one of these factors had been discussed openly by the Commission of Inquiry. Burnett therefore may well have received instructions from Singapore in dealing with the suspect enemy vessel. These matters never attracted the attention of the inquiry and despite RAN's Naval Faculty identifying the position of *Trocas* at 0700z on 19 November, navigational experts could not foresee that it was patently obvious that less than four days sailing was required to the tanker's rescue position at latitude 24°06'S at the speed allocated – regardless of the two longitudinal positions stated.

The story of the action as first told by Eldridge continues until this day. It is a story that has been constrained and deprived of the totality of all the evidence. Based entirely on the views of just a few, the public have been deceived, principally by the Director of Naval Intelligence, Commander Long, who had managed to influence those he selected to disseminate the facts. The story as told has evolved exclusively from Eldridge and Gill, and now with the imprimatur of the Commission of Inquiry. This is an indictment on those willing to continue to uphold the falsity of an alleged chance encounter.

CMDR Long also appeared to have unconditional authority to dispose of naval records in 1945. Today, the Archives Act of 1983 and amendments thereto in 1996, demand that a person must not engage in conduct that results in the destruction or disposal of a Commonwealth record, or of its transfer and custody to another file. Alteration to a file is strictly forbidden, particularly in the event that judicial proceedings were likely to follow or requests for freedom of information are made. Nowadays severe penalties apply.

Consideration to the fiasco must also be given to the fact that Australian prisoners of war in 1941 were incarcerated in enemy POW camps, for example, in North Africa, Crete and Germany. These prisoners and those in Australia were to be treated with respect under the rules of the Geneva Convention, regardless of the crimes they may have committed. It is also noted that during WW2 very few imprisoned Axis or Allied POWs were sent for formal trial for fear of retribution by their enemies.

But the problem for CMDR Long (and the RAN) was that the Admiralty had received a full account of the action from Eldridge, which had effectively exonerated Detmers of any wrongdoing. It was thus expedient for the Navy to maintain his innocence throughout the war years and beyond in case accusations resulted in retribution against Australian POWs overseas. However, this did not alleviate the Commission of Inquiry of its responsibilities in thoroughly exercising its duty with impartiality 64 years after World War II had ended. Instead, the inquiry promoted its foreshadowed and desired objective by broadly countenancing the views expressed by Eldridge and Gill.

When establishing the facts by means of fact-finding, a great deal of evidence can be ruled out. For example, Eldridge, Gill and the Commission of Inquiry believed that the *Sydney* had taken well over an hour to overhaul the raider; that both the cruiser and the raider steamed parallel at some 14 knots and that the raider had torpedoed the cruiser at this approximate speed. This is nonsensical because the location of the *Kormoran* wreck site is now beyond doubt and the navigable parameters are only 8 nautical miles from the turning point on sighting the cruiser to the battle site.

In some instances, the inquiry portrayed the action in sequence, but failure to correctly account for the positions through which the raider had sailed prior to sighting the cruiser renders some findings invalid – this, merely because the inquiry failed to establish the distance travelled by *Kormoran* to the site of the engagement. As a result, the speed of the raider from the turn-away position to the battle site and the speed at which the raider fired the torpedoes cannot be substantiated.

That fact-finding is again notably deficient in the inquiry findings is typified by the conclusion that the *Kormoran* transmitted two distress signals to Geraldton on the 500 kilocycle maritime distress frequency. In fact, the first was sent to Perth Radio at Applecross (transmitted in whole degrees) and gave the approximate location of the raider when she had sighted the *Sydney*, but to suggest it was sent to the emergency shore station at Geraldton is to concede that the enemy had known the frequency on which to report the suspicious cruiser. After being advised of the frequency by Applecross, the second Q signal sent two minutes later on 500kcs had been acknowledged by Geraldton Radio, this time giving the latitudinal and longitudinal coordinate to the nearest mile. The coordinate 111°15'E had been detected in full by Geraldton, but the inquiry had not been diligent in ascertaining the precise position of where the raider had turned away, insofar as having failed to reason why the action reports had all quoted the point at which the raider had crossed 111°E, course 025° being the key to explaining the parameters of the battle site.

The inquiry asserted that *Kormoran* only fired two above-water torpedoes during the initial action, one of which struck the cruiser. Whilst it is true that one torpedo hit, the navigable parameters of the raider so described establish that the vessels must have been almost stationary at the commencement of the action. In fact, three torpedoes had been fired, one from underwater before the declaration which struck the cruiser, followed later by two from above-water, both of which passed short of the *Sydney*'s bow. This was confirmed by the decrypted 1945 action report by FRUMEL and from recent taped statements from *Kormoran* crewmen, which had led the 1998 Senate Inquiry to conclude that the underwater torpedo played a major role in defeating the *Sydney.*

Further dissemination of the navigation revealing that Detmers had submitted to the superior cruiser well before the *Sydney* had closed on *Kormoran* also demonstrates the fallibility of many of the inquiry's conclusions. And the notion that the *Sydney* was close abeam starboard of the raider when Burnett first signalled for the secret letters to be supplied is demonstrably false. In fact, this signal had been originally requested at a distance of some 7 miles in accordance with Admiralty instructions – this, immediately after seeking the call sign name of *Straat Malakka*. But Detmers had not told his crew at their battle stations of this development until the vessels were abeam of one another, announcing to his crew that as they could not supply the secret letters, he had no option but to open fire. Crewmen later agreed while being interrogated that Detmers himself had informed them of this while at their battle stations.

By far the biggest mistake made by the inquiry was the conclusion that the *Sydney* was not at the first degree of readiness or action stations, though her main 6-inch guns and port torpedoes were bearing on *Kormoran* (as evidenced by the raider's survivors). The inference is that the cruiser's four 4-inch anti-aircraft guns were not manned. But according to an ex-crewman of the *Sydney* (and Detmers) they would rarely be manned in the case where there was no possibility of attack from the air when arresting a lone enemy vessel in mid-ocean. And in consideration that Detmers would abide by his decision to submit to the cruiser's demands and not to secretly engage while under surveillance by breaking the rules of sea warfare, the level of readiness of the cruiser had been undoubtedly commensurate with the danger imposed.

Captain Burnett had taken certain precautions if a gun battle was to have ensued, but in manning the 4-inch AA guns, which were dangerously exposed, the gun crews had little chance of survival. This also applied to the open-mounted 0.5-inch AA machine guns. Unquestionably, Burnett had made ready his most powerful 6-inch weapons, the raider having been effectively bailed up while preparations were being made to board the enemy vessel in order to confirm her status.

Criticism of Burnett's actions by the inquiry for getting too close to the *Kormoran* has not been fully understood by most observers. Burnett's intention was clear – to board and capture as quickly as possible the almost stationary vessel which could not reply to the secret letters first demanded at a distance. The result was that the underwater torpedo, which ran true and which could not be detected when launched, had struck the cruiser just as the raider had de-camouflaged and opened fire. Detmers had simply launched this torpedo in advance, well before he had given the order to de-camouflage. It was a desperate attempt to circumvent his ship being captured.

Joseph Burnett's perceived carelessness in approaching the raider has been generally accepted by the public. On the other hand, it has been contentious for those who have studied the action in detail. But the manner in which Detmers had surprisingly delivered his underwater torpedo was simple in the case of a straight-running torpedo. While abeam of the cruiser he was only required to turn the vessel instantaneously to port, release the torpedo and then re-position the raider to take advantage of his pre-aimed guns, as discussed in the POW camp. Both vessels had been parallel, but in a matter of seconds the cruiser was suddenly on the raider's starboard quarter. Except for a few, this discreet manoeuvre had been barely noticed by *Kormoran*'s crewmen.

On returning almost abeam of the cruiser, the order to de-camouflage had been given while the underwater torpedo was well on its way to striking its target. It was then that the raider's first guns fired and the above-water torpedoes were in the process of being launched. Yet very few of the crew would have witnessed that the underwater torpedo had been discreetly fired off, but after re-positioning the raider some of those at their battle stations and elsewhere could clearly see the track of the torpedo running towards the *Sydney*.

Eldridge wrote that the story as told by Captain Detmers and other prisoners seemed to ring true. He could not fully commit to the truth of the action, only that the story appeared to be true. In this respect, decisiveness was seriously lacking. However, his report to the Admiralty on the action was in essence quite definite and it has become resonant with many other reports by the Navy, including that of the Commission of Inquiry. This had all been due to Detmers's story per se and only because it was said to have been frankly told.

Whether by fact-finding or by weight of evidence, the story of the action between the *Sydney* and *Kormoran* as portrayed by the inquiry is now seen in a completely different perspective, the key factor being that Burnett was fully cognisant that he was dealing with an enemy vessel. It was not friendly, the vessel had turned away when sighted, she had not proceeded to identify herself as instructed and she had continued to evade the easily recognised British cruiser. Besides, his VAI showed that no vessel was expected to be anywhere in the area.

But what is relevant here is that the *Sydney*'s lookout (35m above sea level) was positioned higher than that on *Kormoran* (25m). Thus, the cruiser should have observed the raider well before the raider had seen the cruiser and have witnessed the raider turn away in avoidance from 025° to 250°. Plainly, the evasiveness displayed by the errant vessel per se caused Burnett to order the vessel to routinely stop after specifically requesting the vessel's name, but more so because it could not reply to the secret letters assigned to the disguised *Straat Malakka*.

The inquiry was also inordinately fixated on discrediting a number of witnesses called to give evidence (as noted in the transcripts), particularly those who contested the Navy's version of events. Notwithstanding, the real intention should have been to examine each matter in detail, and for example, the hitherto unexplained message purportedly received from Geraldton on the night of 19 November, and issues related thereto. Instead, verbatim narratives and SWACH log entries were all that was required to ascertain that the message was sent much later. A more thorough investigation would have exposed the falsity of this finding. Similarly, the inquiry should have identified the German SMHEA worker who posed as a member of the crew of the *Kormoran*, but it was too obsessed with deriding the faulty memory of the claimant some 50 years after the event.

It has often been said that there are aspects of the engagement which are unknown and probably unknowable. Yes, it will always be the case that conflicting evidence will inevitably draw such a conclusion, particularly if crass uncertainty prevails. This is why so many observers have challenged previous findings because they could not accept the word of some German survivors in preference to others, whether they were officers or not. Thus, if the body of evidence from the Germans had been generally consistent rather than elusory, the German story as a whole may well have been readily accepted. Lingering doubts cannot be reconciled, as any juror would attest.

Given that the Commission of Inquiry may have been unaware of the role played by C-in- C China in this incident, the very fact that the raider had desperately tried to evade the cruiser should have led the inquiry into at least considering that some of the evidence given by senior officers of the *Kormoran* may have been questionable. But failure to undertake the necessary preparatory work to establish the truth or otherwise was to result in preconceived and pre-emptive outcomes which, in turn, delivered the same discredited status quo findings portrayed by F Eldridge and G Hermon Gill.

Captain Joseph Burnett had borne the blame totally. He was unfortunately victimised and he had paid the ultimate price for the disaster. Yet there are, in fact, aspects of the engagement that are unknown. For instance, the full extent to which C-in-C China was involved in directing the *Sydney* to its eventual fate and, was he (Burnett) ordered to capture the raider?

The answers to these questions cannot be explained, and because not one of the *Sydney* crewmen survived, the accusations made against Captain Burnett could not be defended by him or anyone else. History shows that formal proceedings are likely to be instituted when disaster strikes, particularly while on a routine assignment. But in this respect, survival can make a difference.

Take, for example, Captain Turner, Royal Navy reserve officer and master of the liner RMS *Lusitania* who, in May 1915 was harshly treated by the prosecuting Admiralty for the torpedoing of his vessel and for the huge loss of life while en route from New York to Liverpool. He was accused of not following his orders (sound familiar?), but years later he was exonerated by an independent Court of Inquiry. Captain McVay of the USS *Indianapolis* also parallels Turner and Burnett as a scapegoat.

Likewise, had Captain Burnett survived the battle, these two instances above raises the prospect of court action of being taken against him. He, too, would probably have been accused of not following his orders and for not sinking the enemy vessel when he had the chance, regardless of the advice that C-in-C China may or may not have given him. After all, his judgement was paramount in dealing with the vessel that lay before him. But as 'judgement' is defined as displaying good sense at the time, Burnett had decided (or had been ordered) to board the raider with all his main guns and tubes trained on the enemy ship. But unknown to Burnett, the Admiralty, et al, *Kormoran* possessed underwater torpedo tubes aligned abaft the beam. This factor alone determined the final outcome of the battle.

Drift analysis has now an aura of infallibility about it. This is because the International Sea and Air Rescue Organisations have honed their skills over the last 20 years. In Australia, NATSAR have assessed that various objects drift at a prescribed angle relative to the wind and current. Instead, many researchers and authors contend that these objects drift with the wind alone, thus misconceiving the reality of the drift direction, for example, of the *Kormoran*'s final hours.

Although well and truly overdue for release, British archives have yet to reveal to the public details of the Royal Navy's exploits in Singapore for the period during the HMAS *Sydney* crisis and Australian archives are devoid of material that could explain the actions of C-in-C China. Nonetheless, despite these encumbrances, the auspiciousness of the untimely sailing schedules of *Largs Bay* and *Trocas* has, in the meantime, provided a firm basis on which to evaluate the ever-present extent of C-in-C China and RAN involvement in the affair.

The report on the Commission of Inquiry's findings has largely remained unchanged, however, for at least the past 18 months, a 'redevelopment and upgrade' has been promised. But as to whether it will affect the report itself, especially those items in the National Archives that contain crucial evidence, we will wait and see the results. But curiously it will be interesting to gauge what variations, if any, are deemed necessary in order to make changes to the original report first issued in 2009.

Finally, the most disappointing outcome of the rather comprehensive analysis by the Commission of Inquiry is that some relatives of the *Sydney*'s deceased have been led to believe they now have closure on the matter. This can only be true in the sense that they believed the inquiry findings were brought to finality due to the broad and seemingly thorough examination of the evidence.

And for those attempting to seek the truth – they have been masterly misled.

❑ ❑ ❑

www.ingramcontent.com/pod-product-compliance
Lightning Source LLC
Chambersburg PA
CBHW070430170726
48291CB00002B/441